OCCUPIED
EARTH

OCCUPIED EARTH

STORIES OF ALIENS, RESISTANCE AND SURVIVAL AT ALL COSTS

EDITED BY RICHARD J. BREWER AND GARY PHILLIPS

POLIS BOOKS

Hunter X – Part One and Part Two by Richard J. Brewer and Gary Phillips
Do No Harm by Rachel Howzell Hall and David W. Hall
Pike Street Pick-Up by Adam L. Korenman
Union Day by Lisa Morton
How the Game is Played by Rob Hart
Strange Alliance by Cliff Allen
Hope by Matthew V. Clemens
Location, Location, Location by Howard V. Hendrix
Letting Go the Ghosts by Marsheila Rockwell and Jeffrey J. Mariotte
A Day in the Life by Richard M. Johnson
Second Coming by Craig Faustus Buck
The Devil You Know by Jessica Kaye
Johnny and the Warehouse Women by Nathan Walpow
Traitor by Adam Lance Garcia

Cover design by The Cover Collection
Interior design by E.M. Tippetts Book Designs

ISBN 978-1-940610-52-8
eISBN 978-1-940610-57-3

Library of Congress control number: 2015939333

First Trade Paperback edition October 2015 by Polis Books LLC
1201 Hudson Street
Hoboken, NJ 07030
www.PolisBooks.com

TABLE OF CONTENTS

INTRODUCTION

Alien invasion. World in jeopardy. The fate of humanity at risk.

The story of Earth facing an alien threat has been with us for well over a century. H. G. Wells' book *War of the Worlds* stunned readers in 1897 as mankind faced imminent destruction from a hostile invasion by the inhabitants of the red planet.

Completely outmatched by the Martians and their huge machines of destruction, humanity is saved from annihilation by common microscopic germs that humans are immune, but to which the Aliens are fatally vulnerable. Conversely, in Michael Crichton's classic novel The Andromeda Strain, Earth is threatened by a biological microorganism from "out there" to which we are the vulnerable but are saved when the virus mutates into a nonlethal form.

Over the years speculative fiction has shown the Earth threatened by deadly plants, *Day of the Triffids*, sentient seeds, *The Body Snatchers*, extraterrestrial children, *The Midwich Cuckoos* and even elephant-like warriors, *Footfall*. But with each invasion, each tale of ultimate world doom, human kind ends up victorious. By hook or by crook, simple human pluck or just damn good luck, the people of earth come out on top and the world, as we know it, continues.

But... what if....?

What if we didn't win? What if they came, they saw and they conquered? What then? What would life be like under the rule of an alien species? Who would those aliens be, what would they look like? What would they want with us and our planet? What kind of society would we find ourselves in then? This was the discussion that led to the birth of the Mahk-Ra invasion and the stories in this collection.

These fourteen original stories look to answer that what if question; what is the world like now, years after the invasion. They explore life in a world that is still familiar, but ultimately different. People still get up and go to work, do the shopping, fall in love, have families, but the resources and freedoms that are taken for granted today are not so abundant. Twenty-five years into the occupation there is an entire generation that has only known life under alien oppression. Some of the younger populace are pressed into Mahk-Ra military service and taken away to fight in a far off, great interstellar war, while others are left on the planet to survive as best they can.

But humanity continues to function, to do what they have always done under direst of circumstances, they endure. There are still crimes being committed and officers of the law to solve them, small acts of heroism and big acts of political intrigue, and the indomitable human spirit continues in the form of an organized resistance, created by humans who have never accepted defeat at the hands of the alien overlords and dream of, and fight for, a free Earth.

It is into this world that the authors have set their stories. Through their eyes we see the day-to-day struggles of humanity. A harried EMT finds a second chance at life in Rachel Howzell Hall and David W. Hall's, *Do No Harm*. While in Mathew Clemen's *Hope*, two plainclothes detectives, partners, a human and an alien, prove that it may be a new world order but old world crimes carry on, as they race against time to track down a political assassin. *Letting Go the Ghosts* by Marsheila Rockwell and Jeffrey J. Mariotte take us to a Native American reservation for a unique perspective from an already occupied nation dealing with their newest occupiers. While Howard V. Hendrix's *Location, Location, Location*, shows that resistance always begins as a concept.

Fourteen tales of adventure, intrigue, suspense and of the strength of the human spirit, told by an exceptional gathering of writers, each giving their own particular take on a world that may be under the dominion of the Mahk-Ra, but one where humans still fight, every day, in ways big and small to make it their own.

Down, but not defeated. Resistance is all.

Richard J. Brewer and Gary Phillips

HUNTER X

RICHARD J. BREWER
AND GARY PHILLIPS

PT. 1
SURPRISE

I t was Paul Harper's birthday and he was not happy. The day, *his* day, had actually started off well. Really well. His family had made him a special breakfast of ham, eggs and pancakes. His wife must have been putting aside ration cards for months in order to pull such a meal together. It was like the days before the war. It was also possible that she had bought the hard to get food off the black market, but he didn't want to think along those lines. He knew his wife loved him, but he didn't want her loving him to foolishness. Now, that warm Norman Rockwell meal was hours in the past…right now he was wet, cold, bleeding and trying to figure out who had just tried to kill him.

Earlier that morning, with the memory of his breakfast still in his head and stomach, Special Agent Harper arrived to work at the Seattle FBI office smack dab on time. He found his partner, JoHannas-ra, waiting for him at his desk. The seven feet of Mahk-Ra held a brightly wrapped package in his hand that he held out to him. Harper gave the alien a bemused smile.

"What's this?" he said.

1

"It is customary to celebrate the day of one's birth with a gift," said JoHannas. "Happy birthday to you, Agent Harper."

"Just don't sing," said Harper as he took the gift and proceeded to tear away the wrapping. Under it he found a two pound vacuum packed can of prewar coffee. He looked at his partner with a genuine look of surprise and gratitude.

"Han," he said. "This is… I can't accept this."

JoHannas raised a hand in protest. "It is little enough."

Harper leaned in and spoke in a low voice.

"Look I appreciate this, honestly. But I know what this stuff costs and it ain't cheap."

"Please, think nothing of it. Especially do not worry about the cost." A rare half-smile came to the alien's lips as he said, 'I… know a guy, who knows a guy."

Harper barked a laugh. Three years as partners and JoHannas-ra still occasionally managed to catch him off his guard. "Okay," he said. "You can keep the details to yourself. I'll just say thank you and we'll leave it at that."

He opened the bottom drawer of his desk and put the coffee away. Then, thinking about it, he locked the drawer. It wasn't that he didn't trust his fellow agents, but….Arabica beans. Harper's thoughts were interrupted by their deputy director.

"Harper, JoHannas!" he said. "In my office."

Deputy Director Ben Bellusci was five-feet, five-and-a-half inches of I don't give a shit what you think, just do your fucking job. At sixty-seven, he was old enough to remember the times before the Occupation and to know that those times didn't matter anymore. He had been an FBI agent when the war broke out, had fought the Mahk-Ra invasion, had gone along with the armistice and Earth's eventual surrender and afterward he returned to the Bureau, a changed Bureau, but one where he worked his way diligently up the ranks to his present position.

Harper and JoHannas entered the deputy director's office. Bellusci sat behind his functional metal desk. He picked up a folder and did a quick glance at the inside papers before holding it out to JoHannas. He did not offer the agents a seat.

"I need you two to do an escort run," he said.

"Who to where?" said Harper.

"Some hotshot, big deal Mahk-Ra is christening the new cruiser out at the docks," he said. "Massatataa, Mafasstass?"

"Masstas-ra?" said JoHannas. Harper could hear the respect in his partner's voice. "Major General Masstasra is a war hero. He is highly revered by our people for his bravery in several significant and dangerous campaigns. His service to the Empire is legend."

"Yeah?" said Bellusci. "Well, I never heard of him. Where was he during the war?"

"He was not serving in this system," said JoHannas. He didn't elaborate more than that.

It was well known that the Mahk-Ra was engaged in a prolonged conflict far away from the Earth's solar system, but they were notoriously reluctant to talk about it. However, every year a certain percentage of the planet's youthful population -- 18 to 25 year-olds -- were drafted into serving in the empire's military. Most were used to help maintain the huge mother ships that orbited the planet and as repair crews for the damaged space cruisers that would arrive from time to time from parts unknown, and a select few were sent off to those unknown parts as soldiers in the great expansion of the empire. Most of them were never heard from again. Those that did return, with only a few exceptions, lived in secluded enclaves and had little contact with the general populace. Where they served, what they saw, wasn't a subject of public conversation – though rumors had gotten around.

"Christ, Ben, they do this to us all the time" said Harper. "We've got cases to work on."

"And they'll be here when you get back," said Bellusci. "This is what you get for being the first Mahk-Ra-human investigative team, a shining symbol of interspecies cooperation. Harmony among the species and all that. The networks love that shit, looks great on the evening news."

"I could shoot Han in the leg while on camera," Harper said. "That would go a long way in showing inter-species harmony. Then maybe they'd leave us alone and let us do our work."

JoHannas gave his partner a look.

"What?" said Harper. "I thought you guys heal fast."

"Enough," said the deputy director. "These orders come straight from the Needle. You want to argue with them, I got a number you can call."

Harper started to speak but decided not to.

"That's what I thought. So this is how it goes, you two escort this Mafasstass or whatever the hell his name is to the space port. He says his blah-blah-blah. . .whatever, does whatever he's gonna do and then you escort him back to the hotel, or wherever, and you're over and done and out. Tomorrow he's on his way out to who the fuck cares and you're back to work. Those are the orders. Now get outta here."

Two hours later Harper and JoHannas were in the back seat of an armored Lincoln Town Car limousine, a slight rain spotting the car's windshield, facing their Mahk-Ra VIP, Masstas-ra, who, at 7 feet, 5 inches barely fit inside the car. The old world form of transportation was a concession to the human public. They loved to see such a reminder of the old days and it was good publicity for the Mahk-Ra to be seen using it.

"It is an honor to meet you," said JoHannas in the formal High Blade Mahkanese. "Your actions in combat are well known and an inspiration to all Mahk-Ra."

Masstas-ra waved a hand dismissively. "What I have done, I have done for the glory of the empire. No more, no less," he said, with an inflection that sounded like he'd said it a thousand times. "If this trivial ceremony can help pacify the relationship between the Mahk-Ra and these humans then it is my duty to be here. I was on my way home to Ra-Prime when the order came to detour to this Ra forsaken rock of a planet. The sooner we're done and I can be on my way, the better."

"Well," said Harper in the same language, "I don't know about my partner here, but I guess you and I can agree on that last point."

Masstas-ra was visibly taken aback by the Earthman's ability to speak Mahkanese, but he recovered quickly.

"I am merely frustrated, Agent Harper," he said in English. "I have not been back to the home world in many years. This was an unexpected and, yes, unwanted change to my itinerary. I am sorry if you took offense."

"Forget it," said Harper still in Mahkanese. "I think we all had things we'd rather be doing than what the higher-ups have us doing today."

"This is actually a rather historic event," said JoHannas to Masstas-ra. He was studying a hand-held computer tablet. "The christening of the first Mahk-Ra battle cruiser, comprised completely from Earth materials and constructed by a 90 percent human workforce is something to be remembered, and given that the ship will be bearing your name makes your presence even more significant."

"I am surprised that the ship doesn't bear a human name," said Masstas-ra.

"Progress is one step at a time," said Harper. "I don't think the Mahk-Ra are ready at this point to follow a ship called 'The Benton' or 'The Bieber'.

"Bieber?"

"Justin Bieber, a great Earth hero from before the Mahk-Ra arrived," said Harper. "He was held in the highest esteem by our people, much like you are respected today."

"Like your George Washington or Ulysses S. Grant." said Masstas-ra.

Harper took a beat before he replied.

"Yeah," he said, "Exactly like that."

Masstas-ra settled back in his seat. "How long will this ceremony take?"

JoHannas checked his electronic pad. "We should have you back to your ship within six hours," he said. "Once we arrive at the docks you will take the stage. There will be a short series of speeches from various officials, and then you will be introduced. You will deliver your speech and then push a button that will cause a bottle of champagne to swing from a ribbon and shatter against the hull of the ship, officially naming it the "Masstas-ra" and declaring it ready for launch. There will be some photo opportunities and a short reception following. Afterwards, we will escort you back to your shuttle and you may continue on your journey."

"And what does the shattering of this bottle of "Sham-pane" against the hull of the ship have to do with its launching?" asked Masstas-ra.

While JoHannas tried to explain this old maritime tradition and the superstition surrounding it, Harper looked out the side window to see the towering Mahk-Ra war vessel waiting at the Military Space Port of Seattle that now took up so much of Elliot Bay. It was, to say the least, impressive. Five years in the making, hundreds of workers toiling round the clock. Even with the rain sheeting down its sides, Harper could see that its black hull was polished to a mirror finish. As they drew closer, the sheer size of the ship was almost overwhelming. It rose, high into the clouds, dwarfing everything around it.

They arrived at the docks to find a large crowd awaiting them. Word had spread that the famous Masstas-ra, the Mahk-Ra warrior hero would be there. This was a once in a lifetime chance to catch a glimpse of this legend, whose exploits were taught in schools and the subject of books and films. Despite the cold wind and rain, the crowd had grown to hundreds of humans, Mahk-Ra and Mahk-Re waiting for them.

The Mahk-Re were the lower class members of the home world. To most people's eyes the Ra and Re were damn near indistinguishable. Over the years Harper had learned that there were slight physical differences between the two that he and other practiced observers could note, but if in doubt the overall arrogance of the former was always a dead giveaway. Personally it made no sense to him, but the societal division between the two races was a wide chasm that went back for countless generations. Harper had often reflected that such divisions had long existed on Earth as well -- though they weren't as pronounced since the arrival of the alien overlords.

Looking out the window at the gathered crowd, it seemed to Harper like everyone was holding an umbrella, magazine or some damn thing over their heads to shield themselves from the rain; no one's hands were empty. Harper didn't like it. It would be too easy for remnants of the Red Spear to have a hitter or two in such a crowd. Harper knew that JoHannas would be having the same thought and when the three of them climbed from the limousine to the cheers of the crowd, they both scanned the faces around them, searching for any potential threats as they moved Masstas-ra toward the waiting podium. So intent were they at observing the crowd that it took them completely by surprise when the explosion erupted in front of them, throwing them to the ground and taking out most of the stage where Masstas-ra would have been sitting had they been just a little faster.

JoHannas was the first to recover. He pulled himself to his feet, straightening his sunglasses with one hand while reaching for his bleater with the other. A stunned Masstas-ra was on his hands and knees, shaking his head trying to clear it. Harper, a gash on his forehead and blood running down his face, crawled over the rain soaked pavement to the downed alien, his hand pulling his own weapon, an old-school 9 mm Glock. He staggered upright, wiping the blood and water from his eyes.

7

Grabbing Masstas-ra by the arm, he helped the shaken alien to his feet. All around them, people were screaming and running away from the blast site in uncontrolled panic. True to their training, Harper and JoHannas took up protective positions on either side of Masstas-ra.

"We have to get him out of here," said JoHannas.

"Copy that," said Harper. "Let's get him back to the car."

Moving quickly, shoving their way through the surging crowd, Harper gave some small thanks to the fact that everyone was at least moving in the same direction. They reached the limo intact and without hesitation Harper whipped open the door while JoHannas pushed Masstas-ra into the back of the vehicle and then climbed in behind him, followed closely by his human partner.

"Get this car moving," said Harper to the driver as soon as the door was shut.

"But the people around us, sir."

"Will get out of the way," said Harper. "I'm not telling you to mow anyone down, just get us moving."

"Yes sir."

Slowly the car began to move forward, picking its way, with the help of one of the escort skimmers, through the crowd of people and aliens. As they moved, a path gradually began to clear in front of them. Harper put his head back against the limo's car seat and shut his eyes.

"And many happy returns of the day to me," he said, and then added with a sigh, "Moses on a pony."

- TO BE CONTINUED -

DO NO HARM

RACHEL HOWZELL HALL & DAVID W. HALL

Take calculated risks. That is quite different from being rash.
George S. Patton

5:50 P.M.

yawned as the middle-aged white man bled to death on the sidewalk.

Hot dogs wrapped in bacon or...?

Hot dogs not *wrapped in bacon?*

I yawned again, pushed back my sweaty blue baseball cap, then peered at the shuttered liquor store behind me. Smelled like urine and spilled malt liquor. *The more things change...*

Meanwhile, the 65-year old man—Seth Friedlander, according to his I.D.—kept dying.

Carotid artery. Ain't no comin' back from that.

Andreas, crouched beside the patient on the bloody sidewalk, pressed useless pads of gauze against the man's neck. Sweat and blood glistened on my partner's tawny-colored arms.

We both ignored the two Mahk-Ra over-sheriffs monitoring the call.

The September sun sat low in the cigarette-smoke sky. The

little light that broke through the cinders reflected on a fallen alien ship four miles from where I stood. It spanned from Olympic Boulevard all the way north to Wilshire, and rose just as high. The new skyline of Downtown Los Angeles. No more fancy 90-story skyscrapers with rich men's names on top. Anything over twenty stories had been blown to shit.

Back under the old skyline, lookie-loos would've crowded us. *Man down?* Camera phones up and out. Selfies with the body in the background. Now, nobody gawked or hung around. Folks were more scared of these Mahk-Ra mo-fos than the LAPD.

What a world, what a world, what a world.

Back under the old L.A. skyline, Mr. Seth Friedlander would've died a more dignified death. In a hospital bed. At a beachside condo. A final squeeze of his nurse's ass, and a 'good night, sweetheart' and that was that. Now, his bloody Italian loafer sat in a gutter. Now, a size 15 combat boot worn by some sum-bitch from some planet way over there had trampled on his bloody silk tie. And now, his classic Tag Heur watch was being hocked by a thug who specialized in all things pre-Occupation.

Life had changed for Mr. Friedlander. So had death.

Or maybe grilled chicken. Better for my heart.

I glanced at my digital wristwatch: seven minutes to six.

The man on the ground finally stopped breathing.

Andreas craned his neck to look at me. "Call it, Joe."

I lifted my scarred brown wrist again. "Five fifty-five." Then, I reached into the back of the rig, grabbed a white sheet and tossed it to Andreas. Eyes on the ground. Eyes on the vic. Eyes anywhere except for the strange gaze of the Mahk-Ra over-sheriffs who now monitored the scene. And us.

Their eyes. Couldn't see the whites of the Mahk-Ra's eyes cuz they didn't have any. All pupils. Just black. Strange shit.

Fortunately, these two mocks still wore their sunglasses. In an hour, though, once the sun set, those sunglasses would come off. And then, those eyes…

Scared me more than their weapons.

"Just don't look at 'em, Joseph," my mom, Porsche, had instructed me so long ago. But kids don't listen, and so I looked. Nightmares until I hit my twenties, and by then, there was other shit to fear.

Once the meat truck rumbled off to take Mr. Friedlander to the county morgue, I climbed behind the rig's steering wheel. Kept my attention on the alien cops now questioning my partner. Ready to jump out if he needed me to. Certain death? Yeah. But he was my partner. He was all I had.

The mocks towered over Andreas, and strong enough to bench-press Sherman tanks. Not that height and strength mattered when they all carried those Piecemakers.

Andreas Saldana was taller than me, six foot three easy, and built like a heavyweight boxer. Born just a year or so before *they* came, he'd grown up in East L.A. and didn't remember that life at all. He did remember burning buildings. Corpses left in the streets. The vibrations in his silver baby teeth as alien ships roamed the skies in search of more shit to blow up. Andreas didn't know that 20th- century and early 21st century people in his neighborhood had been scared of ELA13 and Avenues who had wielded AK47s and Uzis to kill each other.

Sunrise, sunset.

And now, Andreas slammed himself into the passenger seat. "Fuckin' mocks."

"What they say?"

He screwed up his pug face and sucked his teeth. "Wanted to know why we didn't stop for the mocktard back on Vermont."

"What you say?"

"That another crew took the call."

I flushed. "So, you lied."

"Yeah, I lied."

I grit my teeth and ignored the burn in my belly. "They write us up?"

"They can kiss my butter-Rican ass, man. I been on for three days. I look like I care?" Andreas plucked his flip-phone from his shirt pocket.

"You'll write the run report?"

"Yeah, yeah. Mr. Friedlander dead so he don't give one fuck about no report. You decide yet?"

"Yep." I turned the rig's ignition. The rumbling engine made the steering wheel quiver beneath my palms. "Dogs with bacon."

Sure. Why not?

6:45 P.M.

Static and chatter burst from the ambulance's radio but no calls came for us, 87 CHARLIE. As I drove the rig east, I spotted an alien ship just a mile away, hovering about one-hundred feet from the ground. "That's gotta be about twenty semi-trucks-long," I said, awed by the engineering.

"What's it doing now?" Andreas asked.

The ship's spotlights were shining into apartment and business windows. Inside, people probably stood facing those lights, eyes squeezed shut, hands held up, prayers on their lips.

"Reminds me of police helicopters that used to patrol where I grew up," I said.

Coliseum Avenue. Palm trees. Apartments. Jungle Bloods.

"My grandpa told me about them helicopters," Andreas said. "He called 'em 'ghetto birds.'"

"Yeah." I squinted at the Mahk-Ra ship. "But these fools, though. They're worse than the cops. They don't fuck around. If you run from 'em, you die and ain't nobody marchin' in the streets demanding justice."

Andreas snorted. "Fuckin' mocks will shoot you even if you *don't* run. They roll up on you with them pulsar-things and just... *BAM!* You ain't you no more. Gone like tears in the ocean."

I tore my eyes away from the ship and considered the passing neighborhood. Historic Koreatown. Everybody squatted here now, though, and Koreatown was now Little Armenia, Little Ethiopia and Pico Rivera combined.

Black, white, asian, hispanic, blue-eyed, brown-haired... Arm in arm, hand in hand, chatting and laughing, like those Coke commercials from the 80's. All of humanity had united once the 7-foot freaks with black eyes had landed. World leaders — *earthlings* — had come up with different ways of moving and living. Solar power. Desalinization. No nuclear. Fuck nuclear. But we still got around and did shit without a lot of oil. Had babies with whoever wanted one, just to be sure we'd still be here fifty, 100, 2,000 years from now. All because of the Mahk-Ra.

Thanks but fuck y'all anyway.

So different from the Los Angeles of my childhood. Yeah, there were still cell-phone towers and grocery stores and nail shops, but since Iran, Iraq and all of the Middle East had been cut off of from America, from the U.K., from anybody not *them,* oil no longer flowed as freely as it used to. Not a lot of cars now. More walkers. More bikers. A good thing in some ways. And if cosmic dust and human ashes weren't still polluting the skies, the oceans would stop rising, and polar bears would get to fuck around on the ice again.

I chuckled.

Andreas glanced at me. "What's so funny?"

"Polar bears."

"Heard about them, too. Like dodos and shit."

I nodded. "Yeah. Like dodos."

Andreas's phone chirped and he smiled. "Aww, yeah."

I tossed my partner a look. "Must not be Alizé."

"Nope. My sweet-baby Letty." He opened the phone and cooed, "*Estoy caliente y te deseo,* baby."

At a red light, I plucked my own phone from my shirt pocket and peered at the cracked glass.

No voice-mail. No missed calls. Not even from a telemarketer hustling Mahk-Ra insurance protection plans. Looking at my phone, it was like I no longer existed. In many ways, I didn't.

With a shaky finger, I pressed MESSAGE. Phone to my ear, I squeezed my eyes shut and waited to feel the hurt of living.

"...supposed to get drops for the water. We can't drink the water without the drops, Joseph. Boiling ain't enough, okay? You don't know everything. I read, too." Destiny had taken a deep breath and had then slowly released it. "And hurry up, okay? Kiara's scared. Get the—"

"Daddy," Kiara had shouted. "Daddy, the lights ain't comin' on. Hurry up and come fix the lights!"

Hot tears filled my eyes as my wife's and my ten-year old's voices surrounded me like fiery mist. Not the most romantic message but it had been Destiny's last words to me. And Kiara's.

Just one more chance. Lord, give me one more chance.

My everyday prayer. If God gave me one more chance, I wouldn't stop this time at The Cork for beer and wings and the Raiders. This time, I'd stop at the army surplus store and buy those water purification drops. This time, I'd be at home and I'd hear that ship approach and I'd throw Destiny and Kiara into the F-10 and drive until the gas tank hit 'E,' somewhere up near Solvang. *Just one more chance.* This time, I'd save them.

Fifteen years had passed since then, and I still couldn't tap the DELETE button to erase Destiny's message. I needed to hear. I needed to hurt. I needed to remember that I didn't come home until nine o'clock that night, and by then, my home on Haas Avenue had been consumed in flames just like the six other bungalows on that part of the block. Courtesy of the Mahk-Ra version of an electromagnetic pulse bomb with a fire back. So powerful that it had denied me my family's ashes.

And now, I only saw Kiara and Destiny in my dreams. The

sober ones, at least.

7:28 P.M.

The line at Doggy-Style wound west on Pico like a slow-moving snake. The aroma of onions and bacon called folks as far west as Robertson Boulevard in Beverly Hills. Fifty years ago, those snobby sumbitches wouldn't have driven east of La Brea. But Doggy-Style mixed charcoal and wood in their barrels. Sure: infrared also got the job done, but the meat didn't taste *grilled*.

"We're pulling up now, baby," Andreas whispered into the phone. "Is it wet? Yeah, baby… *Diantre!*" He chuckled. "My, my, my."

The radio squawked. "87 CHARLIE," the dispatcher called. I reached for the handset.

Andreas swatted my hand. "Next one. Earthlings gotta eat."

Like all EMT-Paramedics, Andreas and I didn't have to queue up for food. At least that perk hadn't changed since the Occupation. Out of the stuffy rig, I inhaled and filled my lungs with greasy air. Nothing like the smell of charred meat in the evening. Smelled like… 2012.

Trudy, the owner and head cook of Doggy-Style, had served with me back in Operation Free Earth. She could handle an M16A4 better than the spatula she wielded on her truck. And now, she grinned at me, and the pearly scar running from her right ear to beneath her chin tightened into a smile of its own. "No grilled chicken today?" she asked. Her voice tinkled like the Italian-glass earrings I'd given Destiny on our tenth wedding anniversary.

"Nope," I said. "Dogs and swine."

"Me, too, Tru." Andreas gazed at a trio of women sitting just a few yards away on the hood of a red and black Camaro. "Skirts up to there. Shirts down to there. Looking at them makes

15

my little Dre go pitter-patter."

Down the line, a man cried out, "Hey!"

A mock wearing torn jeans and a tight T-shirt stood in front of a red-faced muscle-head in camouflage shorts and a gray beater.

"This ain't gonna end well," Andreas whispered.

"You can't fuckin' cut, dude," Camo Guy complained to the mock's massive back. "I know y'all supposed to be our lord and savior and shit but you on the street now and —"

The mock's left hand struck Camo Guy in his face and we all heard something crack.

The crowd gasped.

Camo Guy collapsed to the sidewalk as blood spurted from every hole in his face.

Andreas muttered, "Damn."

I groaned and made my way toward the bullshit.

"Be careful, Joe, " Trudy shouted.

"I'm hurt," the mock told me. He held up his giant hand — the middle finger now zigzagged.

"Looks like it's dislocated," I said.

Camo Guy writhed on the sidewalk, lost in blood and bone. At least he was still alive. For now.

"Hold still," I told the alien, taking his hand.

A bearded line-dweller shouted, "What the *fuck*, man? He ain't even hurt and you're treating him *first*? That's bull —"

The mock reached for his waistband and pulled out Big Baby, Piecemaker's little sister. "What's that? You sayin' something?"

Line Dweller's mouth popped close. No one else in the line complained. No one even *left* the line.

On the count of three, I snapped the alien's finger back in place. "Better?"

The Mahk-Ra flexed his hand. "Yep."

Then, in accordance with the law, Andreas tended Camo

Guy's broken nose.

Five minutes later, Trudy passed us Styrofoam cups filled with red punch and vodka. "On the house. You need it more than anybody."

Andreas chugged half of his cocktail before leaving the window. Full of liquid courage, he sauntered over to the women relaxing on the Camaro. "Ladies," I heard him say. "How are y'all this fine e-ven-ning?"

Still waiting for our dogs, I wandered over to the group. I recognized the chunky mulatto as Andreas's girl, Letty. The two other women eyed me, and their pointy, pink tongues licked the sides of their cracked, painted lips. At nearly sixty years old, I still had a square jaw and my height, low-cut salt-and-pepper hair and good teeth (most of them my own); but my heart hurt and I hunched when I walked and my smile felt as real as a polyester. For some women, though, especially in times like these, that was enough.

For the gray-eyed chick on the Camaro — *Carla? Darla?* — it had been plenty. Two weeks ago, we had rolled around the back of the rig. She had tasted like onions and penicillin, and over those ten minutes, I'd wanted to vomit. Miracle of miracles, I came just in time. Afterward, Carla-Darla had asked for my number. I'd lied and told her that a Mahk-Re had stolen my phone.

And now, I muttered, "Hey," barely meeting Carla-Darla's murky eyes and feeling gaggy from just remembering our time in the rig. Almost overcome with fatigue and the dull funk of depression, I watched Andreas flirt and flex his muscles for Letty, and tried to ignore the nagging twist in my gut. Because Letty was half-human, half Mahk-Ra. A product of what happened whenever Imperialist males from this world, and now, other worlds, landed on foreign soil.

Then you get the power. Then you get the women. By force, most times.

17

Couldn't trust Letty even if her momma had been born and bred in Echo Park. If Andreas decided to dump her ass and be a good husband to Alizé for once in his life, Letty would lash out and declare war. Report him just out of spite. Or kill him.

Human. Alien. Half and half. Dog. Crazy bitches be crazy bitches.

8:49 P.M.

I climbed back behind the ambulance's steering wheel.

Andreas slipped into the passenger seat with a sigh and a smile. "That's better."

"You're an asshole," I grumbled as I strapped on the seatbelt.

Andreas sucked his teeth. "Can't help it. Letty got great tits, man, and her *choca* is umm-umm-magically delicious."

"Great tits? Them rolls of fat?"

"Fat with nipples is called 'tits' in my book. And for real: you need to hook up with Theresa again, man."

Theresa? Where the hell did I get Carla-Darla?

"So what, she smell like a deli in a pharmacy," Andreas said, shrugging. "It ain't like it's 1985, man, when bitches smelled like Opium and Obsession and shit."

The nerve above my left eye twitched. "So I hook up with her again. And then what?"

"And then what, *what*?" Andreas shook his head. "Who say you gotta get all close and shit? That ain't the point. It's just fun, Pops. You remember what that is, right?"

No. I tasted my dinner again. "I'm not goin' there with her. *Especially* with her. It's pointless."

"Whatever, man." Andreas pulled out his flip-phone and dialed. "Stick to your sock and lotion. I don't give a..." He smiled. "*Amorcito. Precioso.* Just thinkin' 'bout you, baby."

Precioso? Had to be talking to the wife.

The radio blurted, and the dispatcher said, "87 CHARLIE.

18

Respond Code 3."

A blast of static and then…

Silence.

Not even white noise.

Dead air.

And then…

That familiar rumble in the sky.

"Hello?" Andreas said. "Baby, you there? Hello?"

The walls of my stomach vibrated and the skin across my face tingled. The metal fillings in my back teeth buzzed, alive now with electricity.

Andreas glared at his phone. "What the *hell*, man? They ain't supposed to come so fuckin' close."

I leaned forward to look up and out of the windshield. "We got some cowboys."

The rig's cabin darkened and shimmied.

Andreas dipped into his shirt pocket and plucked out a joint. "We should report this," he said, striking a match.

Trudy's cocktail had slowed my thinking, and I rubbed my forehead. "And then what?"

He offered me the joint.

I pushed his hand away and watched the darkened streets around us.

The ship coming in so low at full power had caused this ten-square mile section of Los Angeles to lose all electricity. The food truck. The street lights. Grocery stores. Even jacked up the natural electricity that kept people alive—heart, nervous system, brain signaling. Twenty-percent of the *old*-old folks, the coots born in the 1970's, dropped dead when those ships re-entered on a whim like this fucker had—the power sap screwed with their pacemakers. Last year, during the EMT graduation ceremony, Mayor Corbin Ortiz had collapsed right there on the grandstand as he congratulated the new class of medics.

During the first invasion, Mahk-Ra forces hadn't used all

of their wizzy-wig weapons and technology. Too much *BANG!* and there'd be nothing on earth left. And what kind of idiot destroyed the place he wanted for himself? So they had fought us — and won — with one hand tied behind their backs. But after one fatal mistake involving unleashed alien-ship power and the resulting death of the president of one of Earth's last superpowers, Mahk-Ra powers-that-be decreed that ships would only use their secondary engines, and no EMP drives *at all*, within 300 feet of a populated area. And nearly every Mahk-Ra captain heeded this ordinance.

But now, jerks like the one now navigating the ship above us, hated seeing the Ferrari parked in the garage and wanted to rev the engine. He had punched the EMP drive, who the hell knows why. Guess he wanted us earthlings to remember that he had the whole world in his hands.

Assholes existed in every galaxy.

Pungent smoke wafted from Andreas' nostrils and drifted toward me. "Hope that Code 3 ain't bleeding to death," he said, slumping in the seat.

I pushed it all back. Even sipped some of the weedy air, just so the numbness stayed with me a little while longer. I stared at the ship's ass and its yellow landing lights slowly retreating northeast, behind what remained of the Santa Monica mountains.

9:22 P.M.

My fillings stopped buzzing.

The sherbet-colored street lights popped back on.

Radio noise filled the cabin.

Time for the living to collect the dead.

"You there, 87 CHARLIE?" the dispatcher asked.

Andreas grabbed the handset from the dashboard and keyed the mic. "Yeah."

"What happened?"

"Mock ship came in strong. Where we supposed to go again?"

"5639 Curson. Sending it now to the CAD."

"Curson?" Andreas cocked his head. "A little far west for us, ain't it?"

The dispatcher chuckled. "Had to send a lot of rigs over to the old Forum. Beyoncé concert."

Andreas flipped the siren's switch. "When that bitch gon' die? What is she? Seventy?"

The apartment complex known as Park La Brea had been built at the end of World War II. Located between 3rd, Cochran, 6th and Fairfax, this complex boasted 18 13-story apartment towers and 31 two-story townhomes. The luxury apartments built in the early 2000's (and held together by spit and staples), had crumpled during the first battle of the Occupation. But the older buildings, having survived 20th-century earthquakes and riots, survived the big battle and every skirmish since. Back in the day, mostly older people had lived in this more than 100-year old development. As a young EMT, I drove up in here all the time, and on most of those trips, left with silent sirens.

After the invasion, though, and because of constant electrical outages and changes in the way we lived, Park La Brea now experienced a 50 percent drop in occupancy. The rent was still too damn high — not because of its location but because the damned things were literally fortresses.

It took a lot of swerving and braking to reach Curson — some drivers had died after that ship's re-entry and their stalled vehicles still blocked every third intersection. But we got there and I raced through Park La Brea's main entrance.

A cluster of grim-faced tenants huddled together on the dried lawn of 5639 Curson, one of the townhouses near the complex's center. Arms crossed, the neighbors threw worried glances at the rig and whispered to each other. No one spoke

21

as Andreas or I grabbed our med kits and rushed to the open front door.

The parquet wood floors were cluttered with video game controllers and flip-flops, blankets and remote controls. The aroma of fried meat wafted in the air and a dirty plate full of chicken wing bones had been abandoned on the sofa.

"EMT," I shouted.

"Up here!" a man shouted back.

Andreas and I considered the flight of stairs that would take us up to the owner of that voice.

"Pretty narrow," Andreas said. "Hope we don't need the stretcher."

The hot dogs and bacon bubbled in my stomach. "I hope a lot of shit, Dre," I said, starting up the stairs.

At the top of the second-floor landing, I shouted, "EMT," again.

"In here!" the man called out.

I made a left into the first doorway.

An elderly white couple stood just inside the pink-walled bedroom. Next to them, a gray-faced white man wearing the jersey of a basketball team that no longer existed hugged a trembling black woman wrapped in a yellow kimono.

A nighttime breeze was drifting in through the open window, lifting the gauzy rose curtains. The top corner of a 'Reading is for the Birds' Big Bird poster flapped in the draft. And a male Mahk-Ra, just under seven feet, lay on the floor. His crimson-gunmetal-colored blood gushed from a wound hidden beneath his EVER RIDE A MAHK? T-shirt. There were scratches on his face. A Big Baby, tucked in a holster, glistened with his blood.

"Oh, *shit*," Andreas muttered. "He dead?"

The alien's chest moved up... down... up... His breathing sounded like gravel caught in a vacuum cleaner.

"Not dead yet," I said, "but—"

And then I saw her.

A toffee-colored girl lay in the bed, lost in pink sheets, a pink duvet and pillows. Eleven years old, maybe twelve, with sandy-brown braids draped around her head like a halo. She wore a vintage Rihanna T-shirt and dachshund-printed flannel pajama bottoms. Blood was caked beneath her fingernails.

My breath caught and my heart shuddered—Kiara had adored dachshunds. Kiara had worn braids in the summertime.

The girl's lips were turning blue but her chest still moved, but not in the rhythmic way her chest should've been moving. Nor was she breathing the way she should've been breathing. With the purple bruising around her thin neck, she wasn't supposed to be breathing at all.

"Her..." the man said.

I placed my kit on the floor, then turned to the voice that had guided me here.

"Her name's Promise," the woman said.

I glanced around the bedroom at the drying Mahk-Ra blood speckling the walls and baseboards, lamps and bedpost.

"Can't..." the man said, shaking his head. "This is... crazy... I just..."

"You the dad?" I asked.

"Oh my..." he said, eyes glazed, pacing now. "What did we...?"

I snapped my fingers in the man's face. "Are. You. The. Father?"

He found my eyes and focused. "Yes. Flynn."

Eyes still on Flynn, I pointed to the woman in yellow. "Mom?"

He nodded. "Mackenzie."

Andreas pointed to the unconscious alien. "Y'all didn't tell 911 that one of them was down."

Flynn shook his head. "No. We... no."

"Cuz that *thing*..." Mackenzie swallowed and her angry

eyes glistened with silver tears. "I *told* you, Flynn. I told you."

Flynn's nostrils flared. "Shut up, Mack. You've told me enough."

"It *ain't* enough. I *told* you that we shoulda left this place right then, and —"

"It's not right," Flynn shouted. "They can't do whatever they want. They can't take our daughter."

"You shoulda known," Mackenzie whispered. "It doesn't matter what planet he's from, a woman knows that look." She turned to me. "She's *eleven*. A baby. I told him that I didn't care who he was or where he came from. Didn't matter cuz he pushed his way into *my* house and stormed up the stairs to take her. "She twisted her lips and spat, 'it's my right.' That's what he told us. And that's when I got... got..."

Anger depleted, her knees buckled. Flynn caught her before she collapsed to the floor. She inhaled and slowly exhaled. With a shaky hand, she held out the Glock.

Andreas and I gaped at the ancient weapon, then gaped at each other.

"I had no choice," the mother said. "I wasn't about to let him take her. Not this one. Not today. Not ever."

Stunned, I pointed to the old couple huddled near the doorway. "Who are you?"

The man cleared his throat, then futzed with his wire-rimmed glasses. "We live next door. We heard the commotion and... We don't know..." He nodded toward Mackenzie and Flynn, then he and his wife left the bedroom.

Promise's chest rattled and her breathing sounded strained.

"She needs a trach," Andreas said. "And we need to call —" he pointed to the alien — "in cuz..."

"I know," I said. "Call it in and I'll clear some space."

As Andreas contacted dispatch on his shoulder radio, I pushed the bed to the wall and piled all the dolls in the corner. My eye caught a small, brown-crusted object sitting atop a tie-

24

dyed teddy bear. "Found a bullet," I said, leaving the bloody stub of metal in its spot. "Okay, let's move her to the ground."

Andreas paused, and said, "Umm…"

"Let's move her," I said, bass in my tone.

Behind us, the Mahk-Ra's wheezing intensified.

I kneeled beside the girl and found the soft spot on her bruised neck. Slid my finger down until I found that dent, the place where I'd make the first cut.

Andreas handed me a scalpel.

With a firm grasp on the cutting tool, I made the horizontal, half-inch deep cut.

Mackenzie gasped.

Flynn whispered, "It's okay, babe."

I made another cut through the trachea, then whispered, "I'm in."

Andreas handed me a blue straw.

Holding my breath, I slipped the straw into the incision I'd made.

Soft sucking—she was breathing again. Her eyes fluttered open.

I smiled and whispered, "What's your name, sweetie?

Her lips moved but she could only whisper. "Promise."

Kiara.

"I'm just gonna bandage you up now," I told her. Gauze. Tape. A pat on her braided head. "All good."

Mackenzie darted over to the bed as I moved to the floor.

"How's this asshole doing?" I asked.

Andreas's hands were covered in weird-colored Mahk-Ra blood. "She shot his ass up. Left side. Right shoulder. Fuckin' knee cap. I cleaned 'em, packed 'em, but all them bullets had to have hit something so he'll probably need surgery." He jammed an I.V. needle into the alien's arm. "Lookin' at his face, seems the girl got in a few licks."

Sirens screamed in the distance.

"So… he's gonna live?" Flynn asked.

I nodded, then walked over to the bedroom window. "Yeah."

Red and blue lights from fast-moving cars reflected off windows near the complex's apartment windows.

Mackenzie whispered, "He'll know that I shot…?"

I turned back to face them. "Yeah. He'll know."

"But our baby," Flynn said. "She's gonna live?"

The sirens sounded closer.

"Yeah," I said, "but they're coming."

Flynn squared his shoulders, then took the Glock from his wife's hand.

She started to protest, but he placed a finger on her lips. "I'm not scared, honey. Just… go, okay?" He turned to me. "You'll take Promise to the hospital?"

I squinted at him. "You know—"

He nodded. "I know. And I'm ready."

Andreas and I jammed down the stairs and pulled the stretcher from the back of the rig.

The engine in the patrol car roared in the distance, bringing the Mahk-Ra closer to us.

We ran back up the stairs.

Mackenzie held Promise in her arms, but was now struggling to walk. "She's gettin' to be heavy," she said with an apologetic smile.

I plucked Promise from her mother's hold and ran back down the stairs. I slipped the girl into the foot-well of the passenger seat and placed a finger to my mouth. "Be very quiet, okay?" I whispered. "Don't move. Don't talk. Don't let anybody know you're down here, okay?"

She nodded.

Two patrol cars raced down Curson.

I ran back into the townhouse and dashed up the stairs. "They're here."

"Where's my baby?" Mackenzie asked, eyes wild.

"Don't worry," I told her. "She's safe."

Andreas rolled the injured Mahk-Ra on to his right side.

I slipped the board beneath him.

Boots clomped onto hardwood floor.

I strapped the alien to the board, and on a three-count, I lifted my end.

Boots clomped up the stairway.

"EMT," I shouted. "We're coming out."

Three Mahk-Ra over-sheriffs jammed into the small bedroom. No one wore their sunglasses and now, those black-black eyes searched our faces.

"What happened?" the tallest one demanded. His name tag said, "Gabe," and several bars decorated his shirt's epaulets. "What do we have here?"

"A dead man if you don't get outta the way," Andreas said.

"Move," Gabe ordered the other two.

The over-sheriffs stepped aside as Andreas and I carried their injured species-mate to the awaiting ambulance.

"Talk," Gabe demanded of the parents.

Out of the front door, and cool night air hit my face.

"Let's get the fuck outta here," Andreas whispered.

We slid the mock into the back of the rig and my partner climbed in beside him.

I slammed the door and hopped into the passenger seat.

Promise still hid in the foot-well.

At the townhouse next door, the two neighbors watched us from their front lawn.

She was smiling.

He was not.

The burning in my stomach returned. *Not good.*

"You okay, sweetie?" I asked Promise.

Wide-eyed, she nodded.

I turned the key in the ignition, and glanced in the right-

27

side window before pulling away from the curb.

At the complex's main entrance, more red and blue lights reflected off apartment windows. Sirens screamed and echoed through the empty streets.

"They sending everybody?" Andreas asked.

"Probably." I eased the rig past the Hertz's place and slowly exhaled.

What songs had Beyoncé warbled over at the old Forum? 'Love on Top?' Or her classic show closer 'Single Ladies'? Mom had loved that one.

Behind the rig, car tires screeched. Lots of car tires.

"Oh, *shit*," Andreas squawked.

I glanced in the rearview mirror.

Another patrol car, and then another, careened around the corner and stopped behind the first patrol car. Three more mock over-sheriffs, each clutching Piecemakers, jumped out of the cars. Two stormed inside 5639 Curson while one stopped on the sidewalk.

The neighbor-couple whirled around to beat it back into their townhouse.

Too late.

An mockover-sheriff pointed at the couple.

I braked as horror gripped my heart.

They froze and slowly turned to face him with their hands lifted in the air.

The mock spoke.

The woman shook her head.

The man nodded. He said something… He smiled…

The mock spoke again.

She dropped her hands.

Her husband, still smiling, brought his hand around his wife's shoulders. Then, he pointed in our direction.

The mock followed the man's finger, then raced into the townhouse to join the others.

"That fucker," Andreas said. "He just sold us out. He just—"

A woman screamed.

This far away, we could hear her scream. And that chilled my blood.

Dazzling white light burst from Promise's second-floor bedroom window.

A woman wearing a yellow kimono raced out of the townhouse's front door. Her arms flew in the air as the rest of her flexed and froze like she'd been dipped in nitro.

"Shit!" Andreas shouted.

I jerked in my seat. Tasted pennies—blood. I'd bitten my tongue.

"Both of them?" Andreas whispered.

I glanced down at Promise—her eyes were closed, and her thin fingers rested on the bandage around her throat. No longer feeling the rubbery hardness of the gas pedal, I drove toward 4th Street. My pulse slowed as the scene in the rearview mirror became a pinpoint and then...

Another pulse of white light brightened back there at the pinprick.

And then, another pulse of light.

The neighbors?

The mocks knew that Andreas and I had saved the girl. A girl who was, legally, supposed to belong to the mock in our rig, or worse— be dead.

But...

I'll get another chance.

"Now what?" Andreas asked from the back.

I caught my partner's eyes in the rearview mirror. "They'll come for her. Which means..."

"They'll come for us."

I nodded.

"And you're *cool* with that?"

I didn't say anything.

Andreas gawked at me, then turned to gawk out the rear window. He sighed, then said, "Well…" He pounded the door.

I slowed to a stop.

He tossed me one last look, then muttered, "Fuckin' mocks." He pushed open the back door and jumped out of the rig.

The door slammed closed as my partner of three years disappeared into the wilds of Occupied Los Angeles.

The injured alien laughed at me. "Don't worry. He's gonna die just like you will."

I sat there a moment, my mind finding its way to the answer. I glanced down at Promise.

Lightly snoring—she'd fallen asleep.

Do it.

She didn't hear me climb out of the rig and open the back door. Nor did she see me slip the empty hypodermic needle into the crook of the mock's elbow. She didn't know anything about old-fashioned air bubbles.

"Bad air," I whispered.

I left his ass somewhere on Hauser, near an overfilled Dumpster. No last words. No last look.

Now, go.

Heart in my throat, I climbed back into the rig and raced southeast. Destination: Compton. Not many mocks there. The safest place now for the human race.

One more chance.

PIKE STREET PICK UP

ADAM KORENMAN

L uc sucked his fingers as a powerful wind gusted through the street. Even with a shirt, hoodie, and jacket, the cold was unbearable. The smell of filth permeated this part of the city where municipal service was spotty. Garbage was piled high at the corners of buildings along with the dirty snow. Seagulls picked at it. The trash forced pedestrians to cluster at crossings as they trudged from one sidewalk to another, all under the impatient gaze of late-morning traffic. For Seattle's residents, it was inconvenient. For Luc, it was opportunity.

Just a few more, he thought. He watched a dump truck rumble up the street. It was only a few feet from the corner when a small boy darted out in front of the vehicle. The driver blasted the horn, screeched his brakes, but didn't have time to stop. Luc, already in motion, grabbed the kid and fell back onto the sidewalk, the truck missing them by inches.

"Jesus," Luc said, breathless. "What the hell are you doing?" He turned the kid around to reveal a dirty face and a mess of brown hair. "T.C.?"

31

The boy frowned. "Luc? Shit." T.C. pushed away and brushed at his raggedy clothes. "I wasn't looking to get saved by you."

Luc groaned. "You gotta stop playing this game. One of these days, you're gonna come up short a Good Samaritan."

T.C. grinned and saluted with a bony hand. "Yes, sir." He spun around and took a step when Luc caught him by the collar.

"What the shit?" He gawked at Luc's outstretched hand for a beat before pulling a worn leather wallet from his pocket. "Just practicing."

Luc was about to answer when something caught his attention. The thieves froze in place as two Civility Patrol officers passed within spitting distance. They wore matching black suits with *CP* stitched in gold over the breast. Both Mahk-Ra were tall, well over seven feet, and had the same dour expression.

Luc swatted the boy on the back. "Best clear out." He watched T.C. run down the sidewalk for a moment before returning his attention to the pedestrians. Fifteen long minutes later, the mark arrived.

He was heavyset, dressed in a brown business suit with a long overcoat. A leather briefcase dangled in one hand. Luc's green eyes lit up as he put the man through the inspection. *Dressed nice, but that doesn't mean anything. A poor man in a fancy suit is still a shitty take. Newer clothes, though, so that's a point. Fat, and who can stay fat on these rations? Three points. Expensive briefcase, that's four. But looks like he's in a real hurry. Add two.* He counted in his head. *Over five. Sweet.*

Four points or less was either too risky or not a good enough take. Luc approached the intersection, his whole body tingling.

The sign on the pre-occupation era signal switched to an orange walking figure and the crowd moved. Luc kept pace, pulling his hood down around his head. He stared at his feet and cracked his knuckles. *Fifteen feet.* He licked the inside of his teeth and breathed frigid air through his nostrils. *Ten feet.* A familiar fear built in his stomach. He looked up. *Go!*

He was just another pasty office worker. His jowls wobbled with each step, and he'd missed a spot shaving under his chin. Luc advanced, stepping out a little too far with his right foot. He tumbled forward, twirling his hands to regain his balance. The two collided, spinning around in an awkward dance before stopping. Luc blushed.

"Oh my gosh, I'm so sorry," Luc said. He brushed the mark's coat and squeezed his shoulders. "Jesus, what a klutz."

"It's no problem. I'm fine."

"Seriously, man. Did I hurt you? Gosh, I shoulda' been watching where I was going."

Rolling his eyes, the mark turned and scampered to the other side of the street. Luc continued his stroll. He turned down an alley, and then cut left through an abandoned market. Stalls lined the wide street, their awnings drawn and windows sealed. The stench of rotted produce and fish lingered. Luc ducked behind what once was a butcher's stand and pulled out the mark's leather wallet. His feet crunched on broken glass and empty streak injectors.

Luc had to bite down on his tongue to keep from shouting. Over two hundred dollars in paper money. He tucked the bills into a small pocket of his pants, then slid the wallet through a crack in the stall. He left with a spring in his step.

At the end of the small street, just before the turn toward the subways, Luc stopped. His eyes narrowed at an unwelcome sight. The local street element resorted to tagging their turf in a battle for artistic supremacy; actual violence meant contending with the CP -- or worse, Talon. The graffiti on the wall facing him didn't belong to any of them. Luc traced the figure: a red circle with the letters RIA in the center. *Resistance Is All.*

Lost in thought, Luc stepped from the alley and collided with another pedestrian. His fingers reflexively dipped into the gentleman's jacket. When Luc looked up, his hand snapped out.

The Mahk-Ra glared down at the pickpocket. The alien's dark eyes were hidden behind opaque sunglasses. Strange, dark blue splotches covered half of the mock's face and hands — Luc could only wonder what caused them — while his head was completely hairless. The occupier wore a tailored suit with *CP* stitched on the lapels. .

"Sorry," Luc croaked.

In a cold voice, the Mahk-Ra replied: "Watch where you are going, Earther." Large hands gripped Luc's shoulders and shifted him to the side. The alien walked past without another word.

Luc watched it turn the corner before releasing his breath. He collapsed against a storefront window, sucking in lungful's of air and letting them out in panicked spurts. *Fuck me, that was close. Jesus.* Luc looked down at his hands and saw a palm-sized black disk between his fingers. He marveled at the case for a moment before realizing what he had done. *Oh shit.*

THE LARGE WAREHOUSE hadn't been built for comfort, but it was home. Rickard had inherited the underground haven from his former boss — or taken it over, more likely. A shanty-town of metal and cardboard and cloth erected over time, climbing two stories high. Now there were schools, markets, and even a theater crammed into the space. Almost four hundred people resided there, and they worked to make it more livable all the time. With working water, adequate heat, and strong-arm security, it was a hell of a lot better than life outside on the streets.

Luc chewed his thumb and groaned. "How much longer, man?"

Rickard didn't look up. He wore jeweler's glasses over his regular set, which made his blue eyes cartoonish and large.

Silver streaks ran through his once black hair and beard. He held a glittering gem at the end of a long pair of tweezers while his other hand shined a bright light. After a moment, he set down the stone and leaned back on his stool. Rickard brought his gaze over to Luc. He placed his calloused hands over his stomach.

"It's good to see you, too."

"I know it's short," Luc began.

"And yet you came home anyway."

Luc rubbed the back of his neck. "I can get the rest."

Rickard took off both sets of glasses and rubbed his eyes. "You sure about that?" Before he had come to America, he had been an interrogator with the British Royal Marines. Or so he claimed. All that had been long before the Trick or Treat War. "Do you know how much you still owe me? Because I do. I've got it right on my board. Three thousand, not including interest."

Luc bit down on his thumb a little harder. "I would have hit more, but I ran into CP. I came back here to lay low."

That got the older man's attention. He leaned forward and glowered. "You mean to tell me that you rubbed shoulders with the law and then dragged ass back to my goddamn shop?"

"He didn't follow me," Luc sputtered. "Gave me the shark eyes and went on his merry."

"Just like that?" Rickard whistled. "Tom, are you listening to this shit?"

From behind one of the shelves, an imposing figure emerged. He stood just over seven feet of taut muscle. His skin was dark gray. *"Adame dun.* I heard." Tomo-Re wore only loose-fitting pants tied with a wire cable. Dirt and grease covered his body. He stared at Luc without emotion.

"And have you ever known CP to pass up a thief?"

Tomo cocked his head to the side. Strands of silver hair clung to his sweaty head. "The Civility Patrol responds to all cases. That is their mandate. It is unlikely they would pass this one along."

Rickard raised his eyebrows in Luc's direction. "What do you have to say to that?"

"He wasn't fucking there. Are you going to take his word over mine?"

The older man rose to his full height and came around his desk. "Kid, you ain't always the most honest player in the room."

Luc's eyes burned. He dug through his pockets. "I'm telling the truth. How else would I get this?" He pulled out the black disk and waved it in the air.

Rickard and Tomo stared at the onyx object, their mouths agape. The old man finally reached out and plucked it from Luc's fingers. He examined the disk, tracing its curves.

Luc paced. "I told you. Didn't know what I was doing 'til it was done. And the mock never felt the lift."

Rickard squeezed the center of the disk until it emitted a loud click. The two halves opened like a clamshell. Inside, resting on black foam, was a small silver cube. The edges were rounded and the sides were pockmarked in flecks of emerald. The smell of anise wafted around them.

"Fuck me sideways. Streak." Rickard picked up the cube and sniffed. He coughed suddenly, his entire face turning red. "Shit, that's about as pure as you get." He continued to hack, catching his breath a minute later. "Christ, Luc. You know the rules. I don't want this crap in my house."

Luc stammered. "I didn't know, Rickard. I swear."

Rickard grabbed Luc's chin in his fingers and pulled the younger man's face in close. "Look. I'm damned impressed you managed a nick like this without getting your throat slit, so I'm inclined to be lenient. But you fucked up bringing this shit here. I want it gone. Not dumped nearby. Not hidden in one of my safes. Gone. Do you understand?"

Luc nodded.

"Say it, Luc. I need to hear the words."

"I understand, sir." Luc's lower lip trembled.

Rickard smiled and pushed Luc away. He went back to his desk and selected another stone from a small pile. Flipping down his jeweler's glasses, he examined the rock for imperfections. "Steer clear of patrols, boy. You get caught with that mess, I don't know you."

Sunset brought bitter cold and snow flurries. Pedestrians doubled over, hoping to make it to shelter before they froze. Luc shifted from one foot to the other, his toes numb yet burning at the same time.

One mark, that's all I need. More than once, he saw a promising candidate, only to find a mock nearby. The occupiers had an innate ability to spot a lift, and they had a unique definition of justice. Luc felt the bones of his left pinky, massaging the spot where the joint jumped to the side. Lesson learned.

His hand dipped into his pocket and fingered the smooth disk. *Streak.* Rickard called it the 'bane of the broken.' Streak had arrived in the city about the same time the Red Spear started their operations. The way the rumor went, the drug was introduced by the aliens as a way to dull the population. *Now that's a terrifying thought.*

The sound of clicking heels drew his attention. Luc searched for the source and froze. There, weaving through the crowd, was the most beautiful woman he'd ever seen. Her thick coat was buttoned to her neck, and a plush scarf fluttered behind her. Luc stared, enchanted.

Hey fucker! Snap out of it. He blinked, focusing on the woman and starting his count. *Make-up, and that's expensive as hell. Two points.* He watched her move, admiring the sway of her hips. *Hands in her pockets, but she's wearing gloves. Something worth checking? No, don't guess.* He tallied the score. *Not enough.* The woman paused for a brief moment and glanced around the intersection. Her tongue touched her upper lip. *Fuck it.*

Luc rehearsed the movement in his head as they neared. Getting into that coat would require finesse. He searched the crowd until he saw an opportunity. Seconds later, Luc made his move.

His first step brought him in-line with a plump woman. He feigned a hit, rolling off her ample arm toward the street. Luc dragged his back foot, waiting until it caught on someone else's shoe. Using the momentum, he stumbled out toward traffic, pinwheeling his arms and shouting. At the last moment, Luc reached back and snatched a passing arm, pulling himself away from the asphalt. He ended up inches from the mark's face. Her perfume swarmed him.

"I'm so sorry, I was just trying to stop my fall."

The woman wasn't angry at all. "It's fine. Are you OK?" She was a little shorter than him, maybe a few years older, and even prettier up close.

"Yeah, geez. Just not my day." His fingers dipped into her pocket, sliding out as their bodies separated. A perfect bump. "Thanks for the save."

She disappeared into the crowd. Luc walked to the end of the block and ducked into a corner, snickering. He opened his gloved hand and his pulse quickened. He'd hoped for a wallet or maybe a piece of jewelry. Instead, a small red card rested in his palm. Hand lettered on it was the word GOTCHA.

"Nice lift, kid."

Luc looked up in time to see a fist rocket into his face, and the world exploded into stars.

THE ROOM STANK of sweat and piss and blood. Overhead, florescent lights flickered and snapped. Dead bugs packed one end of the fixture, casting a clumpy shadow toward the corner. Luc observed it all with one eye shut and an ice pack pressed against his head. There were no chairs, so he rested on the floor with his back against the bare concrete and waited. An hour later, the door opened. The woman from the street walked in, wearing a change of clothes. She looked down at Luc and frowned.

"I'm sorry for the rough treatment. Augustus is…zealous."

"Where am I?"

"East of the city."

Luc nodded. "You're Red Spear."

"What's left of the district cell," she said. "I'm Scarlet."

They both turned as the door opened and a mean-looking man entered. He wore a pistol in a worn holster on his thigh, and looked at Luc with a mixture of malice and apathy. The young thief couldn't help but stare at the long scar running from the man's eye to the back of his shaved head.

"That was a pretty sweet move on the street, my man. The way you looked so embarrassed. So sincere. And that pull?" He snickered. "You've got a gift."

Luc turned his face away. "Please don't kill me."

The man smiled wide. "No need to fear, brother." He sat down on his hands. "I'm Augustus. Who are you?"

"Luc." He tasted bile. "Luc Dufault."

Augustus tilted his head back and forth. "Well, Luc. I got a question for you." He pulled the black disk from his pocket. "Where did you get this?"

Luc held his breath. "I found it."

Augustus bared his teeth. "Not fucking likely." He dangled the disk in front of Luc's nose. "This is a mock case." He squeezed the sides and the disk opened, revealing the silver cube. "And *this* is streak. But I'm sure you knew that."

"Please, I didn't—"

"Don't fucking lie to me."

Scarlet pushed away from the wall. "Augustus, come on."

"I can smell a junkie a mile away." He lifted the cube out of the case, rubbing the sides. His thumb came away glittering with residue. "Do you need a hit? Are you coming down right now?"

"Don't." Luc edged away. "Look, I'm sorry about before. What do you want from me?"

"Your talent." Augustus slapped Luc hard on the leg. "We're planning something big, Luc. And we need you. A quick dip or two and you're free to go."

"Free?" Luc asked. "Whatever you resisters are planning, the rest of us will pay for it."

"And you're better?" Augustus snorted. "How many people lost ration tabs because of you? Or hard earned cash?"

"They may have gone to bed hungry, but at least they woke up."

Augustus grimaced. "He sounds like you, Scarlet."

She ignored him. "This is important, Luc."

"Don't bother." Augustus licked his teeth. "Go help the others prep. I'll finish here." He waited for her to leave. "I'll send someone to grab you tomorrow afternoon. Don't leave town."

Two very large men entered the room and lifted Luc up.

"Drop him off somewhere safe," Augustus said, putting the closed disk container in Luc's shirt pocket. He faced him, looking almost remorseful. "It's pretty cold tonight. You'll need something to keep you 'til morning." Augustus then said, "Sweet dreams, *ladrón*." He blew powdered streak into Luc's nostril. A single breath later, the world exploded.

LUC HIT THE ground hard, rolling twice before stopping. He barely heard the van speed away through the drug-induced fog. The world bucked and churned, and Luc could only grip the concrete beneath him and hold on for dear life.

After a minute -- or maybe an hour -- he managed to get to his feet. The small strip of sky overhead flicked between deep purple and pale green every time he blinked so he tried not to do that as much.

That made him laugh, but when he did his teeth tried to escape his mouth. Luc chased them around the alley, cramming them into his pockets with a curse. He licked his vacant gums and tasted blood, then vomited golden gems onto his shoes. *I should hide these for later.* Luc covered the jewels with garbage. When he was done, he sprinted headfirst into the nearest wall.

LUC WOKE STIFF and freezing. He squinted blind from his makeshift bed. A layer of ice coated the outer blankets and cracked noisily. His face ached, and the tips of his fingers were dark blue. He looked around, trying to get his bearings. A nearby trashcan smoldered, providing little heat. Unmoving bundles of wool peppered the alley, piled together for easy cleaning.

The smell of garbage lingered in the air. Luc pulled his coat over his nose and mouth and shuffled from the small corridor into the street. He rubbed his red eyes and touched the tender areas of his bruised face. His nose felt thick and throbbed painfully. The previous day's events trickled back into memory. The disk, the pretty mark, Red Spear. Luc's tongue scraped against his dry mouth. He was relieved to find he still had his teeth.

"You're alive." T.C. appeared from behind, wrapped in a blanket. "I've seen some rough trips, but that was wicked."

Luc tried to speak and regretted it. T.C. handed him a cup of milky water and he gulped it down. "What happened?" Luc croaked.

"Streak, if I had to guess. Which I don't. You were sweating

41

silver."

They turned the corner and emerged into a bustling pavilion. Stalls, carts, and barkers filled every inch of space. The crowd was a mix of humans and working-class Mahk-Re. The aliens towered over the Earthers, but wore the same expression of desperate need.

"Fresh flour," one man shouted. "Just off the farms. Only four ration tabs."

Another shook a knot of rat corpses. "Meat. Fresh kills, boiled for your safety. One tab gets you two rats."

An old woman pushed a cart through the center of the scrum. A black pot sat in the center, bubbling over with foamy broth. "Soup. Stave off the cold. Three rations or ten dollars."

T.C. licked his lips as they shuffled near the vendors. Luc felt inside his pockets, fingering a few crumpled bills – money he'd held back from Rickard. His stomach rumbled as he passed the soup cart. "Excuse me," he said. "I'll take two, please."

The woman ladled a steaming portion into a large cup and handed it over.

"Keep the change," Luc said, handing her a bill, feeling magnanimous.

They disappeared into the crowd. T.C. sipped at the soup, wincing as he burnt his tongue. Luc held his cup in one hand and took a gulp. The broth favored onions and leeks, but went down hardy. He sighed gratefully.

"You forget how good soup tastes," T.C. said. "I think this makes us even."

Luc shook his head. "Not by a long shot."

The kid grinned. "Happy to have you owe me one." They stopped at the outskirts of the market. "I need to head out if I'm gonna make my quota. See ya around, Luc." He started off, dodging the bums that peppered the sidewalk. T.C. stopped after a few yards and turned around. "Hey. Whatever you got into last night, don't do it again."

"Giving me advice now?"

"Just…this place would suck more without you." Downing his soup in a long gulp, T.C. took off for greener pastures and fatter wallets.

Luc reached the warehouse at dusk. He caught his reflection in a window and shuddered. Both eyes were black and bruised, and his nose was swollen. At least he had gotten all of the silver and green flecks off. A strong wind had kicked up from the north and howled through the man-made canyons of the city. The thief just reached the door when a gust pushed him into the building. Inside was warm and humid. Luc heard voices echoing from down in the main hall and went to investigate.

Rickard and Tomo sat at the old man's desk, sharing a bottle of *Bebasura*. A medium-built man in a long coat stood sentinel straight opposite the two. Nearby, an even more imposing Mahk watched the conversation unfold. Both strangers wore golden shields on their belts. Though he couldn't see it from this distance, Luc knew the letters FBI would be emblazoned across the metal. Like every cop in history, they looked perpetually pissed off.

Rickard smirked. "They're not squatters, Agent Harper. They're tenants, and you're welcome to look at my records.

The agent sighed. "Why do you act like we're on the same side?"

"We are," Rickard said. "I have the best interests of this city in mind. Look out there. Industrial ventilation, six generators and a full maintenance section. This isn't some shanty-town. This is a licensed halfway-house for deposed citizens. All the papers are in order."

"How many of these Earthers are criminals?" The Mahk stepped forward, his black eyes narrowing.

Rickard's nostrils flared. "Joe, you and I go back, so I'm going to forgive the discourtesy. Crime's dropped in my slice of the city since we opened our doors. People steal less when they have full stomachs and somewhere warm to sleep." He gestured to Tomo. "I'm even building bridges with the Mahk community."

JoHannas-ra approached Tomo. "*Parke ron cholo ap?*"

"Yes," Rickard interrupted. "Tom is employed of his own free will. And no, I don't appreciate you trying to speak to my assistant in Mahkanese. You think I'm some fucking degenerate, doesn't know his Core Mahk from his Elder? *Akina far*, arsehole." He glared at the other agent. "I thought we were pass this bullshit, Paul."

Harper's face darkened. "This is a murder investigation, Rickard. At least pretend to give a shit. Six humans dead on the wharf."

"Sounds like a light day for the wharf."

"One was a veteran." That quieted the old thief. "Sergeant Samir Pratel, 105th Legionnaires. He should have been on a reintegration compound, spending out his days in peace. Worse yet is the company he kept: Red Spear." Paul handed Rickard pics of the bodies. "Talon won't be far behind, and you don't want that heat."

Rickard tapped his chin. "How long ago were the bodies found?"

Paul sifted through his notes. "A few day ago, but they're two months old."

Luc heard a sneeze and realized with horror that it was his own. All eyes turned toward the shifting shadow by the entrance.

"Come in, boy. You might as well join the grown-ups." Rickard's eyes bulged for just a moment when he saw Luc's face.

"Lucky Luc?" Paul said. "Jesus, kid. You grew up fast."

Luc's face reddened. "Yessir, Agent Harper."

Ignoring Luc's damaged face Harper asked, "How many stamps do you have now?"

Luc squirmed. "Three."

"You gotta take better care of yourself kid." Now he reached a hand out to acknowledge Luc's bruises. "You can only be Lucky Luc for so long. Sooner or later the luck runs out." He turned to face Rickard. "Major, I'm here as a courtesy, so can you stop dicking me around?"

Rickard chewed on his lip for a moment before answering. "I'm not saying anything, you understand?"

"I remember. You don't help cops."

Rickard nodded. "Good. I have noticed that Lake Wenatchee had some unsavory types hanging around the last few months. Might be worth a look."

Paul smiled knowingly. He gestured for his partner to lead the way out. "Appreciate the tip, Major." He looked at Luc with affection. "Stay out of trouble, punk."

Luc actually grinned. "Catch the right crook...pig."

After the agents were gone, Rickard shot Luc an odd look. "Looks like you picked a fight with a truck. Where's our little secret?"

"Gone," Luc lied. "I was gonna warm up and get back to work." *And help the rebels.* "Why did Harper call you 'Major'?"

The old Brit gave a sour look. "Didn't you know I'm part of the Queen's Royal fucking Guard?" He rolled his eyes. "Harper and I go back to before this world got so shitty. At the time he didn't know my name, so he referred to me as Major. When we finally met, it just stuck."

There were grains of truth, Luc could tell, but Rickard always held a few cards back. Luc knew better than to pry. They shared a comfortable silence for a moment before the older man spoke.

"Listen. Don't worry about rent. Warm your bones, drink some *Bas*, maybe find a pretty girl from the quarters." He tapped the gory photos as he talked.

The sudden burst of kindness worried Luc, but he was too tired to be suspicious. "Thank you, sir. I appreciate it."

"Good," Rickard said. He seemed relieved. Rickard disappeared into his shop, staring at the pictures of the dead rebels. Moments later, he started into a hushed argument with Tomo.

Luc shuffled over to his bunk and stripped down. He relished heat from the generators; his fingertips were still purple. Even his lumpy mattress never felt so soft. The smell of wok-fried vegetables and steamed buns drifted up from the Chinese quarter in a moist cloud. Luc's mouth watered. The onion and leek soup seemed a lifetime ago. He gazed into the shadows and imagined that he could see the stars shining through. He closed his eyes and let exhaustion take him.

Hours later, when he was sure Rickard was asleep, Luc slipped out of the warehouse and made his way to the old market. Two rebels emerged from the shadows when he arrived. An Asian man with a scarred face held up a hand.

"Luc?"

The thief nodded.

"I'm Chen, and this is Lilith." He pointed, and a stocky older woman appeared. "We're headed to the Union district."

Luc shivered. "What about the curfew?" The work slowdowns on the dock had resulted in a curfew being imposed.

Chen and Lilith shared a grin and walked away. Luc lingered a moment.

"Guys? That wasn't an answer. Guys?"

THE OLD TRAM tunnels were abandoned a decade before and had become a covert transport line for the resistance. Using hand-powered carts, they could move around the city without interference.

Everyone on the team wore work clothes and -- except for Luc – light armor underneath. The black disk pressed against his chest; he had meant to get rid of it like Rickard had wanted but right now the weight of it oddly comforted him. Lilith and Chen sat on either side and worked the cranks. Chen hadn't spoken since they boarded, but Lilith hadn't stopped talking.

"No, it was the cheerleader's mouth." Everyone laughed. Her husky voice somehow made the dirty jokes even better.

"Where do you get these?" Luc asked.

Lilith beamed. "Scarlet and I hid in this caved-in bookstore in Newark. Stayed there about a year. Never was one for reading shit, so I stuck to joke books. Kept us sane." She punctuated the remark by clearing her nostrils over the moving tracks.

Five minutes later, Chen stopped the tram near an old platform. Scarlet and three large soldiers waited for them. She pulled Luc off the cart and stared into his eyes.

"Luc, this is Silo and the Twins."

The thief's eyebrows furrowed; the two men looked nothing alike.

Scarlet chewed on a protein bar. "Do you understand how this is going to work?"

Luc nodded. "Chen briefed me. Only sorta impossible."

"You'll be fine. It'll be crowded."

"That's not always better." He swallowed a lump down and followed the group out of the station. They walked in silence, and Luc practiced his movements in his head. When he looked up again, they were there.

Gastropod had once been a stylish pub, serving all types of customers. After the Occupation, it became a favored haven for those who had been members of the International Longshore and Warehouse Union Local 19. The Mahk-Ra had outlawed unions outright but there were still plenty of old timers around who now and then encouraged work slowdowns like the current one underway. Just enough to get attention for certain safety demands but not enough to have the Talon move in. `

There were casuals around, those seeking day work unloading a ship or even those who would have been called scabs back in the day, seeking work during this period but also to curry favor with their alien masters. Human and Mahk-Re workers populated the pub, the dark interior was packed to the brim, and loud music blared from the jukebox. A slender Mahk-Re stood guard outside. Dockworkers were allowed the privilege of moving about during the curfew, provided they had their papers.

"Make it quick," Scarlet said. "We got a schedule."

Jesus. Luc let out a breath through his nostrils. He tightened his stomach and stepped from the shadows, walking with purpose. The huge Mahk at the door held up a hand. "Curfew pass."

Luc handed over the forged document. He didn't have time to worry. The bouncer tossed it back without a glance.

"Move it."

Inside, the noise was deafening. Luc held his hands over his ears and walked to the bar. The stench of stale beer, greasy rations and sweat overpowered him. Everyone in the pub wore colorful ID cards. Red badges were security, yellow for fuel, and green for maintenance. Only white badges worked for their target. The risk was great; stealing from a dockworker meant hard time.

There had to be a hundred blue collar humans and aliens in the bar, and more than half wore white cards on their coveralls. Some of the IDs were dull, almost gray, and others glowed white. Those were the active cards, the ones with valid passes for work. Luc honed in. He cracked his fingers and licked the inside of his teeth. A familiar feeling grew in his stomach, much stronger than usual. His ritual had to be cut short. There was a strict time limit, and Luc didn't plan on being left behind.

The first dockworker slammed into his shoulder. Luc rolled, feigning drunk, and ran his hands down the man's chest. The badge snapped off under his palm and slid into his pocket. A few stumbling steps later he fell onto a table, knocking glasses to the floor. Three men shot up, swearing and swatting at him. Luc fended them off, slurring his words and slapping at their shoulders. They finally shoved him to the ground, where he disappeared into a sea of legs, along with three new badges.

Luc recovered, brushing crushed peanut shells from his back. He spotted a rough-looking man, a shift supervisor judging from the markings on his badge, chewing on a roll of jerky in the corner. The front of his badge gleamed in the dark room. Luc weaved his way to the grizzled old timer. One hand snapped out, catching a half-drunk bottle of *Bebasura* off the bar. Luc grinned glassy eyed.

"How'r'you doin, boss man?"

"Goddamn Director of Ports shut down negotiations again." The supervisor leered down at Luc. "You better be off shift, asshole. I'm not gonna get jammed up because you can't hold your shit."

Luc wobbled his head back and forth. "I'm fine. Jussa lil bit ta drink."

"Idiot." The older man grabbed Luc's collar. "Let's get you out of here before you get yourself killed."

Too easy. Luc's free hand dropped the beer bottle, catching a hold of the retaining pin on the badge clasp. The bottle shattered, spraying the supervisor with stinky foam. He pushed Luc away in disgust, and the badge came off with him. Luc made it to the exit. He was ready for another go when strong hands wrapped around his throat.

Cold air blasted him in the face. Luc flew into the alley behind the bar. Garbage and snow piled up on the walls, cushioning the impact. He took a second to catch his breath and rose to his feet. Two stone-faced men stared back. Both wore shining white badges.

"Fellas."

"Who the fuck are you?" one growled.

Luc hunched a shoulder. "Heard there was extra hands

needed around here."

"Try again." The second one sneered. "I saw you take an ID."

Shit. "Look guys, this is all a little misunderstanding."

"We'll see how that story holds up with the mocks." The first man approached.

"Wait!" He reached into his shirt. "I've got money. I'll give you everything I've got."

Both closed in until Luc could smell the rot in their teeth. "Money, *and* the badge."

"Of course." Luc brought up a clenched fist and set it against his chest. The men leaned in closer, blinking at him. Luc opened his palm and blew crushed streak out in a cloud, directly into their eager faces.

The powder sprayed all over the dockworker's eyes and mouths and they dropped. One held his throat and hacked, the other twitched on the ground as though electrified. Luc grabbed both of their IDs and stuffed them in his pocket. He rejoined Scarlet and the other rebels, never looking back.

THE DOCKING MOOR towered over the intersection of Pike Street and 6th Avenue. Onyx metal glistened under various spotlights, swaying in the heavy wind. Elite shock troops in silver power-armor patrolled the grounds. Luc chewed on his cheek and quietly panicked.

"With the badges and uniforms, we'll walk right in." Scarlet peered around the corner of the alley in which they stood. She glanced back at the team. "We just need access to the ship."

Luc kicked his feet to try and get some warmth into them. "Well, you guys should be good to go. I can make my own way home." He managed one step before Chen caught him with a palm to the chest.

"You're not done yet, thief." Scarlet pointed toward the

ramp. "There's still one more badge to grab."

Chen handed Luc a dockworker's uniform.

"I got you what you needed," he said as he reluctantly stepped into the loose fitting clothes. "What else do you want?"

As they watched, a Mahk-Ra emerged from the office. He wore a sharp black suit with *CP* stitched on the lapels, and, to Luc's shock, his skin sported blue splotches and his scalp was hairless.

"That," Scarlet said, "is Portus-ra. He's the Adjudicator for this territory."

Chen leaned in. "And the head of CP for the city." He spat. "Mocktard fuck."

Scarlet nodded. "He has the access pad for the ship. We need it." Before Luc could argue, she pushed him out of the shadows and toward the ramp.

They walked in a tight pack, crossing the distance to the first checkpoint. Two armed soldiers halted them. A quick scan of their IDs showed all were active and they went through. The next few minutes were a blur as they passed three more inspections, all without more than a second glance. The mocks had human-control down to a science, and didn't argue with a valid badge.

Overhead, the wind turned into a shriek and a freight ship called the Overseer arrived. With twin bubble domes over the front and a long hull, the ship earned the "Dragonfly" moniker. Six jets fired in rapid succession, halting the controlled fall and bringing the massive vessel to bear. It hovered over the surrounding buildings, buffeting the ground with powerful blasts of heat. After a few minutes negotiating the crosswind, it settled down on the moor with a thunderous clank. Docking lines dropped all around the ship and the rebels sprinted out, lashing down the craft to keep it stable.

"Go now." Scarlet hissed, appearing out of nowhere at Luc's side. "If Portus gets in first, we're done."

Luc swallowed, but his dry throat turned it into a gag. "He'll recognize me."

Scarlet took him by the shoulders. "What do you mean?"

"The disk. The streak. I took it off him."

She gasped, then recovered. "If you pulled once, you can do it again. Just pray he thinks all Earthers look alike."

"What if something goes wrong?"

"I won't let anything happen to you. Now go."

Luc marched toward Portus-ra, his stomach in knots. The Overseer's engines were still winding down as he approached, but he could just make out the sound of the Adjudicator's voice. Portus had two soldiers standing before him and barked orders into their faces. Luc couldn't understand the dialect except for every third word or so. He knew passable Mahkanese, but this sounded more like Elder or High Blade.

He ran the game without thinking. *Dressed very nice, so that's a point. Focused on his job, two points.* The Adjudicator gave him a brief glance. *He's a Mahk-Ra and hates humanity, minus a million fucking points.*

Portus waved off the two men and faced Luc. Luc withered under the icy gaze.

"Yes, Supervisor?"

Luc glanced down and saw he'd taken the supervisor's badge. *Great.* "Sir, I...uh...needed to ask about the..."

Portus seethed. "Spit it out, Earther."

"The negotiations," he blurted. "We never finished our previous conversation."

"There never was one," Portus retorted. "Get your team working, docker, or see your passes revoked."

Luc touched the back of his teeth with his tongue and ran through a dozen scenarios. All of them ended with his neck snapped. Portus grew more annoyed. "Excuse me, *sir*, but this isn't going to wait. I've got sixteen crews yammering to end this. That doesn't even touch the ones at home or in bars, not pulling shifts and not getting paid." He felt possessed.

"You have sixty seconds, human." Portus crossed his arms and set his jaw.

Luc's mind churned so fast he felt dizzy. "Every day, ships bypass the port and head up to Anchorage. That's food and supplies for the city that we desperately need, not to mention movement of resources. This, ah, intractability is strangling Seattle."

"And what is your suggestion?" Portus asked. "Would you have us acquiesce to this rabble?" He fingered an object in his pocket.

Luc watched the alien's hands. *He checks it. I'll need to slip something in there.* "Either that or find yourself a new set of scabs. I'll pull every crew off the docks, and you can have CP run the shifts. Or you and the Director's staff really negotiate so we can settle."

Portus sneered, hissing through his teeth. "Your sixty seconds are up. Back to work. Now." He strode toward the office door.

Luc held his breath and lunged forward. He grabbed Portus' shoulder and braced. It all went too fast to register, but he suddenly found himself face down in the dirt, his arm screaming in pain. Portus had a knee pressed into Luc's spine and held the younger man's arm at an extreme angle.

"You touch me, filth? You must care little for your life."

"No," Luc spat. "I just care about my workers." The ground dropped away and Luc slammed into the wall of the ramp. Portus held him a foot off the ground effortlessly. "No work, no money. No money, no food." Rickard's words came out of his mouth. "People steal less, work better, harder, when they have full stomachs and somewhere warm to sleep."

Portus looked ready to split the thief in two, but softened at the last second. He lowered Luc to the ground and leaned in inches from his face. "I'll take it under consideration. Now get back to work before I grind you into powder." He straightened and stormed off, never noticing Luc's fingers slipping out of his coat pocket.

After Portus was gone, Luc checked the object in his hand. The access pad was a flat disk, about the size of his palm, and shimmered blue in the light. It wasn't a perfect match for the streak container, but it was close and the alien hadn't seemed to notice.

Like most Mahk-Ra vessels, the Overseer was clean and built-to-form. The corridors were bright and uniformly grayish blue. Colored stripes ran along the walls leading to different areas of the ship. The signs were in Mahkanese, but helpful pictures guided the human crew. It didn't take long to reach the immense cargo hold at the end of the craft. The room stretched back a hundred feet and was filled floor-to-ceiling with crates. A strange smell permeated the hold. *Licorice.*

Scarlet stopped the group at a pallet of unmarked boxes, her brow furrowed. She unlatched the nearest one and dipped her hand inside, coming back with small bags of white powder.

"Chems?" She went from crate to crate, opening the containers and peering inside. "What the hell is going on?"

"What were you expecting?" Luc asked.

"Bleaters. Explosives. This was supposed to be a weapons run."

Luc shrugged. "Isn't this a good thing? You wanted to go all Robin Hood anyway. We can hand this out on the streets."

Scarlet shook her head. "We didn't bring refrigerant. This stuff would spoil before we got it home." She looked around, suddenly alert. "Where are the others?"

She found them a few minutes later toward the back of the cargo bay, next to a series of broken crates. Each man carried two full backpacks, and they were busy loading up a set of duffle bags with brown boxes. When Silo saw Scarlet approaching, he whispered to the others. They stood in a line, blocking the crates behind them.

"What did you find?" She asked. When they didn't answer, she crew cold. "Seriously, can you cut the bullshit?"

They stepped aside, and Scarlet's face darkened. She reached into the broken crates and pulled out three disks. Inside were silver cubes specked with emerald shards.

"Streak? Jesus, what are you doing?"

Silo nodded to the other men and they resumed loading up the drugs. "Augustus gave us orders: Gather as much as we can, then get back to the harbor site."

"And when were you going to tell me?"

Silo rolled his massive shoulders. "Wasn't gonna." He sighed. "It's nothing personal. I've been with Augustus a lot longer than you. He's family. Let's go, we got enough."

One of the men -- Luc called them Unibrow and Goon -- held up a large briefcase and shook it. Something inside rattled. "What about the calling card?"

"Hey, asshole," Silo hissed. "How 'bout you be a little more fucking careful?"

Luc's blood ran cold. "Is that…"

"We can't," Scarlet said. "I don't know what chem's are in these crates, but if we blow this ship, we could poison half the city."

"Not half," a voice said. "But close enough, if they weren't inert in this current form."

They turned to face the new voice and saw Portus-ra standing between the crates, flanked by armed shock troopers. One of them had a portable facial recognition scanner clipped to his belt. Luc figured that's how they'd been made; one of the cell members present had previously been ID somewhere. The Adjudicator smiled like a cat with a mouse. Luc raised his hands, but the others trained their weapons on the aliens. Portus-ra held the black disk streak container that Luc had switched in his pocket.

PIKE STREET PICK UP

"You've quite the skill as a pick pocket." With contempt he tossed the drug container to Luc who caught it in one hand "A pity that ability went to waste."

Staring at him, without thinking, Luc returned the disk to his shirt pocket.

"Please," Portus said. "Put your guns down and surrender. Your night of fun is over."

Scarlet had a fierce look in her eye but fear shined through. Sweat dripped from her temples and ran down her cheeks. Luc's mouth was cotton dry, and he focused all his energy on not coughing or making a sound while the standoff ran its course. The soldiers sneered and grunted and rattled their rifles. For a minute, no one moved. Then Unibrow hollered and fired.

Everything exploded into noise and light. Luc dropped to the ground, trying to make himself as flat as possible. Bullets snapped and zipped inches overhead. He looked to the side and saw Goon take a bleater blast to the chest. His face a mask of pain, he fell to the floor. One of the agents caught a burst in the head and dropped, followed quickly by the other. Portus remained in place, but his grin was long gone. Silo slung his rifle and stalked over, drawing a long and heavy-looking blade. Before anyone had a chance to speak, he buried the knife into Portus' chest and left it there. The alien gave a disappointing squeak and collapsed.

Luc felt hands under his arms and was hoisted to his feet. Unibrow, sporting a spray of red across his face, pushed Luc toward the door. The thief stopped next to Scarlet who was staring at her fallen comrades

"Come on," Luc said. "Time to go."

They ran ahead and caught up to Lilith, who had her arm over Chen's shoulder. Lilith had a hole in her stomach and was struggling to keep up. Luc took the other side and urged them forward, sweating and grunting from the effort. There was a persistent ringing in Luc's ears, one he knew would never go

56

away.

Cold air hit them like a fist. Luc was blind as he went from the bright ship to the darkness outside. The soldiers milled about, not paying any attention to the humans on the ramp. If they'd heard any of the noise from inside, they weren't showing it. Luc didn't wait to be found out. He led the way, stumbling every few feet as Lilith's energy faded. Her skin was pale as a sheet, but she refused to lose consciousness.

Ten minutes went in a blur. One moment they were running through the streets, the next they were stumbling down frozen alleys. They finally stopped to catch their breath. Luc rested Lilith against a wall. He edged out of the alley and looked down the empty street toward the moor. Still quiet.

"We can't stay here," Luc said to no one. After a moment of silence he looked back. "Hey! What's the plan?"

Scarlet knelt by Lilith's side, holding her hand. The woman managed a brief smile. Scarlet faced the group. "We can still make the harbor. Where's Parker?"

Luc didn't understand until he noticed Unibrow was gone.

"Didn't make it," Silo said. Black scorch marks covered his back, peeling the armor and clothing to reveal red blistery skin beneath. He didn't seem bothered. "I'm headed to the harbor, but you should go home." He held up a hand to ward off Scarlet's protest. "Augustus has some sensitive stuff there. I don't think he'd like you getting involved."

"Like hell," Scarlet said. "We're sticking together and I'm getting some answers."

"He'll kill you." Silo let the words hang there a moment. "Comrades or not, he will kill you."

Scarlet sneered. "Let him fucking try."

She'd just finished the breath when an immense shockwave slammed down on the group, followed by a deafening thunderclap. Luc looked up, gasping. A blue mushroom cloud rose from the ramp. The Overseer's fuel burned bright and hot, even from this distance. Alarms sounded around the city and cries of pain could be heard echoing down the street. Luc watched, awestruck, as the ship keeled over and smashed into an adjacent building. Glass and brick fell to the pavement below.

Luc didn't wait to be told this time. He grabbed Lilith's arm and pulled, grunting with effort. "Come on, Lilith. We have to keep moving. The whole city is awake."

"Luc," Scarlet said.

He ignored her, wrapping both hands around Lilith's torso to get more leverage. Blood oozed over his wrist. He tried several times to get her up, but just didn't have the strength. "Damn it, Lilith. I need you to help me." Then he looked at her face. Lilith's eyes were fixed and vacant. Her skin was the color of the snow around them and her breath no longer fogged in the air. Luc eased her down and backed away, his stomach lurching.

Scarlet took his arm, pulling toward the other end of the alley. He protested, or at least thought he did. They stripped off their armor and left it behind; it was slowing them down and drew too much attention. The padded gear was dropped in the snow drifts next to the garbage, the bloodstains, and the lifeless body of Lilith McCoy.

"I'M REAL SORRY about this." Augustus sucked on his cigarette and moped. If the snow had any effect on him, he wasn't showing. The resistance leader walked a few paces behind the trio, his pistol pointed at their backs. Next to him, Silo—who Luc had learned was named Silofski—seemed remorseful but had a look of *I warned you* written on his face. He'd pulled his gun on them when they'd reached the harbor.

Scarlet, Chen and Luc walked in a line between rows of shipping containers. Off in the distance, the sirens of the first responders still echoed in the night. Most of the city was focused in one direction, which left no one to care about the scene playing out on the docks.

"You were never supposed to come here," Augustus said. "Never. This was my shop, Scarlet." He indicated the pile of duffels filled with pure Streak. "My retirement. Leave the fighting to the zealots. Do you think the Cause wants to be associated with this? Hmm? Do you?"

Luc bit down on his tongue to keep from whimpering. The fear he'd felt at the ramp seemed like butterflies in his stomach compared to this. Augustus wore a long knife on his belt, but also a pistol. Luc prayed for the bullet. In this temperature, he probably wouldn't even feel it.

"You piece of shit." Scarlet's shot daggers with her eyes. "I trusted you. I followed you. Prat was right."

Anger flashed onto the cell leader's face. "Pratel was a lunatic. Always going on about the 'mission.' How'd that work out for him? I kept us together. I kept us alive." He let out an exasperated sigh. "Christ, Scarlet. I've fought the mocks for 20 years. I've buried more brothers than I can count. I wasn't about to go out like that. I deserve better."

"And becoming a drug dealer is better?" She spat on the ground. "The others will come down on you for this."

He snorted. "Let them. I've got an army now."

"You killed Prat." Luc barely recognized his own voice. "Didn't you?"

Augustus's face grew mean as he approached the thief. "Yes. Prat wanted to die fighting the Mahk-Ra. He would have, along with all of us, if I hadn't stepped in."

Scarlet shook her head, tears rolling down her cheeks. "You sonofabitch."

"I didn't enjoy it, Scarlet." He sounded remorseful. "Prat was my friend. He was appointed because he was special. A genuine super soldier, fresh off the alien front, but he was too aggressive. Too willing to sacrifice."

The group arrived at a small strip of concrete adjacent to the water. Ice and frigid waves lapped at the harbor. "We were fine before he got promoted. Before we started his wild crusade. I didn't have a choice. If I hadn't taken him out, we'd all be dead. You hear me?"

"Yeah, we hear you." Chen grimaced against a cold gust of wind. He stopped near the edge of the pavement. "We all hear you. What's the point of telling us all this, if you plan to kill us?"

Augustus smirked, his face calm. "I didn't want to carry your bodies all the way to the water." He pointed his pistol and fired in one smooth movement.

Chen shouted as the bullet pierced his chest just over the heart. He fell backwards, grasping at air. His body hit the freezing ice and broke through, sinking into the frozen depths.

"Fuck," Luc shouted. "Jesus, man. What the hell is wrong with you?"

Augustus turned the pistol on the thief and frowned. "You were really amazing, *ladrón*. I'm sorry it has to end this way."

Luc squeezed his eyes shut, but the gunshot was still deafening. He was right; he didn't feel a thing. After a few seconds, he was brave enough to open his eyes. Augustus still had his pistol out, but he was looking toward the far end of the docks. Two figures stood in shadows. The taller carried an enormous machine-gun and pointed it at the group. The smaller held a revolver, and smoke trailed from its barrel.

"I'm sorry too, Augustus." The small man spoke with a crisp British clip, his voice aged by years of yelling and drinking and smoking. He wore a high-collar overcoat and fingerless gloves. "If I'd known you'd take Pratel's appointment so personally, I would have handled it better."

"Major," Augustus started. "I can explain."

Luc watched as the two men stepped into the light. He didn't understand what his eyes were seeing. It was impossible.

There was just no reason for Rickard or Tomo to be here on the docks.

"I think I heard enough," Rickard said. He nodded to Tomo and the Mahk-Re crossed to Silo and relieved him of his weapons. "Honestly, I don't know what to say. Now, why don't you let Scarlet and this young man go so we can talk."

Augustus kept his pistol trained on Luc's chest. His eyes were wild, and he was sweating despite the cold. "I don't think I can do that."

"Enough people are dead because of you, Augustus. I think it's time to stop."

Hoarsely the deposed cell leader said, "Eat me, old man."

Rickard lowered his head and Tomo leapt forward.

The alien was fast, way faster than anything that large should be. A panicked Augustus fired blindly, missing Tomo. But Luc had tracked the gun's twitching barrel. Before he knew what he was doing, he was airborne, leaping hard to the side. He watched a flash of bright light explode in front of the gun and something slammed into his chest, knocking his breath away.

Luc landed on his side on the snowy ground, gasping for air. Scarlet dropped down to cradle him, tears welling in her eyes. Luc's head rolled to his shoulder in time for him to see Rickard approach Augustus. Tomo had the rebel on his knees. Rickard raised his revolver.

"Thank you for your services, Augustus. They are no longer needed."

The darkness swarmed his vision, and Luc's last thought was that it felt too warm. He slipped away to the sound of a single gunshot.

THE PAIN STARTED in his chest and spread outward like angry fire ants. It took a minute, but he was eventually able to open his eyes and make out a few shapes. Well, more colored blobs than anything else, but it was better than nothing.

Luc tried to prop himself up on one arm, but the pain swatted him down. This wasn't his mattress; that was immediately apparent. The normal lumps had been replaced by comfortable springs and new fabric. He settled back onto a pillow and fought down a wave of nausea. His stomach rolled and bucked.

"Just too stubborn to die, aren't you?" Rickard shuffled over, scratching at his beard. He looked relieved.

"What happened?" He rasped.

Rickard got a cup of water and a bendy straw. He stuck one end between Luc's chapped lips and held the glass in place. "You did some stupid things, made some bad choices, and ended up with less than pleasant company." He set the water aside.

Luc brought his hand to his head and found an IV line running from his wrist. "You killed Augustus," he said.

"He was an arsehole," Rickard said. "A useful one, but I never should have...Well, we all make mistakes. Now I've remedied that one."

The room spun faster. Luc gripped the sides of the mattress and held on tight. "I was shot."

Rickard smiled at this. He'd been waiting for the big reveal. Reaching behind his back he produced a familiar black disk and held it up to the light. One side was still as smooth and flawless as the day Luc had stolen it. The other side now had a sizable dent just off the center. "One in a million shot, kid. Lucky these things are so damn sturdy. Now, I'd be lying if I said I wasn't a little upset you kept this. But it saved your life."

"Sorry I lied," Luc said.

"I lied first," Rickard said. "I never wanted this life for you. It's too short, and damn if I haven't grown fond of you." Rickard placed a hand on Luc's good shoulder. "Rest easy, son. Tomorrow, we can share secrets." He lumbered off toward the living quarter, disappearing into the colorful network of tents and stalls.

Luc understood there was a grain of truth in what Rickard said. He'd figure out it had been him to tell Scarlet and Augustus who he was and his expertise. That day he picked her pocket was a set-up, a way for them to "recruit" him for the job. Another hand appeared and caressed his cheek. Luc followed the arm up until he saw Scarlet's bruised but beautiful face. Her lips parted, offering just the hint of a smile. "You're just full of surprises."

"I try." He grinned, but a surge of pain erased it. "I'm sorry about Lilith and Chen."

"They were amazing. I miss them already." She wiped her eyes. "Thank you for saving me."

Luc nodded. "Any time."

Scarlet sat down on the edge of the bed. "A great thief and heroic?"

He placed his hand on her leg and looked into her eyes. "And available." He flashed his teeth.

She laughed, covering her mouth. "Luc, I've got a resistance to plan. There's not a lot of time for…anything else. Besides, after last night most of us in the Spear are going to do some serious laying low." She stood up. "But I hope this isn't the last I see of you." Scarlet bent down and kissed Luc's forehead. She started for the door.

"You'll be back," he called out. "Won't be able to stay away for long." Luc watched her disappear around the corner. He snickered and held his hand to his face. There, in between his fingers, was the travel token he'd lifted from her pockets.

He licked his lips and waited. "Yeah, she'll be back."

THE END

UNION DAY

LISA MORTON

was twelve before I got to dress up for Halloween.

Those of us born under Mahk-Ra rule knew October 31st as Union Day, the commemoration of the invasion and eventual conquest of Earth. We knew it as a day of military parades and speeches. We didn't really celebrate it; we endured it.

But our parents had known it as something different and they'd told us stories about a holiday in autumn when they'd put on costumes and gone to neighbors' houses and collected candy. Dad had even taught my little brother Marcus and I how to draw pumpkins on that day; we didn't have real pumpkins (the Mahk-Ra didn't consider them an efficient food source) but we had paper and orange and black pens. Sometimes it was strange to realize just how different the world had been for our parents. How the world had been a place where joy was freely celebrated on special days, not ground out of us by the dull stomping of army boots.

All the time I was growing up, whenever my parents talked about how things had been before the invasion, their voices got soft, almost whispering. They were afraid, of course, because the Mahk-Ra were always listening, but I think it also made them sad; sometimes you could hear them choke up a little. In that way, they seemed like most of my friends' parents. Some, like my best friend Teryn, had only a mom; or there was our friend Steve, who was being raised by friends because both of his parents had been taken away. They had plenty of other reasons to be sad, so why dwell on a past they couldn't have back?

Even though they still had each other, my mom and dad didn't seem so different from anyone else. My dad had fought in the war twenty years ago and had lost part of a leg; he still had the same fake foot they'd given him back then, although now it was so scuffed and chipped that it made him walk with an uneven stride. My mom always said that the missing leg had probably been a good thing because the Mahk-Ra didn't conscript humans who were already injured. And they'd never taken Mom because she was a few years older than Dad and they only took young people.

I knew they'd probably take me some day. They'd decided early on that I was "special" because I did better on a lot of their tests than other kids did. They pulled me out of my school and put me in a different one where, aside from the usual stuff like math and science and English, we also learned how to speak, act, and fight like the Mahk-Ra. At first I hated being separated from my friends and forced to work harder than them, but after a while I got used to it. We were taught their history and learned about their "great campaign to unify the cosmos."

But at night, when they sent us home, we learned *other* things.

We lived in a two-room apartment in a big complex, along with a lot of other families. Teryn and her mom lived across the hall from us. All of our apartments were outfitted with monitors that supposedly watched us as much as we watched them, but a lot of them had broken down years ago and had never been fixed. Dad said we had it easier nowadays than the first few years after the conquest, when the Mahk-Ra had locked down everything. "They used to arrest people for just humming old songs," he said.

We sometimes thought we were happy in our little rooms. At night, kids played with each other and made fun of their Mahk-Ra teachers while the adults traded memories from the old days. But they did it in those quiet voices while glancing over their shoulders.

It turned out they were right to do that because not long after I turned twelve, the Mahk-Ra started cracking down again. Teryn and I traded stories we'd heard, about friends of friends suddenly disappearing. We gossiped and chattered because we knew it would *never* happen to us.

Except it did.

Every few weeks, there was a big market held in a different place in our neighborhood. The new location was passed orally; computer networks weren't safe. People found an empty building or neglected vacant lot somewhere and set up tables where they traded everything from home-grown vegetables to memory sticks full of forbidden music and movies. I'd never been allowed to go ("too dangerous," Dad had told me), but sometimes one of my folks found out where it was and went to get something. Mom had heard it was going to happen in an old parking structure one Saturday night in October, and she'd gone down there with some herbs she'd picked in an overgrown field a few miles away. She'd meant to swap them for some meat, but then she found something she thought was even more important than food:

An old book. The kind printed on paper pages and bound between heavy pieces of board. The kind the Mahk-Ra had destroyed by the millions when they'd taken over.

We never even knew what book it was, because about the time Mom was handing her canvas sack of leaves over in exchange for the book, Mahk-Ra over-sheriffs came charging through. A lot of people ran. Some screamed and hid. The Mahk-Ra shot three people trying to escape and everybody who was left – including Mom – stopped and put their hands up. The Mahk-Ra rounded up 32 people, led them to a waiting hover-truck, and took them to a detention center to await trial. Which of course was a joke, because a Mahk-Ra "trial" for human conspirators consisted entirely of a computer assigning a sentence.

For trading in black market items, the sentence was usually five years in a RZ camp. Most people in labor camps died before they completed their sentences.

We heard about all this third-hand. We knew it must be true only because Mom hadn't come home. The next day we saw her picture on the news channel.

It was October 27th. Union Day was four days away. Dad found out from a friend in the FBI that Mom would receive sentencing on November 1st and be moved immediately to the camp three hundred miles away from where we lived in Sacramento. We'd probably never see her again.

I suddenly hated the Mahk-Ra. Up until then they'd seemed almost like big jokes that we didn't really take seriously. I knew they'd hurt my dad during the war, but those were surely *different* Mahk-Ra's, not like the ones who taught us and read us the news and handed us our weekly rations at the Distribution Center.

Now I began to fantasize about killing them. I'd steal one of their pulse rifles, gun down the guards around the Detention Center, and get my mom out. Then I'd kill more of them, just to teach them a lesson.

After that, I'd lead a rebellion to get them off our planet forever.

Dad was gone a lot during the days after Mom's arrest. Sometimes he came home with other men we'd never seen before. They'd huddle together over our kitchen table, going over plans they'd gotten of the Detention Center. Apparently it had once served another purpose, as some kind of office building; one of Dad's new friends had worked there and still remembered the layout pretty well. The men and my father talked all night, about how many guards there'd be and how to get a pass-card for the locked doors and how to get Mom out before more Mahk-Ra arrived. My dad got big black circles under his eyes because he never slept.

On the 30th – the day before Union Day – all the Mahk-Ra at my school were involved in preparing for the big celebrations. In honor of the day, school would be closed, but we'd be expected to attend the festivities.

Like hell I would.

That night I couldn't sleep. I got up and came out into the main room. Dad was alone, sitting, looking at something. He was crying. That scared me almost more than anything, because I'd never seen either of my folks cry before. I was glad Marcus was asleep, because he was only eight and the sight of Dad crying would've freaked him out.

"Dad...?"

He looked up, sniffling. "Oh, R.T." Everybody except the stupid Mahk-Ra called me "R.T."; only the aliens insisted on using my real name, which was Artemis. I hated that name, and couldn't believe my parents had given me something so dumb, although I did like the stories I'd heard about the Greek goddess of the hunt.

Dad said, "Hey, come over here, I want to show you something." Dad gestured at something on the table. I joined him and saw an old-fashioned photo printed on paper; it showed a boy about Marcus's age dressed in black with a white face and holding a big round orange thing with a jagged black grin. The boy was kind of baring his teeth, which looked big and fake and pointed.

Dad had shown us this photo before, and it had always made us laugh, especially when we realized the kid with the crazy teeth was *him*.

"That's you on Halloween, right?"

Dad sniffled and nodded. "Yep. I was Count Dracula. Back before we had Union Day – before the invasion happened and the Mahk-Ra came – it was the best day of the whole year. You could dress up however you wanted on that day. And neighbors gave you candy."

I never knew what to say to that. Candy was a rare delicacy in our world. Today, the Mahk-Ra had given each of us one piece of state-sanctioned sugar candy, wrapped in little papers that read "Celebrate Union Day!" on them. The candy wasn't very good – it was just crystallized sugar – but we cherished it like it was the most amazing thing ever.

Dad gazed down fondly at the photo. "We'd eat so much chocolate it's a wonder we didn't explode. I really miss chocolate..."

I tried to imagine a world where you could be whatever you wanted to be – a hero or a monster or a princess - and in return you were rewarded with an unimaginable variety of exotic treats, but it was too far away from anything I knew. "Sounds like fun," I said, knowing how weak that sounded.

"It was the best. Sometimes we'd play pranks, run around like little demons throwing eggs at houses or hiding behind bushes and suddenly leaping out to scare our friends. Your mother loved it, too. She told me she once dressed as the Bride of Dracula, so I guess we were meant for each other."

That brought reality crashing back down. We were no longer in the world in that photo, but in one where mothers could be arrested just for trying to bring a book home. "What's going to happen to Mom?"

Dad sagged. "I don't know, baby. A group of us are going to try to get her out tomorrow. If we wait any longer, they'll move her to the labor camp and we won't have a chance. But what with it being Union Day tomorrow, we're hoping maybe enough of the Mahk-Ra will be distracted that we'll have a shot."

"Won't they still be guarding the Detention Center?"

"Only the outside, and our sources tell us there are only four of them scheduled. If we can just get past them and get in, we know where she is. And if we can get her out, we can alter her identity chip so they won't be able to I.D. her. But..."

"But what?"

"There are only three of us. Even with Union Day happening, it's going to be pretty slim chances." Dad cleared his throat and turned to me, very serious. "If anything happens to me tomorrow, I've already talked to your Aunt Marcia about taking you and Marcus..."

I made a face – I didn't like Aunt Marcia. She was Dad's sister, but they didn't look anything alike and I don't think he especially liked her, either. She worked for the Mahk-Ra as a Community Leader, which basically meant she finked on anybody she didn't like and the Mahk-Ra paid her for it. She always had a fake smile that creeped me out and I didn't doubt that she'd turn me in if she thought she could get an extra helping of milk for it. "Dad, we're not going to live with Aunt Marcia."

He said, loudly, "Artemis, listen to me!" I did, because he'd used my full name, and he only did that when it was bad or important. "You're twelve; your brother is only eight. You can't live alone. Now Marcia didn't have to agree to look after you, but she did –"

I interrupted him. "Dad, did it ever occur to you that maybe Aunt Marcia's why Mom got arrested?"

It took him about three entire seconds to say anything. "Why would you think that?"

"Because a few days ago when she came over for dinner, she

mentioned how much she missed fresh eggs and Mom made a comment about the upcoming market in the parking lot."

I watched as the pieces clicked together in Dad's head. "Damn. Damn. Damn." He got up and walked away, keeping his back to me. I looked down at the table, at the picture of him in that silly outfit, and I thought about what he'd told me. About Halloween, and kids running around in costumes and playing pranks, and –

"Dad!" I jumped up as he turned to look at me. "Dad, we can help - Marcus and me. We'll do just what you did on Halloween – we'll wear costumes and throw silly things and run around. I'll bet we can distract those guards at the front of the Detention Center enough for you to get in."

Dad smiled, but it was a sad kind of smile. "R.T., I appreciate the creative problem solving, but your mother would never forgive me if I put you in that kind of danger –"

"We won't be in any danger! We'll just run in, scream and jump around, and run off again. We'll have stuff over our heads so they won't be able to I.D. us."

"Masks."

"What?"

Dad sauntered up. "A disguise for your head is called a 'mask'."

"Right. We could make some masks out of bags or cardboard."

Dad was really thinking it over now. "You know, that kind of distractions not a bad idea, though. I'll bet I could get one of the guys to-"

I cut him off. "The Mahk-Ra would just shoot an adult who did it – but even they won't shoot little kids."

He didn't say anything, so I pressed my advantage. "Let us do this. Marcus and I – well, we want Mom home as much as you do. We should be able to help." When he still didn't say anything, I added, "And if the Mahk-Ra *do* catch us, maybe they'll just send us all to the same labor camp. That'd still be better than living with Aunt Marcia."

Dad gave one quiet laugh before gesturing at one of the kitchen chairs. "Okay, I'm not saying I'll let you do this, but let's talk."

I sat down.

An hour later he said yes.

In the morning, I told Marcus all about Halloween. By the time I was done, he was screaming, "I WANT HALLOWEEN!"

He and I spent the rest of the morning working on our costumes. We went to a nearby garbage dump and scavenged a large burlap potato sack, a length of cable, a battered metal tray, a stained man's jacket, a plastic bucket with a hole in the bottom, a two-foot section of pipe, and – the major score – a full-face gas mask with a crack running through the plastic that covered the eyes. We carted everything home, laid it out on the living area floor, and Marcus grabbed the pipe, thrusting it out like a sword. "I want to be a soldier!"

We made Marcus a soldier outfit by using the cable to attach the metal tray to the burlap sack, and cutting eye holes in the bucket and strapping it to his head. If we'd had some paint and a little more detail, it could've passed for the cheap armor they stuck earth recruits in for their first combat mission.

For me, I just wore the old jacket, which was so huge on me that it hung to my knees, and the gas mask. Marcus eyed me, puzzled. "What're you supposed to be?"

I thought for a few seconds and answered, "A gas mask salesman!"

Marcus frowned; he didn't think it was funny.

Next, we made our arsenal: A handful of pebbles in an old tin can made a noisemaker. We didn't have eggs or toilet paper to spare, but we found some foul-smelling sludge near the dump that we scraped into sheets of old paper and carefully wadded up inside a backpack.

The parades would start at noon. We had to be ready by then, because the troops that were usually quartered inside the Detention Center would be out strutting with the rest of the Mahk-Ra. At eleven, Dad came in, looked at us, and burst into laughter. "You two look great! I wish I had a camera."

We went over the plan again. Marcus didn't really listen, but I knew he'd be fine. His job was to run around and scream like a maniac, a role he was born to.

At eleven-thirty, Dad had to go. He got down on his knees and gathered us up in a big hug, one arm for each of us. "I'm really proud of both of you," he said. "But I want you to be careful."

"Let's just get Mom back," I said.

Marcus shouted, "Happy Halloween!"

Fifteen minutes after Dad left, we took off our costumes. Marcus whined, "Why can't we just leave them on?"

"Because, dummy, somebody might see us and report us before we even reach the Detention Center."

He kicked his foot, sullenly. He was *ready*.

We left the apartment, each of us lugging a big pack. As we closed our door behind us, Teryn and her mom came out of their apartment. "Hi," she said, before spotting our packs and adding, "What're you carrying?"

We hadn't even left our building yet, and already things were going wrong. What were the chances of running into my best friend right then? I thought fast. "Oh, just some stuff we have to give to Aunt Marcia."

"Oh." Teryn wrinkled her nose; she'd met Aunt Marcia once and her opinion had been no better than mine. "So you're not going to the parade?"

"We are, but over by her place."

Teryn's mom tugged at her. "C'mon, Teryn, we'll be late. Let's go."

"Okay. See you later, I guess."

"Right. 'Bye."

Teryn and her mom strode off. Marcus looked up at me, frowning. "You never said we were going to Aunt Marcia's place."

"I just told her that, moron, because otherwise she would've asked us to go with them to the parade."

Marcus nodded. "Ohhhh. Okay."

He wasn't always the brightest. At least the Mahk-Ra would never put *him* in a special school with extra work.

The Detention Center was about eight blocks away. The parade had started by the time we reached the street, and the sidewalks were lined with onlookers who were waving little paper flags on sticks that we'd all been issued. Mahk-Ra in gleaming armor, tall and proud, marched down the streets in perfect unison as military music blared out of speakers on the buildings overhead.

Marcus and I had come prepared – we pulled out our own little flags and waved them overhead as he pushed through the rear of the crowd. It wasn't easy weaving in and out of all the spectators, but nobody paid any attention to two kids waving their flags.

We hadn't counted on the crowds and we were a couple of minutes late reaching the Detention Center. We went by it once, and sure enough, there, at the top of a short flight of steps leading up to the main doors on the front of the big concrete building, were four Mahk-Ra with pulse rifles.

Dad and his two friends were on the street nearby, waving their own flags. I approached and nudged Dad from behind. He looked down, nodded once, and went back to cheering the troops on.

At the end of the Detention Center building was an alley lined with dumpsters. It was empty. I pulled Marcus down behind the first bin and shrugged out of my backpack.

Marcus asked, "Now?"

I grinned at him. "Now."

He lowered his own burden and dug into it excitedly. I helped him pull on his burlap "armor" and "helmet", then cautioned him to wait until I got on my jacket and gas mask.

"You got your rattle?"

He held it up and shook it, and I nearly flinched at the terrible racket it made. I checked my own weaponry: the pack full of sludge-bombs.

We were ready.

"Remember, Marcus – you take off running when I tell you to, okay?"

"Yeah, yeah, I got it. Let's just GO."

He ran off, full of prankster spirit. I just hoped he'd actually listen to me when it counted, then I ran out after him.

The people on the street were intent on the parade, and nobody noticed us until we reached the bottom of the steps leading up to the Detention Center. My mask was hard to see through clearly – the crack split my view in half – but I made out two of the Mahk-Ra looking down at us curiously.

Marcus darted up the stairs, shaking the homemade rattle joyfully, shouting "Happy Halloween!" over and over.

The Mahk-Ra all looked down at him, perplexed. That's the thing about them; the Mahk-Ra just don't get humor at all. If you hand them something deliberately ridiculous, it kind of short circuits them for a few seconds.

Marcus went nuts.

He darted around their feet and between their legs, a blur of motion and energy and noise that could be heard even over the piped-in marching music.

The Mahk-Ra looked down and tried to back away. The commander ordered Marcus to stop.

He laughed and jumped up and down, shaking the rattle.

One of the Mahk-Ra started to lower his rifle.

My heart jumped into my throat and for a second I froze.

But the Mahk-Ra in charge made a motion, and the rifle went up again.

I caught a glimpse of Dad watching, too, and knew he must've been as nervous as I was.

And that was my cue.

I hopped up the steps, yelling the phrase Dad had taught me: "Trick or treat!"

The four Mahk-Ra turned away from Marcus to focus on me. That was when I threw the first sludge-bomb. My aim was good, and it hit the closest Mahk-Ra in the chest.

The expression on the alien's face as he looked down at the gooey mess and then *smelled* it was priceless. I couldn't help but laugh, even though I knew it could get me imprisoned or killed. I laughed because I felt powerful, for the first time in my life. Ironically, hiding under a mask had liberated me, and I felt wild and free. I'd never felt this way before.

I threw the next missile. It hit another soldier in the leg. My third lob was a direct hit, and the Mahk-Ra commander blinked as he wiped dark brown filth from his face.

Oh, he was *mad*. He yelled and gestured.

I didn't need six years of studying their language to know he'd just said, "*Get them!*"

I turned to run. If I'd stopped to think, I might have imagined a pulse ray burning my back, sending me crashing down to death; or the humans on the sidewalks siding with their captors and encircling me, trapping me.

But instead I was filled with the joy of the Halloween spirit. I was invincible. I laughed and ran.

The humans parted, giving me room.

I heard a crash. I couldn't resist stopping to look back.

Two of the Mahk-Ra had tripped and tumbled down the steps. Six feet away, Marcus pointed at them, shaking with laughter.

I understood: The little demon had tripped them.

I waved to him to join me, and he ran up. "C'mon!"

The Mahk-Ra picked themselves up and came after us – *all four of them*. This was better than we'd hoped. They might have no sense of humor, but they could certainly get mad.

We *flew* down that sidewalk and cut into the alley. As we ran, we tore off our costumes and tossed them into the dumpsters. We heard the Mahk-Ra coming behind us, but we still had a good lead on them. We reached the other end of the alley and turned right. We pushed through the legs of the mob, and I handed Marcus one of the flags I'd saved from the pack. Other kids had lined up at the front of the crowd, so they could see the parade. We were just two more, dutifully celebrating Union Day in state-approved style.

I heard the Mahk-Ra behind us, but we were indistinguishable from the rest. We'd made it.

We stayed there until the parades ended and the crowds started to dissolve, heading back to their homes in the late afternoon.

...

Dad was waiting for us at home.

Mom was with him.

...

It turned out we'd actually done our jobs a little *too* well, and had put one wrinkle in the plan: Dad had originally been planning to knock one of the Mahk-Ra out and take his pass-card. Fortunately, though, there was one other soldier none of us had known about stationed just inside the door, and he came out to see what had happened when his four fellow guards disappeared. Dad had taken him down with one blow from a lead pipe. Nobody noticed, since everyone else was watching the parade.

The rest had been easy. They'd found Mom quickly and gotten her out. Once they were two blocks away from the Detention Center, they'd removed her identification chip, ground it underfoot, and inserted a new one.

It turned out that one of Dad's new friends worked for the Red Spear and they got us out of Sacramento with some forged transfer papers. We were shocked to find out how big the Red Spear was, and how well organized. By the time we wound up in Atlanta, on the other side of the country, I knew change was coming – maybe not this year, or even next year, but sooner than the Mahk-Ra thought.

We lived quietly, though, with our new names and our new apartment. But when October came around, Marcus started talking about Halloween again. Dad tried to hush him up, but he wouldn't be dissuaded. So we made him a costume – this time he wanted to be a vampire like Dad in the old photo.

We went to the Union Day parades in the afternoon, with everyone else, then we came back to our new, bigger apartment, and we all giggled and teased as we helped Marcus into his costume, with a cape made from a black plastic trash bag and white makeup that had once been chalk dust.

At about eight o'clock, we were surprised by a knock on our door. We opened it to find two kids there, one dressed in a makeshift spacesuit and the other as a soot-smeared hobo. "Trick or treat," they cried, holding out cloth bags.

Marcus saw them, shrieked, "Trick!" and ran to join them.

I still had some of the Mahk-Ra issued candy left over from the day's celebrations, so I tossed one piece into each of their bags. "Happy Halloween," I said.

I meant it.

THE END

HOW THE GAME IS PLAYED

ROB HART

Gaige-ra moves his pen as if he was carving something intricate. He is always and forever taking notes. Many think it's because he's methodical, his precision being a testament to his skill as a leader. Others believe he does it to increase pressure on whoever is addressing the Mahk-Ra High Command. That he enjoys making speakers simmer in the silence.

If that's the case, and Jaylon-ra assumes that it is, then the tactic works.

Ten feet and a trillion miles away, the back of Jaylon-ra's neck grows hot. A tiny muscle next to his eye twitches. He had mentally prepared himself for a variety of scenarios: Applause, dismissal, laughter, reprimand.

He was not prepared to be written at for three full minutes.

The other members of the High Command are also uncomfortable. They fidget in their seats at the horseshoe-shaped table, looking at each other, at Gaige-ra sitting at the head. Their brows arched and their mouths turned up, wondering when their leader is going to speak.

Jaylon-ra can't take his mind off the encroaching feeling of dread that he can feel circling the boundaries of the room like a predator.

Gaige-ra places his pen down, carefully lining it along the edge of his paper. The entire High Command freezes in anticipation. Jaylon-ra holds his breath.

"I remain unconvinced," says Gaige-ra. "There is far too much risk here, for too little perceived gain."

There's murmuring and head-nodding from the High Command, all of them working very hard to visibly agree with Gaige-ra's assessment. Jaylon-ra winces, and glances at Paul, his human affairs advisor, whose face is blank as a stretch of sand.

"I know this plan is... unorthodox," Jaylon-ra says. "But you have said, on several occasions, that we must think creatively if we are to blunt the Red Spear."

"Yes," Gaige-ra nods, eyes looking up and away, like he's trying to recall if he did, in fact, say that. "But what you're suggesting..."

"I'm not asking that we hold a real election," Jaylon-ra says. He pauses, realizing he interrupted Gaige-ra. He searches the leader's wide, flat face for signs of disapproval. He sees nothing, and wonders if that's good or bad.

Jaylon-ra continues, "All we have to do is give the humans the appearance of a choice. If we can make them believe it, and I'm elected anyway, then they'll have no one to blame but themselves."

Gaige-ra clasps his hands together in front of him. "This opponent you're suggesting... Councilman Mancuso. His cousin is currently incarcerated for orchestrating Red Spear activity in Chicago. A close childhood friend is suspected in a Red Spear bombing. These are troubling instances of dissent."

Paul clears his throat. Everyone in the High Command looks up at him.

"If I may," Paul says.

Gaige-ra looks at Jaylon-ra. "You're using the translator? This is highly unorthodox. Humans are not permitted to listen in on High Command meetings. You know this."

"I understand that," Jaylon-ra says, regretting that he didn't make that clear up front. "But he is a trusted advisor and integral to this plan. I would not have included him on this meeting if he didn't offer valuable insight."

Gaige-ra frowns, seething. "Fine. He may speak."

Paul clears his throat again. "You're... sir. Every person on this planet has some tenuous connection to the Red Spear. Councilman Mancuso backed us when we did the curfew. He backed us on the school integration program. He has been with us on a number of extremely unpopular votes, and he's never let us down. He's an old man who wants to take care of his district. He understands how the game is played."

Gaige-ra clenches his teeth. "And how is the game played, *human*?"

"It's politics one-oh-one," says Paul, not ruffled by the disdain in Gaige-ra's voice. "There's a reason his district gets awarded more discretionary spending than anyone else. If anything, he owes us on this."

Gaige-ra gazes at the ceiling. Then he sighs and leans forward. "Leaving the New York City Council in place was an experiment. Even with their veto power removed, we hoped this gesture would mollify the uprisings. Perhaps even engender some trust. Out of fifty-one seats, we had hoped to elect a dozen Mahk-Ra council members by now. There are three. Worse, human on Mahk-Ra violence has risen in the past year."

Paul steps forward, a little surer of himself. Jaylon-ra is worried. He's watched humans killed for less. He's been a very good human affairs advisor. It would be a shame to see him incinerated.

At least he looks presentable, in his pressed suit, his blonde hair carefully swept back. Gaige-ra values neatness.

"District races are different from citywide races," Paul says. "We've run the numbers. We know the Mahk-Ra will vote in high numbers. Even taking into account a surge from human voters, based on our projections, the voting machines only need to dump every third human vote, and we'll take the election in a walk."

"I would not put this plan in front of you if I wasn't confident it would work," Jaylon-ra says.

Gaige-ra puts his hand flat on the desk. Breathes deep.

This is it. Jaylon-ra leans back in his seat. He had high hopes when he woke up this morning. He worked over this plan for a month. It was supposed to impress the High Command enough that maybe, just maybe, he could serve out one more four-year term and then get the hell off this planet. Get promoted to someplace that hasn't been strip-mined to oblivion, where you could get a decent meal more often than on special occasions.

Gaige-ra looks up and there's something on his face that looks almost encouraging.

"We lost three shipping facilities in that region this month alone," he says. "Clearly something needs to be done. We fight them and they fight back and nothing gets solved. Perhaps we can try this plan. I'm not so sure, but your record has been... fairly consistent."

Jaylon-ra is so shocked that his mouth falls open. He tries to regain his composure, express some form of gratitude, when Gaige-ra sticks a thin finger into the air. "But understand that if it fails, you will be held accountable."

As Jaylon-ra and Paul absorb the warning, the hard-light hologram displaying the Command disappears, and with the blue-tinted glow of it gone, the room is plunged into darkness, illuminated only by cloud-choked sunlight drifting through sheer blinds.

Jaylon-ra looks out on the empty expanse of the crumbling

City Council chambers. The scratched wooden desks and leather maroon chairs, patched with strips of red duct tape, are pushed off to the edges of the room, revealing a maroon carpet that's worn pink from foot traffic. The statue of Thomas Jefferson against the far wall, dinged and chipped, looms in the shadows like a ghoul.

Once, apparently, this room was grand. Now it reeks of mold and old books. It looks like the shell of something that moved on a long time ago.

This is what Jaylon-ra is stuck with if he fails.

The enormity of that thought makes his stomach flip.

He gets up from his chair and turns to Paul, who is fumbling around in the jacket of his suit for his pack of cigarettes.

"Some days," Jaylon-ra says, "I hate being the mayor of New York."

. . .

Councilman Mancuso picks up the final slice of pizza from the round aluminum tray, folds it, and takes an aggressive bite, one ear tilted toward Paul, who's finishing his explanation of the plan.

Jaylon-ra surveys the empty restaurant. With the lights off it's dark, made darker by the glare of the sun streaming through the front window. The chairs are turned on to the tables, and the proprietor, a stooped old man, is slowly mopping the floor of the kitchen. Every few minutes someone wanders up to the window and peeks in, then shuffles away, head down.

Paul says, "If you go along with this, we'd be willing to entertain some big asks for your district. Within reason, of course. We might have to space them out a bit or make some gifts to surrounding districts, so it doesn't look like a quid pro quo, but you'll be rewarded."

Mancuso puts down the half-eaten slice and wipes his face with a napkin. His hands are as thick and heavy as the rest of him. A former football player who became a personal injury lawyer. An old school politico and currently the longest-serving member of the City Council. He's held the Coney Island-Gravesend-Bensonhurst seat ever since term limits were abolished, right before the Makh-Ra settled Earth. His hair has gone gray but his eyes are sharp, his smile natural and his handshake firm.

Mancuso picks up the stub of pizza and points it at Jaylon-ra. "You know, before you mocks got here, this place used to be open until three or four in the afternoon. They only stayed open as long as they had fresh ingredients for the pies. Now, they're lucky to make it to noon, twelve-thirty." He takes another bite, and through a mouthful of dough says, "Still the best pizza in the city, though. By a mile."

Paul bristles. "We would appreciate it if you didn't use the term 'mocks.' It's offensive…"

Jaylon-ra puts up his hand to silence Paul. "I've heard worse. So, Councilman, what do you think of the plan?"

"I get asked about this place all the time," Mancuso says. "People come up to me in the street and say, 'I haven't had a Tosto's pie in three years because of these fucking mocks, taking away the things we grow and we build'. And they ask me why I support you. I tell them, what choice do I have, right? I can fight you and get nothing, or I can go along and I can take care of them. Best of a bad situation. Not everyone sees it like that. Some asshole is planning to primary me in two years."

"If you're hesitant…" Jaylon-ra starts.

Mancuso shakes his head. He pops the crust into his mouth, chews, and swallows, then takes a long drink of wine from a paper cup. He wipes his hands and his face with the napkin again, and says, "Elections are tough. You don't know that, because you come along and turn the mayor into an appointed position. And you're the one who makes the appointment. I still have to run for my seat. If I even agree to this, I need a promise.

If things go south for my re-election, I want a job across the hall. Make me a commissioner of something."

Paul says, "Humans don't get to be commissioners. That's not how it's done."

Mancuso arches his brow and looks at Jaylon-ra. "You're the fucking mayor. You'll make something up. But I don't want to find myself out on the street if this is the thing that pushes me over the edge with my constituents. Do you get me?"

"We can work something out," Jaylon-ra says.

"Okay then," Mancuso says. "Good. Now, there's some things you need to understand, if this is going to work."

Jaylon-ra nods. "I get that."

"No, you don't." Mancuso smiles, offering his hand to Jaylon-ra. They shake, and Mancuso pulls him forward, lowering his voice. "If I get out there and roll over, the people are going to figure out what's up. This is a fight. We have to go at this like we're going at it, you know what I mean?" He throws a glance at Paul. "I don't want to be seen as some prick willing to sell out his species for a paycheck, you know?"

Jaylon-ra tries to pull his hand away and Mancuso pulls him closer, puts his other hand over their clasped fists. "I used to chair the Finance Committee, back when the Council and the mayor negotiated the budget. All of this stuff was worked out behind closed doors, you understand? But the public hearings, the people wanted to see you were fighting for them. So I would call up the commissioners the night before, let them know, I was going to scream at them about some stuff. Funding for cops, firehouses, things like that. Something good for the papers. It's no hard feelings. That's just politics. Now do you get what I mean?"

Jaylon-ra nods, still trying to pull away. Mancuso lets go and sits back.

"You don't get the politics end of this, you mocks," Mancuso says, eyeing Paul again. "You don't understand how the ground game is played. You march in and topple governments. You don't work with them. You never developed this skillset." Mancuso points to himself. "I can be helpful, you know what I mean?"

Paul tries to speak but Jaylon-ra puts up his hand again. "Your experience here can be invaluable, Councilman Mancuso. Our ultimate goal here is to save lives. People are dying because the Red Spear can't accept reality. We're not even asking anyone to kneel. Just to stop. We're working for the same thing…"

Mancuso waves his hand. "You don't need to sell me. Saving lives is good. What matters is what you can do for my district."

Paul asks, "What will it take?"

"Let's start with a school," Mancuso says. "I need a new middle school."

Paul's jaw drops. "That's… that's impossible. Sourcing the concrete alone… we'd literally have to take it off an outbound supply ship."

Mancuso shrugs. "You want your plan to work? I'll play along. I'll do your dance. I need a school. I need to show my constituents that I got something out of it."

"The whole point of this is to conceal what we're doing, not advertise it," says Jaylon-ra.

Mancuso shakes his head. "You really don't get it. Look, let me explain something to you. Back when I chaired Finance, I used to get the most discretionary funding, besides the Speaker. And the papers would beat me up. They called me the 'pork-chop pol.' They said it was a corrupt system that awarded some people and punished others. But my constituents didn't give a shit. They'd come up to me and say, 'You must be doing something right, because you got more money for us than anyone else.' What matters is that I can deliver for them."

Paul tries to say something but Jaylon-ra interjects. "Maybe we can make this work…"

"Good," Mancuso says. "Because the school isn't the only

thing on my list."

. . .

Jaylon-ra peeks around the heavy, gray curtain. They had chosen a catering hall in the College Point section of Queens because of how difficult it was to get there; the 7 train was shut down two years ago and the Q65 bus only ran during rush hour.

And yet, the hall is packed, a few hundred deep easy, people spilling out onto the sidewalk in front. They've had to set up video monitors procured from local schools so the people who couldn't get inside could at least watch.

On the makeshift stage beyond the curtain, there's a small table between two podiums, where the moderators are reviewing their notes. Alison Mertz, a human junior political reporter from NY1, and Ronel-ra, the Mahk-Ra editor-in-chief of the *New York Post*. Mancuso insisted there had to be one of each, in order to keep up appearances.

This campaign has been a crash-course in the minutiae of New York City politics. Back in the day, there had to be one Democrat and one Republican at everything. At the polling sites, if you had a Russian interpreter from the Republican party, you needed one from the Democratic party. Inspecting ballots? You need a lawyer from each party present. If one party is in charge of something, the other party can level charges of corruption or coercion.

The presence of a human inquisitor not party to the plan adds a heavy layer of unease to the proceedings. Which is made worse by the signs being lofted by the humans in the crowd.

SHAM! SHAM! SHAM!

DE-MOCK-RACY.

GO HOME MOCKS.

Along with some other less polite phrases.

There are Mahk-Ra in the crowd, too, towering over the humans, but outnumbered three to one, a number Jaylon-ra can't help but dwell on. They don't have signs, either.

Paul appears at Jaylon-ra's side and asks, "Are you ready?"

"Maybe. I like to think that reason and good sense will prevail here."

"Well…" says Paul. "Try to work the crowd a little, too."

The human moderator starts her introduction of the debate format — asking the audience to hold reactions until the end, that candidates would be given sixty seconds to answer questions and the option of a thirty second rebuttal. Jaylon-ra steps on stage as Mancuso enters from the other side, his smiling dazzling in the harsh white light.

There are far more boos than cheers.

Mancuso feeds off the electrical energy of the crowd, his eyes wide and bright, his chest puffed out.

They meet at the center and shake hands. Mancuso pulls Jaylon-ra close and says, "Remember what I said, okay? It's all part of the show."

Jaylon-ra nods, wondering if that's a reassurance or a threat, and takes his place at the podium. Ronel-ra leans into the microphone and says, "The candidates will each give a brief opening statement. We flipped a coin back stage, and Mayor Jaylon-ra won. He has chosen to go first."

The crowd goes silent, all eyes cast toward the podium. Jaylon-ra clears his throat and says, "Thank you all, for being here. It's so good to see so many… brave New Yorkers out here today. Now, I understand that the past two decades have been difficult. In my time as your mayor, I have learned that New York is a strong, proud city. This election is about choice. We want you to tell us what you've chosen. This is about the people. I believe that I offer the best plan for governing, and I trust by the end of this you'll see that."

There's a smattering of applause from the Mahk-Ra in the audience, followed by an explosion of boos from the humans. Ronel-ra leans into the microphone and says, "Please hold all reaction until the end. The more noise you make, the less questions we can ask. If you can't behave, you will be ejected."

The crowd falls silent. Mertz says, "Councilman Mancuso?"

Mancuso smiles. "Thank you, Alison, Ron. And thank you everyone, for coming out today. I see some people from my district. That was one hell of a trip to get here." Laughter from the crowd. "Now, look, I was born on this planet, you know? I understand this city. I've been on the Council for years. I've been elected over and over again. I didn't just march in and take my job, like my opponent did." He tilts his head toward Jaylon-ra. More laughter. Ronel-ra looks flustered. "This is New York. This is the greatest city in the world. And together we can put it back where it belongs: Under. Human. Control."

A roar goes up from the crowd, so loud that the stage vibrates under Jaylon-ra's feet.

Ronel-ra tries to regain control but can't be heard over the cheering. He waves his hand and a dozen Makh-Ra cops, garbed in black riot gear and carrying batons, stream out from behind the curtain and line up along the front of the stage. They stand at attention as one, boots slamming into the floor, and the sound of it quiets the room. Ronel-ra leans into the mic again. "The next person who raises their voice before this is over will be ejected. This is the only debate scheduled and we aim to maintain order."

Alison is smiling at all of this, which Jaylon-ra can't help but notice. She leans into the mic and, perhaps taking a cue from the signs, says, "The first question seems to be the most obvious. Mayor Jaylon-ra, what do you make of the charges that this election is being put on as a show?"

Jaylon-ra begins to talk but Mancuso moves to the microphone and clears his throat. "I'd like to field this one, if I might." He makes something that looks like a wink, though it could be a twitch, and Jaylon-ra leans back, getting that same hot feeling on the back of his neck that he got when he presented this plan to Gaige-ra. The thing he felt so sure about suddenly sitting just beyond the grasp of his fingertips.

"I don't blame you for not trusting the mocks," Mancuso says. Some of the Mahk-Ra in the audience growing visibly angry at the slur. "Hell, I don't trust them. And you know what? I've worked alongside the mayor and his friends since they got here and I still don't trust them. You better believe I'm watching them every step of the way to ensure this is a fair election. That's what you deserve and it's the only thing we will accept. So I have to ask: New York, are you ready to take back your city?"

And at this, the crowd descends into madness.

The front line of humans push into the Mahk-Ra cops, who are ready for the assault, swinging their batons down onto exposed heads. Ronel-ra takes a shoe to the face. Toward the back of the room, there's the sound of something crashing and breaking. Jaylon-ra freezes, unsure of what to do.

Call for order. Dive into the crowd and get between the Mahk-Ra cops and the humans. Something. Anything.

The decision to act is made for him when his security detail yanks him from the podium and through the curtain, carrying him to a van idling behind the building. Paul jumps in just as the door is pulled shut and they lurch away from the curb.

"That got out of hand," Paul says, as a cavalcade of rocks pelt the outside of the van.

· · ·

Jaylon-ra hitches up his coat against the biting October wind and trudges down the street, fallow warehouses flanking him on either side. Only half the streetlights are working, and in a solitary pool of yellow light he sees one of his campaign signs torn up and lying on the sidewalk.

He nudges it with his foot, considering the tag line under his name.

YOURS IN SOLIDARITY.

Underneath that, in felt marker, someone has written: BULLSHIT.

Two more blocks and he's at the address Paul gave him. There's a small gray door ajar, so he steps through, into an office full of tan filing cabinets and loose papers, where Paul is sitting at a desk, two steaming cups of coffee in front of him, his head in his hands. Jaylon-ra takes the light and sweet coffee, sniffs it, and takes a sip. Not bad for three in the morning in the middle of an industrial stretch of Brooklyn.

Paul looks up, his eyes red, his hair disheveled. "We have a problem."

"I assumed that, considering you got me out of bed and dragged me to the middle of nowhere. Is it worse than a riot at the debate?"

Paul nods and takes a deep breath. "The voting machines are bricked."

"What does that mean, bricked?"

"They're useless," he says. "The techs were running a software update and now the motherboards are all fried."

"How could that even happen?"

"Honestly? We're not sure." Paul takes a long swig of his black coffee, then winces. "It could be age. They're old. But one of the computer guys noticed some weird bits of code. He can't be sure, but he thinks they might have been hacked."

"How can a hacker disable hardware?"

"Computer chips have a failsafe to prevent overheating. If they get too hot they shut down. It's a safety feature. But Andres, he's the computer guy, he said these chips are so old they don't have that failsafe. He said it wouldn't be too hard to drop in some code ordering the processors to overclock. With no thermal emergency shut-down procedure, they burn out."

"The Red Spear?"

"Maybe," Paul says. "I don't know. Maybe."

"So we replace the machines."

Paul stands up, puts his hands on his hips, looking down at the floor, like he's bracing himself. "There are four thousand. We don't have the resources to replace even a third of them. And if we could get everything we needed, the election is two weeks away. I'm not even sure we have time."

"If we call off this election there will be riots."

"I understand that."

"And after the riots," Jaylon-ra says, "after a human is elected mayor, we will both be executed."

"I understand that. We have one other option, but it's not a great one."

"And...?"

"Follow me."

Paul leads Jaylon-ra to the back of the office and through a series of concrete hallways until they're in a sprawling warehouse, so big the edges of the room disappear into the darkness. It smells like motor oil. Before them stands row after row of hulking boxes covered with opaque plastic tarps. Paul pulls one aside and reveals an ancient machine that's a foot taller than Jaylon-ra, with rows of small white boxes and a giant red lever across the front.

"What the hell is this thing?" Jaylon-ra asks, reaching up to touch the side of it.

"These are the city's old voting machines. They've been stored here for years. Honestly, I'm surprised they weren't found and stripped for material. I guess the Mahk-Ra never did a good accounting of this neighborhood."

Jaylon-ra steps forward and pulls at the curtain that hangs from a railing that extends from the top, so that it can be closed around the front of the machine, affording the voter some privacy. "How old are these?"

"They were purchased in the 1960s. Interestingly enough, they were used up until 2010. New York was one of the last cities to comply with HAVA, which was a federal law mandating electronic voting machines. These things are beasts, but they're reliable and they're actually easier to count. And there are so many of them we could still hold the election."

"I sense there's something coming up that I'm not going to be happy about."

Paul grimaces. "These can't be hacked. Completely analog. At the end of the night you flip a switch and it shows the total on each line and the poll watchers take them down. In the end, the vote will be the vote."

"So," Jaylon-ra says. "What you're saying is, now this is an election."

...

Jaylon-ra fights to maintain his smile as the man in the gray suit hocks a wad of spit into his proffered hand.

He's always prided himself as being one of the rare Mahk-Ra who's actually fond of humans. The campaign trail is severely degrading his outlook.

He shakes his head at his security detail, two broad-shouldered Mahk-Ra in black suits who are ready to pounce. It would be bad optics to have them beating on a human three days before the election. Especially considering the number of people clicking on their camera phones.

Jaylon-ra takes a handkerchief out of his coat to wipe his hand, and calls after the man, "I wish only to have a reasoned discussion. I know you have strong emotions about this..."

The man doesn't even turn to acknowledge him, just trudges on down the street.

The sun has a finger hold on the horizon as the rush-hour crowd streams around Jaylon-ra and his team of volunteers at the top of the R train steps. All of them human, low-level staffers at City Hall, looking for a leg up in the administration. He had hoped the presence of human volunteers would make him seem approachable, but all it's done is won them withering looks and rude comments.

The Financial District should be a friendly neighborhood, too, considering the pile of tax breaks the Mahk-Ra have given to investors, but his reception here has been the same as it is in the rest of the city: A running scale of ambivalence to anger, with the occasional person willing to talk.

Very occasional.

And even then, Jaylon-ra doesn't expect he won any votes today.

Jaylon-ra takes one of his palm cards and skims over it, wondering if they could have done something differently. In his headshot, he looks rigid and stern, unsmiling. Maybe he should have draped his suit jacket over his shoulder, rolled up his sleeves, looked more relaxed. Mahk-Ra can look threatening when they try to smile. Maybe he should have tried it anyway.

The colors are nice, at least. Blue with yellow text. He'd seem Mancuso's, which are blue with white text. He'd been worried about the similarity, but Paul said most politicians use blue. Even the Republicans, who operated under a red banner before regressive policies and inter-party squabbling destroyed the line twenty years ago, used blue on their palm cards.

Blue is supposed to be calming.

A woman in a heavy navy overcoat comes up the steps. Jaylon-ra positions himself in front of her path, slightly off to the side so as not to block her way and appear threatening. "Miss, I'm the mayor, and I was just wondering, can you tell me how I am doing?"

The woman laughs. "It's 'how'm I doin.' Don't steal a line from Ed Koch unless you're going to deliver it right." She pushes past him and walks down the street.

Paul comes up behind Jaylon-ra, sucking on a stub of a cigarette. He takes out a fresh one, chains off that, and places the new one between his lips, letting the old one fall to the sidewalk.

His suit, normally pressed to a razor's edge, is wrinkled, and there's a heavy white stain on the front.

An old man shuffling by looks at Paul and mumbles, "Fucking traitor."

Paul ignores that and looks at Jaylon-ra. "Confab?"

Jaylon-ra hands his pile of palm cards to a volunteer and says, "Let's say fifteen more minutes and we'll move on to Brooklyn."

The volunteer nods and rushes to confront a new crowd of commuters coming up the steps.

When they're alone, away from prying ears, Paul says, "Things are coming along. We're sending broken machines to high-turnout senior housing. Since they vote in higher numbers, if we move more of them to paper we can dump or replace votes. We're also ensuring there will be service disruptions on public transit. Whatever we can do to keep people from getting home from work on time. Finally, there are two neighborhoods with nearly no Mahk-Ra and high voter turnout, one in Queens and one on Staten Island. We're projected to lose those by ninety-eight percent or more, so we're going to have people posting signs saying you can't vote without a valid, up-to-date ID."

"You don't need an ID to vote."

"The DMV is one of the agencies that's taken a big hit from supply demands," Paul says. "Most people, their IDs are expired. This is just an idea we had to maybe turn some people away."

"What if it gets traced back to us?"

"It's being taken care of by some people who aren't affiliated with us and aren't being paid directly by us. And that's all I'll say. The less you know…"

"Fine, fine. What else?"

"We've got a big report on Mancuso going up on the news feeds tomorrow. Organizations he's given money to that have been accused of impropriety. A letter he wrote to a judge, asking for leniency on a friend who was convicted of insider trading. And there's a rumor he used campaign funds to fix his house. Truthfully, the rumor was unfounded, but that doesn't mean we can't raise the question, plant the seed that maybe there's something to it."

Jaylon-ra sighs. "That's the best you can do? We're going to hang him on things he didn't even do?"

"That's all we could find. Mancuso is actually pretty clean."

"Are we even releasing this with enough time to influence the election?"

"Better now, actually. That way it's fresh in people's minds."

"I don't know…"

"We have to do something to counter the latest flier," Paul says.

"What flier?"

Fear blooms across Paul's face. "I don't have it with me… someone just told me about it. They're being distributed by volunteers, on foot, all around the city. It says the Mahk-Ra conquered a planet called Rigel-8, and after they conquered the native inhabitants, the Mahk-Ra… ate their children."

"What?!" Jaylon-ra clenches his fist, considers throwing it into a wall. He stops himself just short of it. Explosions of anger are unbecoming. He takes a deep breath and says, "First, there is no Rigel-8. Second, the Mahk-Ra have never eaten children. Mancuso is making these claims? How can he do that? Surely we have some recourse here."

"It's an anonymous flier," Paul says. "Even if he personally signed off on it, we could never prove it."

"That son of a bitch. He was supposed to take the fall."

"He knows we're using the old machines," Paul says. "He's must have put it together. I'm pulling out all the stops, but we have to be prepared…"

"I know," Jaylon-ra says, putting his hand on Paul's shoulder. Paul recoils a bit, surprised at the touch. His eyes go wide and soften like he's interpreting it as a sign of brotherhood, when really, Jaylon-ra just wanted to convey the gravity of the situation. "I'm sitting down with the High Command tonight to give them an update. I'm not looking forward to the conversation."

"How much are you going to tell them?"

"I'm still figuring that out. Not too much. We have three days. Maybe we can still pull this out."

"Do you want me there?" Paul asks.

"No," Jaylon-ra says. "Go home and sleep."

. . .

The hall has taken on the quality of a deflated balloon. Limp and devoid of air.

Streamers are strewn on the floor, paper plates from the buffet spilling out of the garbage cans. The blue-on-yellow ELECT MAYOR JAYLON-RA sign hangs over the stage like a taunt. There are small pools of people scattered about the room, but three quarters of the crowd has already left. Rats abandoning a sinking ship.

Paul is slumped in a chair in the corner, an extinguished cigarette hanging from his mouth, his jacket crumbled on the floor at his feet. Jaylon-ra can't tell if he's breathing hard, snoring, or sobbing.

A panel of analysts argue about the election on NY1. Jaylon-ra can't hear what they're saying over the blaring strains of *Don't Stop Believin'*. Who the hell picked this song?

If the members of Journey were still alive he'd have them rounded up and hanged.

The numbers displayed in a box underneath the analysts are white and glowing and rigid. He wants to believe they're not true, that it's a trick of the screen, but there they are.

Councilman Mancuso: 72 percent.

Mayor Jaylon-ra: 28 percent.

Ninety-four percent of precincts reporting.

Mahk-Ra alone were supposed to make up 40 percent of the vote. Aside from the occasional sympathizer or malcontent, a Mahk-Ra would never vote for a human. Which means his people didn't even come out to vote for him. Maybe they thought the race was locked up.

A strong presence at the polls might have driven humans away. Their ignorance cost him the election.

Their ignorance. Paul's. The weather. Jaylon-ra looks for something or someone to blame besides himself. Not that there's much.

He takes a long swig of the only thing left to drink at the bar. Well whiskey, no ice. It tastes like battery acid and it scorches his throat on the way down. He breathes deep. His phone buzzes. He pulls it out and steps onto the balcony, away from the music, where he can get a little quiet. The cold wind whistles and bites at him.

He presses the red dot on the screen to answer and puts the phone to his ear.

"I figured you might not know about this part of the process," Mancuso says. "It's called the concession call. You're supposed to call the person who beat you and congratulate them. And you promise you won't contest the election."

"There's still time."

Mancuso laughs. "Look, you can win all the rest of the precincts and every paper ballot. The race is over. Seems there are still some things humans are pretty good at. Take the night. Tomorrow your weird little assistant can call my chief of staff, and we can set up a meeting. Talk about transition teams."

"What if you were to say you didn't want the job? Like a sudden health problem, or you just truly thought I was a better leader…"

Mancuso laughs again. "Now you're stretching. Look, I'll be honest, I never wanted to be mayor. Not before you mocks got here. Not my thing. Too much pressure, you understand? I was happy to do my job and go home. But now… now it's just been handed to me, I'm supposed to say no? I'll promise you this. I'll give you a top position in my cabinet. Show the people that I want to work with you. Keep the Mahk-Ra leadership happy." He clears his throat, and his voice takes on an edge. "As long *you* know who the fuck is in charge."

"If those machines weren't broken," Jaylon-ra says, "this would be a very different conversation."

"Well," Mancuso says, the word trailing off. It's quiet, and Jaylon-ra thinks they've been disconnected, but then Mancuso continues, "You know how it is with the elections. Once it gets going… things start overheating, you know what I mean?"

"Wait, what?"

"Go have another drink. We'll talk tomorrow."

"No, what did you mean, about things overheating…"

The line goes dead.

Jaylon-ra sticks the phone in his pocket, looks out over the city. From his vantage point on the balcony of the Woolworth Building, he can see a large running stretch reaching to the north. He tries to imagine how it looked with all the buildings lit up. That's how it used to be, in old photographs. Now, some buildings are power-rationed and circuits overload, so only half the skyline is lit at any given time.

It was a good run. His frustration with the process and with the planet aside, it was nice to be in charge of something so big, and even now, with half of it turned off, and even for a human city, so grand and beautiful and alive.

His phone buzzes again.

Jaylon-ra holds his breath and puts it up to his ear.

"So." Gaige-ra says, "Tell me again how the game is played."

STRANGE ALLIANCE

CLIFF ALLEN

He stood watching them. His lips lifted in the thin smile that frightened everyone who saw it. Which was stronger, he wondered, the stink of fear as he approached, or the flood of hatred when he'd gone?

That was the catch. What if he didn't go? What if he stopped to chat? That was where the hate dissolved, leaving only a black pool of fear. None of these people knew how deep or black that pool could get. Not until they had dived with him, to the smothering depths.

Benton was human though those who had endured his close scrutiny would argue otherwise; those who had survived. He was the only human with the rank of Talon Officer among the Mahk-Ra. He was a terror worse than the invaders. He had executed his own brother with a shotgun blast to the head. Since then, he had stacked up enough bodies to become second in command of Talon, the dread secret police.

His reputation was made at the Battle for Barnard's Star. Through resourcefulness, force of will, and the wholesale expenditure of human troops he had turned a military disaster into a strategic and tactical triumph. When the command center had taken a direct hit, it had been he who had dominated the rattled Mahk-Ra junior officers, and rallied the Mahk-Re non-coms to his service. He had battered the enemy off those worthless balls of rock circling around that dismal little dwarf star and chased them out of this sector of the empire.

The Mahk-Ra had been faced with a cultural dilemma. They admired courage. They admired leadership. Here stood a human. They could either accept the superiority of this member of a subject race or make him one of their own.

The mirthless smile bent his features. So, he was adopted as a Mahk-Ra because their built-in assumptions could find no other recourse to an anomaly like him.

Adopted, not accepted. Feared by humans because he was almost Mahk-Ra. Hated by the aliens because almost wasn't good enough. Feared and hated by all, because he could take any of them into dark, windowless rooms, and do whatever he liked. Even high ranking Mahk-Ra were not immune to his attentions.

He stepped from the shadows of the arch onto the sun-dappled walkway. As his Mahk-Re bodyguards fanned out to take flanking positions people recognized him, and the walkway emptied. The former occupants had scattered to stand on the lawn to either side.

They seemed to yearn for invisibility. They stood, almost universally, with their arms to their sides; heads tilted; eyes down to avoid crossing his gaze. It was almost a bow, Benton thought. He accepted it as such.

His booted feet shocked the silence as he moved forward. His long thin shadow was the gnomon indicating his progress. Each time his shadow licked one of the bowing forms they shivered. He took time to notice them. They stiffened as he neared, relaxed when he moved on.

His pace slowed. A pretty young woman caught his eye.

Even with her head down, face half-hidden, she was quite appealing. He let his gaze linger. His smile thinned to the point of no return. His eyes half closed as he regarded her.

Sergeant Chobuc-re noticed the change and gave the silent order to cut the young woman from the herd.

As his guard began to move in, Benton spotted a tiny hand coming around low on the woman's skirt. A small upturned face followed. A pretty little girl of perhaps three regarded him, frankly and without fear. No human had dared look at him in such an open manner in years. Curious, he signaled Chobuc-re to stop.

They appraised each other for a moment, the monster and the moppet, and then she actually stepped around her mother and onto the walkway.

The woman grabbed for the child but dropped back when Benton's guards surged forward with their weapons up. None of them assumed innocence. A very small girl could be a very large bomb. Benton was a prime target for terrorists.

He waved his hand again and they stopped. This time the muzzles of their weapons did not drop, but remained steadily on the small figure as she looked up and said, "Hi! Are you a-scared?"

Benton rocked slightly, surprised by the level of perception implied by the non-sequitur. Or, maybe, just a little girl venting her own apprehensions?

"What makes you think I have a reason to be afraid?" he asked.

"Um ... dunno, um, you just looked kinda scaredy standing there, and you shouldn't," she said sincerely. She reached up and took his hand.

Benton felt a kind of shock at the touch, and then, "Chobuc-re! Stand down!"

"But, sir ... " the sergeant began.

Benton's voice turned so quiet the menace of it bleached the walls of the courtyard. "Now, Sergeant."

"Sir!" The muzzles deflected; the guards stayed rip-cord taut.

The little girl tugged on his hand, and to the shock of everyone present, including himself, he bent to one knee beside her. She whispered, "Arthur says that if you're a-scared, all you have to do is pretend you're not. Pretty soon you won't be."

"Arthur?" Benton drew a breath, regarding her.

"My Grandpa, Arthur."

Benton nodded, blinked, and nodded again, "Is he right?" His voice was almost wistful. "Is that the secret?"

She leaned in with a conspiratorial look in ... her ... eye ... no. No, not three. Older. Seven? Eight?

"Not always," she said quietly, "but surprisingly often."

He pulled back, "Who are you?"

She smiled up at him, "Um," three years old again, "They call me Ranny. Who are you?"

"Ranny? That's an unusual name."

"Short for m'other name, m'big girl name," she motioned for him to lean in, "m'secret name."

"Secret name? You have a secret name?"

She nodded.

"What is your secret name, Ranny?"

She whispered in his ear, "Secret."

He paused, and then said, "Look, Ranny, my job is keeping secrets. I'm very good at it." He tried to look friendly but achieved harrowing. "You can tell me."

She regarded him for a solemn moment, nodded, and then said, "Araneae."

He studied her.

"Araneae Webb." She smiled up at him.

His lips quirked up enough to be scary. After a moment he said, "I'll just call you Ranny."

"Ev'buddy does," she sighed.

He stared at her for a long minute. There was a mystery here. This strange little girl was a mystery. He hated mysteries. Mysteries needed to be dismantled; screamed to be dismantled.

"Ranny," he said, "I can't spend any more time talking with you. Not just now. I have a meeting. I'm on a very tight schedule. We will talk again, I promise. Longer next time--much longer. Until then will you do me a favor?"

"Um, what?"

"Do you see how all these other people are standing?"

Ranny looked around the courtyard and said, "Um, the ones with the guns?"

"No," he said firmly, "no, the other people."

"Uh huh."

"Do you think you could stand like that if you tried? Stand like that every time you see a Mahk-Ra, or someone dressed in a uniform like mine? Could you?"

"Fer how long?"

Was she bargaining with him? "Until they're gone," he said.

"Maybe," she said, then added, "But not ever 'n ever."

Then, as if she had made her point, she turned and stepped off the walk. She dropped her arms to her sides, bowed her head reverently, and became an angel at an altar. It was a pose so pure as to be almost a satire of his instructions.

Benton stood, nonplussed. How had this little girl stolen the initiative? He turned to the mother and said, "You. Up here."

A gasp escaped her. Her knees buckled as she stepped onto the walkway.

"Please, sir," she began, "she didn't know; she's so young ... "

He held up his hand, and the woman stopped in mid-sentence. "What is your name?"

"Marilyn, sir."

"Marilyn," the name sounded like the punch line to a dirty joke as he spoke it, "do you imagine I intend to punish this girl for her ignorance?"

The woman struggled before deciding the safest course was to say nothing.

Benton said, "No, no, Marilyn, this girl is in no way to blame."

"Oh, thank you Si--", His hand lashed out with a slap that knocked her to ground.

He towered over the cowering woman. "It is you who must be punished."

The woman groaned, her quaking hands rapping noisily against the concrete of the walkway. He paused, listening to this paradiddle of fear. He began to tap his toe in counterpoint. The frightened woman quieted to silence.

He smiled his deaths-head smile, and said, "Yes, you must be punished. I've only had a few minutes with Ranny, and yet she seems quite able to understand what is wanted. You have failed as a mother. It's your duty to teach her proper respect. Sergeant!"

"Sir." Chobuc-re towered at his elbow.

"I'm running late for my meeting. Take charge of this. I want the girl escorted safely back to her grandfather. His name, I believe, is Arthur Webb."

He turned, "Ranny ... " She had modified the pose. She stood as before, but now the middle finger of each hand was pointing proudly above her curled knuckles. The angel had become a vulgarity.

He frowned. Did she understand what she was doing? He hoped his guard wouldn't recognize the rudeness of this purely American gesture. He wanted to deal with the girl in his own time.

He tried again, "Ranny, do you know where your grandfather lives?"

She kept her head bowed, arms at her sides, and middle fingers standing proud. She nodded yes.

"Delivered unharmed, Sergeant, you understand?"

"Sir." Chobuc-re said nothing about the pose.

"This woman will have a week of workhouse duty. Nothing that will damage her, Sergeant. I plan to give her my personal attention. You will schedule at least once a week with me, beginning when she's done at the workhouse. Mother and daughter."

Chobuc-re cast a knowing look at the woman, and turned his curiosity off in regards to the little girl. It was not his place to judge.

Everything went swiftly after that. Chobuc-re detailed a guard to take care of the woman and child; got on his com link with the Muni's to arrange air transport for Benton and the remaining bodyguards, and a few minutes later they were landing at the compound in the Reserved Zone just east of Vancouver.

This was definitely Mahk-Ra country -- Galactic technology everywhere, alien entertainment, luxury digs for the new overlords; no humans allowed unescorted. Well, that last specification did not apply to Benton. Living in a zone reserved for the Mahk-Ra was his not so subtle, but very important, statement of power.

As they arrived, they saw a Mahk-Ra troop ship rising from the spaceport at the center of the Reserved Zone, the gravity fields built up around it into a shimmering heat-wave pattern before it zoomed off almost faster than the eye could follow.

As Benton entered his Penthouse, Leann met him with a perfectly prepared drink. Minutes ago he was miles away talking to total strangers, but a perfectly made drink was waiting as soon as he stepped through the door. Either she spent the entire day mixing and discarding drinks just to be ready for when he returned, or she had a pretty impressive intelligence apparatus of her own.

Leann did not disappoint.

"I hear you have a new girlfriend," she said. "Not developing an interest in younger women, I hope." She used the voice that could make an unwary man's pants bunch at the crotch. Unwariness was not one of Benton's failings.

It had been less than ten minutes, and she already knew about his encounter with Ranny and her mother. She definitely had a source inside his guard. Chobuc-re? Possible, but he thought the sergeant too smart to put himself between them.

Chobuc-re had been with him since Barnard's Star. Benton trusted him as much as he was capable of trusting anyone. He owed his life to the sergeant many times over. Who then?

Time would tell. It always did.

They were total contrasts. Leann, voluptuous beauty personified; Benton, skeletal and severe. She a pure sybarite; he Spartan, only interested in luxuries where they enhanced his ability to exercise power.

Power.

That was the aphrodisiac in the relationship. Each finding ways to satisfy needs, and achieve goals through strategic use of the other. No love nest. There was sex whenever he wanted; Leann was highly skilled. But, no, more a mutual power base.

Leann had outlasted her predecessors. She rarely let her fear of him show, which suited him, and her courage in pursuit of avarice was impressive.

She possessed a ruthlessness that nearly matched his own, perversions that exceeded him, and she was up to something he hadn't figured out yet. He had taken steps to rectify that deficit.

He hoped she remembered that her power flowed from his. It might get messy should he have to remind her. Messier still if she had found a way to change the direction of flow.

"Arkum-ra's here," she said leading the way to the living room.

Benton set the untouched drink on a table, and followed her in.

"Ah, Benton!" Arkum-ra turned from the shaded window facing a magnificent view of the spaceport. "I was wondering what might be keeping you. We must hurry, time is short."

Benton held up his hand. "A moment, Arkum-ra." He turned to Leann, "My dear, I believe you have some urgent errand that calls you away?" He smiled his most disquieting smile, "I wouldn't want to detain you."

She stared at him expressionlessly. Her chin came up and then she flashed a smile that could steal men's souls. "Why, how sweet of you to remember. Yes, most urgent and far out of earshot." Her expression turned acid as she left the room.

"With respect, Arkum," Benton's voice was a perfect blend of respect and menace, "I've warned you of the dangers of talking about our business in front of others."

"But, surely, Leann ... "

"Would use it like a knife at my throat."

Arkum-ra was an experienced power player. Much of his upbringing had flowed around obtaining and holding power; physical and psychological. He pursed his lips, then nodded, "You suspect Leann may be ready to expand her horizons. How? It would require an extraordinary alliance. She couldn't offer the same ... liaison? ... that she has with you. No one of sufficiently high rank would risk it. I certainly wouldn't."

Benton spoke into his communicator. "Now." he said.

He turned to Arkum-ra, "I assure you, the risk is in your head, I haven't planted any booby traps on that lovely body."

"Perhaps you have, my friend. Consider: If Leann makes a move, and you're still alive ... Well, I don't have to elaborate on the possibilities for vengeance, betrayal, and blackmail. If you die? One would always worry how many of the skeletons you've buried she might be able to dig up. Neither situation makes for a comfortable alliance. Or, dalliance, for that matter." He shook his head, "No, one must be cautious, of course, but I think you are far too obsessed by it."

"Easy for you to say. If anything goes wrong, the worst you'd face is a reprimand; a recall to the home world; and a stiff fine. I'd be relieved if my punishment began with public evisceration."

"Benton, you exaggerate."

"I do not. There's mortal danger here, Arkum. You know as well as I that my cold-blooded, rat-bastard boss would ... "

"Stop! Don't talk this way in front of me, Benton. Tamar-Ra is from an ancient lineage, and above reproach. Don't test my friendship."

"Okay -- my old-blooded, rat-bastard boss," Arkum-ra clenched his jaw, "would accept any excuse to get rid of me. He's humiliated by having a human second-in-command. It shames him. He wants my destruction; the grislier the better. He's not like you, or the few other Mahk-Ra who accept that courage and intelligence may elevate one above his natural station. Nor, I might add, does he share the kind of business interests we share. He would gladly hold the knife during the evisceration."

Arkum-ra didn't dispute the verity of the argument. "It's true," he said, "there are not many Mahk-Ra who would mourn you." He shrugged apologetically, "I promise you on my word, Benton, I have never spoken of this enterprise outside your hearing."

"No, of course not, but remember that Leann is not above selling either of us if the price is high enough, and her safety from me is assured. As head of Talon, Tamar-ra might be willing to pay that price. Fortunately, this will all be over in another hour."

"Less," Arkum-ra said, "We're running late. The container holding the contraband must be aboard the Ra-Prime passenger liner no later than forty-two minutes from now. My agent on the crew expects to receive the container late, and will get it loaded quickly, with no manifest, and no invoice. It will not exist in any record--but only if we can get it there before departure."

Benton's communicator chimed. He tapped the connection, listened for a moment, and said, "Good." He disconnected.

"We can discuss this further on the way to the warehouse," he said. "I've just gotten word that Leann has arranged a meeting of her own. With Tamar-ra."

"So quickly?"

"There's more. The meeting will be here, in my penthouse, in thirty minutes. I think she plans to walk in and discover us still deep in our schemes. She'll spring, whatever it is she has, in front of me, knowing it will bring my destruction. A remarkable woman."

Arkum-ra looked appalled, "Benton! We must get out of here!"

"Absolutely. The first step is to get rid of the evidence. Get those art masterpieces of yours aboard that liner and off-planet and it'll be hard to prove we've done anything wrong, no matter what Leann thinks she has. Did you arrange for transport?"

"Yes, the van will be waiting in the vicinity of the warehouse. As you suggested, the driver doesn't know the exact location, but he will be close by."

"Good. Let's go. I'll see about arranging the assassination on the way. Won't be easy. Time is short, and this building is quite secure."

Arkum-ra gave him a horrified look.

Benton curbed his exasperation, "No! No. Not Tamar-ra, that would bring down the wrath of god."

"But, who ... Oh."

"Exactly. Plug the leak. Now, with respect, shut up while I make a few calls."

Benton rang for the bodyguard and began tapping an encrypted number into his communicator as the two of them rushed from the room.

Less than three minutes later they were in the air headed for the vast warehouse district to the north of the spaceport.

"No luck," Benton said, "there isn't enough time to get anyone into position."

Arkum-ra said, "But, Benton, it doesn't matter. We're out of the building. By the time they can track us down the shipment will be gone. We're safe."

"Um," said Benton, "not really. You see, I'm about ninety-eight percent sure that Leann has a spy in my guard."

Arkum-ra looked around, "What? You're certain?"

"Ninety-eight percent."

"Then they know where we are. Where we're going."

"They may know where we are, but not where we're going. Not yet."

"But we're leading them straight to ... ," Arkum-ra pulled himself up to his full Mahk-Ra arrogance, and said, "My friend, I assure you, if we meet the worst, I shall do so with honor."

Benton replied, "And I assure you, I have no qualms about jettisoning honor to avoid meeting the worst."

Arkum frowned. Benton waved it off, "No, forget it. Let me think."

After a pause, he stood and moved forward in the transport. "Chobuc-re," he said.

The Mahk-Re sergeant turned to face him. Big, even for a member of his race, he towered over the human.

"Sergeant, I have no doubt about either your loyalty or your honor and I intend no insult. I must ask a question."

The Sergeant loomed silently above him.

"My life may depend on your answer."

In a motion so fast that if Benton hadn't seen it before it would have seemed like magic, Chobuc-re drew the machine pistol from the holster at his side. Benton tensed. The sergeant stood with the weapon in his hand, muzzle pointed down.

The sergeant said, "We are sworn to your protection, sir."

"Yes."

Chobuc-re's presence seemed to push the oxygen from the cabin.

"I'm sorry, Sergeant," Benton glanced at the pistol, "I believe Leann has placed a spy in your company."

Chobuc-re tensed the mountain of muscle he called a body. "Is this an accusation, sir?"

Benton heard other weapons being drawn.

"Not of you, Sergeant. Never. My trust in you is absolute. Nevertheless, I believe there is a spy. What is your best assessment?"

Chobuc bowed his head, the pistol steady at his side, and said, "If this spy exists, sir, you believe your life is in jeopardy?"

"If he can report my position, I am a dead man."

Chobuc-re raised his head and looked slowly around the cabin. He paused as his eyes met those of one of the newer bodyguards.

Benton jerked as the pistol arced up level with his head, and fired a single round. He twisted to follow the direction of aim and saw the bodyguard slump to the deck, a pistol half drawn. The boom had been earsplitting, the silence after, deafening.

Benton looked around. Every Mahk-Re on the transport had a weapon drawn, pointed at the dead guard.

Arkum-ra sat silently, watching.

After a long pause, Chobuc-re said, "We are sworn to your protection, sir."

Benton swallowed, and nodded. He started back to his seat.

The sergeant said, "A moment, sir." He reached down, stripped the communicator from the dead guard, and handed it to Benton. "You may trust us with an exact location, now."

Benton winced, and gave directions for the landing.

As the transport altered course and descended, Benton entered his override code into the dead guard's communicator. He scrolled through the last several days. Very informative, the two most recent calls being imperative. Chobuc-re's judgment had proven correct once again. He showed the readout to Arkum-ra.

"He has contacted Leann since we left your home," Arkum-ra said, "and this other encrypted number. I don't know that coding."

"I do," Benton said, "Tamar-ra."

Arkum-ra considered this, and nodded, "The spy had two masters, clever move. Do you think Leann is aware?"

"No, she hasn't had much chance to play this particular side of the game. Not at this level. Old Tamar and I have been at it for years. Each of us has occasionally managed to plant someone on the other, but the agents fail to thrive. This time, the luck of timing worked in Tamar-ra's favor. A few more weeks might have revealed his agent to me. One wonders if Leann's deal is quite as good as she believes. Tamar won't pay off if he doesn't have to."

Arkum-ra snorted, "Rat-bastard."

Benton smiled his mirthless smile and said, "Indeed."

"This means they know where we are, Benton."

"No, they knew what direction we were headed," he checked the time stamp, "twelve minutes ago. I don't doubt Tamar has dispatched a squad to chase us down, but I'm very careful about the automated traffic control system. I never use it. That doesn't make me invisible, but it does make me hard to track. Now that we're down among the buildings, they'll have to make visual contact to find us."

"Homing devices?"

"Possible, but not likely, my guard is quite diligent."

Arkum-ra glanced at the dead guard, and nodded.

The transport spiraled to a landing in front of the warehouse where the contraband artwork waited. As they climbed out of the vehicle Benton said, "Chobuc-re. We may have visitors coming. They are not welcome."

"Sir." The Sergeant began to deploy the guard.

"Arkum-ra, call that van, please. We need to get the container loaded and on its way." Arkum-ra nodded, took his communicator out and strolled up the street to make the call. Benton turned to the large roll-up door, and rang the bell.

The door to the warehouse rattled up to reveal a large plastic container already sitting on a loader. The paunchy non-descript man opening the door paled when he saw Benton. He glanced at another man driving the loader, but continued to work. The man on the loader nodded to Benton; kept his face blank and his hands down behind the control panel, out of sight.

Benton tried to hide his surprise, but he recognized these men. The man on the loader was, "Wasp", the head of the shooters and bomb throwers arm of the Red Spear. The other man was known as "Bee", a thug and assassin. Their presence here meant trouble, and there was no sign of the regular warehouse crew.

Benton looked toward Wasp's hidden hands, and then out to the street to see how close Chobuc-re and the rest of the guards were.

Chobuc hadn't finished positioning the troops, and the ones that were in place were all looking away from the warehouse, not in. The Sergeant would be back, but a lot could happen before then. Arkum-ra was still out of sight down the street.

He turned his attention back to the two men. "So, what are your intentions, gentlemen?"

Bee and Wasp turned their heads in unison. It was their turn to check out the proximity of Benton's bodyguards. Wasp's hands were still hidden.

Bee glanced at Wasp, who nodded.

Grabbing for his courage, Bee said, "Here's the deal, Benton. We have reason to believe this crate and your pet mock might be attacked. I'm told we don't want that to happen." He cast a dirty look toward Wasp, who just smiled back. "We're here to handle the problem. We didn't expect you. We don't need you."

"Nor I, you," Benton said.

Bee continued, "So, here's the deal. You and those bodyguards of yours climb aboard that fancy transport and haul out of here. We'll see that the mock and his crate of fucking posters get to the spaceport, safe and sound. No trouble from you; no trouble from us."

"A tempting offer, Mr. Bee, but ... "

Wasp cut in, "Benton ... ", and was, himself, interrupted when Arkum-ra stepped through the door.

"The van's on its way, it'll be here momentarily. We should have ample time to get to the spaceport."

Benton bobbed his head, watching the two terrorists. Arkum-ra's presence complicated things, and Chobuc-re would be in soon, Benton needed to put a stop to this.

Arkum said, "Is something wrong?"

"Everything's in order," Benton said, "but these two gentlemen are concerned for the health and safety of you, and your shipment."

"Really? Why?"

Bee's exasperation boiled over, "Look, all we want to do is get Benton out of here, get you and this crate full of advertising crap out of here, and then get out of here ourselves. For Christ's sake!"

It was an unfortunate choice of words, Benton thought. No one spoke to a member of the Mahk-Ra gentry like that, and certainly not regarding his artistic judgment.

"Crap?" Arkum-ra was outraged. "These works of art are priceless. The two Joe-the-Camel posters alone are worth a fortune; mint condition, pre-occupation examples of anthropomorphism, both. The Disney's, the illustrated Aesop's, the Bee selling breakfast cereal ... ," Bee sputtered, " ... are all worth substantial sums. Taken together, this lot is worth enough to purchase a small asteroid to retire on in the home system, and still leave enough to tow it into a nice stable orbit around one of our outer planets. The fact that you're unable to appreciate the artistic irony of a pre-contact subject race depicting themselves as animals only proves the point! Crap?"

When Arkum-ra paused for a breath, Wasp spoke up, "Please, sir, forgive my feeble minded assistant. He's fearful because we believe word of this transaction has leaked out," Wasp glared at Benton, "and we anticipate unwelcome guests at any moment."

Whatever Arkum-ra had been about to say choked off, and became, "Benton. Tamar-ra has tracked us."

Chobuc-re had been attracted by the shouting and came in with his machine pistol drawn. Benton was beginning to lose track of the number of ways this could go wrong, when Chobuc hit the unit alarm in response to Arkum's last statement.

Before Benton had time to explain the mistake and cancel the alarm, a large van glided up to the warehouse.

Bee shouted, "Too late!" and hurled himself behind the loader.

The back of the van burst open, and the sergeant practically threw Benton behind the metal track of the roll-up doors. He covered Benton with his own body-armored torso. Arkum-ra took up a similar position on the opposite side of the doorway.

A heavily armed mob rushed from the van, firing as they came. They weren't Talon, they were humans. Humans with guns? What the hell was going on?

Bee rose up from behind the loader with a rifle, and began to fire. He only got off a couple of rounds before his head exploded, and he fell back. He would not be getting up again.

Wasp also had a weapon. He brought the muzzle up and began to calmly and methodically lay down a field of fire. He was firing out the door at, what ... his own fellow terrorists? What was so important about those damned posters? It couldn't just be the money.

The attacking terrorists were caught in a deadly crossfire.

Between Wasp's methodical firing pattern, Arkum-ra's uncanny accuracy with his civilian model automatic, and Benton's bodyguards, it wasn't even a contest. The bastards had never had a chance beyond surprise, and Benton's group had just been put on alert by Chobuc-re. It was over as soon as it started.

As the last body fell, Chobuc-re turned and pointed his pistol at Wasp. He said "Drop your weapon. Now."

It didn't matter that Wasp had just helped fight off an attack. The fact that he was human and had a gun made his life forfeit.

Wasp whipped the gun up to take aim at his would-be captors. Suicide by bodyguard? Didn't matter. The sergeant had no trouble at all putting a round through Wasp's elbow. The gun went flying, Wasp tipped over backwards, and Chobuc-re was on top of him before he hit the floor.

Benton stood looking down at the man as the others rushed in and began to stop the blood flow and improvise a bandage.

Arkum-ra walked up, "Well, that was exciting. I haven't been in a good fire fight for a long time."

Benton looked up. "Oh. Arkum," he checked the time on his communicator, "now that your driver seems to have gotten himself killed do you think you can handle the van by yourself?"

"What?"

"I don't think your contact aboard the passenger liner would be particularly happy to see me, or any of my bodyguards."

"Good point. Yes." He raised his voice, "Sergeant, recruit some help to get this container into the van."

Chobuc-re looked at Benton, who nodded. The sergeant climbed aboard the loader and trundled away.

Arkum-ra said, "I'll drop off the cargo, and then I'll go ho ... Well, no, I don't think it would be smart to go home. Maybe, I'll just find a quiet little bar at the spaceport and await your call, shall I?

Benton nodded, and Arkum turned and strode out of the warehouse.

Benton walked out to the transport and watched as Arkum-ra squeezed into the van and drove off. Wasp was led out, handcuffed despite the useless arm, and brought over to him.

Chobuc-re stepped up, "Shall I call this in, sir, have someone else take charge of the scene, and the prisoner? We've stopped the bleeding and administered pain blockers, but he should seek medical care if you intend to have him treated."

"No, Sergeant, not yet. I have reason to want to avoid unnecessary attention for just a bit longer, but I would like to get away from this mess."

"We shouldn't leave the area unsecured, sir. There are a lot of weapons lying around."

"Quite right. I'll tell you what, Sergeant; let's take the transport up to the roof of that building at the end of the street. It'll give you a clear view of the area and I can have an informal chat with our prisoner."

"Sir."

In short order, the transport set down amid the pipes, wires, antennas, and other junk that usually accumulates on top of large utilitarian structures. Chobuc-re stood by the open door of the transport while the rest of the guards fanned out to take up various vantage points among the clutter.

Benton leaned out, "Sergeant, why don't you stretch your legs for a bit. Maybe you could go over and keep an eye on the massacre scene down there in the street."

"I should remain with the prisoner, sir."

"Sergeant," Benton let a sinister edge creep in, "while it is entirely possible that I'm growing feeble in my advancing years, I believe that even I can manage an essentially one armed man in handcuffs."

While clearly unhappy with the idea, Chobuc-re couldn't come up with a convincing counterargument. He strolled away to refine the positioning of his troops.

Benton sat back in his seat, looked at Wasp, and said, "Are

you going to tell me what the hell that was all about down there? Who were those assholes with the guns?"

Wasp gave a sad shake of his head, "Those brave patriots were another cell of the Red Spear, whose only fault lay in bad timing." He hesitated before continuing, "They'd seen your mock buddy hanging around the warehouse inspecting his artwork and planned a short, unpleasant, surprise party for him if he came back. We heard about their plans too late to stop them. We came to warn you about the attack."

Benton snorted, "Despite the fact you didn't know I was going to be there?"

"Bee didn't know you were going to be there."

"Ah, and of course, you didn't tell him. You wouldn't tell your ring finger what your fuck-you finger was up to."

Wasp clucked his tongue, "Watch your language, Kenny. You know I can still kick your ass, even in my present condition."

"You know, Arthur, after I've killed someone it's kind of hard for me to take their threat to kick my ass seriously."

"But I've been a pretty active ghost."

They smiled at each other.

Benton said, "You know, I still regret that."

"What?"

"The poor bastard whose head you made me blow off out there at Barnard's Star. In my nightmares he's got your face."

"Well, I've got his name--fair enough."

Benton said, "I wish it could have been you in this uniform instead of me. I'm just not made for this."

Arthur shook his head, "I'd say you were doing pretty well. Besides, it could never have been me. You were the Mahk-Ra hero."

"But I didn't do it for them. Barnard's Star is less than six light years from here. If the Mahk-Ra had fallen there, that whole bloody slaughter would have come here next. I fought that battle for us. I was fighting for Earth."

"You still are. Having you on the inside is worth more than a thousand bombs. The people out there may never know it, but you are probably the greatest hero in human history."

"The greatest monster in history, you mean." There was sudden anguish in Benton's voice, "I'm not a hero, Arthur, I'm a ... a ... sometimes I don't know when I'm pretending and when I really am a ... . I don't have a choice. Being a monster buys me power. But it's so dirty. It hurts so much. It scares the shit out of me."

Arthur said, "I'm sorry about that, but no one's hands are clean, kiddo. It's a time for dirty hands. The historians will apply soap where it's needed later."

"But you don't know what it's like to take people down into those cells below Talon HQ and pretend that I enjoy doing the things I have to do to them; torturing people in their own living rooms in front of their kids and smiling while I do it; other things. I'm not even sure it's for a good cause anymore." Benton lowered his head and whispered, "I'm afraid all the time. I wake up every morning shivering with fear at what I'm becoming."

They sat quietly for a few minutes.

Arthur said, "About this monster thing ... I know for sure that you're not a monster. Foolproof way of telling."

Benton leaned forward. "Tell me."

"The fear. You said you were afraid you were becoming a monster. That's not something monsters worry about, Kenny. As long as that fear is there you're as human as ... I was going to say as I am, but I'd hope better for you than that. Now, if you mention it again I'm going to ignore you." Arthur smiled, "I used to be pretty good at that--drove you crazy."

Benton said, "If I could have gotten you into one of those dark little cells back then ... ," and the two brothers laughed together for the first time in nearly two decades. They both knew it would be for the last time, it had to be, but it felt good.

After a while Benton said, "Okay. Okay, then tell me what's up with that container full of posters."

Arthur smiled, "This is something brand new. It's never been tried before. It's the brainchild of an agent I've only recently become aware of, though I suspect she's been active for a decade or more. You met her this morning."

Benton nodded, "I thought so. I'm sorry, Arthur, but I decked her and had her arrested. She was tapping out the recognition code so hard I was tempted to give her a snare drum."

"Really?" Arthur said, "She didn't mention ... Oh, I think I see the confusion. The woman you hit was not the agent, Kenny. She was handpicked to attract your attention, by the agent. Who else was there at the time?"

"Only that disturbing little girl."

"More disturbing than you know. First of all, not little, well, not young; at least twenty-six, maybe older. Proportional dwarf. Probably should have been receiving hormone treatments about the time the mocks showed up, and didn't get them."

"But ..."

"I've seen her as both boys and girls ranging from three or four up to about nine or ten. Totally convincing. She's most often a girl, so that's what I'm going with, but who knows? Twisty brain inside that little head."

"But ..."

"I know, it's hard to get your mind around. Oh, by the way, don't let her play 'guess my age' with you. She'll crawl into your brain and turn it into a pretzel. Always, and I mean always, remember she's an adult and any of that shifting age crap is purely for effect. Welcome to my world, she's your new contact."

"I don't think I'm following this."

"You'll get used to it. The girl's a genius, the best tactical and strategic thinker I've ever seen, with the possible exception of you at Barnard's Star, but she seems to think sideways, and upside-down. I think you two will get along."

Benton decided he would decipher that compliment later, and asked, "So, what is this plan?"

"Long before I became aware of her, Ranny had developed a web of scientists, engineers, theorists; some of the brightest human minds on the planet. She refers to them as her 'Boffins'."

"Ah," Benton said, "World War Two England. Bletchley Park, etc."

Arthur shrugged, "If you say so. Anyway, she put a simple question to them: instead of using the makeshift arsenal the resistance has at present to fight the enemy, was there anything inherent in Mahk-Ra technology that could be used as a weapon, or as a trigger for a weapon? Today we're going to test what they came up with."

"Test?"

"Well, yeah. We needed a Mahk-Ra gravity drive for the thing to work, and we don't have one of those. The first time we get to use the weapon is also the first chance we have to test it."

Benton sat back in his seat, "And that's the brilliant plan? Test a weapon? How exactly is this thing supposed to work?"

"I'm not in the 'need to know loop', Kenny, but this is the gist. The Boffins came up with this combination of inks, papers, plastics, and so on; impregnated with whatever magic juju chemists and physicists play with, and then made a bunch of perfectly ordinary counterfeit pre-invasion anthropomorphic artwork."

"Counterfeit?"

"Well, some of it's real, but you miss my point. This stuff can get past any detector the Mahk-Ra have, they're just posters. But, when they're packed together in a certain configuration, and then subjected to a gravitic field like the one our theorists think the Mahk-Ra use ... well, something interesting should happen." Arthur sat back and smiled.

Benton said, "Have you been spending a lot of time in the

sun lately, Arthur?"

"I said it was a test. The worst that can happen is the ship will take off normally, and you and your friend will be filthy rich. The best we're hoping for is that when the crate self-annihilates it will cripple the ship and cause a crash. And in case you missed it, the important word in there was, 'self-annihilate'. It leaves absolutely no trace of itself. The thing that brings the ship down will be a malfunction of the gravitic field."

"Okay," Benton said, "so we're rooting for interesting. Let's hope it works."

Arthur smiled, "Time will tell," he said.

Benton laughed out loud at the echo of his father in Arthur's voice. "It always does," he said in response.

Benton checked the time on his communicator. "I hope Arkum made it, that passenger liner is going to be taking off any minute now."

Arthur said, "We should have a pretty good view from here."

As Benton turned to look out the open door, Arthur slammed his cuffed hands into to the back of his brother's head. The pain to his shattered elbow was excruciating, but the blow served its purpose. Benton fell through the door, sprawling face first onto the roof of the building. Arthur sprinted for the low wall at the roof's edge.

There was a shout, and the Mahk-Re bodyguards raced to intercept him. He leaped to the top of the wall, seemed about to jump, and then paused looking toward the spaceport.

Benton propped up on his elbow, staring across at his brother. As Arthur turned around to face the approaching Mahk-Re, Benton could see the Ra-Prime passenger liner rising in the distance behind him. Gravity waves began to build around the ship, but instead of resolving into a smooth heat-shimmer, the field seemed to fragment. It twisted, clumped, separated. The roiling gravity waves began to emit visible light;

stronger and stronger; shining brightly. Benton could feel the gravitic distortion. Arthur swayed on the wall, thrust his cuffed fists into the air and shouted, "Resistance is al--"

The ship became sun-bright. Benton rolled on his side, brought his knees up, and covered his head. A huge weight crashed down on him as the world came apart.

It seemed to go on for days. It was a giant's baby rattle with him inside. His ears popped, and then ached, as the pressure wave tried to scrape him from the rooftop.

Finally, the brightness faded, the noise subsided, and things seemed to settle. Benton tried to sit up, but couldn't manage it. He realized that Chobuc-re was laying on top of him, also trying to roll into a more upright position. Benton got his hands on the sergeant's back, and pushed. Chobuc-re teetered into a kneeling position and drew his machine pistol.

One of the sergeant's arms was distorted in a way that could only mean broken bones. He had lost his spectacles and was squinting through barely slit eyes. He seeped blood from dozens of cuts, nicks, and abrasions. His right cheek was beginning to swell from the blow that had taken his eyewear. The pistol was level as he twisted this way and that trying to scan in all directions at once.

Benton sat up.

Chobuc-re immediately started pushing him back down, "Sir, stay low."

"Sergeant," Benton said, "any snipers that were out there are hamburger. Relax. There's nothing to shoot."

"Yes, sir." The sergeant continued his squinty-eyed back and forth sweep.

Benton reached up to grab the door frame of the transport, and realized that the door was missing. He looked around for the first time. Devastation. Beyond doubt, his very large bodyguard had just saved his life. Again. If he had been exposed to the beating Chobuc-re had just endured it was unlikely he'd still be alive.

He dragged himself up into the transport and reached across to the convenience compartment for his sunglasses. He turned back.

"Sergeant. Face me."

"Sir."

"Chobuc-re, this is a direct order," he placed the sunglasses on the Sergeant's face, "you will wear these until proper eyewear can be obtained."

"But ..."

"An order, Sergeant. I know these aren't as good as you need, but they're better than you have. Wear them."

"Yes, sir."

Benton stood and looked around. Arthur? Gone. Not escaped ... just gone. He tried to locate the other six members of his guard. Two were clearly dead. Two more, unsteady, but working to extricate the fifth who was trapped in debris. The sixth was wherever Arthur had gone.

Benton felt strange. Exhilarated. He felt like he was thinking more clearly than he had for a long time. He ordered Chobuc to stay seated where he was until the others could administer first aid, and walked over to the wall Arthur had been on. He looked toward the Reserved Zone.

The Boffins had been off on the power of their device by several orders of magnitude. This hadn't crippled one ship; it had nearly obliterated the entire spaceport. Other ships, large and small, were scattered around like beer cans after a frat party. All the buildings in the Reserved Zone were gone, burning, or fatally wounded. Windows would be shattered all over the Vancouver area.

It was a blessing the explosion had happened at the heart of the Reserved Zone. The very nature of the Zone worked in their favor. A huge percentage of the casualties would be Mahk-Ra, not human.

Benton sighed. Arkum could not possibly have gotten clear of all that destruction. "Goodbye my friend," he said, "I'll miss you."

Through the floating dust and smoke, he tried to locate the building that had carried his penthouse. The only candidate that seemed in the right position was several stories too short, and quite ragged.

Tamar-ra was a self-important, over-inflated, pain in the ass, but he had one virtue. He was addicted to punctuality. Benton glanced at the time and smiled an almost natural smile. Old Tamar had probably had time to finish one perfectly made drink and share a few anecdotes about Benton's shortcomings with Leann before the world ended.

Goodbye Leann. Goodbye Penthouse. Not that he would miss either very much. Leann had become a liability, and as for the other; he just didn't care that much. Time for a new start.

Ranny, and her "mother" would be the beginning of that.

His brief talk with Arthur had shown him that he was too isolated. He needed someone to talk with. Someone with the intellectual capacity to keep up, and who knew the truth about him. That would be Ranny. While he didn't underrate his late brother's willingness to lie through his teeth anytime it suited his goals, he did trust Arthur's evaluation of Ranny's capacities. As for Marilyn the Mother, well, she had been hand-picked to attract his attention; she would probably prove quite interesting in her own right.

He heard the sound of emergency vehicles in the distance.

For now, as the ranking Talon Officer on Earth in the absence of the lately departed Tamar, he had to consider the coming investigation. With Tamar-ra missing, and he certainly was that, Benton might be able to stretch the investigation out for a couple of weeks before a new Mahk-Ra Commander took over.

The question would be, "Is Tamar-ra dead? Or, perhaps in

the confusion, had he been kidnapped by some opportunistic faction of the Red Spear?"

Who could tell? All avenues must be thoroughly explored. He chuckled.

Benton was quite certain there would be no evidence whatsoever of terrorist involvement in the explosion. He could be very thorough. A few people might have to die under torture, a few unfortunate overdoses of truth drugs, some people shot while trying to escape. These were details. He could handle them, now. Arthur had helped him there, too.

The investigation would show that the explosion could only have been a horrendous malfunction. Solely down to some Mahk-Ra engineering failure. There was no need to repeat the Iranian lesson. No need to punish humans.

They would get away with this clean.

They couldn't afford to use the weapon again soon, it was too hard to deploy, and too easy to counter, but it was in the arsenal. The Boffins knew it worked. In time they could improve on the delivery system. We would use it again. Not soon, but someday. Someday.

He couldn't wait to talk with Ranny about the possibilities. They could wait it out together--the three of them; the monster, the child, and the "mother". This felt like the first big step on the road to a free Earth.

He smiled.

Time would tell. It always did.

HOPE

MATTHEW V. CLEMENS

Detective Eric Blocker knew the call was trouble when it came in. The whole town knew the police were on high alert because Mahk-Ra governor Aquinas-ra would be in for a visit tomorrow, yet someone had committed a murder. When the first officers on the scene wouldn't give any details over the radio, Blocker knew they were in some deep shit. If the victim was a human, the radio would have been flooded with information. When a Mahk-Ra was murdered, though, the first responders, especially the humans, clammed up. Killing a person was tantamount to a severe misdemeanor, but murdering a Mahk-Ra was serious shit and it rarely occurred.

The DPD detective, his dark hair a bristly cap, his green eyes the color of the Mississippi River on a good day, rode shotgun while his Mahk-Ra partner drove. The unmarked car's emergency lights were on, siren blaring, as they sped toward the crime scene, LeClaire Park. It was a green space squished in between downtown and the Mississippi.

Davenport, Iowa might be the backwater of all backwaters, but it did have the distinction of being the place where the big river flowed west instead of its usual south. Even the invaders hadn't been able to change that.

SteVannas-ra, Blocker's partner, who seemed to grudgingly tolerate the nickname of Steve that the Earther had hung on him, sawed the wheel to avoid a car that felt no need to get out of their way. Because of the Mahk-Ra's sensitivity to light, Steve wore sunglasses anytime he was outside.

Steve stood better than a foot taller than Blocker's six-one, and had an easy fifty pounds on the Earther's two-ten. Steve was also fastidious in his personal habits, at least compared to Blocker. His uniform was always clean, like he had just stepped out of a Mahk-Ra recruiting poster. Blocker usually looked like he'd slept in his clothes. At least Earther detectives didn't have to wear uniforms, one of the old-time traditions left in place by the Mahk-Ra to make the transition seem smoother.

"Who the hell commits a murder when the governor is coming to town?" Blocker asked.

His attention still on his driving, Steve said, "Many Earthers do not have your mental acuity."

Blocker shot him a look, but the Mahk-Ra's face was passive as he wove in and out of traffic. The duo had been partners for the better part of two years, worked dozens of cases together, and Blocker still had trouble telling if Steve was being serious or simply screwing with him.

"Still," Blocker said, ignoring his partner's possible sarcasm, "pretty ballsy to kill somebody when we're all on edge and out in force already."

"Seems like just the sort of thing the Red Spear would do. What would you call it in your sports metaphors?"

"A grandstand play," Blocker said.

"Yes," Steve said. "A grandstand play, does that not seem to be the obvious scenario to you?"

Blocker shrugged. "I thought we might let the evidence lead us to the killer."

"Of course, but the mathematical probability that the killer is a Red Spear member is in at least the eighty-seventh percentile, maybe even higher."

The Mahk-Ra liked to think they had higher intellectual gifts than the Earthers, but the truth was when they started spouting numbers like that, they really weren't any more accurate than the average TV weatherman, Blocker reflected. While all the aliens did that to some extent, a way of showing their superiority, Steve had risen statistical hyperbole to an absolute art form.

"That means there's a thirteen percent chance it wasn't Red Spear," Blocker noted.

"Not particularly good odds," Steve said, pulling the car to a stop in a parking lot just on the town side of the green space that abutted the river.

Blocker had grown up in this once thriving community. Before the invasion, there had been a third of a million people in the metro area that covered both sides of the river. Now there wasn't even half that.

He also had gotten the hell out of here at his first opportunity, but that, too, was before the invasion. He had migrated to Seattle, and gotten accepted to the police academy there. He hadn't been on the street six months when the Mahk-Ra invaded. Something inside him, sense of duty, loyalty to family, his concern for his ex-girlfriend, Hannah Perez, *something* had drawn him back here right after the invasion.

Being penniless in a war-torn nation, it had taken him a while to work his way back from halfway across the country. By the time he got home, the fighting was pretty much over. Several friends from his youth, including Hannah, had joined the Red Spear and were actively working for the resistance. When it came time for Blocker to make that decision, his parents had been the ones to persuade him to rejoin the police department. The decision to turn his back on his friends had been a difficult one, but, in the end, he knew he had done the right thing.

She had made it clear that she wasn't interested in taking him back even before he told her about joining the police, but for him that didn't matter. You don't get to pick who you fall in love with and he loved Hannah. Being away from her had made that even more clear for him, even if the fire had faded for her.

The last thing she said to him, eyes brimming with tears, had been a single venomous word, "Traitor."

Now, they were on opposite sides of the law. Any hope he had of returning to a life that included Hannah and his other friends was gone. Instead, he found himself working with those who wanted to stop them.

Even though Steve walked at a slower rate than his fellow Mahk-Ra's, Blocker still found himself quickening his pace to keep up as they strode toward the crime scene.

Ahead of them, Blocker could see crime scene tape marking off a big rectangle. Cops, both human and Mahk-Ra, manned the perimeter to keep the gawkers and press back. Further inside, drones little bigger than footballs, alternately hovered or sped around to get a different perspective as they photographed and video-recorded the crime scene. Blocker was surprised to see not one body, but three, each of them covered with a tarp. Each tarp was big, bigger than one needed for a human. The victims were Mahk-Ra, all of them. Three dead aliens. Blocker's gut turned to ice. This was the sort of thing that got entire towns exterminated as payback.

One of the drones turned from the body it hovered above, and on its underside a laser beam shot out toward the top of the Davenport Bank building three blocks away.

Blocker and Steve paused to watch the drone take off overhead, following the laser to the bank.

"Sniper," Blocker said. "A sniper good enough to take out three Mahk-Ra before they could take cover."

"If the rest of my existence is spent on this rock, I will not understand how that is an honorable way to deal with an opponent," Steve said.

Blocker shrugged. He was not going to get drug into an argument about the ethics of combat with one of the aliens that had not only defeated his species and now ran the planet, but had wiped Iran completely off the map for having the temerity to fight back. "Maybe we should go see what we've got first."

Steve took the hint and led the way forward. While the humans gave the Mahk-Ra detective a wide berth, the crowd all seemed intent on filling in to bar Blocker. He had to shuffle between onlookers who grudgingly moved aside to let him through.

One guy muttered, "Mock lover," as Blocker passed.

Another voice, one the detective couldn't identify, said, "Traitor."

Swallowing his anger, Blocker just kept pushing through the crowd.

At the tape, a uniformed human, Marty Jensen, raised the yellow and black band for them to go under. Steve practically had to squat to make it and when he stood straight, he glared at Jensen.

Blocker reached up and clapped his partner lightly on the shoulder. "It's not an affront, Steve, he's short."

The Mahk-Ra detective seemed unmoved by that fact.

Blowing out a long breath, Blocker said, "Okay, you caught us, Jensen grew up short so he couldn't raise the tape any higher. It was a plan by his parents just to fuck with you."

In spite of himself, Steve managed half a smile. "You are vulgar, even by the meager standards of Earthers."

Blocker shrugged. "Yeah, I am."

"You also make a coherent point."

"Ya think?"

Still having trouble adjusting to the sarcasm of Earthers,

Steve simply said, "Frequently."

They approached the nearest Mahk-Ra body. His queasiness grew. Aquinas-ra was not exactly a benevolent governor, if they didn't catch the sniper fast enough, he just might exact a more widespread "justice" than simply executing the killer and all of his or her family. He had wiped out smaller settlements for the murder of a single Mahk-Ra. Some rulers kept order with a steel fist, Aquinas-ra favored more of a scorched earth authority.

When they got to the corpse, Colonel Stanis-ra was waiting for them, and even with the obligatory sunglasses, Blocker had no problem reading the colonel's anger in his face. He knelt next to the victim, a hand on the corner of the sheet. Looking up at them, his voice icy, he said, "I want the killer delivered to me in the next twenty-four hours, no excuses."

The colonel was normally a prick, but this seemed excessive even for him. In the military set-up of the Mahk-Ra, he was like the mayor, police chief, and officer in charge of Mahk-Ra forces in the area all rolled into one.

"Who are the victims?" Blocker asked.

Pulling the sheet back on this one, the colonel revealed the face of Aquinas-ra.

"Shit," Blocker said. "What the fuck is he even doing here? Are these his body guards?"

Blowing out a foul breath that rose into Blocker's face, the colonel said, "They never even got their weapons out of their holsters."

"But they weren't due here until tomorrow," Blocker said.

"The governor and his team arrived last night. This morning he wanted to do a surprise inspection of the riverfront, just he and two guards, no commotion."

"Why the riverfront?" Blocker asked.

"I informed the governor that we needed to beef up security here to keep Red Spear smugglers from using it to land supplies. He wanted to see for himself. The rebels killed him to protect their supply lines, I suppose. It will do them no good, we will squash them like the insects they are."

"How did they know he was here, though?"

"Spies," the colonel said. "That is for you and SteVannas to ferret out. The two of you need to deliver me the sniper or I will be forced to punish more than just the Red Spear. Now, get to work!"

As he and his partner moved closer to the governor's corpse, Blocker couldn't help thinking that while killing the governor would be a coup for the Red Spear, it just might get the whole town wiped out if he and Steve couldn't find the sniper within the colonel's time limit.

Kyla, the blonde bombshell who led the local Red Spear cell, was crafty and audacious, but she was smarter than to make a play like this. Like him, she had grown up here. She wouldn't risk the whole town, not even to be rid of Aquinas-ra. If Red Spear cell members were behind this, it would have to be a splinter group. Someone who didn't give a shit about the repercussions.

Staring down at the dead governor, a good size hole in the Mahk-Ra's forehead, Blocker thought about the past. The same Earth, but a different world. Summer days in his youth made up of playing baseball on green grass, the sun high in the sky. There were the easy smiles of his friends as they ran all afternoon chasing fly balls or stretching singles into doubles. Life had seemed so simple then. Now, everything was complicated. Every-fucking-thing. Blocker ran a hand over his face and blew out a long, exasperated breath.

In the distance, at the bank building, he could see the crime scene drone flying around, taking photos. He hoped the little bastard found something because he had few avenues that looked anywhere near promising. There were no witnesses at this end who would have seen anything helpful. One or two might have seen the window or the muzzle flash, but the drone's computer had already calculated all that and was taking photos of every square inch of the room the shot came from. The machine even had a mechanical arm that allowed it to collect small pieces of evidence if it found any.

Steve seemed perfectly content to stand there doing nothing until the drone returned. Blocker was less patient.

"Maybe we ought to head over there ourselves," he said. "We're going to want to see it in person, anyway."

Steve just looked at him, then past him toward the bank building. "The crime scene investigator returns, even as you speak."

For reasons beyond Blocker's understanding, the Mahk-Ra detective insisted on referring to the drone as if its job made it a sentient being.

Blocker turned to see the drone speeding back to them through a sky so blue it almost hurt his eyes. "Good," he muttered.

Within a minute, the thing was hovering between them.

"Well?" Blocker asked, addressing the drone.

"There is evidence," the machine said, still hanging there, the four motors on its corners whirring quietly.

Blocker couldn't understand why they couldn't make the voice less tinny and robot-like. He had seen the Iron Man movies when he was a kid, and the robot that assisted Tony Stark sounded like a real person. This thing sounded like a broken drive-thru squawk box. "Which is?" he asked.

The drone ran a video of its exploration of the room where the shot had come from. The machine flew in through a window left open by the killer.

"Fingerprints on the frame or the opener?" Blocker asked.

"No," the drone said, then restarted the video that would pause anytime one of the detectives asked a question.

From the drone's POV they watched as it flew into an empty office -- empty of no desks, chairs, or even an old coffee pot. It

HOPE

looked like it hadn't been used in years.

Steve asked, "Any sign of Mahk-Ras in the office?"

"None," the drone reported.

Blocker looked at his partner who seemed very pleased with himself that he had eliminated an entire species with just one question.

The video rolled again, and finally, Blocker saw "the evidence." Lying on the floor, near a wall, to the right of the window where the shot had come from, was a casing from a 50 caliber bullet, just the type that had killed the governor.

"Any fingerprints on the casing?" Blocker asked.

"No," the metallic voice answered.

A tiny alarm went off at the back of Blocker's brain. Something weird there. "Any fingerprints anywhere in the office?" he asked.

"None."

Blocker didn't like that. Why would an assassin be so careful about not leaving fingerprints behind yet leave the shell casing? It was like asking to be caught.

"What about DNA?" Steve asked.

"Affirmative," the drone said.

While the drone was an Earther invention, the ability to have them capable of instantaneous communication throughout the Internet, all telecommunications systems, both human and Mahk-Ra, had been an upgrade the aliens had engineered.

"Where was it?" Blocker asked.

"Skin cells on the edge of the casing," the drone reported.

Blocker asked, "DNA on the casing but no fingerprint?"

The drone fluttered in the air, the equivalent of a shrug.

"Have you identified the source?" Steve asked.

A still photo replaced the paused video on the drone's screen. Blocker tried not to react as he looked into the brown eyes of the woman he loved, Hannah Perez. No one on the force knew of their past, and no one on this planet or Ra-Prime knew that he was still in love with her.

"I know this Earther," Steve said. "She is suspected Red Spear."

Shaking his head, Blocker said, "This feels wrong."

Steve just stared at him.

"This doesn't feel wrong to you?"

"Wrong?" Steve asked. "How? We have the DNA, we have a suspect, we have only to arrest her."

The colonel came over. "You have evidence?"

Steve brought him up to speed.

"I think we should go look around the office," Blocker said.

"You have evidence," the colonel said, his voice hard. "Go, arrest the woman. Bring her to me."

"But..." Blocker said.

The colonel silenced him with a look.

For a race that thought themselves intellectually superior, the Mahk-Ra had a limited outlook. They had the tenacity of cockroaches after a nuclear bomb, but their tactics were simplistic - attack. They moved ever forward, simply overwhelming their enemies with sheer numbers and perseverance. When it came to seeing a possible frame job for a murder, well, Steve was trapped by thousands of years of Mahk-Ra genetics.

"What if she isn't guilty?" Blocker asked. "What if it's a set-up?"

The Mahk-Ra detective shrugged, something he had learned from his Earther partner. "Then she is a suspected enemy of the state and we will bring her in anyway."

Blocker frowned.

Steve eyeballed him. "Right?"

"Yeah," Blocker said, maybe a little too quickly. "We bring her in."

Hoping it wouldn't come to that, Blocker turned to the drone. "Last known address for Perez, Hannah."

The drone said, "Sent to your mobile device."

Looking at the address, an apartment uptown, Blocker figured they wouldn't find her at home. He had, since he had been back, kept tabs on her and knew she had left that apartment a while ago, but it was still in her name so she could be there, he supposed.

While Blocker didn't know for sure what he would do if she was guilty, until he knew for sure, his instinct was still to protect her. The set-up just seemed too neat. There was no way a Red Spear assassin would leave a shell casing behind, especially one that was laying in plain sight – especially Hannah.

In the meantime, he wondered if there was a way to warn her, just in case.

He scoured the park looking for a runner, one of the dozen nameless kids Kyla used to communicate with the Red Spear agents in her network.

Early in the invasion it had become clear that the Mahk-Ra could use any electronic communication to track and target the Earthers. The armed forces were annihilated early on, but the Red Spear had gone old school almost from the beginning.

Kids, like a latter day Fagin's army, were used as messengers, lookouts, eavesdroppers, and even sneak thieves. They were just children, but with the very life of the planet at stake, the Red Spear felt it necessary to use every resource available.

Especially in this cell, Kyla tried to protect the children, but there was danger every time they stepped outside, just as for the adults. Even though she mothered them, Kyla was also the one who had to send them out, and if Aquinas-ra was in town, she would have runners in the area to pick up whatever info they could.

If he could somehow catch one of them, maybe he could get a message to Kyla to send an E-1 alert to Hannah. E-1 was Red Spear code for go to ground until further notice.

Finally, he spotted one hanging near the tape that held back the rubberneckers. Thankfully, he wasn't near any of the uniformed officers.

"We should at least interview a couple of the onlookers," Blocker said. "Just in case one of them saw something."

"If you want," Steve said. "I know what I need to know, I'll be in the car."

Blocker approached, and though the kid looked nervous, he didn't bolt. He was maybe twelve or thirteen and had the same blond hair as his leader. The detective wondered if the resemblance was more than a coincidence.

"Hey, kid."

The boy pointed to himself, raised his eyebrows. He looked like he was about to make a break for it.

"Don't run, kid, I don't want to chase you."

The youngster's clothes were clean, but his hair hadn't seen a comb for a while, and his sneakers looked like he had run here from San Francisco.

Nodding back toward the corpse as he closed the distance to the kid, Blocker asked, "See anything?"

The boy shook his head.

Leaning close to the kid, his voice barely a whisper, Blocker asked, "You one of Kyla's?"

The kid's eyes widened for a second, then he shook his head. "I don't know what you're talking about."

"Okay," Blocker said, voice still low. "But if you happen to run into anyone named Kyla, tell her she needs to get an E-1 message to Hannah ASAP."

The boy just stared at him.

"It's not a trap. Tell her Blocker sent you."

Looking skeptical, the boy said, "I have no idea..."

Blocker cut him off. "Clock's running, kid. In thirty minutes it might not matter what you say." Taking a step back from the kid, Blocker let his voice rise a little. "So, you didn't see anything? Get your ass to school."

The kid needed no further encouragement. He turned

and sprinted away as fast as he could. Turning to the other onlookers, Blocker asked, "Any of you see anything?"

Nobody had. Letting it go, but giving the kid as much head start as he dared, Blocker finally trailed after his partner to the car.

Steve sped north, headed for the shitty neighborhood on the far side of town. Half the population was gone, the economy was depressed, and there wasn't a lot of prosperity left here, but the Colony Park neighborhood had been a beehive of illegal activity that required regular visits by the police, SWAT, and once the National Guard, even before the Mahk-Ra invaded.

On his belt, Blocker's cell phone chirped. He pulled it up, looked at a number he had never seen before. Still, he took the call. "Blocker."

The voice on the other end was soft, just the hint of an accent. "Do you know who this is?"

Kyla! The Red Spear commander had received his message. She had some balls, calling him while he rode in a police car with his Mahk-Ra partner. He couldn't keep his eyes from cutting to Steve, who was focused on the road, and didn't even seem to notice that Blocker was on the phone.

Letting out a breath, forcing himself to calm down, he said, "What's up?"

"You drew the killing of Aquinas-ra."

It was not a question.

"So?"

"We're being blamed for it, aren't we?"

There was no anger in her voice. She probably had assumed all along they would be blamed for the murder. "Yep."

"We didn't do it," she said, her voice matter-of-fact.

"That's my thinking, too."

There was a moment of silence while she considered that.

He had met her once. A long-haired blonde who leaned to ponytails, she had light blue eyes that could lull you into thinking you weren't dealing with a woman who had both a genius level IQ and a mean streak.

"Really?" she asked. "That's interesting."

He wanted to tell her about the faked evidence, but not while Steve was listening in.

"Well, if you didn't let the puppy out, who did?" he asked, hoping she would follow along with his lost puppy analogy. It was the only thing he could think of on the spur of the moment. The Mahk-Ra had decent hearing. It was possible Steve could hear Kyla's voice on the other end, though Blocker was pretty sure he wouldn't recognize it. At least that was his hope.

"Not sure," she said, "but I'm looking into it."

"So, you'll let me know if you find Bogie?" he asked.

There was a long silence. Blocker knew she had figured out what he meant, so the only reason he was waiting for an answer was because she was weighing her options. Finally, after what seemed like a minute, she said, "Yeah, I think I will."

"If I get a chance, I'll try to look for him, too."

He couldn't say more, but he hoped she would figure out what he meant.

After a moment, she said, "You're not looking for the 'puppy' now?" The word sounded funny when she said it.

"Nope, different dog."

"The one in your message?" she asked.

"Yeah," he said quietly.

"You won't find her, or any of them, for that matter."

"Good."

"You're wasting time," she said.

"Can't be helped, but as soon as I'm done with this, I'll find time to help find Bogie, okay?"

"It's going to have to be, isn't it?" she asked.

He was getting ready to reply when she clicked off. He hoped she was right and that Hannah wasn't just sitting at the address they were headed to.

"Bogie?" Steve asked, eyes still on the road.

"Lady friend of mine," Blocker said. "Her puppy has gone missing. She was hoping I could help her find it."

Steve gave him a sideways look. Was he suspicious?

"What?" Blocker asked. "I'm a detective."

Something like a grin tried to break out on Steve's face, but he suppressed it. The Mahk-Ra did not smile much, and Blocker was pretty sure that laughing aloud was a capital offense.

The mood turned serious for both of them as Steve parked the car in front of the address they had been given by the drone. They got out of the car, checked their weapons. While Steve had a Mahk-Ra handgun, a Piecemaker it was called on the streets, Blocker stayed old-school carrying the Glock he had gotten when he became a Seattle cop.

They stood before a two-story building that held twelve apartments, four per floor, a third of them in the basement. The faux brick facade was cracked and chipping off, the windows were all filthy, and emergency calls, either police, fire, or both came in on the average of better than two a day on this block.

At least they wouldn't have to try to clear the tenement on their own. Steve already had the remote off his belt as Blocker opened the trunk. He was barely out of the way when the drone took off and buzzed a couple quick circles overhead as Steve reacquainted himself with the controls.

Unlike the crime scene drone from this morning, this one was both armored and armed. The only thing it couldn't do was open doors. They would advance slowly, the drone clearing every apartment. Blocker hoped Steve would follow procedure, clearing the apartments from the bottom up. Hannah's place was at the top in the back. If they started at the bottom, the people coming out of their apartments would be bitching and moaning. That would warn whoever was in an apartment yet to be searched. In this neighborhood, there was always an uproar.

Already, a few people had started peeking out from

behind curtains Blocker saw, and a couple of brave souls had ventured out on their front stoops, but bystanders wouldn't be a problem. Cops weren't exactly out of the ordinary here, so nobody looked too eager to get in on the action. They were just watching because it was break from the usual boring bullshit of their lives, and having a real Mahk-Ra detective on the block *never* happened. They would watch, but this was one time they wouldn't come out to cheer on either side.

"Ready?" Steve asked as they approached the door, the drone buzzing like an angry insect just over their heads.

Blocker was near the knob of the front door now. He nodded, twisted the knob and threw the door open, careful to remain to one side of the door. The drone went inside, hovered for a second as Steve looked at the monitor on the remote control to make sure no one was waiting to ambush them on the stairs. There were two sets, one on the right down to the basement, then five stairs on the left that led to the first floor.

The drone swooped down into the basement while Blocker kept his pistol aimed upstairs. Steve took the drone past the basement apartments and Blocker could hear the faint whir of the machine's blades.

"Clear," Steve said, standing behind Blocker. "Moving to the first floor."

This wasn't simply a progress report, but also a warning to Blocker not to shoot the damned thing when it burst into view at the top of the stairs. Having covered the basement level from front to back, the drone had gone up the back stairs and was now flying back toward them on the first floor.

The buzz grew louder, then Blocker saw the drone about the same moment that Steve said, "Clear."

Without hesitation, Steve took the drone up to the second floor. Blocker wasn't waiting around either. He was right on the machine's heels as it went up the final flight of stairs. The hallway was clear, and when one door on his right cracked open, Blocker leveled his pistol, then the door immediately slammed shut.

He could hear Steve's feet pounding behind him, and he wanted to get inside first, just in case Hannah was there, he didn't want the Mahk-Ra killing her with the drone before they even had a chance to question her. They wanted her alive, but if by some miracle she was inside and took a shot at the drone, Steve might simply react. Mahk-Ras were not known for their patience when they perceived a threat, even if it was only to a drone.

The last door on the left was Hannah's. The drone hovered in front of it, as Blocker came up, panting. He tried the knob, locked. Without hesitation, he threw a shoulder against the door and the cheap lock shattered in the flimsy frame, the door swinging drunkenly open. The drone swept past and went toward the two bedrooms in the back.

His momentum having carried him inside, Blocker swept his gun around the vacant living room. Even though he was certain she had abandoned the place weeks ago, her scent lingered in the air. The Mahk-Ra might not know what it was, but Blocker knew it was her. He prayed that she wasn't here. He moved to his left, past the ratty dining room table, and into the minuscule kitchen – empty.

Steve was at the door now, and the drone was working on the second bedroom. She wasn't here or Blocker would have heard gunfire by now, he was sure of that much. As quietly as he could, he let out a sigh of relief.

"She's not here," Steve announced.

Blocker gave him a look. "No shit."

Then he heard something, footsteps behind them. He looked at Steve. The Mahk-Ra had heard it, too.

Turning toward the broken door, too loudly Blocker asked, "Who's there?" Something in Blocker's gut twisted. He hoped whoever was in the corridor wasn't Hannah coming back for something.

A voice in the hallway, a male voice, yelled, "Fuck!"

Steve raised his weapon toward a spot on the wall about where the voice had come from.

"No," Blocker hissed, trying to keep his voice low. "We take him alive, we can question him."

Obviously, Steve didn't like this plan, but he said nothing.

Blocker crept to the door, his gun up. He peeked around the door, saw a wisp of long, black hair, Hannah! But he was sure the voice had been male, what the hell?

He had the door blocked and Steve couldn't see into the hallway. The Mahk-Ra pressed against him, trying to see over his head, but Blocker used a hip to keep him back.

Blocker yelled, "Freeze!"

The face became more clearly visible as the suspect looked up, and Blocker realized it was a boy, a teenage boy with hair almost exactly like Hannah's. The kid didn't hesitate, he turned and ran.

His prey, younger and more limber, flew down the stairs three at a time. Blocker took off after him but not before taking a quick step backward, causing Steve to trip and fall over the leg of a chair.

Blocker ran hard now, trying to keep up, but the kid was a whole flight of stairs ahead of him and pulling away.

The detective figured the boy for one of Kyla's gang of messengers, but if he was, he was on the older side. He wore a grimy T-shirt, ripped jeans and sneakers held together with duct tape around the toes, and he was fast.

The teenager was out the front door and going left before Blocker could even get to the last landing. Turning, the detective took a calculated risk and went down the back stairs and out the rear of the building. He wasn't going to outrun the kid, so he had to hope the young man decided to curl around the building in hopes of disappearing in the apartment buildings to the north.

Blocker burst through the door into blinding sunshine and turned right. In three quick strides, he was at the corner of the building and pulling to a stop. He heard the kid coming and didn't risk taking a peek.

Listening close, his heart hammering, Blocker waited until the kid was nearly on him, then stuck out a stiff arm, clotheslining the boy, and dropping him to the ground with a hard whomp, the air exploding out of the kid's lungs.

Pressing his advantage, Blocker dropped on top of the boy, pinning him down. The detective knew he had only a short time before Steve would be joining them, and the Mahk-Ra would torture the kid to find out if he knew where Hannah was.

"Let me up," the kid shouted, struggling against the bigger man holding him down.

"Stop fighting," Blocker said.

The kid fought harder.

Where was Steve? The Mahk-Ra detective had to be on his way, didn't he? Blocker didn't want to hurt the kid, but the boy wouldn't stop struggling.

"Kid, stop!" He pinned the kid down tighter.

"Screw you, cop!"

"Look, I need to talk to your boss."

"I don't have a boss," the kid said, squirming harder, but running out of breath now.

"I'm going to let you up, let you go."

The kid looked skeptical.

"But I need you to tell Kyla to call me."

"Fuck you."

Blocker heard the drone in front of the building. That was why Steve wasn't out here, he could cover more ground with the drone. Shit. They only had seconds now.

Rising off the kid, Blocker said, "Look, just deliver the message. Let Kyla decide for herself. Tell her to call Blocker -

soon!"

Blocker heard the drone heading toward them now.

"Go, kid, run!"

Then the boy heard it too. He didn't need to be told twice, he was a vapor trail headed north.

As the drone came around the building, Blocker shouted, "Hey, kid, stop!"

The boy didn't even turn to look. Blocker was putting on a good show for the drone's camera, and the kid either knew that or didn't care. He was gone.

Steve ran up next to him and the drone sped after the boy.

"Stop or I'll fire," Blocker yelled as the drone flew past him.

The kid was almost to a building now. Blocker fired at the same instant that Steve made the drone dive to get a better angle and fired the drone's machine gun. It was probably just bad luck that Blocker's shot struck the tail of the drone and sent it momentarily off course. The drone's shots went harmlessly into the air, missing the boy. By the time the drone righted itself, Blocker knew it would never catch the kid. One of Kyla's kids who lived to be a teenager, like this boy, knew how to evade a drone once he had that big a head start. Blocker was sure the kid would be fine, but the question was, would he deliver the message? And, if he did, would Kyla call him?

Steve turned to him, and though his partner's anger was apparent, the Mahk-Ra managed to keep his voice even. "You shot my drone, Earther."

"Earther" was a term of derision to Steve and though he used it for most people he only used toward Blocker when he was pissed. Blocker suppressed a smile.

"Sorry, but you're the one who dove it into my line of fire."

Watching the monitor, Steve used the joysticks to fly the drone between the apartment buildings to the north.

"Seems to be working fine," Blocker said, careful to keep any trace of humor out of his voice.

"The steering is off by at least 8.34 degrees."

"That's not that much."

Steve shot him a look. "The boy has disappeared, perhaps we should call in a team to sweep all those apartments until we find him."

"That's going to take a lot of time," Blocker said. "I thought we were after Hannah Perez, not some anonymous kid."

"He is our best lead."

"What are the odds of that lead panning out?"

"Less than twenty percent," Steve admitted. "Do you have a better plan?"

"Yeah," Blocker said, turning toward their car and having no idea what the hell his better idea would turn out to be.

He was sure Hannah was innocent, but the clock was running and Colonel Stanis-ra wasn't going to cut them any slack on his twenty-four hour order for bringing in the killer. Blocker wondered if turning in Hannah would be the only way to save the city. The plan to frame the Red Spear, Hannah in particular, was a brilliant one. Get them to not only apprehend the wrong person, but someone who would never be believed, no matter how much she protested her innocence, and was part of an organization the Mahk-Ra was out to destroy anyway.

That was when it hit him. Who stood to gain the most from the death of Aquinas-ra and the capture of one of the Mahk-Ras' biggest enemies? Only the Mahk-Ra would benefit, and of all of them, whoever took over for Aquinas-Ra was the most likely suspect. But who would that be?

"Wait," Steve said. "The drone is not back yet."

Blocker kept walking while the Mahk-Ra recalled the machine. The whole way to the front of the building, Blocker's mind raced as he tried to think of anything that could serve as enough of a lead to mollify Steve. Even as he considered that, he tried to figure out which Mahk-Ra would have the most to gain from Aquinas's death. Only in finding the real shooter, and whoever was behind the frame, could he hope to save both Hannah and the city.

He unlocked the trunk, and when Steve got back to the car, the drone settled down into it. Blocker closed the lid while Steve reattached the remote to his belt.

"So, you were saying?" Steve asked.

Going around to the passenger side, Blocker said, "We figured she wouldn't be here."

"*You* figured."

"Either way, she wasn't here."

"So, our next stop is?"

They were already driving back toward the main north-south drag, Brady Street.

Grasping at anything, Blocker said, "You remember that strip bar over on the west side?"

Steve was nodding now. "The one where the Red Spear used to meet."

"Worth a shot?" Blocker asked, wanting the Mahk-Ra to feel like he was in charge.

"Did not the Perez woman work there for a time?"

"Bartender, not a stripper."

"Then yes, it is as you say, 'worth a shot.'"

The strip club, a long cement bunker called Boobies, wasn't as classy as its name. It aspired to seedy, but couldn't rise even that high. A canvas tarp had been pulled across the front window, and the stage was the size of a porta-potty without the door, but with the odor.

Blocker let the Mahk-Ra lead the way. The alien detective would put everyone in the joint on their guard. Nobody would probably talk anyway, but with Steve leading the way, their silence was virtually assured.

By letting Steve deal with the few customers, the only bartender, and a couple of lonely strippers, Blocker bought himself a little bit of freedom, just in case Kyla got his message and decided to call.

The bartender had never heard of Hannah, and the customers around the bar weren't going to admit to knowing anyone on the planet whether the interrogator was a Mahk-Ra or not.

Blocker checked his watch for the fourth time since they entered, exactly six minutes later than the last time. The cell phone in his pocket vibrated.

To Steve, he said, "Going to the john."

His partner nodded, and Blocker strode toward the men's, trying not to walk too fast as the phone vibrated again. Once inside, he passed the three vacant urinals, checked the two stalls to ensure his privacy, then locked himself in the larger one before finally pulling out the phone.

He clicked the button, said, "Blocker."

"I heard you wanted to talk to me," said the seductive voice on the other end, Kyla.

"Yeah," Blocker said. "Our friends will want someone to pay for what happened this morning."

There was silence on the other end. Blocker kept his ears open to anyone coming into the bathroom, too.

"If not the real killer, then Hannah, and if not her, the whole fucking town, maybe."

Her voice arctic, Kyla said, "I'm not giving you Hannah."

"And I'm not asking for her. I do want to know if you have any idea who the shooter was, though."

Another long silence, another glance at the door hoping no one, especially his partner, came into the men's room. As the silence dragged on, Blocker tried to pick up sounds outside the bathroom. He knew he didn't have a lot of time. When she still didn't speak, he said, "Look, Kyla, everything you've worked for, this asshole is going to destroy it. Are you going to stand by and let that happen?"

After a pause long enough for him to wonder if she was still there, she said, "No."

Speaking in a rush now, he said, "The evidence all points to Hannah."

"She didn't do it," Kyla said, her voice rising.

"I know," he said, his own voice rising, plowing over hers. "Just listen, will you? I may only have seconds. It's a frame. I know it, but the Mahk-Ra are convinced that because the evidence ties to Hannah, and she's Red Spear, that means she's guilty. If they don't find her, or if we don't find the real killer, they may torch the whole fucking town, understand?"

"Yeah."

"I'm tied up with my partner chasing Hannah. I need you to find the trigger man."

"Why would I help you?"

"Because fighting back isn't just about killing Mahk-Ras, it's about saving human lives and you can maybe help me save the whole city."

That shut her up.

"I think a Mahk-Ra is behind this," he said. "One of them that wanted Aquinas out of the way."

"Bullshit. Mahk-Ra don't kill their own. It's not how they're wired, they don't kill for personal gain."

It was all falling into place for him now. "They have been studying us for years, decades, maybe they're learning from us."

"The bad as well as the good," Kyla said, seeing where he was going.

"But without whoever pulled the trigger, I've got nowhere to go, even if I do figure out who built the frame."

"I'll see what I can..."

The men's room door opened and Blocker interrupted her. "I'll come help you look for the puppy as soon as I can get away." He clicked off.

"Are you still in here, Blocker?" Steve asked, his voice

booming off the hard tile walls.

"Can't a guy have a minute?" Blocker asked without opening the stall door.

"You have been in here for well over that duration of time, and who were you talking to?"

"A woman, the same one from this morning. I'm trying to get lucky, but she's all wrapped up in her missing dog."

"Bogie?" Steve asked.

Blocker flushed the toilet, to keep up the illusion, before coming out of the stall. "Yes," Blocker said. "Fucking Bogie."

"Your species and your insatiable sex drive," Steve said, shaking his head. "No discipline."

Blocker moved to the sink to wash his hands. "Getting laid is more fun than discipline."

"The mindset that made it easy for us to conquer you. No discipline." Steve opened the door and the music from the strip club blared in. "I have a lead on Hannah Perez's whereabouts. We have to go."

Blocker fell in step, well, as best he could with a partner a foot taller.

When they were outside, and Blocker's ears were no longer being assaulted by the music from the club, he asked, "Where is she?"

"One of the dancers said Perez had a boyfriend that lives on Marquette Street."

The idea that she had a boyfriend tugged at something in his gut. That thought bothered him more than they might actually be closing in on her.

Blocker went back to what he was thinking about when he was talking to Kyla, the Mahk-Ras' learning from the Earthers. "Which Mahk-Ra stands to gain the most from Aquinas's death?"

Steve blew out a long breath. "We have evidence. We have a suspect. Besides, what you're thinking, that is not the way of the Mahk-Ra."

"Humor me."

After only a second's consideration, Steve said, "Stanis-Ra is next in line, why?"

"Because he was the one that kept us from going to the sniper's nest."

"Because we already had evidence to follow."

"Okay, but the only evidence was the casing. Where is the rifle? How did someone get it in and out without anyone noticing? Why didn't we see the security recordings?"

"We may have overlooked those things, yes, but we had a trail to follow."

"We've been at this all day and most of the night and no one has called us with any information on either thing. You don't think that's weird?"

The Mahk-Ra went silent, and Blocker let him mull all that over as his cell twitched, which meant a text had come in. Blocker took a quick look.

> The "boyfriend" knows the trigger man.
> The dancer is with us.
> Be careful, might want to keep you alive. K

So, he had been right and he was a step closer to having the killer in his sights, if he trusted Kyla. Big "if." She had trusted him, though. He needed to figure out how to spring the idea on Steve, and that wouldn't be that simple.

To make matters worse, they were pulling up in front of the house now. Assuming that Kyla's setup was complete and Hannah wasn't here, the only thing they needed to do was get Hannah's boyfriend to tell them what really happened. He wondered why Kyla had put the word "boyfriend" in quotation marks. Was this a setup, too?

"What's the guy's name?" Blocker asked.

"Richie Panten. He's an informant."

"Informing about what?" Blocker asked.

"Red Spear activity."

Blocker knew the guy. He was an asshole and had about as much to do with Red Spear as Steve did. Now he knew Kyla was on the up and up, Hannah wouldn't date Panten if he was the only man on the planet. Panten might have tried to inform on Red Spear, and now Kyla was getting her revenge, and saving Hannah at the same time.

Steve was out of the car now and Blocker was struggling to keep up. Steve had the drone out of the trunk and in the air before Blocker caught up.

Night had settled in and the streetlights weren't much help. A splinter of light leaked out the edge of the blinds on the living room window of Panten's house, but the rest seemed dark.

"I'll go around back and find a way for the drone to get inside. Wait here, and if he comes out the front, he's yours," Steve said.

"Yeah, got it," Blocker said. He had no intention of obeying his partner but he put on a good show until Steve rounded the corner of the house and was out of sight.

Instantly, Blocker tiptoed to the front door, gingerly opened the screen and silently turned the knob of the inside door. It turned, unlocked.

Blocker let out a breath as quietly as he could, then slipped his Glock from its holster. Holding it at his side, he eased the door open an inch. Through the gap he could see Panten sitting on a filthy couch in his skivvies, his greasy hair hanging to his shoulders, his skinny, bare chest sprouting maybe three curly hairs. The room stunk of sweat and the joint that hung loosely from the loser's lip.

Before Blocker could get into the room, the drone appeared from somewhere in the back of the house, causing Panten to sit straight up, his hand going behind the cushion.

The drone's mechanical voice said, "Richard Panten, you are under arrest. Freeze!"

Panten didn't. He rose, lurching a little, gun in hand. The drone fired, the sofa cushion where Panten's head had been exploded in a cloud of puffy crap. Even before the fluff had reached the floor, the drone was turning for a second shot.

The stoned Panten didn't stand a chance as he tried to bring his pistol, a .357, to bear on the drone.

Panten's back was to him and Blocker saw his chance. He came in hard and fast and clubbed Panten over the head with his Glock. The guy went down just as the drone's second shot buried itself in the wall next to Blocker's head.

"Hey!"

The drone backed off and its metallic voice, manipulated by Steve, said, "Sorry."

They searched the house, but there was no sign of Hannah, just as Blocker had expected. Still, Steve pushed the topic with Panten.

"Who the hell told you she was my girlfriend?" Panten whined. "Hannah Perez has never even spoken to me."

Steve looked pissed. It was clear to Blocker that the Mahk-Ra detective didn't believe a word he was hearing.

"Look," Panten pleaded from the backseat, "I know who really did it. It wasn't Hannah."

"When we get back to the station, we will teach you not to lie to us," Steve snarled.

"I'm not lying."

"Then how do you explain your girlfriend's DNA on the shell casing?"

That stunned Panten into silence.

Something cold coiled in Blocker's stomach. This guy was supposed to get Hannah off the hook and instead the dumb son of a bitch was tightening the noose. Had Kyla sent them off on a wild goose chase while she got Hannah clear? If that was true, the whole town would pay. He couldn't believe Kyla would do that. They were still missing something.

Twisting around in his seat, making his voice as menacing as Steve's, he said, "The governor has been assassinated and someone's going to pay. Might as well start with you. You know the penalty for murdering a Mahk-Ra?"

"Death," Panten said, his voice barely above a whisper.

Blocker pulled his gun. He couldn't shoot Panten through the bulletproof Lexan that separated the front and back seats, but his goal was to scare the shit out of the loser, not kill him.

"Tell me why I shouldn't have my partner drive us down to the river and we'll just get this over with."

Panten's eyes went wide. "Wait, wait, I brokered the goddamned deal."

"What deal?" Blocker asked.

"Between the shooter and the one who hired him to cap the governor."

"Who did the hiring?"

"I can't tell you that, he'll kill me."

"And the shooter?"

"They would both kill me. I can't tell you!"

"He's lying," Steve put in. "He's making it up as he goes, trying to save his girlfriend."

"No," Panten shrieked. "I told you, she's not my girlfriend."

They were getting closer to the station and Blocker knew his time was running out.

"Drive us to the goddamned river and let's save some time. He's got nothing to tell us, let's just kill him so we can get back to work, find someone who will help us close this case."

Finally, his voice tiny, Panten said, "It was a mock."

Steve glared at him in the rearview.

"No offense," Panten added lamely.

"That's impossible," Steve said.

"It was," Panten said. "A Mahk-Ra hired a shooter from out

of town. A pro who goes by different names and faces way I hear it."

"No," Steve said, his voice colder than usual. "It is not the Mahk-Ra way."

Blocker saw only one way to save Hannah and maybe bring the killer to justice. If it didn't work, well, best to not think about that.

When they got to the station, Blocker practically ripped Panten out of Steve's hands and, yanking the suspect by an arm, drug him inside. He bypassed booking and the interrogation rooms.

"Where are you going?" Steve asked, the one struggling to keep up, for a change.

Blocker all but ran the suspect down the hall to the office of Stanis-Ra and burst into the colonel's office without so much as a knock.

"What is the meaning..." Stanis-Ra blustered as he rose from behind his desk.

"Blocker, what are you doing?" Steve called from behind them.

Even Panten was talking. "What the hell?"

Still holding Panten by the arm, Blocker said, "Colonel, you said you wanted Aquinas-Ra killer brought to you within twenty-four hours. We brought you the man who set up the killing."

"But Hannah Perez..." Stanis said.

Again, Blocker cut him off. "She didn't do it. For that matter, neither did this asshole, but he set it up."

"What are you saying, Detective?" the colonel asked, his eyes wide, staring at Panten.

Steve hung back by the door, totally unsure of what Blocker was doing.

Blocker was as far out on a limb as he could be. The only thing left was to play out the bluff. "Panten here says you paid him to kill Aquinas-ra so you could move up."

"That's a lie," Stanis roared, but his eyes weren't on Blocker, they bored into Panten who shook his head feebly.

"I didn't tell them, Stanis," he pled. "I didn't."

Stanis' hand went to his weapon and he drew it. Blocker's gun was still in its holster and his right hand gripped Panten. He figured they were both dead.

As Stanis' weapon came up, there was an explosion from behind Blocker and as he watched Stanis drop his gun and sag to the floor, Blocker realized Steve had shot the colonel. Spinning, Blocker saw Steve standing there, shock on his face, like he was just realizing he had drawn and fired.

"You were right," Steve said, quietly.

Blocker shrugged. "Even though Mahk-Ra aren't supposed to covet, Stanis did. He learned it from us. It's one of our biggest weaknesses. All that observation..."

"He learned too well," Steve said.

This was the first time Blocker had ever seen pain on Steve's face. Another lesson learned from the Earthers, he supposed. They grilled Panten for most of the night, but he was of no help with identifying the sniper's real identity, the guy was a frickin' ghost and already in the wind. Afterwards, a Mahk-Ra guard marched the petty criminal into the alley and shot him behind the ear. Blocker felt bad for the guy, Panten was nothing more than a patsy but it was either him or maybe the whole city.

Exhausted and feeling shitty about Panten's death, Blocker left the station with the idea that he might get a couple hours sleep before his next shift started. A call from Kyla changed that. He got her up to speed on what had happened. Two Mahk-Ra officials were dead, and a couple of Mahk-Ra bodyguards. Panten had been the only Earther to die, though. Even though she would never know it, Blocker had even managed to save Hannah. Not a bad day's work. Kyla gave him a bit of information as a thank you.

Instead of going home, Blocker went to a shabby neighborhood near the railroad tracks that bisected town. There was a homeless shelter there. Looking in through one of the windows, careful to stay in the shadows, Blocker saw a woman pouring coffee at a makeshift bar, chatting with the homeless people on the stools before her. Her hair was short now, streaked with purples and reds to hide her even more, and she wore glasses that he knew she didn't need, but it was Hannah.

She smiled and something in his heart froze for a second.

He could never have her. He could dream, he could hope, maybe someday, but they were still on opposite sides, as far as she was concerned. Still, there was hope. That was what Red Spear was really about, what Blocker knew he was about, the thing he lived for...hope.

HUNTER X

RICHARD J. BREWER
AND GARY PHILLIPS

PART TWO
THEY CALL ME HUNTER X

O f course the bomb went off prematurely. That's what I get for buying second-hand timers from the East Emerald Double Dragons gang. But that's what was available given the window of time I had and with the recent gutting of the local insurgents. Now the mocks were on point and on the move. Logic demanded that I should call it a day, but this was the last chance I was going to get to take a shot at that fuck, Masstas-ra. I'd been informed he was scheduled to cycle back to Ra-Prime later today, and who knew where after that. It was now or never.

I knew he hadn't been hurt because he hadn't even made it to the stage when the device went off.

Fuck.

I'd planted the bomb in a coffee urn just to the left of the stage. Unlike the timer attached to it, it was a nice piece of tech. The thing gave off a false organic signature, thus evading scanner detection.

Nice.

There was some comfort in that it seemed I'd iced that bastard, the Director of Ports, up there on the stage. That now late bastard had him a taste for Earth pussy and frequented a nearby seaside pleasure house that also had a casino attached. Bribing his regular girl so I could plant a bug in her boudoir wasn't a big deal. She hated the prick and his sick demands. But he was smitten with her, telling her all sorts of bullshit about setting her up in Madrona, the gated Potemkin Village just off the shores of Lake Washington and reserved for quislings and assorted sell-outs. He loved to go on about himself, how nothing in this sector could function without him. After sex and plied with Irish whiskey, one of his other weaknesses, it didn't take too long to learn the plans for the christening ceremony.

Not only did I get him, but a few other high-level mocktards as well were also sent to the happy hunting grounds, but not the one that mattered...the one responsible for what happened to my wife and daughter. No, I'd missed him.

It was a good thing I'd altered my usual M.O. and hadn't planted myself on a roof with my rifle to pick off strays as they ran from the blast area. The mocks already had their drones in the air, buzzing and whizzing about the rooftops and upper stories of the various buildings. Fortunately there was the cold-assed rain coming down. For all their sophistication and fancy gadgets, the rain played havoc with the machines, and yet they chose Seattle as the seat of their government.

Dipshits.

I moved out from among the humans and mocks who had come outside from the hiring hall to take a gander at the commotion. A couple of Civility Patrol dickwads barreled past, pushing and shoving everyone out of their self-important way. Of course everyone scattered for cover when the bomb went off. But as there were no other explosions, their curiosity overrode good sense and they had started to drift back out into the open. I'd been hanging around the docks for the past three weeks, dressed appropriately enough to avoid suspicion. I'd even picked up a few days work off-loading ships.

I couldn't believe it when I heard that the battle cruiser being finished was going to be named for that righteous fuck, that so-called war hero Masstas-ra.

Christ.

But when I heard that he was going to do the christening, well, that was just too good an opportunity to pass up. They were making a big thing out of this being the first battle cruiser built entirely of Earth materials. But what it really meant was that the empire was in trouble. The messy war they were engaged in over in that other star system was finally taking its toll. Resources were being stretched thin. They meant to bleed Earth of any and all resources in this fight of theirs.

The showers had turned to a drizzle. I milled with the crowd along the dock area, bumming a smoke while keeping an eye out as they evacuated the docks. One of the perks of working the Port was the ability to get real cigarettes, copped fresh from cargoes being readied for export straight from those hillbilly labor camps. Our overlords rightly considered tobacco a filthy habit, but they also understood that for humans pressed into off-world service, and increasingly under pressure by the Mahk-Ra, the things did seem to aid in relieving stress.

"Think it was the Spear?" the beefy dude I got my cig from said under his breath.

"Who knows," I said. "Some of them do be swinging a set. Could be stragglers, left over from the recent scrubbing, figuring on payback."

"Yeah, I hear you," he said, producing a vicariously induced grin. Then just as quickly, it was gone. You never knew who you were talking to. Who was looking to turn someone in to the Community Leader or some other rat-fuck snitch kiss-ass functionary in order to make Brownie points with our alien masters.

With that in mind, the dockworker quietly stepped away from me and I from him. By now several shock troopers had assembled and were trying to regain some order while Masstas escaped. Technically the space port is several klicks away from what was now Seattle proper. The Red Spear cell had recently been neutralized and the few members left alive had been sent off to the RZ camp in Phoenix. So the mocks had felt pretty safe to do their propaganda-rich christening.

Suckers.

It's not like I didn't know I was playing out a string that would ultimately end in my death, but I'm not suicidal. I had a pulsar pistol on me and I could have charged that shithead while he was still recovering from the shock of the explosion. With the mini-bomb on me, a phone grenade, I could have probably fragged enough troopers to pull it off before I got blasted to ribbons. Still, training is training. Recon your surroundings, what are the possible value-added on sites and availables in completing your mission.

"Move back, clear a perimeter of 100 meters," the sergeant of the shock troopers yelled out. He was big, even for a mock, seven five or more and a weight lifter. Because of the rain it was pretty overcast, some of the troopers actually took off their sunglasses, their big, black eyes roving about, scanning for trouble.

Watching the crowd right after the blast I spotted my quarry making his way to the vintage car he'd arrived in. I recognized his babysitters, a human and a mock, from files I'd procured on the black market a while ago. The human's name was Paul Harper, an agent for the FBI. The mock, his partner, JoHannas-ra.

Interesting.

I moved off along with others who didn't want to be in the vicinity in case matters went south and the shooting started. It looked natural, not any way out of the ordinary. Down a nearby side street of warehouses, robot forklifts and cargo tenders went about their business unloading sealed shipping containers. Some of these were being loaded onto flatbed trucks. I walked over to a bobtail where a guy in a rain-slicked parka was munching on a sandwich. He was at a loading dock of a frozen fish warehouse, sort of isolated as the robots piled pallets of processed fish bricks into his truck.

"What was all that about?" he said chewing on his faux roast beef and motioning back from where I'd come.

Hunching a shoulder to distract him, I used a stunner minirod. I shocked him in the chest and he doubled over, I followed that up by socking him so hard in the head he folded like a busted out gambler. Filching his key fob from his pocket, I saw that it required a security code. I stomped a boot on his knee and he gritted his teeth.

"Give me the code," I demanded. I flashed my butterfly knife, flipping it open and closed rapidly.

He talked and then I gave him a good boot in the head to unconsciousness. When the mocks interrogated him later, maybe they'd believe he had nothing to do with this. Maybe he'd only get five or six years in a labor camp, but more likely he'd get sent out over the water to Blackwell's Island, the super max prison where incorrigibles of all stripes resided on the blackened volcanic rock. I drove off in his truck after using the control on the fob to command the robots to cease loading and close up the rear of the truck's cargo bay.

They weren't going to wait for air transport as that would be precious minutes of exposure. They had pushed Masstasra into the antiquarian limo he'd arrived in and were moving out. I was sure, despite its looks, the damn thing was probably armored and possibly outfitted with defensive weapons. There was a skimmer leading the way through the crowd and another following. I didn't need to chance shadowing them close as the most logical place to take him was the nearby and fortified

Department of Freight and Transport, less than three miles away.

The mocks are nothing if not crazily efficient and record conscious. Water, road, air and off-world hauling in the service of the empire requires the right paperwork. In this region those come from the D.F. & T. The pertinent electronic document blanks -- never saved on the system but on portable drives - could be used by smugglers or rebels. That's why the transport departments are built bunker-like to discourage incursions – top floor at the surface, several floors beneath the ground.

I had previously mapped out the streets in my head. I took a shortcut and zoomed through a swath of dockworker housing, mostly nondescript concrete apartment blocks that reminded me of the crap housing I grew up in back in Sacramento near the downtown arena where I use to sneak in to watch the Kings basketball team. The area is decently cared for and it was a bitch secreting away one of my caches, but I'd eventually found a spot behind an old senior center.

In a freestanding little used outside storage shed, long in need of repair, I fetched a tool case from behind some adult diaper boxes and took off again. Traffic was light that time of day. I passed an over-sheriff patrol car, a Ra and Re in the vehicle. They gave me the once over and I nodded back, a nervous smile on my mug just like any other civilian hoping to be left alone to do their job without any trouble. They rolled past and I gave the rig some gas, heading back toward the roadway at a clip.

It's pretty much a straight line to the Department and if I was moving that shitheel, that's the way I'd have done it. No rigmarole, no fancy ducking and dodging. No time for that kind of bullshit 'cause maybe there's some floating IEDs around, or some clear plastic, nigh invisible Symtex Bouncing Betties. I figured they'd want to get him safe and secure as fast as possible.

In my case I had a few special items, including an RPPG, a

rocket-propelled pulse grenade launcher. I parked in a handicap zone near the front of a housing complex that bordered the route as I heard the sirens approach. I'd bet the noise hadn't been Harper's idea but Masstas-ra, being the self-important prick he was, would have insisted on the hoopla so that the humans would know somebody important was coming through and to make way.

My phone's lockPick app easily overcame the circuitry of the apartment's entrance gate, and like that, I was inside. The rain had let up for a few minutes and even though it was still overcast and cold, there were a couple of good lookin' babes in spray-on bikinis laying by the pool. They must have been freezing their asses off.

Crazy.

From the bit of chit-chat I heard between them it sounded like they worked at the nearby casino. I tipped my cap to the ladies as I walked by. Maybe they thought I was there to repair the washing machines what with my work clothes and the case I was hefting.

I hurried up an enclosed stairwell and gained the top floor, the third landing, and blew out the lock of an apartment door with my handgun. I lucked out and no one was home. I made my way to a rear window and opened it. The small convoy was coming straight up the road and I got out the RPPG; sited it, took in a slow breath, and let loose the grenade. It struck the hood of the lead vehicle, blowing up the engine and dropping it to the pavement like a rock. The Lincoln, unable to stop, skidded along the wet pavement and T-boned the skimmer at full speed.

Sweet.

Given its armor, I figured nobody inside the limo would have been injured too badly. But now they were stalled on the road and I was that much closer to my kill shot. Staying in the apartment would be sure death as mocktech was already zeroing in on the origin of the assault. Odds were they wouldn't exit the vehicle. They'd sit tight and wait for back up. Then the trailing skimmer hit the limo.

I ran down the stairs. Ascending was a cop, a Mahk-Ra.

The fuck?

Was he one of the uniforms I passed in the patrol car? How could they have responded so quickly?

"Halt. Hands up," he said, his gun already out of its holster and starting to rise.

I shot the deputy in the face, his dark blood staining the compact stairwell's walls. I kept going, stepping over his crumpled corpse. I was traveling light. I only had the one shell for the RPPG so I'd left it upstairs. I wasn't wearing gloves or a DNA blocker. Fuck it. It wasn't like they didn't know me.

On the ground floor it became clear why the cops were in the vicinity so quickly. They'd come to see the two poolside chicks, a regular mid-day nookie run I figured. I didn't have a lot of time to think about it, the other cop had already pulled his piece and started blasting away. I dove behind a row of shrubbery while also tossing one of the flash-bang grenades I had strapped to my ankle under my pant leg. When the device went off, it blew him back into the pool.

"Rickie," one of the women yelled from where they were crouched in a far corner next to a cool-heat unit.

"Really?" I laughed. "Rickie-re?"

Rickie was alive but stunned. Blood was running from his ears as he treaded water in the pool. I bolted from the premises as the rain began again and fuck me if another cop car didn't come roaring up, jumping the curb and skidding mud tracks across the postage stamp lawn. Out came a lone Mahk-Ra deputy leveling his semi-auto shotgun at my head.

No time to reach for the gat I'd re-holstered in the small of my back.

Dumbshit.

I snaked an arm out and the butterfly knife in its custom

housing left my sleeve, the razor sharp blade aimed for his upper body. He swatted it aside with one hand, the other trying to aim his shotgun. But the move distracted him enough to give me the time to cover the distance between us. I dropped down using a leg sweep to up-end the tall motherfucker. He was six inches taller than my six-four.

Still I do okay for a man my age. I sport defined eighteen inch biceps and call on a mixture of fighting styles from wing chun to bare-knuckle brawler. That and them enhancement nanobots my once alien masters saw fit to graft into my nervous system when I was part of Specter Squad Zeta didn't hurt either. Besides, the taller they are and all that. He went down hard to the ground.

He didn't stay down, though. Faster than you might think, given his size, the cop leaped to his feet, as did I. His shotgun was on the ground but like a lot of mocks, he figured to overpower me physically. He crowded in swinging and connected with a left that dropped me to a knee. Only, I wasn't as rattled as I seemed. As he prepared to accordion my skull with his pile driver fist, I hit him in the nads and he groaned, doubling over. Then rising quickly, I jabbed three stiff fingers onto a spot just next to his heart.

This combination of attack put a momentary stop to the fight as the mock struggled for the air that suddenly exited his lungs. But the bastard was tough and recovered faster than I'd thought he would. He managed to land another solid left to my jaw, exploding fireworks in my head, and was looking to follow that up with a right that would probably have put me down for the count, but I moved in under his guard and unleashed an uppercut worthy of Floyd Mayweather back in the day. That momentarily spun those black eyes of his. I followed with a rapid series of edged hand strikes at his head and nerve points around his neck and shoulders that sent him to the lawn face first.

I picked up his hat, and saw a uniform jacket on the back seat of his prowler. Putting them on, I jumped behind the wheel and gunned the engine to life. Maybe if I stayed in the car, hat on, jacket on, the others on the roadway would think I was a cop coming to help – I needed it to work just long enough to fool them and allow me to blast Maastas-ra to Kingdom Come.

- TO BE CONCLUDED -

LOCATION, LOCATION, LOCATION

HOWARD V. HENDRIX

know the mocks' surveillance of us goes back at least to the 1930's. Sure, they must have seen plenty of human entertainments before they invaded. I still don't get their fascination with Hollywood, though. Especially among what I guess is their underclass, the Mahk-Re. But hey, it's good for business, so I'm not complaining.

I wasn't complaining either, that day I sat on a bench outside Delphinion Studios' Stage 1, waiting for Iawan-Re and his daughter Iolawn to be piloted my way by noisy native guide and chief scenarist on their project (and my undeniable acquaintance), Jake Lenfants. Delphinion was built in the 1970's, almost half a century before the invasion. I guess that makes it Old Hollywood, for the mocks. My realty agency had the place "For Sale or Lease."

Glancing around from the bench, I took in Delphinion's four sound stages and associated buildings. The studio complex stood beside a light-industrial cluster of what had once been adult movie outlet stores, now pleasure 'bot emporia, also on land once owned by the studios. Smog-smudged, dilapidated,

170

and dusty in the summer afternoon heat, everything in the neighborhood seemed a throwback to earlier days, earlier tech – yet also at the same time somehow raw and new, as if the pads for the buildings had only yesterday been bulldozed into the stone-and-gravel dry wash in which those buildings now stood.

Jake Lenfants' car wheeled in off the frontage road and up to the gate. I heard Jake buzz down his driver's side window and present bona fides to the security guard. It took a moment for the guard to walk back to the kiosk and start the gates swinging out of their way. In a moment more, they had pulled into a parking space in front of Stage 1, around the corner from where I sat.

"...a real fixer-upper," I heard Jake say. "At least the location's good. Close to the old 210 and Foothill Boulevard."

"And the price is right for the project," said an older male Mock voice – Iawan-Re's? -- in the accented Mahklish some call Mahkanese.

"Which project, doc? The whole Family Odyssey thing? Or just *Home From The Swarming Stars*?" asked Jake, also in Mahklish. He once told me he learned the lingo from his brother-in-law, a guy named Harper whose partner in the FBI was the first Mahk-Ra to be fully integrated into a human law enforcement department.

"The former is a program – technically -- but both, I should think."

"Shouldn't we all," said Jake. In a moment more I heard Jake direct their attention to the studio's emblem.

"I 'should think' that's a fitting sign for your work, that logo."

"Why so?" a female voice (presumably Iolawn's) asked, again in Mahklish .

"It shows the stars of the constellation Delphinus, overlaid on the image of a delphinium flower – see?"

"What's Delphinus?" Iolawn asked.

"Delphinus, the Dolphin, is the constellation between Aquila the Eagle and Pegasus, the Winged Horse, in the human 'constellation' system," said the voice I presumed was Iawan-Re's.

"That's right, doc, but don't steal my thunder," Jake said, before launching into his spiel. "In Greek 'delphinion' means 'little dolphin.' The flower is called 'delphinium' in Latin because the spur made by its sepals was thought to resemble a dolphin's fin."

"So why's it fitting for the project?" asked the female voice. I was surprised to hear that it wasn't Jake who answered.

"Aquila carries the thunderbolts of war," said the Mahk male, "and Pegasus the thunderbolts of inspiration – for poetry, all the language arts."

Abruptly, Jake laughed.

"You some kind of search engine on all things human, doc?"

"Only about certain subjects."

"Then let me do my stuff, okay? Both dolphins and delphinium flowers have long been associated with healing and medicine -- "

"-- and all of those elements will come together in what we'll be doing here," Iolawn said, tumbling to it.

They came around the corner to where I sat, beside the nearest shutter roll-up door, which was down.

"Ah!" Jake said, breezing in and introducing me before I even had a chance to stand. "That square-jawed man with hair like a steel brush is Starr Strewnfield. Sounds like the stage name of an ex-astronaut who went into real estate, which it isn't, though he is."

I was tempted to ask if Lenfant meant his name could be translated as Baby Jakes – and if that might be too close to "Babycakes" -- but I didn't. Jake nattered on.

"Hey, Starr-crossed! I hear the most florid liars are real

estate agents and wine reviewers. That true?"

"I always heard wannabe screenwriters were the worst," I said, shaking Jake's hand and allowing him to drag me to my feet as Jake, simultaneously, introduced me to Iawan and Iolawn, our prospective buyers and/or lessors. I could see my height came as a surprise as I loomed up before Iolawn and shook her hand.

"Oh! You're taller than you look!"

Mahks are tall enough that they aren't used to humans being able to look them in the eyes – or be in any way on the level with them.

"My daddy always said I was big for my size, ma'am," I aw-shucksed, glancing away. I turned and shook her father's hand. "My height's all in my legs -- "

" 'His worth's unknown'," Jake said, " 'although his height be taken.' "

" -- but at least I'm not light in the heels like Kid Jakespeare, here."

"So long as you don't call me Kid Red Spear," he said with a broad wink, as if he were just making an off-color joke. I grimaced. What did he think he was doing, making a crack about the Red Spear movement in front of Mahks? That could get a person picked up by Resistance Zero, and I'd heard what happened in those RZ camps.

"No, just light in the head, buddy," Jake continued, turning back to his Mahk clients. "He's definitely not Hollywood – or even Houston, anymore. Only thing Starr's got to do with rocket stages or sound stages these days is selling the latter."

"Which I had better get to. If you'll follow me . . . "

We entered through the more human-scale entrance beside the roll-up door. We made our way upstairs, so I could show the prospectives the main studio office suites. Jake made tourist-attraction comments on how I was dressed -- "California casual, see? Attire equally appropriate for closing a megabuck deal or going for a morning jog." I tried to ignore him, with as little success as usual.

Over the next hour I led them through the cavernous spaces of Delphinion's four sound stages, my talk full of square footages, heights to catwalks or perms, cycloramas, amps and phase power, silent air conditioning, wireless web, parking, numbers of production offices, conference rooms, kitchens, restrooms, roll-up doors. To break up the litany of physical description and give the clients a chance to take it all in, Jake and I wandered away, tossing the occasional jokes and odd speculations back and forth, when we thought we were out of earshot.

"Hey Starr, you hear what the good ol'boy said when the reporter asked him a question about how the Mahk have orgasms?" Jake asked, standing in a corner draped in cyclorama. " 'I don't know what the big deal is, about that. My wife and I been married near forty years, and she has Mock orgasms all the time!' "

"Here's one for you, Hollywood," I said from the edge of the stage. "How can you tell which starlet on a production is the most clueless?"

"She's the one banging the screenwriter. Very funny. That was old before your parents were born. Hey, speaking of which, you think they ever shot pornos here?"

"The company history says no."

"Yeah, right. I suppose it's just a coincidence there are all those adult pleasure centers next door? You really think this was never a *Destry Rides Again* kind of place -- liquor in the front, poker in the rear? No Stagedoor Johnnies, Backdoor Billies, or Marlene Dietrich-Una Merkel one on one? No? Come on! This place must be positively ectoplasmic with the ghosts of money shots!"

"Maybe you ought to add it to your location-shots tour, Hollywood."

"Studios are not on the location-shots list, by definition," he sniffed. "But then I suppose the only shots you know about are space shots."

Iawan and Iolawn, having appreciated the cavernousness of yet another cavernous sound stage, walked toward the cyclorama. We began to make our way toward them.

"Are you really a human astronaut?" Iolawn asked me as we approached.

"Was," I said, neglecting to mention I had also flown sorties against the invasion fleet. Or that I had done so because, once, years before, looking down from orbit, I had experienced that cognitive shift known as the "overview effect." I had seen the Earth, fragile as a Christmas ornament of pale blue glass dusted with flashing sprites, hanging in a great dark universal tree decked with distant twinkle lights -- and felt the imperative to protect that frail ball against all that might threaten it.

And when the Mahk-Ra blew my fighter apart from around me and I was hanging in space, dying, what I believed would be my last thoughts were simply to wonder why I had left Earth -- the better to see the stars, or the better for the stars to see me. I had told my ex-wife about it – Jake too, once. I don't know if he got it.

"That's ancient history, now. Long story."

"Do you have a background in physics or engineering, then?"

"I taught college courses in both – long enough to learn I was no teacher."

"We might be able to make use of you for our project, as a technical advisor, or on a consultancy basis," her father said.

"What's your project?"

"A contemporary version of Homer's *Odyssey* with an all Mahk-Re cast."

"Sounds interesting. Science fiction? Space opera?"

Father and daughter both nodded.

LOCATION, LOCATION, LOCATION

"Film? TV? Webisode?"

"More a full immersion sort of thing," said Iawan. "It requires military security clearances, too."

"Hmm. I had clearance when I was in the service, and a different type of the same, as an astronaut. And I suppose your Mahk clearance requirements can't be too high, if you've let someone like Jake in on this business."

"I've kept secrets you'll never know, hoss."

"And probably wouldn't want to. I've never worked as a consultant, but I'm interested, especially if there might be something in it for me."

By the time we finished the tour of the complex, exchanged contact info, and gathered together documents for their real estate lawyer to review, it was getting on toward evening. Since the clients were staying in Studio City, Jake suggested dinner at a restaurant called Hugo's. I agreed to meet them all there in an hour.

The food was good – "Ceviche and salmon and pork loin, oh my!" as Jake put it. The watermelon margaritas flowed. Jaw and Jo particularly enjoyed them – especially after surreptitiously spiking theirs with kronch, the hallucinant the Mahk-Re are so fond of.. The same one that the Makh-Ra have long outlawed, also known as "streak" out on the street – and the same one I had never tried before. Out of a sudden sense of comradeship, I let Iawan drip a few drops of the stuff into my last drink of the evening. It lent a slightly bitter tang to the watermelon sweetness of the cocktail.

Despite the fact that it was dark when we left the restaurant and our clients seemed more than a little inebriated, Jake insisted on giving all of us a tour of nearby location shots. The clients agreed. Having endured Jake's "tours" before, I wished at that moment the clients had opted for an autonomous vehicle. I joined them grudgingly.

Shortly thereafter, we were careering through the Southern

California night, up onto freeways and down onto surface streets, headed places Jake seemed to know by memory as much as map. As he drove, Jake regaled us with tales of his industry: How the ever-forthcoming blockbuster bubble would bring about the long-awaited return to mid-size pictures. How the improvements in superlight cameras and handheld processing had done so much to blur the old distinctions between films of "high" and "low" production values. How Mahk crowd-funding and independent production were becoming the price of admission into Hollywood for young directors and screenwriters.

Somehow, we eventually found ourselves moving slowly along quiet residential streets in a suburb called Arleta.

"Iawan," Jake said to the father, who was sitting in the front passenger-side seat, "check the street sign coming up, would you? What does it say?"

"Uh, 'Roslyndale,' I think."

"Yep. This is it." Jake turned right and drove slowly up the tree-lined street. We stopped across the road from a well-lit house fronted with what looked like white French doors. Jake nodded toward the house.

"Okay, name the movie that features the house right there. No helping, Starr. I'll give you a clue: 'Ma-a-arty!'"

Iawan looked to Iolawn questioningly in the back seat, but she could only give him a shrug expressing her utter ignorance.

"Nothing? Not even a guess? How about this: 'Good night, future boy.'"

Iawan looked back at Iolawn, who just shook her head.

"Oh, come on! I'll give you one more clue. This makes it too easy. It's a line from a scene that takes place right there in that driveway: 'Roads? Where we're going, we don't need roads.'"

"*Back to the Future . . . ?*" Iolawn ventured.

"Well for heaven's sake, yes! It's Marty McFly's house from the first movie of the franchise. Let's check out another one.

177

Maybe you'll do better with the next."

We rolled off through the night again. Jake's tales were more interesting to all of us this time, as they were about his own experiences in the world of pitches and treatments, franchises and universes and re-launches. Of being called in to give his "take" on any number of studio properties gathering dust on producers' shelves. Of the myriad ways in which productions could be almost green-lighted -- and then never happen, or be put into turnaround hell for years. Of actors attaching themselves to projects, and then detaching from them. Of directors who got removed from productions two-thirds of the way through filming. Of who screwed whom and why – and who got the screen credit.

Jake was again too busy driving and talking to bother to tell us where he was taking us but soon we had rolled on into North Hollywood, as I informed our clients.

"There on our right is the Mahk-Ra Office of Media Standards . . . "Jake said. And the silence in the car could have been cut with a knife.

Before long we drove up an avenue called Klump to where it t-boned into Dilling street. We stopped near the corner, before what looked like a split-level ranch. With its stonework façade beside the slab of front door, and the tall windows above both, the place struck me as tip-of-the-tongue familiar.

"Okay, this one is both easier and harder than the McFly house. And again, no help from you, Starr. Well? Any guesses?"

"How easier?" asked Iawan. "And how harder?"

"It looks so familiar," Iolawn said, "but something about it's not right."

"Exactly. It's easier because it's from an iconic show of the late 1960's through early 70's, and this exterior shot of it was used a lot. Harder because, since the exterior was shot, it's been through more changes than the McFly house. That front fence and that gate with a lantern on either side, they weren't originally there – the owners put all that in to keep out trespassers. The landscaping's different too. Try to ignore the fence and the lanterns and the landscaping, and just look at the house front. Well?"

The answer did not come to either Iolawn's tongue or her father's.

"Still don't know it? You've got to be kidding! Okay, okay. One hint, then, from Alice: 'If there's anything I can't stand, it's a perfect kid. And six of 'em, yecch!'"

"*The Brady Bunch*, maybe?" Iawan ventured.

"Dingdingding! We have a winner! You're getting better at this. One last stop, then – but let's make it something a bit more challenging."

We were off into the Los Angeles night once more. Jake continued to entertain us with dropped projects and dropped names.

"The longer I listen to you," the still kronched Iolawn said, "the less your Hollywood sounds like a boulevard of broken dreams than a grand maze of roads taken and not taken."

"What do you mean?" I asked.

"The many films and shows produced -- and the far greater number that never saw the light of day or dark of a movie theatre – they constitute a vast multiverse of parallel and alternate universes!"

"The fog of light upon LA," said Iawan, "is the aura of might-have-been productions! Can't you see it?"

For a moment I cog-shifted. The wall screen of reality slipped between channels, and I did see it. A Los Angeles of innumerable virtual universes glowing evanescently around the projector bulb streetlights of what actually became real. A cityscape much less the old song's "great big freeway" than a Mobius highway system at whose every crossroad and cloverleaf the hope of *luck* sprang eternal -- a hope nurtured even in the most dejected wannabe's still fertile suspicion that, although the system might ultimately get you nowhere, at least it would have the good grace to take forever to get you there.

I shook my head. The vision disappeared, but I wondered. Was that kronch stuff Iawan put in my drink kicking in, somehow?

On the concrete roads of an abstract landscape, we didn't have to travel too far to find Jake's next challenge. I confirmed to our clients that we were still in North Hollywood. We pulled up to the curb beside a white painted storefront place on Magnolia, called Power Plumbing.

"Okay, this one's from an iconic sitcom of the 1970's. You can play this time too, Starr. I don't think I've shown you this one, before. This place has been through loads of changes. The building looks a lot different, but the awning's still here. Well? Any idea?"

None of us had a clue.

"Nothing? See the alley next door? A pickup truck filled with junk drives up into that alley, after turning in from the street in front of the Magnolia Market, over there. The building across the alley hasn't changed much either. Any guesses?"

Still nothing.

"The theme song of the show is an electric blues/funk piece recorded by Quincy Jones. Last chance? Nothing? Once I play it, you'll all know. It's a dead giveaway."

"Who's the human search engine now?" Iawan asked, but Jake was too preoccupied with calling up a video on his handheld to hear the question. Jake didn't show the image, but we could hear the theme music. Within the first four chords, Iawan, Iolawn, and I all blurted out, "*Sanford and Son*?"

"Right you are! This location was used twice in the opening credits of the series, part of the montage. "

"Jake, why are you so big on 70's shows?" I asked as we pulled away from the curb. "You weren't even born when those shows aired!"

"No, but my parents were," Jake explained as he passed another vehicle. "They were born the year *The Twilight Zone* first aired."

"See?" I said, trying to keep the annoyance out of my voice. "Now I never would have even thought of chronicling history that way -- or of doing this kind of location-shot windshield tourism, either. I swear, Jake. When you die, other people's lives will pass before your eyes. And they won't even be people – they'll be characters. Your memory's the product of syndication!"

"There's nothing wrong with deep background research. It's all grist for the mill."

"What mill? Doing those 'take' things? From everything you've told me, my take on *those* is that *you're* being taken. They sound like a way for the studios to get new ideas from 'outside' for free. R & D too cheap to pay for. "

"You don't understand the process, Starr."

"And I'm glad I don't. Your 'process' would drive me nuts. You've been at this how long? Twenty, twenty-five years? Your endless process is like a lightning strike in a wet forest – maybe it starts a little burn, but the fire just keeps skunkin' around and never really amounts to much."

"That's colorful, Starr, but it misses the mark. The process would drive me nuts – if I didn't love it. You've got to love the process."

I made a sound of rueful disgust and turned to look out the window. We drove along in silence. It seemed to me that, for Jake, the fame and celebrity of the location shots endowed otherwise mundane places with a sort of *mana*, stardust scattered through an anonymous world. The whole point of Jake's windshield tour was to peel back the surface of the mundane to expose the glamor behind it, as if the Hollywood multiverse was also, somehow, a palimpsest. In a topsy-turvy way, the shots were somehow more real than the locations themselves, evidence of preternatural provenance, of innumerable other possible worlds persisting just beyond the edges of this one.

A sensation of swarming alternate realities overwhelmed me. My mind was inundated by a tsunami of epiphanies, but when it was done I knew that I had left Earth *both* to better see the stars *and* for the stars to better see me. And they had.

When I turned back to the others, I realized that the car was stopped, parked by the side of the road. And something else about the dreamland we moved through – which moved through us -- occurred to me, despite myself.

"I saw it."

"Saw what?" asked Iolawn quietly.

"I saw the Christmas ornament Earth again. Saw my comrades' aircraft exploding under the Mahk-Ra onslaught. Saw the night-lit Mobius highway of Los Angeles from space, three dimensional and more, endlessly opening like rows of diamonds in a rose of diamond. Saw things that haven't happened yet on our timeline. The smoking blue ruins of Delphinion Studios. The smoking blue ruins of Earth. I know saying this might get me sent to an RZ camp, but so be it. They all exist. They're all real."

Jake smiled an enormous smile.

"Now he sees the process! Finally! If he could shift to see the world in overview when he was hanging in space, he could see *this* – I knew it!"

Iolawn and Iawan smiled too. Iolawn nodded.

"From inside a worldline, only that worldline looks real. All the others seem virtual, seem to be might-have-beens. But yes, they're all real, to those who can see them."

"And what you see depends on where you stand, Starr-crossed. Location, location, location."

Each held out a hand toward me. In each palm, like shimmering stigmata, a numinous tattoo shifted, from the image of a spear, to the image of a red rose, to the image of a red circle round the letters RIA. "Resistance is All" – the motto of the Committees of the Crimson Rose and Spear. The Red Spear. The clandestine fighters against the Occupation.

I saw it, and did not wonder if this was all a plot to catch me and send me to an RZ camp. Yet still I had to ask.

"But you! You're Mocks!"

Iawan smiled beatifically.

"We are the Mahk-Re. The Mahk-Ra conquered and occupied our lands before they ever travelled to another planet beyond the homeworld we lived upon. We know what it's like to be might- have-beens. And we still are. But not forever!"

"We can help you," said Iolawn. "We have already helped you. The ship that picked you up in space after your own was destroyed – it was piloted by a Mahk-Re. You can help us. Join us in our project."

"What? The one you plan for Delphinion? But I don't even know what it is."

"Guided oneironautics," said the smiling Iawan. "Dream shifting. The deepest immersion. We will slide sideways the present consensus reality of the Mahk-Ra empire. Change *their* hearts and minds. Change the way they see us Mahk-Re. Change the way they see the Occupation of your world. Shift their reality into *our* consensual hallucination, *our* dream of the future."

"And this whole tour tonight? Was that part of it?"

"In a way," Jake said. "The Mocks really do love our old media. Especially the TV stuff from the 60's and 70's, when their surveillance of us first got just the slightest bit free of government control, and started to gain a popular market back home. The Mahk-Re were instrumental with that."

"We saw how your media shaped and changed who you are," Iolawn said. "How it changed your world. That made us wonder if we could use our version of it to change ours."

"I could have shot-toured you to locations of old shows that more obviously changed collective perceptions of our world," Jake said. "*Roots, All in the Family, M.A.S.H.*, I don't know. But I didn't want to make it too obvious. Thought it might scare you off."

"Your people scare off easy when it comes to dealing with us Mahk-Re," Iawan said, glancing away. "Even many in the Red Spear don't quite trust us, or the soft-power approach we're advocating. Violence is so much more . . . direct. But some have come around. They realize that, to really collapse the wave-form of all the superposed possibilities, to really change the channel, all that is necessary is that we *see* to it. That is what all our sage talk of the 'auras of alternate universe's and 'emanations of parallel realities' must needs amount to. Will you join us, and help us see to it?"

"But what can an old astronaut turned real estate agent do for you?"

"The same thing you did for the Mahk-Ra," Iolawn said, "but with a difference."

In the car by the side of the road, the wall screen of reality changed channels again. I looked at our driver and my fellow passengers and saw that it would be through the wounds in their dreams that the light would enter each of them, and that each of them would enter the light. And that the same might become true for me, for like them I had been born of what's torn.

"Sign me up," I said at last, shaking their hands, hoping against a nightmare of smoking blue ruins.

And nothing changed. And everything changed.

LETTING GO THE GHOSTS

MARSHEILA ROCKWELL and
JEFFREY J. MARIOTTE

K imberly Greymountain looked up as the bell on the door of the Taovaya Cultural Center chimed, expecting to see her son Daniel and mentally preparing herself for Round Two of the shouting match they'd begun earlier that morning. Round One had ended with him storming out of the new building, slamming that same door so hard she thought the glass would crack, even though it was designed to be unbreakable.

But instead of a hotheaded twenty-something with a reservation attitude and big city dreams, two extremely tall, slender men in hats, suits, and sunglasses walked in like they owned the place.

No, not men. *Mahk-Ra*.

The aliens were pale-skinned and big-eyed, so sensitive to the light that they had to wear dark glasses. She assumed that sensitivity extended to their skin, too, since all the ones she'd seen covered almost every inch of their lanky bodies with clothing, but she didn't really know that much about them. They'd landed in 2020 and taken over, like another race of pale-skinned people had done to hers five hundred years previously, and since the Mahk-Ra had largely left her people alone, not interfering with the system of reservations already set up for them in the Americas, it wasn't hard to mentally replace one set of invaders with the other. Life went on for the indigenous, who'd endured, and would continue to endure, long after those who wanted their land left for greener galaxies.

"Gentle . . . beings," she said as politely as she could, glad Daniel wasn't here to see her doing the very thing he'd accused her of earlier: being a red apple—red on the outside, white underneath—and kowtowing to men whose skin was lighter than hers. But funding for the cultural center had come from light-skinned people, and she was not one to look a gift horse in the mouth. Especially if that horse was healthy enough to carry her to where she wanted to go. "Welcome to the Taovayan Cultural Center. How can I help you?"

"You are the owner of this establishment?" The words were smooth, but the inflection was off just enough to make the words sound strange and foreign in Kim's ears, and it took her a moment to grok what the taller of the two aliens was saying.

"What? No. The tribe owns the cultural center. I simply curate it for them."

"But you are in charge?"

"Well . . . yes, I guess you could say that."

"Then this is for you," the other one said, pulling a folded piece of paper from inside his suit jacket. As he handed it over, Kim tried not to flinch when his clammy flesh came briefly into contact with hers, then mentally chastised herself for the exact sort of bigotry her own people had faced for so many years. Still, principles aside, she couldn't suppress a small shudder and a sudden longing for antibacterial soap.

Opening the paper, she saw that it was an offer to purchase the cultural center and the land on which it stood—land that had been part of the Wichita people's history since the 1700's—

and the number included more zeroes than Kim had seen since Daniel had flunked out of his junior year in high school.

"You want to . . . buy . . . the cultural center?"

"No," the taller of the two said. "We have no interest in the center, or the mission, or the petroglyphs."

The "petroglyphs" were probably one of her people's most sacred artifacts — the whole reason there *was* a Taovayan tribe again in the first place, as opposed to just another group assimilated under the umbrella of the Wichita. Not true petroglyphs at all, the stone inscriptions were a sort of Native American Rosetta Stone, combining words from the long-dead Taovayan language with French and Spanish translations, since they had been allied with one nation and at war with the other back when her ancestors had set chisel to stone. What remained of the artifact had been discovered on ancient Taovayan land, along the banks of Texas's Red River, and had promptly been dubbed the Red River Stone, though with its size and thickness, it was really more of a paver, or a tile — nothing nearly as grand as the Egyptian treasure it resembled. The most precious of the Taovayan artifacts in the building, it sat in a glass-walled display case of its own, angled on a foundation of creamy silk and carefully illuminated to best reveal the words and symbols carved into the ochre rock.

Not true petroglyphs, but then the mission wasn't a true mission, either. It was a sized-down replica of the one at San Saba, which the Taovaya, along with other Wichita and the Comanche, had attacked and destroyed in 1758. Built for the conversion of Apaches, their hated enemies, the Catholic mission had been burned to the ground. Unfortunately, her people hadn't known at the time that there were no Apache inside, only Spaniards — including two priests, whose deaths had been immortalized in the 1765 painting, *The Destruction of Mission San Saba in the Province of Texas and the Martyrdom of the Fathers Alonso de Terreros, Joseph Santiesteban.*

LETTING GO THE GHOSTS

The Spanish had tried to retaliate a year later, at the Battle of the Twin Villages—one on either side of the river, not far from where the Stone had been found two and a half centuries later—only to be soundly defeated. But as other native peoples had learned before and since, there was no stemming the inexorable tide of European conquest, and the Taovaya soon ceased to exist in all but memory, subsumed by the Wichita in the early 1800's.

Which made this cultural center all the more vital, and the appearance of these Mahk-Ra all the more terrifying.

"What, then?" she asked, fear giving her voice a belligerent tone long years of conditioning had taught her could only lead to trouble. But she couldn't suppress it—she'd fought so hard to bring her people and their language back from extinction. To lose the touchstone of the newly reconstituted Taovayan tribe now, so soon after their seeming victory—their proverbial rise from the ashes—it was too much to be borne.

"The land . . . your reservation. The mineral rights. This building and the mission sit atop a deposit of uranium, a mineral we find ourselves in need of at the moment. Your Bureau of Indian Affairs has already agreed to the sale, pending approval from you and your tribe. We believe the price offered is more than fair."

Kim bit back her sarcastic reply; ten cents an acre had often been considered a "fair price" for Indian land—when they were offered any payment at all—and she could only imagine what the tribal council would have to say to such a statement, if any of them could stop laughing long enough to compose a response. And though the Taovaya had received federal recognition, they were still technically landless—the acreage on which the Cultural Center and mission stood was not a reservation, but a census-designated place where a concentration of Native Americans once identifying themselves as Wichita happened to live. Still, whatever term the aliens used, it was a legitimate

188

offer, and it was her duty to bring it to the council, no matter how ridiculous. Or offensive.

"I'll discuss it with the council," she said, a polite smile plastered to her face. "Someone will get back to you."

She didn't say when, though she imagined it wouldn't take long for a unanimous "no." Better to give the Mahk-Ra that answer via means that didn't involve physical proximity. She knew enough of her own people's history to know what invaders liked to do to messengers.

The shorter Mahk-Ra nodded and the two took their leave, the door chiming as it closed behind them.

"You can't do it!"

Daniel's voice was loud in the quiet room, ringing off the glass and making Kim jump. He must have seen the Mahk-Ra enter and come in through the delivery entrance in back so he could see and hear what was being said without being seen himself. He was good at that.

"You can't let them take our land!"

She wasn't sure why he would suddenly care; half the time he seemed to want to leave it all far behind. But she had to admit that the other half was a wannabe Indian activist, repeating AIM slogans from long before his birth as if they were brand new. Ah, the inconsistency of youth; it crossed all cultural barriers.

Kim turned slowly to face him, holding the paper in front of her like it was a poisonous snake and only her grip on its head was keeping her and her son safe.

"No, Daniel," she said, the insults exchanged between them earlier forgotten in the face of this new threat. "You're right. I can't."

She looked down at the paper that could alter the fate of her people, feeling echoes of the past, of a hundred other brown hands grasping a hundred other pieces of white paper — full of lies, broken promises, and slow, disgraceful death — and her next words were as much a vow to those ghosts as they were to her son.

"I *won't.*"

###

The council met in a one-room building that had been constructed of concrete block a few years after the Red River Stone had been unearthed, bringing the remnants of the Taovayas back together. It was all the grant money would pay for, and that only with a lot of volunteer labor from the tribe, sanding and hammering nails and laying pipe and painting the blocks. There had been a mural on the west exterior wall depicting tribal history, centered largely around an image of the mission in flames, with thick black smoke roiling into the sky, where it broke apart and became the wings of vultures. As an unmarried teenager, pregnant with Daniel, Kim had thought it was the most glorious thing she had ever laid eyes on. But it hadn't been properly sealed, or had been done with cheap paint, or the wind and weather that scoured the landscape had been too much for it; now, only patches of faded color remained, and she couldn't even make out where those clouds of smoke had been.

"One-room" wasn't exactly true. The large room was furnished with cast-off folding tables and chairs from a church group in Wichita Falls, and at the back of the room was a single washroom. The toilet flushed so loudly that everyone in the room could hear it and the plumbing under the sink had been repaired more times than anyone could remember, although sometimes the old men argued about that.

Kim stood at the front, looking at the five members of the council and other tribal members who'd gotten word of the meeting and had come to find out what was going on, even if—like her—they had no say in the matter. Back when the Taovaya had been a recognized tribe apart from the Wichita, their council had been comprised only of old men. Now there were three female members, including Linda Wahpepah, who had taught Kim most of what she knew about the old ways. For years, Linda had been a science teacher at a white school, but she had finally had enough of that and come back for good. She had taken an interest in educating the young girls about what it meant to be Taovayan, and Kim had taken up the cause with a fervor of her own when Daniel was born. She found the other woman's presence here calming, and the way Linda beamed at her former student, eyes narrow but bright behind thick-lensed glasses, smiling so broadly that her cheeks stood out like ripe plums, made Kim feel comfortable enough to begin.

She talked around the subject for a couple of minutes, complimenting Charley Winterhawk on a new vest he wore, with intricate beadwork done in the old way, teasing Betty Little Sister about the amount of white in her long hair, before finally coming to the point. "I was visited today at the Cultural Center by some of . . . some of them. The aliens."

"Mahk-Ra," Charley corrected.

"Yes, that's right."

"They can kiss my red ass."

The council members burst out laughing, except for Irene Swake, who sat with her arms folded over her chest and a stern expression cemented on her face. She disapproved of profanity of any kind, and, Kim suspected, of every other sort of merriment there was, too.

"That's how I feel, more or less," Kim said when the laughter died down. "But they brought me an offer, and I have to share it with you."

"An offer for what?" Irene asked, obviously glad to get back to business.

"Mineral rights. Uranium, specifically. Apparently what we've got, they need."

"It has never been concentrated enough for use in nuclear power plants or anything else," Betty said. "Even when the council *wanted* to sell it, there were no buyers."

"Not concentrated enough for human technology," Linda said. "Who knows what processing capabilities the Mahk-Ra have? Our uranium might be just what they're looking for."

"They can't have it," Charley said.

"We haven't heard the offer yet," Irene countered.

Johnny Redbird rapped his knuckles on the table. A throat injury had left him perpetually hoarse, making it hard to speak above a loud whisper. He wore his wispy hair in twin braids, which Kim thought made him look like a cartoon, but as a teenager, he'd been an AIM member and participated in the Occupation of Alcatraz Island in 1970, and even near ninety, he commanded respect everywhere he went.

"Let the young lady finish," he rasped. "Let's hear the offer. Then we can decide how to tell them to kiss Charley's ass."

Rather than just put a number out there, Kim read the offer letter in full. When she got to the actual dollar amount, the room went silent. After a minute, Charley let out a guffaw. "What?" he asked when he had caught his breath again. "We aren't actually considering that, are we?"

"That much would buy a lot of furnaces," Redbird said. "Rebuild a lot of houses. Send a lot of kids to school. Put dinner on a lot of tables."

"Johnny's right," Linda said. Kim was shocked to hear her seeming to take the Mahk-Ra's side. "We can't afford to just ignore it."

"Sure we can," Charley argued. "How many promises were made to our people, over the years? How many of those ever happened? We let them take the uranium, and then what? Take them to court when they don't pay up? They're not even from Earth, what makes anybody think they'd accept the validity of any human court?"

"They do follow the law," Redbird pointed out. "They make their own law, sometimes. But once their puppets in government pass those laws, the Mahk-Ra stick to it, and they don't go easy on their own when they break it."

"We're not using the uranium anyhow," Linda said. "What do we care if they take it? If they pay up front—"

"Hah!" Charley said. "They'll write a check, or do a transfer, or something, that they can worm out of later."

Other voices joined in the fray, and Kim's stomach churned as she realized that those in favor of the deal seemed to outnumber those opposed. For Linda and Johnny Redbird to be arguing the way they were shocked her, made her feel like the world had tilted sideways beneath her feet. Finally, Redbird brought his knuckles down on the table again.

"Kimberly," he said. She strained to hear him over the murmuring behind her. "We need to take a vote. Maybe a few of them. Thank you for bringing us this offer, but you can't stay for that part."

He looked out at the other tribe members who'd gathered during the course of the debate—it was standing room only, now.

"Same for the rest of you. We've heard your concerns, and we'll take them into consideration and do what's best for the tribe."

Kim didn't mind getting kicked out with the others. If the council was going to vote to sell a single grain of Taovayan sand to those aliens, she didn't want to be in the room when it happened.

Daniel was waiting for her outside the building with a couple dozen of their closest friends and relatives, who milled around, seemingly aimless. And then a table appeared, and moments later, food and drinks atop it—coffee, frybread, refried beans. Someone produced a drum and started playing and the wait became a sort of impromptu powwow.

"They're going to vote to sell."

"You don't know that," she protested, but her son just rolled

193

his eyes disgustedly, and she couldn't blame him.

They *were* going to vote to sell, and there wasn't a damned thing she could do about it. Daniel rolled his eyes again when she said as much.

"Nothing you're *willing* to do about it."

"What would you have me do? Force the vote at gunpoint? I'd be arrested and they'd just retake the vote, and vote more cautiously the second time around.

"Or maybe attack the Mahk-Ra when they come back? Kill them? They'll just send more, and it'll be the whole tribe that suffers, not just me. Or did you forget about Iran?"

Not that such a thing was possible, of course. In the second week of the Invasion, Iran had struck back with a long-suspected but never-proven arsenal of nukes. They had succeeded in destroying one of the Mahk-Ra's Mother Ships, and for the space between two breaths, mankind felt their first — short-lived — glimmer of hope.

Then the Mahk-Ra responded, converging on the small Middle Eastern nation and spending the next week turning it into a parking lot.

It was a lesson the entire planet had taken to heart — Native Americans, perhaps more deeply than most, with primers like Wounded Knee and the Trail of Tears in their collective consciousness.

"So, what?" Daniel asked, frustration making his question a dagger aimed straight at her chest. "We dance, and wait for a miracle that will never come?"

The Ghost Dance was a sore subject among Daniel's generation, who couldn't understand the depth of despair that had led so many to dance themselves to death, either through exhaustion and malnutrition or through disobedience to the white man. The whites didn't comprehend the dance and so feared it, and conquered that fear most often with a bullet and a muzzle flash.

They had danced for a peaceful end to white encroachment, but in the end it was the white man who remained and they who had passed, becoming like ghosts themselves.

Kim had no good answer for him, and the disappointment she read in his face cut her to the core. Maybe the loss he sensed on the near horizon had finally made him understand what he would be giving up if he left.

"You go ahead and dance with your ghosts, Mother. As for me, I'd rather make them than be one."

And before she could reply, he disappeared into the crowd, drumbeats sounding in his wake like a call to a war that simply could not be won.

###

It was nearing midnight when the unanimous vote was finally reached. The crowd had only grown in the intervening hours, though the youngest and oldest had eventually given in and been taken home to cribs and rockers while their parents and children stayed behind. It was a verdict that affected them all; they would hear it together, unanimous in the vote and united in its implementation, whatever that might be.

As Redbird came out of the building followed by the others, Kim craned her neck, looking around in vain for Daniel. Though he was a head taller than most of the tribe, she couldn't find him.

If he was even still there.

Ignoring the pang his absence brought even as other family units gathered closer to one another to hear the news, Kim turned to face Johnny Redbird, alone in the midst of her people.

He didn't beat around the bush.

"We're taking the offer. With that much money, we can buy other land, build a new Cultural Center, and put all of our kids through college, to boot. We'd be fools to refuse."

"If we even could," someone in the crowd murmured, but it

195

was quiet enough that the words carried.

Redbird nodded.

"Exactly. Now go back to your homes. We'll call the Mahk-Ra in the morning and sign the deal tomorrow afternoon. In the meantime, start figuring out what college colors your kids look best in. I'm kind of partial to burnt orange, myself." The crowd laughed as he made the "Hook 'em, Horns" symbol for the University of Texas, and then began to disperse as he'd asked, the air full of excited, hopeful conversation instead of the complaints and arguments Kim had been expecting.

Redbird was really good at what he did, she realized.

Even when what he was doing was selling out his own people.

The council wanted a check, but the Mahk-Ra wanted a ceremony. The aliens invited the media, and some of their journalists showed up, mostly from the Texas press. They carried sat-cams that could transmit the images back to their respective news organizations, even from such a remote location. Decades after the goal of "universal broadband access" had been declared met, it remained obvious that Native American communities didn't count as being part of said universe.

It appeared that the national and international outlets would ignore the story, as they did most news related to Native American issues. Unless some calamity occurred, they were content to do a story once every half-decade or so, reporting the not-so-astonishing findings that many Indian communities still suffered from poverty, crime, fetal alcohol syndrome, and the other sad consequences of a people hunted nearly to extinction and then occupied.

Kim had expected protesters outside, even if just a handful—and she was firmly convinced that Daniel would be part of the group. She hadn't seen or spoken with him since he had vanished into the crowd the night before. But no protest materialized; a few tribal members had come to see the Mahk-Ra but they were largely supportive of the deal. Even those who opposed it did so quietly, because to do otherwise would risk the wrath of the tribe as a whole. Besides, anyone who didn't like the deal was still going to benefit from it. Still, there was a small law enforcement presence, just in case: tribal police, sheriff's officers from the county, and uniformed Mahk-Ra officers, towering over the rest.

Charley Winterhawk wore his best white shirt and bolo tie under his new vest. The shirt had been patched many times, some of the patches sewn on with colorful thread, and it was frayed at the cuffs, but he dug it out anytime there was an occasion to dress up. Johnny Redbird's clothing was old, powdered with dust, but Kim noticed that his black hat was brand new. As she sometimes did when working at the center, Kim was wearing a traditional dress of tanned deer hide decorated with elk teeth. It closed at the neck and dropped almost to the moccasins on her feet. Modern clothing was far more comfortable, but there was value, she believed, in reminding visitors to the center how the Taovaya had dressed before the coming of the Europeans. She wondered how long it would take for people who lived as far out in the boonies as they did to adopt Mahk-Ra styles of dress, mannerisms, perhaps evolve to look like them through interbreeding, further diluting Native bloodlines. Assimilation seemed inevitable, however hard some tried to fight it.

Seven Mahk-Ra had come, not counting the reporters, and they filed one by one through the center's doors to a smattering of applause from the onlookers. The council members were already inside, as were the members of the press. The ceremony would be brief—a few words from Redbird, a few from the head of the Mahk-Ra delegation, the application of thumbs to a touchscreen that would record the prints to affirm the deal, much as signatures on paper treaties with Washington had done back in the old days. She wasn't sure whether the aliens' thumbprints were as individual and unique as human ones, but if the agreement wasn't any more enduring than those earlier treaties had been, she supposed it didn't much matter.

When everyone was in place in an inner chamber usually used for educational presentations and sometimes crafting sessions for young people—Taovayan council members standing in a semicircle on one side of the buffalo skin-draped table that held the touchscreen, Mahk-Ra on the other side in similar formation, with the glass case containing the Red River Stone behind them, where it would be visible in any news footage—the speechifying began.

This was when Kim was supposed to make her exit—she wasn't part of the council, after all, and had only come to open the Center and get it set up for the ceremony—but when she made to leave, one of the Mahk-Ra held out his hand in a forestalling motion, shaking his head. She glanced at Johnny Redbird, who'd exercised the privilege of age, and been chosen to speak for the tribe. He stood nearest the table on the Taovaya side, and when he saw her looking, he gave a quick nod. Kim moved over near him and crossed her arms while he took a half step forward, the cue for the other participants to pay attention.

"Today marks a new start for our people," he rasped. "A fresh opportunity, provided by our friends, the Mahk-Ra."

Kim wondered how he could utter that phrase without gagging, but he went on. "We have for too long suffered from poverty, from lack of educational opportunity, lack of resources. We inhabit a landscape that no one else wanted. As proud Taovayans, we looked out for one another, we held each other up, we clung to our traditions."

Another lie, Kim thought. She decided not keep count, for her own peace of mind. "But in this world, tradition only takes you so far. We can tend our fields and raise our cattle and sell our crafts, but although that keeps us fed, it does not buy technology for our homes. It does not pay for good teachers for our schools, or for their supplies. It does not send our children to college. It does not finance infrastructure—the canals and irrigation systems that would make our fields more productive and our cattle more numerous, the electricity and broadband that would connect even those most far-flung among us to the modern world. Those things cost money. And that is what the Mahk-Ra offer. Not as charity, for we are a proud people who would never accept that. But in exchange for minerals we do not need and they do. A fair price for necessary goods. We are pleased that after so long, someone recognizes the worth of our land, and in that recognition allows us to improve conditions for all the Taovaya. Thank you, Carrana-ra, and your associates, for your willingness to do business. May we all prosper together."

Carrana-Ra, the Mahk-ra standing nearest the table, stepped forward as Redbird stepped back. "Thank you, Mr. Redbird," he began. His English was good, though thickly accented, and Kim tried to focus on the words, to understand what was said. But before he got another phrase out, something else wormed into her consciousness, and after a few moments, she realized what it was.

Smoke.

Another moment or two passed while she processed that. Taovayans often cooked over open flame, in outdoor ovens or grills, and some homes were still heated by woodstoves or fireplaces. Smoke was not an unknown aroma. But the Cultural Center had an electric furnace, and anyway, it was a warm early evening, with no need for any additional heat.

Linda Wahpepah noticed the smell at the same time. "Is that smoke?" she asked.

"I think so," Kim said. "I'll check. Please continue with the ceremony."

She rushed from the room. Locating the source didn't take long. Thick, grey smoke streamed under the closed door that led to a storage area and her office. She pressed a hand against the door—warm, but not yet hot. The whole center was equipped with an automatic fire-extinguishing system; overhead sprinkler units were supposed to come on, and fans would draw oxygen from the affected area to lessen the chance of the flames spreading and to draw smoke away from anyone inside. But she didn't hear water or fans. A panic switch near the electrical controls could override the automatic function, in the event of a breakdown, and start everything going at once, although it would be building-wide—the ceremony's participants and the press, with all their gear, would be soaked, as would the building and its contents. Still, being wet was better than being dead.

She threw open the door. The smoke was thicker here and it rushed toward her like a train bursting from a tunnel. Above the orderly rows of shelves on which she stored supplies, artifacts that were currently off display, extra merchandise for the center's tiny gift shop, and more, she saw flames scaling the back wall and spreading along the ceiling. Her office was on the right, the fire to the left, so she waded through the smoke and into the small room. The electrical panel was on the wall, just a couple of feet from the door. Yanking open the cover, she found the panic switch and flicked it.

Nothing. No fans, no spray from above. She tried again, with the same result. The rumble of the fire grew louder as it covered more territory, and the smoke became more dense. From the inner chamber, she heard voices raised in alarm, and the scuffling of feet.

She rushed back to the doorway. Tribal members were spilling from the chamber into the center's main display area. "Get out!" she cried. "Go out the front, not this way!"

Johnny Redbird tried to take charge, directing the group toward the center's front door, while others, including the Mahk-Ra reporters, hurried to open it—one while simultaneously trying to film everything. Over the general din, she heard words that chilled her despite the heat at her back.

"It won't open!" someone called.

"Break it down!" A Mahk-Ra voice.

Kim didn't dare leave her position; if anyone tried to come this way in search of the back door, she had to be there to steer them away. The back door was blocked by flames, impassable now, and it was locked and barred. Nobody could stand there long enough to remove the bar and unlock it, not without burning to death. She couldn't see the front doors from here, but she heard banging that she guessed was someone trying to kick it or smash through with a chair or some other object. That wouldn't work, she knew. The doors were glass, but impenetrable by design. The Red River Stone was precious enough to the tribe that despite its overall poverty, no shortcuts had been taken in the Cultural Center's security. In the event of a power failure, the doors would not open. Only the back door could be opened without electricity.

"Shoot it out!" someone called.

"No, don't!" Kim screamed, knowing no one was likely to hear over the sounds of growing panic. Three shots were fired, and a shrill cry testified to what she had feared: bullets only ricocheted off the glass, and one had struck home.

Panic welled inside her, too. Locked in a burning building made to be a kind of small fortress, the heat searing her flesh as the smoke clogged her airways, she knew that even if anybody outside saw what was happening and called the tribe's volunteer fire department, it would be twenty minutes or more before they arrived. She wondered how the various systems could all have failed at once, but with smoke coiling around her head and her heart hammering, she was unable to hold the thought, much less arrive at a rational conclusion.

One thought gripped her with sudden urgency. The Red River Stone. It had survived the centuries, out in the elements.

Now that it had been removed from its historic resting place, the responsibility of protecting it fell to the tribe. Stone could withstand fire, but this was within a structure, and that structure would soon be coming down around them. Falling timbers or ceiling debris landing directly on the case could crush both it and the Stone to dust.

The smoke was so thick, Kim could barely see where the entrance to the inner chamber was, and the roar of the flames drowned out all but the faintest hint of screams from around the front door. She was effectively alone, cut off. Whether anybody else remembered she was in here, or knew she wasn't with the group, she couldn't say. She would grab the Red River Stone, then join the others, to be rescued or die together.

The fire had spread along walls, floor, and ceiling, surrounding her. It had to be close to the main room, if not already there. Deep coughs racked her aching lungs. She stumbled toward the inner chamber, where her people had so recently gathered in what, to many, was a triumphant moment. Now flames licked up the legs of the wooden table on which the touchscreen still sat, its surface free of thumbprints, human or otherwise. The display case stood behind it, against a wall alive with fire. It was locked. She knew because she had locked it, then pushed it so the latches backed up against the wall, where the flames were heaviest now. Instead of trying to move it, she snatched up one of the folding chairs the tribal elders had used and raised it over her head, smashing it down against the glass. The chair rebounded, and the shock traveled up her shoulders. She brought it down again, and a third time, and finally the glass shattered. She tossed the chair aside and gathered the Stone into her arms.

For several long moments, she couldn't see the doorway at all. Smoke filled the room, and no doubt all the rest—maybe the whole world by now. The only light that cut through it was the hellish glow of the fire, and that was everywhere. She would die here, in this chamber, clutching her people's Red River Stone even as the flesh bubbled and crisped and curled off of her.

She had almost given up when a familiar voice broke through smoke and despair. "Mom? Mom, where are you?"

Daniel? She tried to answer, but another coughing fit gripped her. A blurred shape wove through the fog toward her. "Mom? Is . . . that you?" he asked. His voice had a faraway trembling quality.

But it was definitely Daniel. She started toward him, unsteady on her feet, but before she reached him, he fell to his hands and knees. Kim rushed forward, holding the Stone with one hand and trying to bat smoke away with the other, then crouched beside him. His hair was singed, his cheeks blackened. His shirt was smoldering, with visible pinpoints of light embedded in the fabric. She brushed at them, and sparks flew beneath her fingertips. "Daniel, are you okay?"

"Mom . . ." he said again, but his voice faded before he could add any more.

"Hush," she said. "Don't try to talk. Can you stand up?"

He looked at her and shook his head slowly. The whites of his eyes were bloodshot. Mucus trailed down his face. "I'm . . ." he tried, but that was all he could manage. Kim took his hand in hers, pressing the Stone to her chest with the other, and tried to help him to his feet. But he couldn't rise, even with her assistance.

The fire was everywhere. Flaming debris rained down from overhead. The screams from the front were nonstop; she was sure the people—and aliens—who had tried to go out that door were being burned alive. She had no better options—just a back door she couldn't reach, her path blocked by flame.

Well, she'd fought her way through worse things in her life, and for less cause.

Daniel was her son, flesh of her flesh. She couldn't— *wouldn't*—stand by and watch him burn. She was torn, though—

she still held the Red River Stone, the symbol of her people's past and the most permanent expression of the language that was remembered now only by a handful of the old ones. In a way, it felt like the glue that held the tribe together, to the extent that anything did. As much as she had opposed the deal with the Mahk-Ra, it had unified the people again. Most of them, anyway. Now it was surely gone, as was the tribal council. What did the Taovaya have left, besides the Stone?

And what did Kimberly Greymountain have left, besides Daniel?

She set the Stone down, touched it one last time—sadly, reverently. Then she turned and put her hands in Daniel's armpits. She struggled to stand, struck by a wrenching coughing fit. But she pushed through to her feet, raising Daniel to his. "Come on," she said.

She looped an arm under his and around his back, and together they made their way to the storage area. The conflagration was impassable, still; the fire created its own wind, blowing in her face, hot and dry as the dead of summer in all the deserts of the world, all at once. Furnace hot. The Christian Hell hot.

But she had no other choice. It was make her way to the back door, with Daniel, or they both died here. "We're going through there, Daniel. It's going to hurt."

"I . . . I don't . . ." He said something else, but she couldn't make it out over the fire's fury. She thought a straight shot would be best; the floor back here was concrete, and though everything on the storage shelves was either in flames or already burned, the walls were still on fire, and would be hotter than the room's center. Half-dragging Daniel, she made for the door, seemingly miles away.

Her theory seemed sound. The heat was searing. She could smell her own hair burning, and her lungs felt like they had contracted to the size of walnuts; she could hardly catch her breath. But she and Daniel made steady progress toward the door; too slow, but better than none. The screams from the front were no longer audible, and loud cracks and crashes broke through the sound of the fire. The place was falling apart around them. "Come on, Daniel," she urged. "You've got to help me."

As they passed one of the rows of storage shelves, her gaze landed on something that didn't fit. Even under these conditions, with the entire center engulfed, she knew that. She kept the storage area neatly organized. She took a second look and saw a pair of metal gas cans, one lying on its side and the other standing up.

Then Daniel lurched forward, and she had to keep up or risk losing her grip. She was so weak she wasn't sure she would be able to lift him again. But they were almost to the big steel door, and although the smoke was thick in the air, the fire had mostly moved on.

She released Daniel long enough to shove the bar aside and unlock the deadbolt. The heavy door didn't want to give; the walls and jamb had probably warped from the heat, throwing it out of true. But she shoved again, hard, and it opened. She grabbed Daniel and they both fell from the building into blessedly cool, fresh air.

Kim pushed herself to her hands and knees, watching Daniel curl almost into a ball, choking and gagging. His back spasmed with every cough, and she wished there were something she could do. She could barely breathe, herself.

And as she watched her son, a disturbing train of thought pushed into her consciousness.

He had not been at the ceremony. She'd been surprised he wasn't protesting in front of the Cultural Center, but he wasn't, and she hadn't seen him all day.

Whoever had sabotaged the place had known how to disable the fire extinguishing system and the door locks.

Daniel, who had not been at the ceremony—who had been vocally, forcefully, opposed to the deal he thought was a betrayal of the entire tribe—had nonetheless been inside the center, somewhere. As had a couple of five-gallon gas cans.

And Daniel had always been entranced by the story of the destruction of the Mission San Saba.

The conclusion was inescapable.

"Daniel, why?" she asked. "Why?"

He coughed dark phlegm into the gravel behind the center. "...had to pay . . . all of them. You . . . weren't supposed . . . to be here. Came back . . . for you," he said before the coughing overtook him again. "I'm . . . sorry."

"So am I," Kim said. "Sorrier than I can ever say."

The trial—if it could be called that—took place less than a week later. Kim and Daniel and a gaggle of reporters were the only humans present; there was no jury. The proceedings lasted less than an hour, and they, unlike the ceremony that had started the whole thing, were broadcast over all the major networks. And she was sure it had gotten excellent ratings. It seemed bread and circuses weren't just a human invention, but a universal constant.

Like her, Daniel wore his best suit. And like her, his cheeks and hands were scarred, and always would be—a lifelong brand they would both bear, though one for far longer than the other. His black hair was cut short and he wore a white shirt and a grey tie; her dress suit and heels were likewise black, her hair tied back, a chunky turquoise necklace about her neck, the shock of color an act of defiance in the somber courtroom. A reminder of what had been lost—far more than just the lives of five council members and twice that number of Mahk-Ra.

It never occurred to either one of them to pretend they didn't know what had happened. Besides, people knew they made it out the back door, knew the two of them were the only survivors that night. The pretense wouldn't have held up for long.

More importantly, she was Kimberly Greymountain. He was Daniel Greymountain. That name went back a long way, and there was honor in it that had to be upheld. And they were Taovayan, of which there were precious few left, and there was honor in that, too. White man's law couldn't take that away. Neither could Mahk-Ra law. Not poverty, not prejudice, not occupation by this group or that one.

The Taovaya were a principled people, and Greymountains owned up to their mistakes.

After the sentence was pronounced from the bench, Daniel had asked if he could speak briefly to his mother. They met on the courthouse steps. In the west, the sun sank toward the horizon and turned red as it did; a wildfire was streaking the sky with grey and had made for vivid sunsets these last few days.

"I'm going to learn Taovayan," he told her. "Fluently. Every word, every syllable. All the things you tried so hard to teach me, before. And when I have, I'll teach the young ones what it took me so long to know."

Kim looked at him, a seed of peace growing in her heart. Daniel had spoken before about what he, and many like him, saw as the only two choices her people had—make ghosts, or become them. Assimilate or die fighting.

But there was a third choice; there had always been a third choice, and the much-reviled Ghost Dancers had known it, even through their despair.

Make ghosts, be them—or *free* them. The ones you created yourself, the ones that you inherited, the ones that dogged your path, punishing you for reasons you might never fully comprehend.

Let them go. Find the good, focus on that. Make more of it,

when you could, and less of the other, when you couldn't.

It was what Kim had tried to do her whole life; the lesson she'd tried to impart to Daniel and to everyone else who came through the Cultural Center.

She looked away from him and toward where the sun was setting and the bottoms of the clouds were washed with rose and salmon, and tears filled her eyes, blurring it all into a formless mass of pure color. Since before the days of the first Taovayan, that sun had done the same thing, and through all the years of occupation, all the years of struggle, it came up each morning, set, and rose again the next day. The sun and the clouds and the rivers and the rocks and the sand didn't care who had power, who made the laws and enforced them, who occupied what territory. Those things were temporary. One day all the occupiers of Earth would be gone, the Indians who had been on this continent first, and whoever they had come from, and the Europeans who came next and forced the Indians onto smaller and smaller patches of planet, and even the Mahk-Ra. All of them would disappear in time, remembered by no one, all traces of their passing obliterated, but the Earth would still be there.

In that context, what happened to any one individual didn't matter. The tribe — its spirit — would live on, regardless

She smiled and moved to hug him, but a guard stepped between them. "I'm sorry, ma'am," he said. "You can't touch him."

"He's my son," Kim said.

"I understand that, but it doesn't matter."

"All right," she said. She caught Daniel's gaze, and held it. "Goodbye for now."

He started to say something in response, but the guards were impatient, and pulled her away before he could get it out. She glanced back at him once, over her shoulder, as she was marched down the stairs and toward a bus waiting to take her to the public execution site.

"Goodbye," she repeated softly. He was young and full of fire. He had many years to give to the tribe, more than she would have, and he had energy, and now, she believed, he had finally made up his mind. There would be no leaving for the city, not for him.

With her thoughts firmly on Daniel's future and what it could mean for her people — now truly his people as well, for perhaps the first time in his life — she looked at the sun again, perched on the horizon line, and waited for tears that did not come.

A DAY IN THE LIFE

RICHARD M. JOHNSON

F inishing his shave, Robert splashed old school aftershave on his face. It cost him plenty to acquire the real stuff. Reflected in the hotel mirror, he watched the news cast from the halo-television behind him. The flattened out three-dimensional figures reminded him of the way television from his childhood used to be.

Channel 3 was repeating an earlier story about a bombing that had taken place last night in downtown Los Angeles. The Red Spear had destroyed a Mahk-Ra stronghold on the top of the Library Tower by taking the whole building down, demolishing it from its base. Human casualties had been minimal, less than what used to make up an American baseball team before the Occupation and all of them high level collaborators.

Baseball had been outlawed by the Mahk-Ra after the takeover. They said it was to discourage national partisanship, but most humans figured it was because they couldn't understand the game; all that waiting around, that and the fact that the Mahk-Ra could never put together a winning team, unlike other sports where they flourished; football, soccer, basketball --- the last for obvious reasons.

Originally built in 1989, the Library Tower's construction helped stop the demolition of the actual library building. L.A. sold the air rights. The city trusties sunk most of the money earned in that way into saving the city's main library, previously devastated by a massive fire. Its official name had been that of some bank or other, and it changed hands half a dozen times in the last sixty years, but the people still called it the Library Tower.

Secretly, the Tower had been converted into the Talon's main west coast headquarters. Over five hundred officers of the Mahk-Ra secret police, and a lot of alien tech, had been demolished in the coordinated attack. The buildings surrounding the Library Tower had barely been affected. The tall landmark had expertly collapsed inward and pancaked like the old Las Vegas casinos used to do when they were destroyed to make way for the newer, glitzier edifices taking their place.

Ultimately, the joke was on all those casino developers. When the war started, if one could call a fight that only lasted a few months a war, the Mahk-Ra had strategically wiped Sin City off the map in one of their first of many concentrated bombing runs. The Vegas gambit was a strong enough opening statement to catch the world's attention, and make everyone who lived within a five mile radius of Reno, Atlantic City, and Monte Carlo, grab as much of their personal belongings as they could carry and head for the hills.

What the hell did they think the Mahk-Ra were, Robert chuckled dryly. Interstellar holy acolytes, so pious they were only going to destroy all the gambling centers of the world?

Later it was revealed that a large, international military convention was in the city, and the Mahk-Ra had managed to kill off an incredibly large contingent of the military's best strategists -- a huge blow against the world's defenses.

Robert wiped his face with a towel, shook his head, and

meticulously hung the damp cloth back on the towel rack. Despite the changes now in place, he didn't have any problem with the Mahk-Ra. Sure they had conquered the Earth, but as dictatorships go, as long as you worked within the system they set up, you could do pretty nicely for yourself. Hell, Nazi Germany was worse in so many ways. The Mahk-Ra might be sticklers for rules, but they weren't trying to wipe out an entire race. No, humans and other conquered races were now part of the empire.

It was actually nicer in the initial months of the takeover, before the resistance kicked fully into gear, Robert reflected. There weren't any real restrictions on travel until about nine months after the Red Spear became fully organized. Now, because of them, you had to jump through so many hoops to get from one coast to the other, that a trained circus lion would be impressed. Flight was virtually impossible unless you had been checked out many months in advance.

If he was ever caught in a raging snow storm, Robert knew he would never freeze, the sheaf of papers he had to carry to prove he was supposed to be where he should be, would burn for at least a day before the fuel ran out. Not that he would ever burn his papers, God forbid... He'd emolliate himself before he'd burn his travel documents. They were too valuable.

Brushing his teeth, he recalled the torture you had to go through to travel from state to state before his company had arranged for special dispensation for its sales people and technicians. Everyone at the company had to be vetted. The Mahk-Ra even went so far as to have all the people each employee were, or had been, regularly in contact with scrutinized as well.

Robert thought about his poor ex-girlfriend, Larissa Gifford. He'd only dated her for about eight months in college. When the Mahk-Ra had investigated him they found she was friends with individuals suspected of being Red Spear. He'd heard she was at work, ringing up groceries for a customer in his hometown of Fresno, when they came for her. Two uniformed mocks, towering over everyone in the store. They walked straight over to Larissa, told her she was required to come with them, and started to escort her out. Some kid blocked their way, wanting to know what she had done, where were they taking her? Absentmindedly, they knocked him through the store's plate glass window. Supposedly the youth was also suspected of being part of the resistance – but that could have just been talk. It had been a perfect shit storm of events. If things hadn't lined up the way they did, she probably wouldn't have been put through so rigorous a "questioning" process. She didn't survive. Robert blamed the Red Spear and their cowboy methods. Still, he was glad the process hadn't extended back to him.

Turning away from the mirror, Robert went over his client notes. The news shifted to the entertainment report. He had his notes, maps and photos spread across the bed in neat little stacks, arranged in order of importance to the day ahead. When dealing with important clients, he always used hardcopies, not computers. Of course the Mahk-Ra had their eyes and ears and terabytes into everything, but the common folk either didn't know that, or didn't care. As far as Robert was concerned, unless you were stupid enough to plot against them on your computer or phone, the Mahk-Ra pretty much left you alone.

On the TV, a cute entertainment reporter, Felicia Kenway was interviewing one of the beautiful people, a Mahk-Ra model by the name of Chan- ra, was in the middle of breaking up with one of the top human actors, a fellow named, George Huston. George was a good-looking guy who, at six-four, pulled up three or four inches shorter than Chan- ra. Seems Chan had caught George with another human woman, a model named Katrina Kelly who, oddly, couldn't be found for comment.

Unfortunately, George had not taken the time to read up on the Mahk-Ra way of courtship, Felicia told her viewers. Generally, a Mahk-Ra dating a human was frowned upon, but in a few cases exceptions were made; usually regarding celebrities. That didn't simply mean actors and models. The list included quisling politicians, sports figures, war heroes, and a guy named Eddie Michaelson. What made him so special, no one knew.

Reaching for the remote control, Robert boosted the TV's volume. Felicia was speaking with Chan-ra, who was displaying a calm demeanor as well as being dressed in full Mahk-Ra ceremonial garb, which included several ornate items only used for preparing a sacrifice during the ancient Mahk-Ra high-holy days. Felicia explained that when a Mahk-Ra female took a human mate, he became hers. Her property. And if the relationship ended, he had to win his freedom in battle. Chan-rawas hoping that George would at least supply the public with some sport before he died when they telecast their battle.

Robert grinned. What horseshit. He'd taken a three month Mahk-Ra intensive when he first came to Goldberg Mosley and Fitzhugh. There were no high-holy days, no such ceremonial battles or garb to go with it. It was all a show to build up an audience for the event. Like when boxers would trash talk one another before a big bout.

The program then cut to George on the set of his newest science fiction, action film, *Time Warriors*. He talked about how he'd been training for the fight, with his Mahk-Ra costar, KuTak-ra. How he was confident he would be able to hold his own against his former flame. The reporter asked George if he had seen the most recent footage of Chan training and he glanced quizzically at him.

The footage ran onscreen. Chan-ra was in the same outfit shown in her segment. She bowed to the camera, then in her warrior stance, deftly removed the chokota and struck it soundly against the takamo armor she wore. The sound of the vibrating chokota had been known to make the most hardened human soldier wet himself. The high pitched noise was akin to a dentist's drill. The vibrations could felt to the bone. Robert was impressed. He knew the chokota was a crystal-metal hybrid that could, if the need arose, flay with micro-dermal accuracy. What Chan-ra next did to the three beef carcasses hanging from chains wasn't pretty.

Cutting back to George he was still smiling, but his expression had faltered. There was a look in his eyes that told you he knew he still had a hell of lot of training to do in the next two months if he didn't want his sexual organs to be gold plated and used as ornamental jewelry, or his heart to become a new chew toy for Chan-ra's pet bokomo, Max, a monkey-like animal found on Barnard's Star.

George was a better actor than Robert suspected. They'd get in the arena, grunt, swing at each other a few times, maybe draw a little blood, then George would throw away his weapons, declare his undying love and beg Chan-ra to take him back. And she probably would... Unless, George had really pissed the statuesque alien off, then poor old George might just find himself bleeding out during the closing credits of the show. Ah, well, his career wasn't what it was ten years ago anyway. But he'd go out a ratings winner.

Robert turned off the set, gathered his papers, and placed them carefully in his valise, a leather Gladstone circa the 1960's. Reaching for his suit jacket, he was stopped by the chiming of his cell phone laying on an end table. He hesitated a moment before picking it up. It might be important. Someone might want to cancel.

Robert answered. "Yellow..."

"I hate when you answer that way..." The voice from the other side of the secure call replied.

"Hey, Matthew, something up? I was just on my way to my first meeting."

"I thought your first meeting was at ten?"

"Different time zone..." Robert waited. "What do you need,

Matt?"

"The boss wanted me to go back over the specs with you one more time, before you met with the client."

"Come, on, we covered that at least ten times before I left."

Matt, chuckled. "I know, but there had to be a call on the books or Walter would be all over my pasty white ass... So, how's California?"

"Sunny, bright, and dry."

"Lucky, bastard. That snow storm hit here last night. I'm freezing my nuts off."

Robert looked at his old-fashioned wrist watch. "You can always do the next one."

"No thanks! You know I don't fly. You never know when those ass hats in the Red Spear will decide to drop another plane out of the sky."

"Matt that was a plane filled with Mahk-Ra dignitaries. There were no humans on board. The Red Spear aren't out to get regular business Joes like us."

"Still...did you catch the news this morning?"

"I'm here in Los Angeles, hard to miss."

"You anywhere near it?"

"Nope. Happened downtown, I'm out near the beach."

"Santa Monica?"

Sitting on the edge of the bed, Robert put down his valise and double checked its contents. "Santa Monica's too expensive, ever since Malibu and the marina were taken out by that tsunami."

"So, where are you, then?"

"Culver."

Matthew, sighed. "Ah. Near what used to be the old Sony-MGM lot? Where the Mahk-Re built Delphinion Studios?"

"Yeah. What's up? You want me to bring you a tee-shirt or something?"

"Would you?" Mathew said in a singsong voice.

Robert stood. "Look, I'm going to be late. What else do you need?

"You hear about that Iowa thing?"

"Yeah, I heard. Davenport's a tough town. They're saying it was some loser named Panten.

Matt laughed. "Right. You wouldn't know any more about it?"

"I know the rat bastard got what he deserved. And I'm running late. Anything else?"

"How are you getting to the job site?"

"Public transportation. The traffic out here is worse now than it was back when."

"I'd stay off the buses."

"Why?"

"That's how those bastards took down that Library Tower." Robert could hear Matt tapping keys then he continued. "The Red Spear managed to get hold of some public buses two days ago without setting off any warnings. They filled the busses with enough of that explosive the Mahk-Ra used on Vegas and Iran and drove them through the front doors by remote control."

"They used Pax-12?"

"Yes, that and Symtex to set it off."

"Interesting."

"Shit yeah it's interesting."

Robert glanced at his watch again. "How'd they get so much of that material?"

"Who knows? I'm willing to bet that somewhere several Mahk-Ra are missing their heads. I wonder why the hell the Talon used that building."

"The Tower was on a hill, probably a better vantage point to watch from, near the main rail line as well. Plus the Tower was mainly offices. I would think it was easier to convert that into what they needed." Robert stood and picked up the valise

217

again. "Okay, I got to go."

"Be careful, the west coast is getting crazy right now."

"I'm always careful. We good on the package?"

"Yep, just got off the phone with Harold, before I called you. Shouldn't be any problem."

"Good."

"Cool." The line went dead.

Outside, Robert hailed a cab and set off for his first meeting in Beverly Hills. The day was beautiful and the sun was sneaking between the buildings. Beverly Hills was no longer the exclusive playground of the rich it had been the century before. With the Occupation, the Mahk-Ra had taken the opulent mansions for themselves or for the cooperating class.

The cab dropped Robert in front of the Exocore Sunset Business Complex. Looking up, he shielded his eyes from the glare bouncing off the exterior glass of the building. It was a marvel how high they could currently build a structure in California, now that the Mahk-Ra had managed to stabilize the tectonic plates in the earth. In many ways the planet had become a much more pleasurable place to live. Too bad the aliens had come as conquerors as opposed to benefactors, but the Occupation had its benefits as well. If you knew what you were doing.

Work was plentiful, the Earth was bountiful in its riches -- sure, a good deal of our water was taken off-world and now there was rationing. Also the majority of able-bodied were pressed into a far off war – but thanks to the miracles of the Mahk-Ra, air pollution had pretty much disappeared, and they had curtailed many human diseases. Far as Robert was concerned, it was an age of wonders, and he was thriving. Yes, there was oppression. Sections of the world were barely scraping by, but if you stayed on the right side of Mahk-Ra law, life could be very good. All you had to do was to learn to work within the system, to work the system. Those who didn't, suffered. Robert didn't like to suffer.

In the waiting room of the Exocore Corporation, he straightened the magazines sitting on the glass coffee table that was between the two couches. The receptionist looked from her holographic monitor after an appropriate amount of time and again asked him if he would like some coffee or another beverage. Again, Robert politely declined. She eyed his ancient valise but said nothing.

Once through the door that separated the lobby from the rest of the office, Robert's meeting took a little over forty-five minutes to conclude, with him securing a multi-million dollar security equipment sale for several of the Excoree buildings, and an additional service contract. His ten percent commission would come in handy. Especially given his next stop.

After taking the subway to the Valley, Robert walked to where one of the few remaining bookstores in the country was located. The Illiad bookstore covered the entire hidden sub-basement of a ten story building on Cahuenga. The original owner had passed away some years ago, but the book community had banded together and kept it alive. The entire floor was moisture and climate controlled, and filled to the ceiling with books. Aside for a few private collections and a handful of heavily monitored bookstores around the rest of the country, books had pretty well disappeared. Everyone today was forced to carry electronic note pads and read only approved material.

There existed a clandestine group of people who preferred handling a physical book over the Mahk-Ra laundered electronic ones. But since the paper blight back in 2025, and the mass burnings under the Mahk-Ra, few had survived. Because of their rarity, and the fact that most pre-Occupation books were now illegal, made them prohibitively expensive. He had a few hours to kill before his last appointment and how better than to spend those hours in a highly illegal den of paper and ink.

Approaching the building, he reviewed the password in his head. He'd been here before, but he wanted to make sure there would be no trouble. After a series of hidden passageways, and once past the rough looking guard, Robert turned in his Gladstone at the counter. He then wandered the arranged aisles with the euphoria of a child let loose in a candy shop with a wad of dollar bills clenched in their fist. This was going to be a good day.

Nearly two hours later, Robert emerged from the bookstore two blocks away via a disguised exit with an autographed copy of *The Land of Laughs* by one of his favorite authors, Jonathan Carroll. The edition was rated in very good condition, and had cost him slightly over three thousand dollars, cash. He also managed to fetch a fairly beaten up copy of Michael Connelly's *The Concrete Blonde* for around eight hundred, again in cash. It might have been autographed too, but the title page was so faded he couldn't tell.

Feeling very happy with the purchases he'd made, Robert tucked the books into the false lining of his valise. He walked the slightly longer than a mile distance over to Lankershim Boulevard where he knew he could relax and get a bite to eat. He stopped at a nice restaurant bar he was familiar with on the corner of Lankershim and Weddington, sitting near the window so he could watch what was going on out on the street. After the host made sure he had the proper ration cards to eat there, Robert spent the next hour enjoying a Portobello mushroom burger, a tasty microbrew beer and girl watching. Usually he didn't like to sit near a window, because the destitute tended to gather outside and stare at him as he ate. He was finishing his beer and marveling over how this section of the city had remained mostly unscathed from the war when he realized he needed to get to his last appointment. Unfortunately cabs were not as plentiful in North Hollywood as elsewhere in Los

Angeles, so he was forced to ride a bus, despite his friend's warning, to where Universal Studios once stood and catch a cab from there.

Robert got out of the cab about a mile and a half from his actual destination. He took a route predestined long before he arrived in California. He walked briskly through a seedy neighborhood, trying hard not to draw attention to himself. After all, he was carrying thousands of dollars in collectables, and really wanted to keep them -- at least until he had time to read them both.

Despite his mild appearance, he wasn't worried about being rolled for his wallet or his Gladstone. But he wanted to avoid a confrontation given the presence of surveillance cameras even though he could tell that many in the area had been destroyed. Probably by the humans...or could be the Mahk-Re. They liked to prey on people who didn't belong here too.

Walking up Van Nuys Boulevard, Robert passed graffiti covered walls, the telltale circle and letters that were the symbol of the Red Spear. Two buildings later, he entered a large apartment complex that was across the street and south of the Van Nuys courthouse. It wasn't too new. It had been built somewhere in the last twenty years. Waiting for the elevator, Robert noticed the cameras pointing at the entrance when he came in, were also non-functioning.

The combo lock opened after he entered the correct code. The apartment was tidy and non-descript. He stood in the doorway, listening. Robert slid inside and closed the door. He paused again, making sure his first instincts were correct and that no one would surprise him.

Moving to the back of the apartment, Robert opened the door to the bedroom and then to the closet. In the rear of that, where they said it would be, was the equipment bag. Inside he made sure everything they said would be there, was. Zipping it closed, he placed a roll of cash in the sock drawer of the dresser and carrying the bag and his suitcase, exited the apartment.

Taking the flight of stairs at the back at the building, he made his way to the roof. It was fairly level, with a three foot parapet around the edge of the building. He set down the valise. Walking over to the north-east corner of the build, he could easily see the entrance to the courthouse. Lying down below the lip of the roof, Robert extracted from the equipment bag a camouflage tarp painted the color of the roof and a flattened cardboard mirror box. Sometimes, low tech in a high tech world was best. He covered himself with the tarp and quickly constructed the mirror box. He fondly eyed the little periscope toy he used to play with as a kid, then attached it to the lip of the building, its specially coated surface suffusing sunlight from glinting off its surface. Now he could watch who entered and exited the courthouse without being seen.

Next he assembled the sniper rifle and checked the load. Three bullets as promised. If he needed more than three, he knew it would be time to retire. Keeping his eyes on the mirror box, Robert extracted a warm bottle of tea, and after wiping the rim of the bottle with a tissue, opened it. He settled in, keeping his eyes on the front of the courthouse.

It took twenty seven minutes from when he'd taken position on the roof.

A hover transport van pulled up and an armed guard got out carrying a bleater. Within a minute three security drones were in the air. Not thirty seconds after that, the witness was brought out of the courthouse surrounded by more armed guards. They had armor on him, including a protective helmet. Didn't matter. The poor Mahk-Re that the humans were trying to protect was a good head and a half taller that anyone surrounding him. It took only one shot to shatter his head like a melon struck by a hammer. The bullet was made like the chokota, the crystal-metal hybrid. When launched, it activated and vibrated through the helmet's armored shell. The drones all turned in unison and started to coordinate his position.

Robert swiftly hit the button on the mini electronic pulse device that was designed to take out anything in a half mile radius. The drones dropped from the sky like wounded doves, their control chips fried. He chuckled, sometimes high tech in a high tech world is best. Unscrewing the barrel of the rifle, he dropped its segments back into the equipment bag along with the camouflage tarp and the mirror box. He set the mechanical timer on the incendiary device in the bag for three minutes. He was pretty sure no one had seen where the shot had come from, but the fire would take care of any evidence left behind. If they got up to the roof before ten minutes, they'd probably be able to put it out before it caused any serious damage.

Snatching up his valise, Robert ran to the far edge of the building and in one fluid movement leapt onto the edge, then across the three foot expanse of a passageway that separated his building form the next. He dashed across that roof to the far side pulling a zip line from a hidden pocket in his suit jacket and used it to drop down and escape into the alley below, gripping his Gladstone between his legs. Running down the alley Robert made the next corner at the end of the block. There, just inside an electrical breaker room fronted by a metal side door sans latch to an office building, the mag-glide motorcycle was where it was supposed to be, along with a helmet – there was still a helmet law. He strapped his valise to the machine and switched jackets, he had a leather one in the valise, he ditched his dark suit coat elsewhere.

Riding south along Van Nuys, Robert made it to the freeway within minutes. He'd also stripped off and disposed of his wig, latex nose and fingertip sheaths before reaching the freeway. He'd dissolved the latex with acetate and pouring the flammable liquid onto the wig, tossed it down a storm drain, dropping a lit match in after it. His luck was holding and it only took one match. Given the preponderance of dead leaves inside the sewer he hoped things didn't get out of control. It was another drought year in California.

While he rode the motorcycle east along the 101, toward downtown's Union Station, Robert wondered if he'd have better luck taking his alternate escape route via the former John Wayne airport in Orange County, because as Matt had said, things downtown were getting kind of crazy.

Hours later he boarded his plane, his two books hidden securely in his valise. Robert wondered again why so many people were having trouble with the Occupation. He loved the Mahk-Ra. They always paid on time.

SECOND COMING

CRAIG FAUSTUS BUCK

emma didn't need another asshole. She had the one nature gave her; she had her Mahk-Ra husband who worm-holed back home to Ra-Prime seven months ago with all their savings; she had her MR slumlord who demanded a hand job every Friday in exchange for not evicting her for the two months' back-rent she owed; she had her dick-brained human boss who was, at the moment, smirking behind his desk; and she had the MR jerk with the greasy brown comb-over at table ten who'd complained to Dick-brain Dave after Jemma'd slapped him.

"You think I'm going to let you skate for hitting a customer?" said Dave, his face so sweat-drenched it looked like he was wrapped in Saran, even though Jemma had goose bumps from the air conditioning. He took a swig from a still-frosted mug of some foul mix of Melonzade and Jägermeister that he'd invented and spent four years trying to persuade Corporate to put on the menu but, as usual, the Mahktard suits just didn't get it.

"That comb-over put his fucking hand up my crack, Dave. I don't recall that in the job description."

"Allow me to refresh your memory."

Dave pulled out the thick employee handbook, miraculously extant though printed on paper fifty years ago.

The longevity of a cockroach, thought Jemma, like this restaurant.

Dave flipped to a well-worn section and read, "I hereby acknowledge and affirm that the Melonz concept is based on female sex appeal and that the work environment is one in which joking and innuendo based on female sex appeal is commonplace." Dave looked up with a vicious gloat.

Jemma's bile burnt the back of her throat. "Innuendo means wordplay, Dave, not foreplay."

"Tough shit, Jemma, it's not okay to take a swing at a customer, especially if he's MR." He wiped his forehead with his arm and it came away soaked.

"It was a reflex, okay? I didn't mean to hit him. If I'd'a had a little more time to think about it I would have stuck a fucking fork in his chest."

She glared at Dave. He softened.

"Look, I like you, Jemma. You got a nice rack and you're a good waitress, even if you have put on a few pounds. So I'm sorry you don't like it here. It truly pains me to accept your resignation."

She felt her stomach twist at the thought of telling her thirteen-year-old son that they'd have to live out of her rattletrap of a car for a while, despite the fact that even duct tape couldn't stop cold drafts from flowing through the aft-hatch.

"I need this job, Dave."

The smarmy tyrant gave her a grin. "Then get the hell back to work. And no more screw-ups." A drop of sweat dripped from his nose into his Melonzmeister as he took a sip. She wished she could piss in it.

THE LAB WAS bathed in red light allowing Scud-re to work

without the protective dark glasses MRs usually needed on Earth. Above his large eyes, Scud-re's brows began to dance as he validated the gene fragments he'd finally managed to extract from the ancient linen. Glee filled his heart as the data checked out. He'd been working for sixteen hours straight and his stomach was rumbling like one of those primitive internal combustion engines some humans still used, but he couldn't tear himself away from his work to eat. Despite being a so-called aboriginal Mahk-Re, Scud-re was sure this breakthrough would be his ticket home to Ra-Prime.

Humans had labored for thousands of years to decipher the story that now glowed in the view-field implant behind Scud-re's emerald green eyes. Granted he had been working on this bloodstained rag for a year, but most of that time he'd been waiting for his gluon scanner to arrive from Ra-Prime. Earth being just one of twenty-six worlds on the shuttle route from the pater-planet, shipments were routinely delayed — particularly these days. But once Scud-re got the scanner up and running, he'd needed only three days to recreate DNA fragments from the ancient image stained into the sacred cloth.

Since at least the fourteenth century, many humans believed the Shroud of Turin was Christ's burial cloth. They'd even managed to isolate iron oxide from the Shroud, which may have been residue from hemoglobin. But in 1988, carbon-dating proved the Shroud to be a fraud. It wasn't until 2031 that archaeologists, using MR technology, finally discovered Christ's actual burial site. His funeral shroud was among the treasures they unearthed, in addition to contemporaneous writings and artifacts that corroborated its historicity. Now Scud-re had finally extracted the shroud's ultimate revelation.

HE RAN DOWN the hall to his supervisor's office. At six-six and a hundred eighty pounds, he was trim, but he was still winded by the exuberant sprint.

Huxen-ra's office door scanned Scud-re and evaluated his job level, his Mahk-Re ancestry, Huxen-ra's schedule and current activity. Then it did the math and slid open to admit Scud-re without ceremony.

Scud-re's boss was watching 3D-mini soccer players run around on top of his desk, a livecast match from Brazil. "Humans and their games," he chuckled. "I've got three K riding on Real Madrid Bahrain."

"Do your wives know you're gambling?" asked Scud-re. He and Hux had an easygoing relationship, despite the difference in their castes.

Hux shut off the game with the flick of a thought. "What's up?"

"I finally nailed it," said Scud-re, amused by his own metaphor.

"Christ's DNA?"

Scudre replied with a gleeful grin. He dropped into a gelatin chair and felt it jiggle from his excitement.

Hux sat up, suddenly attentive. "The humans are going to go nuts over this, especially the Christians."

"That's just the half of it," said Scud-re. "I'm pretty sure I've got enough shards to sequence his genome."

Hux's huge black pupils sparked. "Are you shitting me?"

"I shit you not. I'm going to get to work on it after lunch. By this time next week I hope to have a healthy clone of Jesus Christ."

"Cloning a human god." Hux spoke slowly, as if rotating the phrase to ponder it from every side. "We can't just jump into this, Scud-re. We need to think it through. What if he's born a mere human? What if he can't work miracles, or whatever it is humans use to identify their gods? An event like that could cause a lot of unrest."

"What are you suggesting?"

Hux continued to ponder. "Or what if he does have divine powers? How would the Muslims react? Or the Hindus? Or the Jews?"

"Are you saying I shouldn't do it?"

"Now don't go disassembling on me, Scud-re. I just have to run this cloning by the powers that be, that's all."

Scud-re's hackles spiked. "Come on. I've been stuck on this dump of a planet for years waiting for a high profile shot like this. It could mean my own lab back on Ra-Prime. This kind of opportunity doesn't come along every day, especially for a Mahk-Re. Please don't tell me you're going to let the brass screw it up."

"We're talking about bio-engineering the Second Coming of Jesus Christ," said Hux. "The backlash could be huge and global. I can't approve this on my own. I have to notify Rhea-ra. It'll be her call whether it has to go any further up the chain of command."

Scud-re wasn't worried about their department head. Rhea-Ra was a biophysicist. But above her level were politicians and they were capricious. Especially with a Mahk-Re involved. The more bigwigs who weighed in, the greater the chance that one of them would find a reason to kill Scud-re's project, perhaps his future.

"Even if this *does* get approved," said Hux, "how are you going to find a huwoman surrogate to carry the clone? You can't exactly advertise, 'Help wanted: Mother of God, preferably virgin.'"

Scud-re was already wracking his brain to answer that question. If he could get the egg planted in some human womb, the political risks of halting the project would be much greater for the powers that be. He needed to find a fecund huwoman who would willingly face an explosively controversial pregnancy with a potentially unhuman baby in a goldfish bowl of global scrutiny. Finding such a female would be no easy task.

But he had to impregnate one fast.

I⊤ HAD BEEN more than seventeen hours since Scud-re had eaten anything and it was affecting his ability to concentrate. So when the young, blonde waitress delivered his deep-fried Philly cheese steak, Scud-re wolfed it down. The fatty fuel flooded his bioburner and relief was immediate. He finished off his third cup of coffee, feeling his mind clear and his muscles pump up. He was trying to catch the blonde's eye for another cup when an office door shot open in back, sending chips of plaster flying from the wall it smashed into. A brunette stormed out, her nostrils flared, her jaw clenched, her anger so visceral it turned heads.

Her Melonz T-shirt was stretched tight across her breasts and knotted beneath them to reveal nicely sculpted abs. Her faded jeans fit her like spray-paint, knees worn, leg-bottoms shredded. Scud-re thought she was pleasantly plump in her rear and her breasts, as befit a huwoman sneaking into her thirties. The woman's molten dark-chocolate eyes were a little too close-set for her face and her nose bent to the left from a break that was never set right, yet somehow she made it work. The woman practically oozed a wild, spicy, real-human spirit that appealed to Scud-re.

The brunette slipped behind the bar where the other waitress was arranging glasses.

"Jemma, where have you been?" asked the blonde.

"Eating Dick-brain Dave's shit."

Scud-re's waitress gave "Jemma" an empathetic smirk. "Twelve's been bitching for unleaded."

Jemma grabbed a fresh pot of decaf. Scud-re admired the way her bicep flexed from the weight. She strode toward table twelve, the steam from her pot wafting behind her like a vapor trail of fury. Scud-re thought this strong, fierce huwoman seemed like the perfect candidate to carry his clone, but he couldn't imagine how to broach the subject, even if the opportunity arose.

Table twelve hosted two grim chemical-blonde octogenarian MRs, probably escapees from the nursing home down the street. Their garish makeup gave testament to their failing eyesight and they clutched their purses like hyenas hoarding carrion. They scowled when Jemma splashed coffee on their table. *There goes your tip*, thought Scud-re.

As Jemma headed back to the bar, Scud-re called out "Miss?" She ignored him. He raised his voice, "Hey! Can I get some more coffee, please?"

In a sudden shift of rage-driven momentum, Jemma whirled on her heels to face him and, as Scud-re held up his cup with an impish grin, she slipped and the entire pot of scalding liquid spilled into his lap.

"I UNDERSTAND YOU had an unfortunate accident," said Dr. Hosep-ra.

Scud-re groaned through gritted teeth as he waited for the anesthesiologist to arrive with some Accupleasure to moderate the agony.

The young doctor raised the sheet to examine Scud-re's groin, gently prodding the inflamed organ. Scud-re screamed.

"Let's not be melodramatic," said Dr. Hosep-ra.

"Will there be any damage to my, uh... functionality?" asked Scud-re.

"It's not like you're human. You should regen by tonight."

Moments after Dr. Hosep-ra left the room, Jemma appeared in the doorway. Scud-re was struck by her effortless sensuality. She was a scorcher in more ways than one.

"I came to apologize," she said.

He looked past her at three human orderlies staring

hungrily, like dogs watching their kibble being scooped. "Come on in," he said.

The hospital-room door considered the issues and slid closed behind her. She put out her hand and said, "Jemma Haley."

Scud-re was too exhausted to raise his hand. She lowered hers with an understanding smile.

A bedpan sat in the visitor's chair so she settled on the edge of the bed, crossing her legs and leaning on one arm with her breasts so close to his face that no amount of self-control could stop him from looking. He'd learned the hard way that human females could be touchy about males staring at certain body parts, but this huwoman didn't seem to mind. His pupils settled in her cleavage where a small gold crucifix hung from a delicate chain.

"I'm sorry you got hurt," she said.

Scud-re resisted the urge to cop some MR attitude, make her sweat over what she'd done. He inexplicably wanted this magnetic woman to like him. "It was an accident," he said.

"I got fired for it if that makes you feel any better."

The gloom in her voice aroused Scud-re's radar. Maybe he could turn her misfortune into a stroke of luck for both of them.

"Makes me feel worse," he said. "Is there anything I can do to help?"

"You could give the bad news to my son." He was dumbfounded. She smiled and said, "Just kidding."

She's fertile, he thought. "I might have a job for you." She uncrossed her legs, then recrossed them in the other direction, as if the prospect of a job offer just an hour after her firing seemed too coincidental for comfort.

"You'd want to hire me after what I did to you?"

"People make mistakes. You're only human."

She laughed. It was an easy, husky laugh. He liked it.

"Okay," she said. "You've got my attention."

"It would only be for nine months. But if you qualify, I could pay you ninety thousand dollars."

Her eyes went almost as wide as an MR's pupils.

"Ninety? As in nine oh?"

"That's right."

"What do I have to do? Murder somebody?"

"Just the opposite: give birth to somebody. A clone. Assuming your womb is functional."

"Surrogates don't make that kind of money. What's the catch?"

"It's... a celebrity."

THE WOMAN WORE black mini-nuke bandoliers that crossed her chest in an X, separating her improbably large breasts to stretch her bra-top so tight her nipples threatened to spike through. But Ozzie's attention was fixed on the bazooka nuke she held against her leg.

"Ozzie?" He must have heard his name but he didn't budge. "Ozzie!"

A rat the size of a Rottweiler raced toward him down the post-apocalyptic street. Ozzie blasted it and swung back before the woman could raise her weapon. Then the world went blank.

Ozzie turned to see his mother behind him, finger poised to air-toggle the wall in case he tried to resume play.

"Why'd you turn off my game?"

"Go wash your hands. It's time for dinner, then homework."

Shoulders slumped, he trudged toward the bathroom to run his hands under water. Jemma pretended not to hear him mumbling something like "friggin' bitch." She surveyed the cramped one-bedroom unit with its cheap Goodwill furniture and wondered what kind of home she could provide with ninety-thousand dollars. Surely someplace whose thin walls weren't cheap faux titanium, and whose ceilings weren't century-old, sadly indestructible cottage cheese.

Jemma stepped into her small kitchenette to decant the cicada chili she'd brought home from Parker Center, a gastropub in the old police department headquarters, now a popular spot for MRs to pick up human prostitutes of every sex and proclivity.

As she zapped the Parker's take-out in the old-fashioned microwave, she contemplated the daunting prospect of another pregnancy. She knew that women were genetically programmed to forget the pain of childbirth over time so they'd be inclined to repeat the experience--some sort of survival mechanism to guarantee reproduction of the species. But Jemma's DNA somehow lost that gene. After more than thirteen years, the pain of delivering Ozzie was still etched in her memory like an epitaph on a gravestone. Delivery was an ordeal she did not want to repeat, especially for a child she'd be giving up at birth.

Ozzie walked in and grabbed a stool by the tiny shelf they used as a table. He took one look at the chili and rolled his eyes.

"Can't we pretend we're a normal family once in a while and go out to McGoogle's?" he said.

"You stop getting D's and F's, you can have a GigaMac every night for a month."

She handed him a NutriCoke from the fridge.

"Why bother?" he said. "School don't mean shit."

"School *doesn't* mean shit."

"What?"

"It's not 'don't mean shit,' it's 'doesn't mean shit' and you mean to say 'does mean shit.'"

"What friggin' difference does it make?"

"It makes the difference between sounding like an uneducated idiot or someone who might talk his way into a decent job."

"Like Melonz? Oops, I forgot. You lost that job."

His sarcasm cut like a laser blade. She swallowed her pride and spooned his dinner into a bowl.

"All the good jobs go to Mahktards anyway," he said.

"You need to be ready. Opportunities come up."

"Yeah? Where's yours?"

She considered telling him about Scud-re's offer but if she couldn't wrap her own mind around it, how could she expect a thirteen-year-old to understand? Especially a kid as bitter as Ozzie. She marveled at how much she loved this insensitive pit of negativity. It was no wonder the MRs found human maternal love so bewildering. She put a hand on her stomach, hoping to feel some sort of premonition, perhaps a sign from God, but all she felt was indigestion.

By noon the next day Scud-re was out of the hospital. He went straight back to work. Jemma was already in the building, two floors down, enduring a marathon gynecological exam. A few minutes after four o'clock she walked into his lab.

"I'm cleared to bear clones," she said, taking a seat.

"I've already sent an advance to your cash account," he said. "It should cover your back rent and more."

"I haven't agreed to the job yet."

"You came in for the physical. I wanted to pay you for that time. But it's a pittance compared to the fee you'll get if you agree to carry him."

"It's going to be a boy?"

"Yes."

She thought about this, but to Scud-re's relief, she didn't ask about the clone's identity. He couldn't believe she wasn't curious but he supposed she might want the child to remain anonymous to make it easier to give him up after delivery.

The door slid open and an auto-cart rolled in.

"Your eggs," said Scud-re. They'd been extracted during her physical. After completing his DNA sequencing, Scud-rewould replace the nuclei in her egg cells with nano-engineered duplicates of the nucleus that gave birth to Christ.

Jemma watched Scud-re take a rack of small vials from the

235

cart. He handled them gently, almost lovingly, as he bent his tall frame to store them in his under-counter freezer.

"You act like they're precious," she said.

"They are to me."

He turned and caught her grinning.

"Will you do it?" he asked.

"I have to do something to keep a roof over our heads."

Not long afterward, Jemma walked out of the restroom in a mint-green hospital gown. Despite all the Mahk-Ra innovation bestowed on humankind, it amazed Scud-rethat no one had reinvented these ridiculous gowns. She hopped onto the table. Scud-repositioned a pantoscan probe--like a marble on a gold wire--over her belly. He swung it gently in a circle.

The pantoscan imaged Jemma's abdominal anatomy above Scud-re'shand, floating in the air in lifelike 3-D. He set the scanner down and reached into the image, double-tapping her small intestines and her bladder. Both organs disappeared, leaving her womb unobscured.

"Panto transparency sixty," he said. Her imaged organs grew translucent so that he could see them both inside and out simultaneously.

"Is this going to hurt?"

"You may feel a little cramping, but not too bad."

He swiveled her virtual anatomy toward him to make it easier to access the image of her vagina. As he orchestrated movements in the air, a snakelike robotic embedding arm replicated his actions inside Jemma, making its own corrections for any unsteadiness in his hands. Ten minutes later she was pregnant.

It was a mechanical conception, but to Scud-re it felt like the best sex he'd ever had.

"Hey, Ma. Where's the brew?"

The question struck Jemma as odd. Why would her thirteen-year old be looking for beer?

She rose from the couch and walked into the kitchen. Ozzie was standing in front of their worn-out refrigerator staring at the empty shelf she usually stocked with pale ale. Someone had invaded her home and taken it.

"You're letting out the cold," she told Ozzie. "No shopping in Fridgie."

He grabbed a NutriCoke and closed the door.

"Yo Fridgie," she said to wake its attention. "Where's my ale?"

"Sorry, Jemma," said the fridge. "Beer has been forbidden."

Those assholes broke into my home, she thought, *stealing my brew and reprogramming my food supply.*

Ozzie left the room and she heard him boot up the living room wall to play one of his real-games. The sounds of gunfire and pulse bursts filled the air.

Jemma glanced at her nip nook. They'd taken her hard liquor, too. They would have needed a Rules and Regs override to violate her private space, and override warrants required more juice than a scientist like Scud-re would have, especially since he was Mahk-Re. What sort of freaky life form was she carrying in her womb that not only caught the attention of Upper Esche, but demanded their intervention?

SCUD-RE NERVOUSLY TWIRLED the pantoscan probe, waiting for Jemma to get undressed. It had been four months since Rhea-ra sent Scud-re's proposal upstairs and it still hadn't been approved. The delay could only mean someone up the chain was raising objections. Scud-re's dick would hit the fan if Upper Esche denied this project and then found out Jemma was well into her second trimester. But that was a risk he was willing to take if it would get him back to civilization. He was sick of kowtowing to the MR military thugs who'd been sent here to run this wasteland of a planet.

Jemma came out of the restroom and walked past him to the examination table, her hospital gown giving him a sweet flash of butt cheeks. She caught him looking and glared.

"You don't look happy," he said.

"Someone broke into my place and stole my booze," she said. "Did you know they were going to do that?"

"Your contract forbids alcohol," said Scud-re. "It can malform the clone." He immediately regretted his officious tone. He didn't want Jemma to see him as a typical MR.

"Who did it, Dr. Scud-re? Upper Esche doesn't even know I'm pregnant."

He looked away, embarrassed to have been put in this position by Rhea-re. Over Scud-re's objections, the department head had insisted on cleansing Jemma's home site of potential fetal toxins before Upper Esche had even weighed in on the project.

"The brass can be a little overzealous," he said sheepishly.

She glared at him with those pools of cocoa and he felt like a turd. Even worse, like a human turd.

"I don't know why I'm making excuses for them," he said. "I'm sorry."

He was heartened when Jemma seemed surprised. MRs rarely apologized to humans. Her expression softened.

She lay down on the examination table. Scud-re swung the pantoscan over her Y-axis, from cranium to coccyx.

"Why is Upper Esche even interested in me?" asked Jemma. "What's so important about this baby?"

"Let me concentrate." Scud-re, side-stepped the question. "We'll talk later." He reached into her virtual anatomy to feel for physical anomalies that the pantoscan might miss. As he ran his hand along her virtual womb, she reached up and grabbed his arm.

"Don't be such a Makhwonk," she said, and moved his hand from her virtual anatomy to her actual one. "Here's what real life feels like."

The soft flesh of her belly seemed electric to his touch. If he could have flushed with embarrassment, he would have. He tried to withdraw his hand but she held it firmly against her.

"You're as close as he's got to a father," she said.

He smiled and relaxed his hand, moving his fingers to gently palpate.

"You're different from the others," she said. "Tender. Sort of caring. Almost human."

He smiled again. "I'll take that as a compliment."

And then the fetus kicked. Scud-re jerked his hand away, as if he'd been burned. Jemma pulled it back.

"Feel the life, Dr. Scud-re. Because you're the one who put it there. You went deep inside my womb and you planted it. You connected my baby to me. You made it mine. It's like we made love, only without the fun part."

His heartbeat trilled at the thought. One of the most unexpected perks for MRs on Earth was the pleasure of passion. Back on Ra-Prime, reproduction was a job, not a joy. Despite MR supremacy in most things, sexuality was a standout bastion of human superiority. Erogenous zones were playgrounds for humans, but minefields for MRs.

Jemma stared into his large green eyes as if trying to decipher a code, then gave him a teasing grin.

"You're a virgin, aren't you?"

He said nothing but his pupils gave him away.

"I knew it," she said, amused. "You can kiss me if you want."

He was mesmerized. He'd only dreamed of feeling her lips on his. He leaned over and wondered, as he kissed his first human, why she closed her eyes. Her lips were impossibly soft and warm and moist and bursting with an energy he couldn't describe. And then the most amazing thing happened: she parted her lips and he felt her tongue. He thought he would melt right there in the lab. He'd never experienced a feeling like this before. His legs trembled. She sensed the strength of his reaction and pulled away to watch.

"Wow," he said. "Is it always like that?"

"Not always," she said, "but when there's an emotional bond... like having a child together...."

Scud-re tried to understand the connection between the kiss and the clone, but the logic escaped him.

"So tell me, Dr. Daddy," she said, "who is this child of ours?"

Scud-re braced himself for a storm. "He's going to make history. His DNA comes from the blood of Jesus Christ."

It took her a moment to ingest the concept, and even then, it didn't quite register. She hadn't been to church in years, but she'd been raised Catholic and still believed in Jesus as Lord. The fact that she was carrying Him in her belly defied her comprehension.

"You're telling me I'm carrying the son of God?"

Before Scud-re could reply, the door opened and Dr. Huxen-ra marched in. Hux started at the sight of a woman in a hospital gown in Scud-re's lab.

"What's going on here?" he demanded.

"Hux, meet Jemma," said Scud-re. "Jemma, this is Dr. Huxen-ra, my supervisor."

Jemma was too staggered by Scud-re's clone revelation to speak.

"Jemma has graciously agreed to be our surrogate," said Scud-re.

Huxen-ra's mouth opened, then closed. He took a moment to compose himself.

"I'm sorry Dr. Scudre," he said, "but Upper Esche has put the kibosh on the clone. They're afraid this birth will turn into a massive disruptor, the kind that sparks human revolts. Two-hundred thousand Mahk-Ra and twenty million humans died in the First Interplanetary War. Upper Esche wants to avoid a repeat."

"They have to reconsider!" said Scud-re. "This birth is too important!"

Jemma saw the interference pattern of fear roll across Huxen-ra's pupils. His ass was on the line along with Scud-re's.

"You're not hearing me, Scud-re. This wasn't just a local decision."

Scud-re's jaw dropped. "This edict came from Ra-Prime?"

"It went all the way up to the Senate of Commanders."

"Hello?" said Jemma. "Don't I get a say in this?"

"No!" Scud-re snapped.

Jemma realized he hadn't told Hux about her pregnancy and was afraid to tell him now. Her immaculate conception had become their dirty little secret. Scud-re was treating her like some dumb high school girl who'd gotten knocked up under the bleachers, and she didn't like it.

"Your Senate of Commanders can eat shit," she blurted. "I'm already pregnant."

Scud-Re looked like he'd been shot in the stomach. For a moment, time seemed to stop.

Then Huxen-Ra's pupils exploded in a virtual fireworks display. He wheeled on Scud-re and shouted, "You keep your mouth shut and terminate this pregnancy today!"

Long-buried beliefs overwhelmed Jemma like zombies leaping from their graves. *Abortion is murder. Mortal sin leads to Damnation. Christ is our Savior.*

"No fucking way," she said. "I'll die before I let you kill my baby."

Dr. Huxen-ra was astonished at the nerve of this uppity human. "If you insist," he said, and stormed out.

Jemma leapt off the table, primed to bury her nails in Scud-

241

re's bleary pupils, a lioness rearing to defend her cub.

"Do you honestly think I would hurt you?" said Scud-re. "We need to get out of here."

They managed to sneak out the back and she took him to the only place she knew where an MR and a human could sit together without drawing attention: Parker Center. The lighting was dim, allowing MRs to remove their glasses. Most of the women were dressed to reveal their wares. Jemma felt like the only female in the room who wasn't trying to peddle a happy ending. The bar was raucous, befitting an inter-species meat market, but the back of the place was quiet as newly-paired couples sought private tables to conduct soto voce negotiations.

Scud-re and Jemma settled into a back booth and Scud-re's eyes scanned the room. A human waitress approached and leaned in to give Scud-re a good look down her blouse as she took their order. Jemma remembered being coached to show "tits for tips" at Melonz. That seemed like a lifetime ago.

After the waitress left, Jemma said, "I guess I can kiss my ninety thousand dollars goodbye."

Scud-re looked up with tremulous waves in his pupils.

"You'll be lucky to live through the night."

"They wouldn't dare. Even MRs have laws."

"This isn't the local cops," he said. "The Senate of Commanders *makes* the law. They *enforce* the law. They *are* the law."

"You're going to let them murder our baby after you felt him kicking?"

"Of course not." Scud-re looked miserable. "But that doesn't mean I can stop them."

Then he saw something over her shoulder and the turbulence in his pupils receded. Jemma turned to see a young woman crossing the room, barely five feet tall and skinny as a stick figure. She had striking blue eyes and jet-black, bowl-cut hair except for a braid that hung down past her shoulder.

The woman slid into the booth beside Scud-re and stared at Jemma.

"This is the womb?" she asked in an unpleasantly high-pitched rasp.

"Who the hell are you?" said Jemma.

She turned to Scud-re looking surprised. "Didn't you tell her?" She had a scar across her throat--maybe a knife wound--and Jemma wondered if that explained the annoying voice.

"Jemma, meet Valerie," said Scud-re, then whispered, "Red Spear."

Jemma was stunned. The Red Spear were the planet's most violent, radical anti-occupationists. How could Scud-re be involved with these human resistance terrorists? He read her expression.

"I'm Mahk-Re," he said. "The Mahk-Ra have oppressed us for centuries. I know what you humans are going through. So I help where I can."

"He's been feeding us intelligence," said Valerie.

Jemma felt a budding admiration for Scud-re, but she still didn't trust Red Spear.

"Why are you telling me this?"

"Because we humans are at war," said Valerie.

"I'm not," said Jemma. "I don't even vote. And I don't believe in terrorism."

Valerie guffawed.

"They're not terrorists," said Scud-re. "That's just MR propaganda."

"That's why we need baby Jesus," said Valerie. "So he can grow up spreading the gospel of humanity and proving the absurdity of MR accusations. With Christ as the face of Red Spear, the world will rally to our cause."

"You think I'm going to let a bunch of armed revolutionaries raise my child?"

"You'll never survive without us," said Valerie. "No one

SECOND COMING

else has the resources to keep you safe."

"Safe? Running from MR Nazis in some underground netherworld? How am I supposed to raise two kids on the run?"

"I know this is all happening fast," said Scud-re, "but your old life ended the second you told Hux about the clone."

"You've got a propaganda bonanza in your belly," said Valerie. "And your other son is in grave danger."

"Why would anyone hurt Ozzie?"

"They'll grab him to control you. It's what they do. Like it or not, you're an outlaw now."

JEMMA RUSHED INTO her apartment, relieved to find Ozzie drinking a glass of tomato juice while actually doing his homework. His implanted temporal node glowed through the skin of his temple as algebra formulas from the middle school satellite streamed into his memory. She could see him straining to understand.

"Ozzie, we have to go."

He roused himself out of in-load mode. "What?"

She snatched the tomato juice out of his hand. "Go pack a bag. Now."

"Where are we going?"

"I'll explain on the way. You've got five minutes to throw some stuff in an overnight bag. Take what you care about, we may not be coming back. And wear your gym shoes; we may have to do some running."

"But..."

The front door slid open, despite redundant security locks, and two MR shock troopers rushed in. The glass slipped from Jemma's hand, smashing on the floor, sending tomato juice spewing like blood. The first MR was a good seven-three or four, wiry and nervous. Jemma could see red sparks in his pupils even through his dark glasses. Behind him came a female, a

244

few inches shorter and thicker in the torso. Her glasses revealed nothing. Both were heavily armed and wore their storm-trooper jumpers with the Mahkanese symbol for "overlord" emblazoned on their collars like silver Omegas.

Ozzie stood up, eyes glued to the intruders.

"Get out of here!" screamed Jemma. "You have no right!"

"Where is Dr. Scud-re?" said the tall one.

"I don't know," said Jemma.

"All right, we'll do this the hard way," he said. Then, to the thick one, "Get the boy."

Ozzie took off. The tall one raised his pulse rifle, but Jemma lunged, knocking his aim off. A blue burst singed through the wall leaving a hole the size of a grapefruit. The other soldier swung her arm into Jemma's brow, slamming the back of her head into the wall. Jemma struggled to stay conscious as Ozzie fled through the back door. The mocks, with their heavy body armor, would never catch him before he disappeared into the streets of the human ghetto. Jemma's last thought before she blacked out was, *Thank God, Ozzie listened for a change.*

JEMMA WAS FLOATING in deep space, her thoughts erupting like popping corn. Would the baby Jesus worship his older brother as younger sibs were wont to do? Would he crawl after Ozzie like a little duckling? Would Ozzie turn the Lord into a video-game addict? Or teach him to hate school and disrespect his mother? Would her new son be able to perform miracles? How does a mom survive the terrible twos with a toddler who can move mountains? How absurd it seemed that she, a woman who couldn't even survive Melonz, was chosen to carry the Holy Embryo.

She woke hard, trying to feel her womb to reassure herself that her baby wasn't hurt. But her hand wouldn't move. Jemma realized she was spread-eagled in mid-air, suspended and immobilized by some sort of force field. She looked around but couldn't see much of the room. The dim lighting implied that she was in an MR facility.

Jemma wondered where Ozzie was. How would he feed himself? Where would he sleep? Not counting his virtual world, he had little experience interacting with strangers. He would be easy prey for the black marketeers and outcasts who roamed the streets. As her fears approached panic, the door slid open and a short MR, barely six-three, walked into the room. He was portly, wearing a dark gray suit buttoned up so tightly that Jemma could see his shirt through the straining seams. His gray hair was close-cropped and he had bushy black eyebrows, below which one of his pupils was cloudy, like a giant cataract.

"Where am I?" she said.

He ignored her. "You can call me Mr. P. That's 'P' for pleasure or 'P' for pain. Up to you."

His speech was precise, unnaturally formal, no accent.

"What do you want?"

"Your clone, of course. After that, you are nothing but an empty vessel to me."

"My baby's not up for grabs."

"Of course he is not up for grabs; he is mine. He is *my* baby now. *My* little god. *My* little guinea pig."

The pressure of the force field amplified the shudder of terror that coursed through her. "What are you going to do to him?"

"Nothing that's not typically human. His formative years will be spent in a string of abusive foster homes. I will ensure he is addicted to drugs by the time he is fifteen. Then he will be incarcerated for an extended stay in an underfunded, understaffed juvenile RZ camp where I will allow him to ripen to the point of rot. Around age seventeen, he will be squatting in a rat-infested vacant hovel in a gang neighborhood where he can make new friends and harden his criminal skills. He'll be arrested and sentenced for a few years in a maximum security penitentiary for an immersive education in racial hatred. I will be his guardian angel through all this to make sure the prodigal Son survives being beaten, sexually abused, overdosed with street drugs, shot in a drive-by and shivved in prison.

"By his twentieth birthday, the Divine Jesus will be a depraved, violent, depressed, ex-con junkie bigot, ready for his grand global debut. I will present the Son of God to you pitiable Earthlings with so much fanfare that every human on the planet will be forced to see how pathetic the false idols you worship are, how wretched they are in the shadow of the glorious Mahk-Ra."

Jemma felt herself being sucked into a black vortex of doom. She made a desperate grasp for one last flicker of faith.

"Jesus won't fail us," she said. "He shall overcome. And everyone, no matter what their religion, no matter what their planet of origin, will witness the miracle and lay down their arms."

Mr. P burst out laughing. "Bravo, Ms. Haley. *Très amusant.* But, in the face of an undeniably fallen God, clear evidence of the absurdity of all human religions, do you really expect any intelligent being, or any human for that matter, to choose faith over what they can see with their own eyes?"

"The Lord works in mysterious ways."

"Be that as it may, His alleged son is already mine. That is not why I am here. There is something else you're going to do for me."

Jemma's heart sank. She'd heard this come-on at Melonz. The thought of having sex with this fat, weasely, Cyclops of a Mahktard....

"You're going to tell me where to find Dr. Scud-re."

She felt awash with relief, her predicament notwithstanding. They still hadn't caught Scud-re. He must have blown his cover and gone underground with the Red Spear cell. Why else would they be so intent on finding him?

"I have no idea where he is," she said.

Mr. P's face scrunched into a frown without the help of his dead eye. Facial paralysis should have been a simple fix for MR doctors, but Jemma suspected his was an intentional affectation to rattle his victims.

"I'm giving you a choice," he said. "I can keep you here in comfort until you give birth and then I'll set you free to go find your teenaged boy and live out your pitiful life as best you can, or I can bind you in the force-field until the progeny arrives, then dump you on a garbage heap, immobilized but fully conscious to savor the sensation of rats slowly gnawing their way through your flesh and into your organs, till death does you in."

She never imagined she could feel so much loathing for another being.

"I can't tell you what I don't know."

Mr. P moved his finger to describe an arc in the air and she felt the force field follow the shape, bending her back into an unnatural curve like a bow being drawn to the breaking point. She shrieked as her vertebrae stabbed into her sciatic nerves, sending an excruciating pain down her spine and into her legs. Mr. P waited a moment, then relaxed the force field.

"Torturing humans is so boring," he said. "Please don't make me do it all day. Just tell me how you were supposed to contact him."

"I wasn't."

He sighed with mock-sadness and rebent the field.

Every nerve in her body felt like it was being shredded by a dull handsaw. Jemma thought her spine was going to snap. She started to weep.

"I guess we'll have to do some permanent spinal damage," said Mr. P, raising his hand like an orchestra conductor.

Jemma clenched her teeth, steeling for the worst. Then an

248

explosive blast knocked a chunk out of the exterior wall. Mr. P turned, surprised. Automatic fire burst through the hole and severed his head from his neck like a scythe. Jemma watched in shock as his head bounced off the floor before his body had time to collapse. She gagged but managed to keep the contents of her stomach from erupting.

Four more explosions simultaneously pierced the wall, then laser torches finished cutting through it, outlining a rectangular hole from floor to ceiling, about the width of a one-car garage. The torches snapped off and the circumscribed block of three-feet-thick fortified wall started to inch into the room. It made a horrendous din as the weight of steel and granite scraped across the rough concrete floor, pushed from behind by a tremendous force.

Jemma heard alarm sirens wail, then the door to the room burst open and MR security guards streamed in, faces hidden behind protective uberglass shields, pulsing blindly through the breached exterior wall. From outside, the invaders perforated the wall with return fire and the room reverberated with the pulsing force of the Bleaters being used by the MRs. Jemma screamed in the crossfire, but the energy field that encased her also protected her from the fireflak.

The massive rectangle was finally forced all the way into the room by a robotic ram, creating a passage to the outside. A gas grenade went off. Red Spear invaders, wearing gas masks and headlamps, stormed in through the passage, some armed with pulse-weapons but many firing Uzis and even handguns. The MR guards, despite superior weapons, were badly trained, outmanned, unmotivated, blinded by the high-intensity lights and overcome by gas. They retreated from the room, presumably to regroup. An eerie silence ensued.

Jemma scanned what rebel soldiers she could see without moving her head. Only two of them were tall enough to be Mahk-Ras, so Jemma assumed the rest were humans. She yearned to see faces, to make human connections, but they all wore gas masks.

One of the rebels keyed something into a touchscreen on the wall. Jemma felt the force field gently lower her to the ground and then shut down. As the field dissipated, residual gas hit her throat, squeezing it closed like a sphincter. She clutched her neck, feeling death closing in fast. She wrapped her arms around her belly, frantic to protect her fetus. Then someone stuck a gas mask on her face and life flowed back with a rush of air. Her panic seemed to disappear into a black hole as her mind slowed to a workable pace.

She looked up at the MR who'd attached her mask. Despite their two faceplates, she recognized Scud-re. He lifted her in his arms and carried her out through the hole in the wall. She'd never before felt so free.

JEMMA LAY IN a hospital bed, hands resting on her swollen belly, thumbs nervously twiddling.

"Relax," said Scud-re. "It'll be over in a few minutes." He took her hand.

"The pantoscan said I'm not due for three weeks. Why can't I just wait?"

"Natural childbirth is too risky. Pre-due C-secs are virtually foolproof with MR surgical apps. Don't be scared."

He bent over and gave her a gentle kiss on her furrowed brow.

She squeezed his hand. "I love you, Scud-re."

She doubted he understood the human implications of her words, but she hoped he'd learn over time.

Valerie wheeled Jemma's bed into the delivery room. The walls were lined with empty safe-deposit box compartments, their doors hanging open. The abandoned bank vault was brightly lit and furnished with the best medical equipment the black market could supply. Everyone wore surgical gowns and sani-filters over mouths and noses. Three obstetricians were in attendance along with a team of nurses.

A short Asian man with long red hair leaned over Jemma. "I'm Dr. Nyne. I'll be your primary physician."

"This place isn't much of a hospital," said Jemma.

"Beats a manger." He smiled. "Now don't worry, you won't feel a thing."

He nodded to a nurse who injected some smart anesthetics into Jemma's bicep. She would remain conscious and mobile but the anesthesia controller would monitor her nerve activity and block any pain.

Scud-re watched with an expression of fatherly pride as Dr. Nyne booted the C-section Bot, initializing the automated procedure. The bot hovered above Jemma's belly, ready to lase.

"Halt!" The voice was booming, startling.

They all turned to see a woman, the spitting image of former Vice-President Angelina Jolie. She stood in the doorway, a gold crucifix tattooed on her forehead, a six-inch gold cross on a choker around her neck.

"Reverend Paylon," said Dr. Nyne impatiently, "we're trying to perform a birth here."

"This is not just a birth, Doctor," she said. "This is a holy event that shall change the course of history and be remembered for millennia. It is the Second Coming of He who is destined to save Earth from the plague that has rained down upon us from the skies. And that creature," Paylon pointed at Scud-re, "is a heathen from the enemy's ranks. For all you know he is here to make sure the baby Jesus never sees the light of day."

"You don't even know him!" shouted Jemma.

"I ask you, Doctor," said Paylon. "Have you even met this MR before today?"

Dr. Nyne's fallen face answered her question.

"I thought not," said the reverend. "And yet you are willing to gamble the future of our entire civilization on this Mahktard."

"I know him," said Valerie.

"Are you questioning the judgment of a regional commander?" said Paylon.

"No," said Valerie sourly.

Paylon gripped her crucifix and signaled for two guards to come forward to seize Scud-re. He struggled against the burly militiamen, but he was outmatched. Jemma jumped off the gurney and grabbed the articulated arm of the C-section Bot. She swung it hard, smacking it into the face shield of the nearest guard. He went down and Scud-re pulled free from the other. Scud-re wheeled toward Valerie who turned away to clear their path to the exit. Scud-re and Jemma took off.

"For the love of God," said Paylon, "do I have to do everything?"

She extracted a concealed mini laser torch from the tip of her cross. Jemma smelled burning plastic as she and Scud-re ran out and Paylon wielded her weapon. They ran down a tubular hall. With the extra weight of the baby, Jemma was already losing steam. She could hear MR pursuers, not far behind and getting closer.

"My body can't do this," she said. "You go on without me."

"I could never leave you here alone," said Scud-re. "We're going to get out of here together. You, me and our baby."

Maybe love wasn't so foreign to him after all. He took her hand and led her into a service tunnel. She prayed they didn't have far to go. Her legs were feeling weak.

A stab of sunlight caught Jemma's attention. She looked up and saw it coming from the grip-notch of a manhole cover. They were under the street.

"There," she said, pointing.

A rusted iron ladder ran up the wall to the manhole. Scud-re scurried up and wedged his shoulder against the heavy steel plate, the tendons in his neck distending from the strain. The cover was starting to lift when a guard rounded the corner and fired a handgun. The bullet went straight through Scud-re's chest. Jemma screamed.

Scud-re's eyes locked on Jemma's, pain sculpting his face. But his pupils retained their fire. The through-and-through hadn't killed him. She prayed it wasn't just a matter of time. Dark green blood was blooming through his shirt at a frightening pace.

Scud-re held a hand to his wound, as if he needed pressure to curb the pain, and gave another heave. The thick metal plate finally flopped over, revealing the sky through the manhole. Scud-re reached down for Jemma, but a guard grabbed her from behind. The other raised his weapon for a second shot.

"Run!" shouted Jemma.

"No," said Scud-re. He raised his hands in surrender. "Not without you."

Paylon strode into the tunnel as Scud-re hopped off the ladder, landing unsteadily. His shirt was completely blood-soaked now, front and back.

"You didn't have to shoot him!" Jemma shrieked. "He's on your side!"

Paylon smirked. "When are you going to learn to act human? He's not our kind." She motioned at a guard: "Lock her up. When she goes into labor, strap her down."

Jemma's fuse lit up but before she could retort she was seized by a sudden contraction. She felt as if someone was wringing her womb. She had strayed too far; the anesthesia controller was out of range. Her agony doubled her over.

"Captain!" barked Paylon. "Time her contractions."

That's when Jemma's water broke. It felt like the forty-day flood was surging from her womb. The service tunnel had become a chaos of babel and bodies in motion. Jemma heard Paylon shouting for the obstetrics team. Then Scud-re was somehow beside her, helping her gently to the ground, wiping her hair out of her eyes.

Jemma was slammed by another spasm of monumental pain. An orderly came running down the hall pushing a gurney. Dr. Nyne and Valerie followed close behind, along with several nurses and, judging by their dress suits, a few Red Spear rebels.

Paylon shouted at the guards, "Strap her down! Now!"

The orderly locked the gurney's wheels in preparation for loading Jemma.

In a trough between tidal waves of pain, Jemma became aware of the hungry stares of the people surrounding. They looked like vultures. Every last one of them wanted to take her baby. *Fuck. Them.*

The guards moved in and she thrashed out furiously, her violence fueled by her pain. An inhuman shriek came out of her mouth that stunned the guards.

Suddenly the tunnel was filled with the rapid-fire sound of serial bursts and five guards went down like bowling pins. The others turned, weapons rising, to see a rogue guard, pulse rifle vibrating. His aim was true, every shot hitting its mark in the throat, just below the face shield. Only one guard got off a responding shot and it was wayward. The others died with their weapons cold. Only the unarmed went unharmed.

Paylon's hand crept toward her crucifix.

"I'll take that!" shouted the guard, and ripped the cross from Paylon's neck.

Jemma's heart did a loop-the-loop at the sound of his voice. "Ozzie?"

The guard raised his face shield to reveal her son. He'd survived the streets. She looked around at the carnage and appreciated, for the first time, the hand-eye coordination he'd developed from his endless hours of gaming.

She was still stooped in pain so Ozzie crouched before her. "You okay, Mom?" he said.

His lip was split and his forehead scraped and scabbed. His

hair was greasy and knotted, his face streaked with filth. She'd never seen anything so beautiful.

Paylon glared at Ozzie. "We saved your life," she said. "You would have been eaten alive out there. We gave you a home."

"You lied to me," said Ozzie. "You said you wanted to save humanity. Then you treated my pregnant mother like shit and tried to kill the one guy who was protecting her."

Ungrateful as always, thought Jemma proudly.

Scud-re turned to Jemma. "We need to get out of here."

"The MRs will kill you," said Paylon. "They'll take the Christ child."

"No one's taking my baby," said Jemma. "Not them, not you."

She rose to her feet and Scud-re helped her painstakingly climb the ladder, the girth of her belly forcing her to ascend sideways. Ozzie came last, his weapon trained on the rebels left standing.

Scud-re pulled himself onto the street, then helped Jemma crawl from the manhole.

Ozzie stopped on the last rung and called down: "You try to follow us, I'll waste you, I swear to God!" Then he, too, scrambled onto the street. As Scud-re pushed the manhole cover back in place it suddenly heated and burned his hand. Someone's vain attempt to pierce the steel with a bleater.

"We're free," said Ozzie.

Jemma and Scud-re exchanged a glance that bespoke the unfathomable hurdles they had yet to clear before they were likely to feel any semblance of freedom.

"At least we're together," said Jemma.

They'd come out in an empty alley, strewn with rat-hole riddled garbage bags spilling rancid food and unidentifiable waste. The stench was overwhelming. Jemma felt like throwing up. They heard the manhole cover rattle as the guards tried to force it open. Scud-re wrestled a hunk of concrete onto the

255

circular plate to weigh it down.

"Where can we go?" said Jemma. Another contraction hit her like a wrecking ball. The cramping knocked her back into a pile of garbage twice her height.

Scud-re knelt between her legs and spread them wide. Ozzie watched stupefied as Scud-re ripped the crotch of Jemma's panties to reveal the dark, wet crown of a large infant's skull straining against an opening half its diameter. Scud-re tried to push his little finger between the vaginal opening and the baby's head but Jemma's flesh was as taut as a snare drum.

She fought to stay conscious through the pain. Her nervous system was in overload, her eyes almost popped out of their sockets and her voice was stuck on auto-scream.

"She needs an episiotomy," Scud-re said in a panicked voice. "Give me that cross!"

"What?"

"Lasers cauterize as they cut."

Ozzie looked confused.

"Just do it!" cried Scud-re.

Ozzie handed over his weapon.

Jemma couldn't understand what was happening. Or why the hell it was happening now. The baby wasn't due for weeks. Why did she feel like the wrath of God was inside her, trying to pry its way out with a crowbar? And in that unbearable moment, she saw the light: the Son of God was coming early to defend his mother.

Scud-re pulled the laser from the cross and laid the barrel against the skullcap to aim the beam at Jemma's perineum without hitting the infant. And then, even though the fetus was still bottlenecked, something caused him to change his mind. He tossed the weapon and dropped his hands beneath the baby. A moment later the Holy infant slid out of Jemma like a bobsled on ice.

"That was one hell of a Second Coming," said Scud-re.

Jemma barely noticed the release of pressure and pain, she was so stunned by the event. Ozzie's childbirth had been natural but it had torn her vagina to shreds. This baby was noticeably bigger than Ozzie had been, yet this birth had left her unscathed, immaculate. The second time around was supposed to be easier, but this seemed too easy. Could it possibly be a miracle?

They all stared at the baby. Waiting for a sign.

"He's not breathing," said Ozzie.

Scud-re lifted the infant aloft and gave it a swat. They all listened intently, as if expecting a Heavenly choir.

Instead, the Son of God began to wail.

THE END

THE DEVIL YOU KNOW

JESSICA KAYE

lijah-ra was the head of security for the Capitol building in Washington, D.C. The Senate and House still held meetings there regarding domestic affairs only, although any Act of Congress had to be authorized by the Mahk-Ra's Seattle command center in order to carry any weight. International affairs didn't really exist. Resolution of any such conflicts had been usurped by the overlords. It behooved the nations that remained to play nicely. Mahk-Ra intervention was invariably ugly, at best.

Elijah-ra's given name was Sorhi-ra. He had been in the second contingent sent to Earth, after the invasion was over and the decisive victory for the outer space warriors had been secured. He had learned most of the languages spoken by mankind before setting foot on the planet. His formal training had been in classrooms with live tutors and furthered at home with electronic media. For idiomatic proficiency, he watched copious amounts of television programs, easily obtained from the intelligence unit's library. From these, he learned that he preferred English and French and so he requested, and was happy to be assigned to, the once United States. Eastern Canada may have been a little better for practicing his spoken language skills since he could have used both languages there but he was a fan of the television programs *Friends* and *The West Wing,* and so had looked forward to seeing what was left of either New York City or Washington, D.C.

He began calling himself Elijah after reading the Old Testament, a storybook he knew humans called the Bible, which he had found in his Washington hotel room, before he had found permanent housing. He had used the Mahk-Ra search engine to learn more about the prophet Elijah. He read about the Jewish tradition of leaving a cup of wine for Elijah on the Passover table, as well as opening the door to let him in, should he wish to slake his thirst. He learned that sometimes there was agreement that the wine level in the cup had diminished and that Elijah must have invisibly sipped from the cup; children were especially susceptible to this belief.

Elijah-ra loved the idea of a dinner guest who was invisible to the other diners. Although he was seven feet tall, he did sometimes imagine himself as a bit of a stealth peace-keeper, casting a benevolent eye over the motley assortment of humankind assigned to his care, just as Elijah kept an eye over those at the Passover table. The creatures should be grateful that a race as superior as the Mahk-Ra had been thoughtful enough to take over their planet, Elijah-ra believed. It had brought order to a disorderly planet and had stopped the squabbling between nations and saved many more lives than it had cost.

There were no rules against changing one's name. The powers that be liked it, if they didn't overtly encourage it. They thought it made their representatives appear to the vanquished Earth citizens to be a little more like them, with names they could pronounce. It made them appear to be just that little bit less foreign.

Despite his chosen name, Elijah was not a prophet like his

Biblical inspiration, but a soldier in this Mahk-ra's army. He was happy in his work. Each day had just enough routine to make him secure in his abilities and just enough variety to keep him on his toes. He even had developed a cadre of friends from his co-workers, both Mahk-Ra, Mahk-Re and humankind. There were all sorts from each species who were thrilled to work on Capitol Hill. Nor was it that unusual any more to see the species mingling. Mixed marriages were few and far between but even that had become less stigmatized. Mahk-Ra highers-up scrutinized the pairings to make sure there wasn't some sort of ill intent in the cross-fraternization. Humans tended to similarly study each couple to try to ascertain whether the human half was in danger of forgetting that he or she was part of the conquered, not the conquering race.

Elijah was not part of a mixed-race couple; his wife, Alina-ra was also Mahk-Ra and she too was stationed in Washington, D.C. Her job was far less exciting than his, he thought. Alina was a curator at the New Alexandria Library. This was the name the Mahk-Ra had bestowed upon what was formerly known as The Library of Congress. The Mahk-Ra archives had recorded the loss of the original Library of Alexandria in ancient Egypt, a library which had been a repository of many books and the destruction of which was considered a great loss to the documentation of culture. The re-naming of the modern dominant nation's repository of all works, great and small, was a sly nod to mankind's early efforts at recording the achievements of its civilization. The proximity of Alexandria, Virginia to the Library of Congress and a sense of humor in the Mahk-Ra Regional Commander in the District of Columbia combined to suggest the new appellation. Alina was a curator, not a librarian, because no one other than a Mahk-Ra was allowed to view or read those books.

At night their routine was familiar to married couples the universe over. They would exchange stories of how their day had been, whether anything of special interest had happened. They might talk about whom they saw at lunch or who didn't show up at work and whether it was due to an appointment, an illness or discipline by the Commander's office. They had a comfortable apartment near Dupont Circle, convenient to work and convenient for their days off, too. They could cross into Maryland or Virginia in no time, to go hiking or shopping at a department store. Occasionally there were outings to the Pentagon, which was less of a pentagon and more of a triangle since the war. L'Enfant had been a clever architect and engineer, instrumental in the layout of the city of Washington, D.C. centuries ago, but his use of traffic circles was more efficient in fooling armies on foot than armies in the air and so not a deterrent to the Mahk-Ra, which had easily attacked the military's headquarters from the airspace above it. There were plans to rebuild in order to provide offices for authorized personnel and to house documents especially germane to sites below the Mason-Dixon line. Some of the Mahk-Ra had even acquired a slight southern accent.

Each workday morning, Elijah and Alina would walk, hand-in-hand, to the Metro stop. They would ride together and alight at the Capital South exit. After seeing Alina to her desk, Elijah would finish his commute by walking through the underground tunnels that linked the buildings. It pleased him that both the Metro and these subterranean passages had been repairable after the Battle of the District of Columbia ended.

All in all, this was just about as great a gig as he had hoped for.

CHRISTMAS WAS NO longer a government-sanctioned holiday but most organizations, whether private or public, were closed. That included Alina's work, but security never sleeps. Elijah reported to work Christmas night to supervise the evening detail.

The entire city was blanketed with snow and, seemingly, with calm. It was pretty nice of the Mahk-Ra, all of the Mahk-Ra thought, not to be hard-nosed about snuffing out the celebrations of any religion. While they completely agreed with the human political philosopher Karl Marx that religion is the opiate of the masses, they disagreed with him as to whether the effect of that opium is for good or for ill. The Regional Commander thought that things were much better when humankind believed some supreme being was looking out for them and would restore a world in which they ruled the Earth once more.

"There is no news to report," Junior Adams, the young day shift guard said to Elijah and his relief, Gene Nohm, a 35-year-old mid-career man. Junior was six feet tall, 23 years old, sandy haired and, by now, sleepy-eyed, having been on duty since 6 a.m. He stood to leave, exiting the chair at the security station by the Capitol's front doors. Elijah and Gene wished Junior a good evening and a happy holiday and then Gene settled in at his post, expertly examining the video monitors in front of him. Gene, also tall at 6 feet, two inches, dark haired and dark eyed, was human; an American native, as was Junior.

It was wise to give indigenous people a sense of control over their own affairs, Elijah reflected. That included having a human/Ra/Re mix in police and security forces. The key was to vet each applicant thoroughly and to repeat the vetting process at least annually. Troublemakers would occasionally manage to beat the system, but not often.

Elijah walked to his office nearby, produced a thermos from his satchel and placed it on the desk, alongside the container with his dinner he'd packed at home to relieve the boredom of being in what was usually a bustling hall. He was already a little hungry. Christmas lunch had been hours earlier and a walk with Alina around their quiet neighborhood had burned at least a few calories. He was constantly watching his weight.

It was important to stay trim and healthy in this line of work and so his appetizer was a mix of raw carrots and celery sticks. He didn't feel sorry for himself. He enjoyed this sort of plain and nutritious food. He found Earth-farmed food appealing; he preferred it to the staples of his old diet back on Ra-Prime.

As Elijah lifted the first carrot to his mouth, he heard a soft noise. It was coming from one of the monitors on his desk, twins to those at Gene's post. Normally these were on visual only but Elijah had turned up the volume on each of his so that any sound in what was supposed to be an empty building would be audible.

Elijah scanned each of the monitors quickly. In the tunnel connecting federal buildings, he saw a shadow near the forefront of the image on one screen. He watched it intently. Did something move? Was someone there?

He moved his hand to his belt to pat his government-issued sidearm and rose from his seat, heading toward Gene. When he reached him, he told him he thought he had both heard and seen something.

"You stay here and keep your eyes on the monitor and keep your radio channel open in case I need backup," he said. Some bosses would have sent the guard but Elijah's credo was that a good overseer needed to remain active in the work he supervised.

The tunnel was empty, except for the unmoving train car used to shuttle Congressional members and their minions from one building to another. The train's doors were shut and it seemed unlikely to Elijah that anyone had managed to board it without making noise or having been seen by himself or Gene. He swiveled in place slowly, to ensure he was the only occupant of the tunnel. Whatever he had thought he had seen, there was nothing out of the ordinary visible there now.

He stayed alert as he turned to head back toward his office. He started at a sound, something like an exhalation. It was a very low, soft noise. He walked to the train, the only place where someone could be hiding. He placed a hand on each side of the car doors, intending to force them open. It was a dicey move. To put both hands on the doors meant his weapon was briefly out of reach. Prior to conscription into the Mahk armed forces, Elijah had been an actuary and calculating risk was something at which he excelled. It was, in fact, one of the reasons he had been appointed to his position. A good Chief of Security is expert at data analysis in order to determine the threats to the regime and the public and to minimize time wasted on red herrings.

Perhaps these were not red herrings. He had seen a shadow and heard a sound coming from a place he knew should be empty. His mind computed the myriad calculations and came up with likely scenarios.

Elijah dropped his hands and resumed the hold on his weapon. He turned away from the train and walked out of the tunnel, out of earshot of anyone who might be hiding in the train and contacted Gene. "I didn't see anything," he said when the guard responded to the call on his communicator. "Did you see anything on the monitors?"

"Just you, boss," Gene said, using the nickname that usually made them both smile.

It was a little patronizing of the guards and Elijah indulged them. He believed work should be as much fun as possible without infringing on one's duties.

"I heard a sound right by the train. I want to investigate but I need you to cover me," the Mahk-Ra said.

Gene didn't hesitate. "I'm on my way."

Gene soon joined his superior in the tunnel. Neither of them liked the thought of leaving the post unguarded but the doors to the building were securely locked, making it unlikely any unauthorized personnel would gain entry this evening.

"Gene," Elijah said softly. "Cover me." He loved saying

that. It wasn't every day he had an opportunity to spout clichéd police phrases.

Gene raised his chin slightly in acknowledgment.

This time, with Gene acting as backup, Elijah put a hand on either side of the doors of the train and pulled them apart.

He wasn't surprised to find a human waiting inside the car, but he was surprised to find that it was Junior, the day shift guard. Junior shakily pointed a gun at the Mahk-Ra and pulled the trigger. Elijah stumbled backward, Junior's bullet having found its target. Gene, firing from the doorway, let loose a round of his own and ended a life.

THE AMBULANCE ARRIVED within minutes of the gunshots and EMTs quickly hooked Elijah up to an IV drip after making sure he was still breathing. The bullet had not severed a major artery. He'd been taken to George Washington University Hospital, the same hospital where, decades earlier, President Ronald Reagan had been taken to save him from a would-be assassin's bullet and where Junior arrived DOA.

In his hospital room post-surgery, a Talon investigator informed Elijah that a search of Junior's apartment had uncovered a journal documenting his attempts to join the local Red Spear cell. They had found details of Junior's scheme to entice Elijah into the corridor with small movements and sounds that he knew would attract the Makh-Ra's attention and then kill him in order to impress the Spear.

Junior had been a fair marksman, but he hadn't prepared long enough to hold his gun steady when aiming it at a colleague. It is so much easier to shoot strangers. This was a common problem with insurgency groups – a wannabe's excitement would get in the way of the time required for adequate preparation.

Later, Alina sat bedside in Elijah's hospital room. She was reading aloud to her husband. His eyes were closed but he was awake and as alert as possible while painkillers coursed through his system.

There was a soft knock at the door. Elijah smiled a wan smile at Gene, who stood holding a small bouquet of yellow flowers. "Hi, Boss," Gene said somberly.

"It's not a funeral," Elijah said, just a little weakly. "Come in. Alina, you remember Gene?"

Alina stood to give him a hug. "Thank you for saving him," she whispered. She turned to her husband. "I'll let you two talk and I'll take a little walk. I'll be back soon."

"Bring some fresh fruits and vegetables, please," Elijah joked. He was on a liquid diet. If something went wrong and he suddenly required another surgery, the doctors didn't want to have to worry about a combination of a full stomach and anesthesia.

She smiled the patient smile of the spouse of a Mahk-Ra who has indomitable spirit and good nature and left the room.

Gene crossed to the window. "I hope you like yellow," he said, motioning toward the flowers and placing the vase on the windowsill. He walked to the chair Alina had vacated, sat and looked at Elijah. "How do you feel?"

Elijah looked intently at Gene for a moment before he spoke. "I feel pretty good, actually," he said. "I am in pain but I'm alive. No serious damage done. It's thanks to you that the medics got to me so fast, Gene. I will never forget that. I owe you."

Gene smiled for the first time since he'd entered the room. "You were brave, Boss. You knew something was wrong and you faced it head-on without even knowing what to expect."

"But I wouldn't be here if it wasn't for you. Thank you for that." Elijah took a breath. He was tired and both thinking and speaking took more effort than usual.

"We're usually pretty good at weeding out the subversives. We missed something with Junior. I wonder if you know what happened? Was he already planning something when he got this job or did he change along the way?"

"Boss, I didn't know Junior was trying to join the Red Spear. He never talked to me about it and I didn't pick up on any clues. We didn't see each other often, anyway, other than for him to hand off the shift to me. It's not as though all humans know what the others are thinking. You know that by now."

Elijah nodded. He did know that. But he didn't know everything.

He almost admired Junior for having planned his attack for Christmas night, a time when there would be minimal, if any, witnesses or collateral damage, as well as for learning enough about Elijah to know that any small movement or sound would prompt him to investigate their possible causes. Slipping into the train car surreptitiously left just enough fleeting movement on the monitors to catch Elijah's eye and the initial noise he had heard must have been that of the train's doors closing behind Junior.

"Still," the Mahk said. "You could have left me to bleed out. You could have rid Earth of one more Mahk-Ra. I'm grateful."

Gene ducked his head for a moment, hiding his emotion. He considered his words carefully for a long moment, then said, "You're right, it's not as though anyone likes being a vanquished people. For a smart guy, it makes no sense to me that you think this occupation is good for the human race. You wouldn't think the Mahk-Ra were better off if another planet had conquered yours."

"Of course not," Elijah said, both surprised and pleased by Gene's candor. "It isn't possible. No one could conquer the Mahk-Ra."

"It's just a hypothetical," Gene said. Talking politics with one's boss was never a good idea.

Elijah got the point. Sometimes he was a little too literal, he realized. "Right, ok. But that's different. Humankind *is* better off than before the Mahk-Ra arrived."

Gene sighed quietly. "Anyway, Boss, I'm glad you are on the mend." Besides, he thought, the Mahk-Ra higher-ups would just replace you if you died and who knows what that Mahk would be like? Better the devil you know. . .

"I'd better let you get some rest," Gene said. "Enjoy the flowers and see you back at work soon." He stood, waved and was gone. He didn't want to be late to the Red Spear meeting. They had to plan how to salvage Operation Bradbury: smuggling books out of what the Red Spear still called the Library of Congress, through the tunnel and to safety in the hands of human curators. After all, not all Red Spear cells were dedicated to blowing things up. Some were dedicated to preserving evidence of mankind's achievements.

But Junior's escapade had turned the tunnel into a Hot Zone, which the Mahk-Ra now would likely keep under strict surveillance. Gene quickened his pace. He didn't want to miss a minute of the meeting.

JOHNNY AND THE WAREHOUSE WOMEN

NATHAN WALPOW

Three in the morning, the doorbell rings, you think mocks, right? Maybe even the Talon—they can afford to be polite. It could happen to anyone, anytime, but it was happening to me. Because who else would be ringing the doorbell at three in the morning?

But, unlike most folks, I was prepared. Had been since not long after the mocks blew Iran off the map.

I jumped out of bed and into the closet. Pushed aside the shirts and pants and my one dress and twisted the little brass hook an umbrella hung from. The back of the closet swung inward. I stepped through, glanced at the hole in the floor leading to my escape tunnel, checked the control panel. Everything showed green. The monitor cycled. Wide angle off the roof: nothing unexpected. Backyard: fine. Inside the main house: nothing but a candle, with faint snores on the audio.

Front door: Johnny P. Jones.

I hadn't seen him in forever. Might have been a little happier if he didn't have four mocks with him. Only—

I zoomed in. Their clothing confirmed what I suspected. Women. Better yet, Mahk-Re women. So weird, but likely not a threat.

I buttoned up my secrets, closed the closet, went to the front door, undid the three locks.

"Hi, Annie," Johnny said, like he'd last seen me a couple of days instead of a bunch of years ago.

"Get them in here," I said.

He stood there like a dumbass, so I grabbed the closest woman's arm and pulled her toward the entrance. No resistance. She seemed numb. The other three followed, and Johnny brought up the rear.

I swiveled my head to see if anyone was looking. No lights on in the main house. Not surprising. One of the tenants was deaf and the other pair were heavy stoners. Out on the street, nothing amiss, unless you counted the panel truck parked with its nose blocking my driveway. Johnny and his harem's transportation, I figured.

I ducked back in, slammed the door, fastened the locks. Turned to Johnny. "Explain."

He shrugged like dropping in uninvited with lower-caste alien invaders was an everyday occurrence. "I kind of rescued them," he said. "I didn't know where else to go."

"You haven't seen me in seven or eight years, and the first person you think of when you 'rescue' a bunch of Mahk-Re women is me?"

"Second. First was Logan, of course. But I didn't know where he was. Didn't know where you were either, but figured you might still be here."

Logan was a guy we'd both worked with before the invasion, a generation older than Johnny and me—me being Annie Kevorkian, former potential art historian—the three of us and an ex-soldier named Vince Bolívar forming a vigilante posse, helping the helpless, that kind of shit. We'd gotten pretty good at it before the mocks showed up. Then Logan disappeared, and we went our separate ways. Johnny went back to petty crime, Vince went off to fight the mocks … and later, to fight for them … and I kept up the vigilante routine as a solo act. Invasion from another star or no, humans still did nasty stuff to one another. And with law enforcement otherwise occupied, somebody had to keep a lid on it.

"Make yourselves comfortable," I told the women. They didn't move. I pointed at the sofa. "Go sit, okay? Gonna be a while till I figure out what to do about you."

They got the picture and in short order their big strong bodies were perched on the sofa, easy chair, and floor. Six-three at a minimum, bodies like goddesses. And excellent posture. They would've been something for humans to emulate if they hadn't shot our planet all to shit.

"Hang out there," I told the women. "Food and drink in the fridge. And for God's sake, stay away from the door. And the windows." Not that they'd go near the windows, at least after the sun came up. None of them had sunglasses.

I grabbed Johnny's arm, swung him around in front of me, gave him a push. "You. Into the bedroom."

"Been waiting to hear that since the day I met you."

I couldn't stifle a smile as I knuckled the small of his back and he hustled into the bedroom. I closed the door, left enough gap so I could see if anything developed out there. "Spill."

"Well …"

"Look, I don't care what you were up to. Just tell me what happened."

He sat on the bed, ran his fingers idly over the comforter. "There was this guy I met, and he was putting together some guys to hit this warehouse all filled with—"

"Spare me the details. You found the women at the warehouse?"

"Uh-huh. We kind of screwed up and the alarm went off

271

and the other guys bailed. I got caught inside. And while I was trying to figure out how to get out, I went to the bathroom."

"Get to the point."

"Turned out the bathroom was next to the room where they were keeping them, and one of them made a noise, and I found this little hole in the wall, and there they were. So I—"

"You got them out, and you brought them here."

"Yeah, but there's a lot more. The fire extinguisher and the—"

"Later. Tell me more about the warehouse."

"You said I should spare you the details."

"Now I'm un-saying it."

"Well, the guy said it was full of TVs, but as soon as we got in I knew we were fucked, because the crates were that weird mock cardboard and they had mock writing on them."

"And no guard?"

"Didn't see one. One of the guys shot out the security camera."

"There's usually more than one."

"Just saw the one."

"Okay," I said. "We have four Mahk-Re women and somebody had them prisoner and now we have to figure out what to do."

"It's okay I brought them here, right? I mean, I didn't know where else to go."

"It's fine, Johnny. What can you tell me about the women?"

"Not much. They wouldn't talk. I think they thought I was in with the guys that had them."

"Mocks?"

"There must've been Earth guys working there too. I saw Fritos bags. You know how the mocks hate Fritos." Given how quickly the MRs had taken to our junk food, their distaste for Fritos was almost legendary.

"They thought you were in on it, they would've overpowered

you and gotten away. Let me talk to them. You go take a shower. You kind of stink."

I pulled out a couple of towels, gave him a shove toward the bathroom, went back into the living area. The women — the mocks had been on Earth long enough that I called them "men" and "women" — were still exactly where we left them. I went to the fridge, grabbed a six-pack of what passed for soda these days, popped open one and put the rest on the coffee table. "One of you in charge?"

"*Quoi?*" The French word they'd somehow picked up for whenever they didn't know what to make of a question.

"In charge," I said. "The leader. The one who speaks for you."

The one in the easy chair said, "The others look to me."

"Good. What's your name?"

"Gar-re."

"Who put you in the room my friend found you in?"

"Mahk-Ra. But after the first night we saw only Earth men."

Gradually, aided by my smattering of Mahkanese, I pried out the story. Each had been working at her menial job, scrubbing decks on a mothership or peeling their equivalent of potatoes, the kind of thing the Mahk-Ra passed off to the Re. Each had felt faint. Each had awoken in a nondescript room, been raped by a Ra and then brought to the hidey hole in the warehouse.

"And since then?"

For the first time, they looked at one another. Gar-re made contact with each, came back to me. "They bring us out, one at a time. Earth men. Two or three, with weapons. They cover our heads and bring us somewhere else. We are raped by other Earth men."

"How many?"

"Three. Four. Wealthy, if their clothing is a sign. Your silk and linen. *Vandash.*"

Vandash was a mock fabric. Like if you made pearls into

cloth. Incredibly expensive. The only Earth people I'd ever known to wear it were collaborators.

"What do you want to do?" I said.

"*Quoi?*"

"We can send you back where you came from—I mean, where you were kidnapped from, you know the word? Or we can make those who did it pay."

"I understand. You have authority?"

"I don't need authority."

At some unseen sign, the spokesperson role switched to another of the women. The smallest of the four, barely six-three and probably under two hundred. She said, "The Mahk-Ra or the Earthers will pay?"

"Both, if you like."

It was rare to see a mock smile. They did it the same way we did—it never ceased to amaze how similar our physiology and facial expressions were—but they usually chose not to.

The smile made her face stunningly beautiful. "Do you know why the Mahk-Re are treated as, what is your expression, second-hand …"

"Second-class citizens."

"That. Do you know why?"

I'd heard stories, but never from the source. "No."

"Nor do we. There are historical reasons, but they are ancient. It is one thing for them to despise us. It is another for them to treat us like animals. Yes, we would like to make them pay."

# # #

The property was Logan's. I'd lived in the guest cottage in the back since a couple of years before the mocks arrived. After Logan vanished, I gave him three years before deciding he was gone for good. Then I started renting out rooms. Even under alien Occupation, you needed an income, and, aside from the occasional liberated wad of cash, freelance vigilantism didn't pay much.

I'd been modifying the place since. Logan was gone because he'd crossed swords with the wrong collaborator and, I was nearly certain, had to flee the country. It was only a matter of time before I did the same, and I liked it where I was. So I'd fixed up all sorts of hidden weapons and perimeter monitors and warning devices modified from liberated mock technology, and I'd dug the tunnel that started behind the closet and let out in the alley behind a 7-Eleven a block away. All of it built with redundant circuitry, redundant hardware, redundant everything. Because Murphy's Law had survived the invasion.

I let the Mahk-Re women clean up, fed them, told them to get some rest. I situated Gar-re on the sofa, the rest—the "short" one was Palkin-re, and I never caught the other two's names—in sleeping bags. Johnny would get the floor. Or maybe I'd let him sleep in my bed. Nothing'd ever happened between us and nothing ever would, but it had been a long time since I'd had a warm body next to me and, long separation or no, I still trusted him more than just about anyone.

We sat down in the kitchen nook. I asked him, "How in are you?"

"Whatever you're up for." There was something in his eyes I hadn't seen since the invasion. "Shit, Annie, I haven't done anything worth talking about since they came. I mean ..." He hooked a thumb in the women's general direction. "The only reason I found them was I was robbing a warehouse. For Christ's sake, a fucking *warehouse*. How shitty is that? But now—yeah, I'm in for whatever you want to do."

"Good."

"What do you want to do?"

"No fucking idea," I said. "We're not dealing with child molesters here. There's organization and probably pulse rifles." I thought it over. "I suppose we ought to go back to the warehouse and case the joint."

"I know someone that might be able to help."

"Who?"

"A hooker."

"I don't know ..."

"Also a mock."

"I know mocks too. I don't think I'd count on—"

"You don't get it."

"What don't I get?"

"The hooker and the mock," he said. "They're the same person."

Living under Occupation, you circle your wagons and keep your friends close and don't venture any farther from home than you have to. You absolutely don't know who to trust. They say that war brings out the worst in humanity, but Occupation brings out far worse. Self-preservation takes over. Think about Marshall Pétain; a World War I hero who led the Vichy government during World War II on behalf of some of the worst evil our planet has ever devised.

Yet whenever you think people have reached the depths, outposts of love give you hope. Japanese war brides after World War Two and cute little *con lai* after Vietnam.

But interspecies romance topped all that.

Our Mahk-Ra overseers viewed it with disdain. But it happened, with both Ras and Res. There were stories of children, though I'd never seen one and my high school biology told me it was out of the question. But who knew? If the invaders so resembled us that we could have, and evidently enjoy, sex with them, were kids that much harder to believe?

A lot of people considered anyone consorting with an MR of the opposite gender a likely collaborator. But it was hard to suspect my neighbor down the street with the Mahk-Re live-in when they were so obviously in love and when the woman made the best damned chocolate chip cookies you ever had.

Once the Pandora's box—pun intended—of interspecies

sex was opened, no one was surprised when prostitution came next. It went both ways: Earth women who sold themselves to MRs and mock women who went after Earth men. In the topsy-turvy post-invasion world, many who wouldn't have been caught dead visiting a human prostitute were just fine frequenting Mahk-Re ones.

Including, I found out after some red-faced stammering, my old friend Johnny P. Jones.

Once he got it that I wasn't going to judge his choice of sexual partner, he proved more than forthcoming.

"Well, yeah," he said. "I mean, there are the things you expect, like the whole strangeness of it all. It's like in the old days, going to a black hooker, or a Chinese one. It's something different you don't get in your regular life, but even more."

"And the things you don't expect?"

His flush returned. "It's a turn-on how they're bigger and stronger than you. And their pus—"

"Enough," I said. "So do you go up to Old Hollywood and let one wave you down, or do you have someone special?"

The look on his face ... and I got it. My old evil-fighting buddy was in love with an alien hooker.

He saw I'd figured it out and suddenly became interested in finding something to drink in the fridge.

I said, "It's okay. None of us was ready for this world. What's her name?"

"Sammie-re. She likes me to call her Sammie."

"Is your thing with Sammie the reason you were so eager to rescue our new friends?"

"Some of it."

We talked about the possibility that Sammie could be of help. But I doubted talking to a voluntary mock hooker was likely to tell us anything about those drafted into service. I got the feeling Johnny had only brought Sammie up because, for whatever obscure psychological reason, he wanted me to know about her. So I said we could talk to her later if checking out the warehouse didn't give us any leads.

When I told the gals where we were going, they wanted to accompany us and kick some ass. I convinced them it wasn't ass-kicking time yet. That we wanted to shut the whole thing down and to do that we had to find whoever was in charge.

I armed myself with a switchblade. The kind that won't show up in a scan. It had cost me a ton and had proven its worth almost immediately. I slipped it into my jacket pocket, grabbed some other gear and threw it all in a gym bag. Looked everything over. Went back to my stash and ensured redundancy.

I made sure they knew not to go anywhere, not even the patch of weeds separating the guest cottage from the main house. It wouldn't do for anyone, even my tenants, to see them. You never knew when someone would turn out to be a collaborator, no matter how well you'd vetted them. Or turn into one when the opportunity arose.

I also showed them some of my home improvements. Not big stuff like the control center and tunnel behind the closet. Nor the cache of water purification pills, morphine, and the like. But I pointed out the switch for the metal shutters for the front windows and showed them a couple of guns hidden in innocent-seeming places.

First thing when we got outside was having Johnny move the panel truck. It wasn't particularly out of place on my nice little residential street, but like I said, when opportunity arose … people changed. I told him to park it around the block, near the 7-Eleven where the escape tunnel came out.

I picked him up in Logan's '09 Impala, which I'd been tending since Logan had gone AWOL. Automobile maintenance was an unanticipated skill I'd picked up, and the car ran sweetly whenever I could get decent gas. I ignored the scratches in the paint, the four inch crack in the windshield, the missing wheel cover. A car that looked too good attracted attention.

Johnny directed me back to the warehouse. It was in an industrial block in the foothills above Burbank. Somewhere along the way I said, "Tell me about your heist. I'm a little concerned you didn't know it was a mock stronghold."

The patented Johnny P. Jones sheepish expression. "I guess we did."

"You *guess*?"

"Okay, we did. But we didn't see any guards and I told you about the camera and there was supposed to be a shitload of *vandash* in there."

"Back at my place you said you thought it was TVs."

"I didn't want you to know I was dumb enough to hit a mock warehouse on purpose." He looked out the side window, up toward the OLLYWOO sign.

"You're not dumb. You've just got lousy judgment. Tell me how you got into the place."

"One of the guys was off-world for a while, a tech for the mock army. He knew all about their locks."

Johnny described the setup inside the warehouse, and it became clear that anyone working there would have known about the women. Which meant they were all involved ... both Earthers and mocks.

I parked a couple of blocks away. Johnny said, "You still got that gun underneath?"

Logan had built a tidy setup beneath the driver's seat. Even if you crawled down and looked, you wouldn't see anything. But if you reached down and pressed a certain doohickey, a gun magically presented itself. I'd built one under the passenger seat too. Like I said, redundancy. Johnny didn't know about that one and he didn't need to. "I do," I said. "But I'm not taking it. I don't expect any shooting."

We went in on foot. Our route took us along one side of a warehouse. Once we turned the corner the loading dock was twenty yards on. Across the road was a big yard filled with girders and tanks and a lot of other crap that would probably sit there forever. One big tank lying on its side had a big red circle with an *RIA* on it. Some resistance fighter had climbed over razor wire to put it there.

There wasn't much activity. No trucks, no pallets. The big sliding doors were down. Two men stood by an open people-sized door, looking at a clipboard. A woman sat atop a forklift, eating a sandwich. One of the men nodded and both went inside.

The woman crumpled her sandwich wrapping, tossed it at a trash barrel, fell way short. She hopped down, eyed the wrapper, decided it was close enough. She was thirtyish, with short blond hair and a swimmer's build. She said, "Help you?"

"We're looking for Vince Bolívar," I said.

"Don't know any Vince."

"He owes my brother here money."

"Sorry to hear that. What makes you think he'd be here?"

"Gave me the address a while back," Johnny said.

"Sounds like you got burned. No Vince here. Fact is, the mocks run the place, so—"

The door opened and out one came. A big one, seven feet plus. He said something in Mahkanese. The woman replied. A couple more back and forths, then the mock said, "No Vince works here. You are mistaken. Leave."

"Are you sure?" I said. "Because—"

He let us see one of those green pistols of theirs, strapped to a wide purple belt. "I will not say it again."

Something I learned from Logan: When your plan runs up against a brick wall, don't push it. Especially when it was a lousy plan to start with. Anyway, I'd already learned something. "Okay, thanks," I said, grabbing Johnny by the elbow and hustling us out of there. At the corner we turned and headed back to the car.

Half a minute later. "Stop."

I whirled, hand on the switchblade. It was the blond woman. Seven or eight yards behind. How the hell had she managed to get so close without me noticing?

She had a Glock pointed at us.

I said nothing. Watched for something that would confirm my suspicion. Johnny opened his mouth. I subvocalized, "Uh-uh."

No tells. Just a smile. She let us look at it for ten or fifteen seconds. Then she said, "Tell me who you are."

"You can't make us," Johnny said. The bravest idiot you'll ever know.

"I think I can," she said, pointing the gun down and shooting off the tip of his right shoe.

He looked down. His big toe wiggled in the sunshine. "Christ," he said.

"Let's not fool around anymore," the woman said. "That could just as easily have been your eye. So just walk and let's get this over with. Van. Over there," she said, chin-pointing at an ancient Econoline across the street.

"Got it," I said. We marched across the asphalt. "By the way," I said, "Aren't you afraid of blowing your cover?"

"Keep moving."

You do what I do enough years, you learn to recognize a cop. The tone of her reaction had told me I was right. Now the only question was whether she was working undercover or whether she was in on it.

The van's rear door opened as we approached. Inside was a Mahk-Ra. He too had a gun pointed at us, another one of those green things.

We climbed in. They made us lie down on the floor. The woman frisked us. There went the switchblade in my pocket.

The Mahk-Ra climbed into the driver's seat and we pulled away from the curb. We didn't go far. Maybe half a mile. Then we made a left and there was the quick bump of a driveway and the light outside went dim. Then a rolling door rumbled down, it smacked into the ground, and we were in darkness.

The mock got out and turned on a light. The back door opened. The woman told us to exit the van and followed.

An auto repair shop. A Tesla was up on a lift, a VW Beetle on the ground. A couple of windows high up in the walls were covered with sheets.

They directed us to a small office off to one side. Two chairs inside. I went left, Johnny right. I expected ropes or electric cords or cable ties, but they seemed satisfied to have us off our feet.

"Who are you?" the woman said.

"I was about to ask you the same thing," I said. "The way I figure it, either you're a collaborator or we're on the same side."

My turn to get the tip of my shoe blown off.

"Damn it," I said. "I've had these Vans since before the invasion."

"Don't ever call me a collaborator," the woman said. A good thing, I judged, because the "ever" implied there was going to be more to our future together than a few questions and a shallow grave. "Now tell us who you are."

"Speak, woman." The first thing the MR had said. "My colleague has little patience."

More good news. Contrary to what you saw in crime movies back when, bad guys seldom referred to each other as "colleagues."

I saw no point in anything but the truth. Tried to make it as succinct as possible. "Four Mahk-Re women were held in that warehouse and forced into prostitution. My friend here set them free. We came back to try to find out who was behind it."

The woman frowned. "I think you're lying."

I considered a reply, decided "No, I'm not" wasn't going to help.

"Helen," said the Mahk-Ra man. "I think it is the truth."

Helen said, "You're an expert judge of Earth people's character now?"

"No. But I have been trained to tell when the truth is being told."

"And I wasn't?"

"Your training is insufficient."

"Yeah, well—"

"Children!" I said. "Don't fight."

"Mocks," said Helen.

"Earthers," said the Mahk-Ra.

Johnny finally found his voice. "Honey, you're wrong and he's right. I rescued them and we're taking care of them. Look at this face and tell me if you think I'm lying."

She did. Shook her head. "Must not be. You look too dumb to fool me."

"Agreed," the mock said. He sheathed his gun and, reluctantly, Helen followed. "I am Kone-ra," he said.

"Helen O'Brian. We're on a joint task force. L.A. County Sheriff's Department and Mahk-Ra security forces."

"Talon?"

"God, no. They can't be bothered with little stuff like a few missing women. Especially Mahk-Re. We're with Vice."

Mocks and Earth cops teamed up? Not so long ago, such a thing would have been unthinkable. But my father, who was shacked up with some Romanian woman up in Tacoma, had mentioned he knew a guy whose nephew was in the FBI in Seattle with a mock for a partner.

"You will take us to the women," Kone-ra said.

"We will indeed," I said. "Can I have my knife back?"

No answer. I didn't push it.

I rode with Helen and Kone-ra in the van. Johnny followed in Logan's Impala. I said, "How long have you been undercover?"

"Four months," Helen said. "But we've been watching that place for nearly a year. We know some of the players, but we don't plan to move until we find who's at the top."

"You knew those women were there, and you let them get pimped out every few days and you let it go on?"

"What can I tell you? The greater good, some such shit."

"You sound jaded for a woman who can't be more than thirty."

"I'm sixty-two."

"And I'm the Queen of England."

"The Mahk-Ra had spies living among us for decades without us catching on. If they could make themselves look like us, how hard is it to make a woman look thirty years younger?"

"Nice perk."

"Can't deny it. But it's easier to work undercover if I look young."

"By the way, how come you weren't watching the place when Johnny rescued the women?"

She shrugged. "Inter-agency screw-up. A little confusion about assignments. Some things haven't changed."

We arrived back at my place, sat in the van while Johnny took his sweet time getting out of the Impala. He was wiggling around in his seat like he was trying to get the belt unstuck. Finally he extracted himself.

We passed the main house and walked up to the guest cottage. I undid the various locks. Pushed the door open. "Ladies! We're back!"

They were huddled around the TV, watching the 15,000th rerun of *Gunsmoke*. People loved Westerns. A simpler time, when men were men and women were schoolmarms.

Then they saw who was with me. I supposed I should have warned them I had a Mahk-Ra along. But this went far beyond surprise.

Utter fear.

I was such a moron.

The guns were back out. Kone-ra's green pistol pointed at

the clutch of women and Helen had the Glock aimed at me. She sidestepped over to Johnny, reached in his pocket, pulled out the underseat pistol. Said, "I wondered what you were doing in the car before you got out. Figured it was something like this."

She motioned him to stand next to me. He did and put his arm around me protectively.

Helen gestured to the TV. "Turn that thing off."

Gar-re's fingers played at the remote. The volume went up, up, and up some more. Finally she looked down and found the mute button.

I said, "You got pretty indignant when I called you a collaborator."

"I'm not. This is, call it a side project, for both Kone and me. Since the mocks showed up our pensions are shit." Kone-ra showed a hint of a smile.

"So you were hanging around hoping whoever took the women would come back?"

"You obliged nicely."

"Is anything you told us true?"

She smiled, seeming genuinely amused. "The part about us being on an inter-agency team. Oh, and the part about a screw-up leaving the place unguarded."

I looked over at Gar-re. "This the guy that raped you when they first took you?"

Her hand was still clenched around the TV remote. She nodded.

"All of you?"

More nods.

I turned to Kone-ra. "Pimping out your people. You must be proud of yourself."

"They are Mahk-Re," Kone-ra said. "They are to me what your dogs are to you."

"Asshole," Johnny said.

"You have a saying," Kone-ra said. "Sticks. And stones."

"What happens now?" I said.

"These will go back."

"To your warehouse whorehouse or to your planet? And us? What happens to Johnny and me?"

"Come on, girl," Helen said. "You can figure that out."

Over on the TV, *Gunsmoke* had given way to *Bonanza*. The four Cartwrights sat atop their horses, chatting with a couple of make-believe Indians. I said, "Herman Munster over there I get. But you? Why are you doing this?"

"Is this the part where the villain's supposed to monologue so the hero can figure out an escape plan?"

I snorted, like I was really amused. "As a matter of fact, we're past that part."

I glanced at Gar-re. She unmuted the TV. The *Bonanza* theme burst forth, loud, clear … and distracting enough to make Helen look away. One of the Mahk-Re women, Palkin-re, the "short" one, jumped her. There was a struggle. Kone-ra went to step in. Two shots rang out. Both women crumpled to the ground.

I pressed the shirt button on my sleeve. My knife popped out, right into my hand. My other knife, that is, the one that lived up my sleeve whenever I left the house, attached there by a mechanism powered by equal parts mock technology and Yankee ingenuity. The one that Helen had missed. The one that had turned out not to be redundant.

In one motion I flicked it open and threw it Kone-ra's way.

It wasn't a great toss, but it was good enough. The knife went into his cheek. As he raised his free hand to his face, he sent a couple of shots in my direction. Both went wide. You try aiming a gun with a switchblade sticking out of your face.

Gar-Re and the other two were on him instantly. No matter how big he was, three against one usually ends up only one way. Then one of the women had the gun, and when Kone-ra continued to struggle she shot him in the kneecap. He joined the crowd on the floor.

I picked up the remote, muted the TV. A promo was on, for *The Wild Wild West*, where James T. West's gun-up-the-sleeve had inspired my knife.

I glanced at Helen. She looked mighty dead.

So did Palkin-re.

"I will make sure," one of the others said. It was a short examination. "Both are dead."

Before I could utter a platitude, Johnny said, "Annie?"

I turned. Blood on him too, leaking out of his thigh. "It's only a flesh wound," he said, and passed out.

I pulled my knife from Kone-Ra's cheek. Slammed it into a stuffed chair to clean the mock off, used it to rip Johnny's pants leg open. A through-and-through. He'd live. I bound it up, dug up the morphine, shot a dose into him.

Kone-ra'd slipped into unconsciousness. "What do you want to do with him?" I asked Gar-re.

"We will find a fitting solution."

"And your friend?"

"Palkin-re will receive the proper respect."

"You don't seem very upset."

"I will be upset later."

I motioned to Helen. "Can you get rid of that too?"

"It will be our pleasure. We will need a vehicle."

"I have just the thing," I said.

The women bound Kone-ra with duct tape. I told them to leave his legs free. Then I made sure Johnny was resting comfortably, found the car keys in his bloody pants, and led the women into the escape tunnel. One had Helen over her shoulder. The second wrangled Palkin-re. Gar-re woke up Kone-ra, got him to his feet, and made it quite clear that she would use his gun on him if necessary. Then she took his sunglasses. I'd dug up a couple of pair for the other two.

We reached the other end of the tunnel and emerged by the 7-Eleven. Right across the street from the panel truck. All the

MRs but Gar-re, dead and living, piled into the back, along with Helen's corpse. Gar-re took the driver's seat. I handed over the keys, mumbled condolences about Palkin-re. Within a minute the truck was out of sight.

I went back to nurse Johnny. The morphine was at work, but he was conscious. "Sammie," he said.

"Case is solved. We won't need her help. How come you grabbed the gun from under the seat?"

"I dunno. Seemed like it couldn't hurt. Lot of good it did. Lot of good *I* did. All I did was get myself shot. Can we call Sammie anyway?"

He was woozy and in pain. But I couldn't help myself. "You do know she's a hooker, right?"

"Course I do. So?"

"I'll call her. Give me the number."

When I told her I was calling on Johnny's behalf, it quickly became clear that, as far as she was concerned, he was just another client. My poor deluded buddy. "Okay, great," I said, and hung up.

I went in to see him. On the edge of consciousness. "She was very worried and said to tell you to get better, and that she looks forward to seeing you soon."

He said something unintelligible and was asleep.

I thought about what came next. I hadn't seen the two crooked cops tell anyone where they were headed, but someone could have been tracking them. Once somebody realized they were missing, all hell could break loose.

I cleaned up the blood, took a shower, made a grilled cheese sandwich. And sat down to make some plans.

TRAITOR

ADAM LANCE GARCIA

"T his will only take a few more moments, ma'am,"
FBI Special Agent Harper said, all apologies.

"No, it's fine," Joanne Adeline said, raising the
fingers of her right hand ever so slightly off her desk. She kept
her face still, even; that was what was needed right now. She
couldn't allow them to see beneath the surface. It would be
unbecoming. "Take all the time you need. Difficult as this is, I
understand you're just doing your job."

The agent's lips formed a line. He anxiously tapped his
pencil's eraser against his notepad. He was human, handsome
for a man in his mid-forties. Adeline had read several reports
about Harper over the years, finding his career impressively
atypical to most other humans. And yet, despite his remarkable
CV, the agent seemed oddly meek in Adeline's company. That
and the softness that rolled over his belt made him terribly
unappealing.

Harper looked to his Mahk-Ra partner, JoHannas-ra, who,
even seated, towered over him. Adeline noticed JoHannas-
ra was consciously hunched so that his height would be less

pronounced. It was an oddly… *human* gesture, one Adeline had never seen before in a Mahk-Ra. Whether it was for her sake or his partner's, Adeline was unclear. Either way, it gave her pause.

"Where was she found?" she asked, breaking the silence.

"In Salmon Bay," JoHannas answered, his baritone voice filling the room, "though we have reason to believe she was murdered somewhere in Broadview. During the riots," he added.

"During the riots," Adeline repeated without realizing. Her eyes had moved to the far windows, looking out to the grey, rolling sky that perpetually hung over Seattle like a shroud. She cleared her throat. "And you're certain it was a non-terrestrial weapon that killed her?"

JoHannas gave her a hesitant nod. "We are."

"That is…" Adeline suddenly noticed she had chipped a nail, that the skin on her knuckles was dry. Her hand was shaking. She gripped her armrest to steady herself. "That is worrisome."

"It is," Harper agreed. He met her gaze and Adeline saw, briefly, a fire of rebellion in his eyes. And here she thought the Mahk-Ra had snuffed that out long ago. He knew who she was, and what she had done. Maybe it wasn't timidity she had seen, but rather anger, hatred at the woman who had sold the world.

She raised her chin. "And what evidence do you have?"

"CCTV footage, eyewitness reports," JoHannas explained. "Some other physical evidence, but I'm afraid we can't disclose it."

Adeline's right eyebrow arched skeptically. "Even to me?"

JoHannas gave her a slow nod and a knowing smile. "Even to you, ma'am."

"Yes," she said, bristling. "Procedure. I understand, but you should know that I already have access to everything in this district. So, please, save me the time and effort of turning my chair," she indicated the computer screen on her desk with a subtle nod, "to bring up the information and tell me what you know."

Harper shifted in his seat before leaning forward and resting his elbows on his knees. "There's little doubt it was a Talon enforcer."

Adeline could hear the anger and resignation in his voice, no matter how hard he tried to hide it. "Yes, I surmised as much."

JoHannas, ever Harper's counter point, kept his tone even, and somewhat clinical. Adeline found it comforting. "We have reason to believe that after your daughter was killed, her body was identified, and rather than register her into the system, the enforcer—or *enforcers*," he clarified, hinting at his loyalties, "dumped her body into the water to hide their involvement both from us, and from you."

For a moment, Adeline rolled the word "daughter" on her tongue, tasting it like a foreign word her mind could not digest.

"Suspects?" she said, at last.

"We don't have any," JoHannas replied with little hesitation. While the Mahk-Ra was much better at hiding his anger than his human partner, Adeline could still feel rage wafting off him. Was this the beginnings of treason or simply the anger of a policeman denied his quarry? It was a fascinating question, if only Adeline had the ability to process it. "Even with CCTV and eyewitnesses, all Talon enforcers were wearing blacked-out helmets which hid their faces. The only way to identify the perpetrator, and their potential accomplices, would require the approval from Ra-Prime and frankly…" He held open his hands to say what Adeline already knew.

"Hm," she sounded through her clenched mouth, unable to find any other response that didn't involve screaming.

"We're very sorry, ma'am," Harper said with sincerity.

Her eyes were beginning to water. Adeline quickly stood to let them know their meeting was at an end. Harper and JoHannas took the cue and followed suit. "Thank you, gentlemen," she said, careful to keep the power in her voice as she tried to blink away the potential tears. She smoothed out her suit jacket. "I appreciate your coming here as well as your candor on this matter."

"I wish there was more we could do, ma'am," Harper said, placing his fedora on his head.

"As do I," Adeline said, hearing her voice break ever so slightly.

"We are sorry for your loss," JoHannas said.

She reached for her phone as the agents headed toward the door, but couldn't remember why she had. "Agent JoHannas," she said.

The Mahk-Ra stopped and turned to face her while his partner left the room. "Yes, Director?"

Adeline stared down at her phone and unconsciously tapped her chipped nail against its glass screen. "Did she... Did she suffer?" she asked, quietly.

The Mahk-Ra gave her a smile that almost looked sad. Even after all this time, the Mahk-Ra still struggled with human facial expressions. "I couldn't say, ma'am," he lied.

"Yes. Thank you."

The agent hung back for a moment, making sure his human partner was out of earshot. He shifted his feet uncomfortably and nervously brushed his finger against the tip of his nose. "Oh, and, um, ma'am?"

Adeline looked up. "Yes, agent?"

Agent JoHannas-ra took off his hat, bowed his head and said, "*T'e toa kee-ray Mahk-Ra See-cha.*" It was a Mahk-Ra sign of respect, of subservience, one rarely, if ever, given to humans. *Sister of the Mahk-Ra, to you, we owe victory.*

Adeline walked out from behind her desk and slowly approached the agent. "*Narrete ka-gree, Mahk-Ra, sin ta,*" she reciprocated. *For the Mahk-Ra, Everything.*

JoHannas-Ra replaced his hat and took a step back, his head held high, giving Adeline his full measure. He was exquisite.

"Thank you, again, agent. Do keep me apprised if anything changes."

"Of course, ma'am," he said, slipping on his sunglasses. "Of course."

The Director closed the door behind him; her hand clutching the knob tightly, her knuckles turning white. She looked across the room to her desk, the mahogany top clean despite the paper-thin computer screen. She looked to the walls, the counter spaces, and the small side tables placed beside the couches and armchairs. She didn't have a photo of her daughter, not a single one. Had they really been that mad at one another? Had Adeline really said all those terrible things before she had stormed out the door forever?

They had dumped her body in the bay.

She jumped when her phone rang. "Answer," she said aloud. The wall screen opposite her came to life, revealing the youthful visage of her assistant. "Yes, what it is, Franklin?"

"Sorry to disturb you, ma'am, but your car is waiting outside. You have a meeting with Grand Commander S'Fek in an hour and you know how he is about punctuality."

"I'll be out momentarily," Adeline said, turning to the door, before pausing. "Oh, and Franklin?"

"Ma'am?"

She thought at what she would ask him and decided against it. She cleared her throat. "Nothing," she said. "I'll see you shortly."

"Of course, ma'am. See you soon." The wall screen blinked off and Adeline felt the silence quickly fill the room and found herself drowning.

The car was waiting outside. A gleaming black Cadillac, a pre-war original model, hand-picked because it reminded Adeline of her grandparents. The engine had, of course, been replaced with Mahk-Ra tech, a necessary change ever since oil was scarce, with so much tanked off-world. Her chauffer stood by the open passenger door. He was young and handsome, as was much of her staff. It was easier that way, they didn't know her, didn't know who she had been. They didn't look at her with the recriminating eyes of those that had survived. They were born into this world and knew no other.

"Good morning, Director," the chauffer said with a smile and touch of his cap.

"The Needle," Adeline said without a preamble. She climbed into the car and let her body sink into the leather seat.

"Very good, ma'am," the chauffer replied, closing the door.

Adeline's home was in Madrona, which, even after all these years, still retained the leafy, small village feel it had had before the war. Part of that was due to the simple luck that combat had never stepped foot within the tree-lined streets, as well as the twelve-foot high, electrified fences and the hundreds of guards that now surrounded the district. Adeline watched the trees, the joggers, the dog walkers, and the children heading off to school through the tinted windows. This was the enclave of the collaborators, the humans who had turned the other cheek when the Mahk-Ra had struck. They were the men and women who had chosen subjugation over revolution, and had become part of the puppet human government that oversaw the planet. It was a time capsule as much as it was a lie.

The demonstrators were already waiting by the gates, as they had been nearly every day for the last ten years. There had been a time when the populace would never had been so emboldened to protest, let alone so close to the home of the North American Director, but these were not the good old days. Several had signs with long, poorly written diatribes of their various grievances, while others simply held up placards with Adeline's face crossed out with a red X. Through the bullet-proof glass, Adeline could hear them, just barely, call her name, call her "traitor." Adeline tried to ignore them, as she had for the last decade, but found herself staring into the crowd as her car rounded the curve and headed toward the highway. Had her daughter been in that mob, shouting obscenities? Had she driven past her every day, and never seen her? And if she had, what would she have done?

They killed her then took her body and threw it into the bay.

Adeline massaged her eyes and desperately tried to push away the needless thoughts. What good would they do now? She turned to the tablet Franklin had left for her in the car and attempted to catch up on the day's agenda.

Outside her car, the landscape of the city quickly transformed from the idyllic refuge of the wealthy and political, to the reality of Occupation. To Adeline's mind, the City of Seattle had never truly been a beautiful city — that honor was given to London — but it once had a certain unique charm that was undeniable. Now, however, the city streets looked more like the remains of pre-war Detroit, crumbling and flaking like lead paint. While some sections of the city were better than others, nearly every building edifice was vandalized with the Red Spear symbol alongside various versions of "Mocks Go Home!" and "Earth for Earthers." Water and food shortages were rampant; looting a common occurrence. The streets were littered with garbage, and the people seemed eternally covered with a thin film of grime. Or perhaps that was simply Adeline's perception of it; it had surely been her perception of humanity as a whole.

There was a strange irony that the Mahk-Ra had chosen the Space Needle as their base of operations on Earth, and Adeline had always quietly wondered if it had been intentional. As the car made the approach, after making its way through the various gates, inspections, and security sweeps needed to enter, Adeline tried to remember what the Needle had looked like back before the war. At the very least, she knew there had been no gun turrets atop the saucer. The chauffer pulled the

295

car up the Magistrate Building—a Spartan building of Mahk-Ra design, the twin black columns lining the entrance the only ornamentation. Adeline finished the last of her daily prep while she waited for her driver to walk around the car and pull open the door.

"Ma'am," he said.

He offered a hand to help her out, which Adeline took. Her knees were not what they used to be. She tucked her tablet under her arm and headed into the building.

The inside of the Magistrate building was cold and dimly lit, better for the Mahk-Ra, who found Earth's sun oppressively bright. Adeline's own eyes had long ago adjusted to the difference, but she was forever thankful for the illumination of tablets and computer screens. There was comparatively minimal security within the building, with only a handful of guards scattered around the halls. Even if the Red Spear were bold enough to try and attack the buildings surrounding the Needle, they would have to fight their way through a number of barricades and kill-zones before they could make any significant damage. And with the gun turrets atop the Needle, air and missile strikes were next to impossible.

"Good morning, Director," Grand Commander S'Fek-ra said, his scarred visage looming over the entrance. He had been waiting for her, which was little surprise, but still an annoyance.

"Grand Commander. I hope I didn't keep you waiting."

"Only thirty-four seconds. It is inconsequential," he said, stubbornly holding onto his Mahkanese accent after so many years on Earth. He turned on his heel and marched down the corridor, his heels clapping against the marble floor.

Adeline did her best to keep stride, a task that was always difficult for a woman of five-one following a seven-foot tall alien; especially one that insisted on having mobile meetings. "I read over your reports," she said.

"Did you? I am always impressed by your ability to do

what is exactly required of your position." S'Fek-ra's position as Earth's Grand Commander, much like his scar, was given as a punishment, an ironic reward for some war-time failure on the other side of the galaxy. He made sure his distaste for this world and its populace was well known.

"I noticed there is little on the agenda to curb the water shortages in the South," she said, ignoring the slight.

"We can't allocate those resources at the moment, not with the recent swell of insurgency in Europe. The South will just have to suffer a little longer. If the local governors ask, simply tell them the new desalination plants will be operational within six-months and apologize, again, for the delay. What is your assessment of the situation in Australia?"

Adeline fought the urge to glance at her tablet. She knew she had read over the Australian report on the ride over, could even visualize the continental map with the large swath of red across it, but the actual report was muddled in her mind.

They had beaten her to death and thrown her body into the bay.

"I'm actually more curious to hear your thoughts on the matter, sir," Adeline replied after the briefest hesitation. "It's been years since I've overseen that sector."

S'Fek nodded, accepting the answer. "An absolute mess. Were it up to me, we would carpet bomb the entire continent and kill off that particular breed of malcontents, but the home-world feels they produce your best soldiers." His lips snarled. "I'm sending down a diplomatic envoy to work out an agreement that will hopefully help quell the tumult, though I have little confidence in their success."

They talked through other local and what once considered "international" matters as they made their way through the halls, with the Grand Commander alternating between praise and outright mockery at Adeline's suggestions. It was part of the daily repartee; a game of one-upmanship that Mahk-Ra seldom afforded humans. Normally, Adeline found she somewhat enjoyed it. Today, however, she found the procedure bristling, and was grateful when they arrived at her office door. S'Fek gave her a brusque farewell and began heading towards his next roving meeting when Adeline decided their conversation was not yet at an end.

"Before you go, Grand Commander," she called after him.

S'Fek stopped short, but didn't look back. "I have a meeting with the Consumptions Department in one minute, Director," he said, impatiently.

"It is in regards to the Broadview Riot," she said without emotion.

He half-turned his head toward her, curiosity breaking through his typically stone face demeanor. "What about it?"

"I was wondering if I could see the Talon's report, there are some discrepancies that I would like to rectify, specifically in regards to the escalation in violence."

A moment passed before S'Fek slowly turned around to face her. "The Talon falls under my supervision. If there's a discrepancy I can easily take care of it. Besides, we've already determined it was instigated by the RS to distract from their unfortunately successful raid on the munitions depot in Beacon Hill."

"I wouldn't want to trouble you. Besides Broadview is part of my jurisdiction, I should correct any oversight that may have occurred. And I would like to see if there's anything I can learn to prevent something like that from happening again."

"Something like 'what' from happening again?"

"A riot of that nature so close to the Needle, instigated or otherwise. Even with our defenses, it's a risk I wish to avoid."

S'Fek studied her for a moment, his large black pupils steady. "It will be delivered to your private computer promptly," he said at last.

Adeline gave him a slight nod. "Thank you, Grand

Commander."

But S'Fek was already walking away. Adeline waited until he had rounded a corner before she keyed open her office door and walked into the waiting room.

Her assistant Franklin was waiting for her, dutifully standing by his desk, with a tablet ready in hand. "Good morning, Director," he said with a thin, welcoming smile. "How was your meeting?"

"As expected," she replied with an exasperated sigh. She walked toward the entrance of her private office. Franklin, always on point, followed after her. The lights automatically flickered on as they entered, revealing a classic wood-paneled room that evoked a lost era of human dominance. Unlike the other rooms in the Magistrate building, Adeline had adjusted her lights to a brighter setting, both as a necessity for her human eyes, as well as a way of granting her some control over her Mahk-Ra superiors. "Did I miss anything while I was with the Grand Commander?"

Franklin adjusted his glasses and he read over his tablet. "Just the usual correspondences. Typical allocation requests, general updates from local precincts. The Eastern governors were hoping to arrange a conference call with you sometime this week."

"Is this in regards to the influx of European refugees?" she asked as she sat down behind her desk and switched on her computer terminal.

"I assume so, ma'am."

"Set something up for later this week. Thursday, perhaps." There was a soft chime from her computer and Adeline froze when she noticed a small notification from the Talon had appeared on her desktop.

"Um. Excuse me, ma'am?" Franklin said with visible discomfort.

Adeline blinked her way back to the present. She raised her

chin toward her assistant, but kept her gaze on the screen. She hadn't expected it so soon, which, to her mind, meant only a small number of unpleasant possibilities. "Yes?"

"If I may be so bold... are you all right? You seem..."

"My daughter was killed during the riot in Broadview," she said before she could stop herself. She wasn't immediately sure why she had let that slip out, but noticed the pressure that had been building in her chest had lessened slightly.

"Oh," Franklin sounded quietly. His face paled, unaccustomed to seeing the normally detached Adeline reveal anything approaching emotion. Adeline doubted he even knew she had had a daughter. "I am sorry to hear that."

"I appreciate the sentiment, Franklin," Adeline said, her demeanor stiffening, "but it is unnecessary. She was simply on the wrong end of a — On the wrong side."

"Ah," Franklin said. He glanced down at his feet, understanding the implication. "Well, if there's anything I can do, please don't hesitate to ask."

"You're very kind, Franklin," Adeline said. "But right now, I just need some privacy so I can take care of the day's agenda."

"Understood," he said with slight bow. "You know where to find me."

"Close the door behind you," Adeline instructed as he walked out.

She waited several seconds after she heard the click of the bolt latching into place before she tapped the notification. A small text message appeared, curt and polite, it simply stated that these were the files she had requested of the Grand Commander. She tapped the message and a dozen or so labeled folders fanned out over the screen. She quickly scanned for the folder marked "IRs," knowing it would be the only thing she'd need to deduce who had killed her only child.

IRs, or Incident Recorders, were recordings from the cameras outfitted in all Talon enforcer helmets. The recordings were stamped with a Talon enforcer's Unit as well as their personal identification number, the date and time, and were used as tools for training and future strategy and tactics, rather than security. As such, the recordings never released to departments outside the Talon or the Magistrate. Even the police weren't aware of the cameras' existence. It was bitterly ironic that the one thing that could help identify her daughter's killers was completely denied to the one department that could truly do anything about it. And while Adeline doubted she would reveal this to either agent Harper or JoHannas, she could, at the very least, use the recordings to help her find the killer herself.

The IRs were organized by Talon I.D., from Twenty-One-Zero-Zero to Eighty-Eight-Seven-Three. Adeline was briefly stunned by the sheer amount of Talon enforcers that had been used that day, forgetting that she had been the one who had called them out. Yes, the riot had gotten that bad and the response had been warranted. A role normally taken by shock troops, use of Talon enforcers to quell a riot was atypical, but due to the protest's proximity to the capital and suspected Red Spear agitation, Adeline had sent out the enforcers to ID and imprison any known RS operatives. She knew that even if she had known her daughter was there she would have made the same decision, but such was the price of governing.

But they had beaten her to death and dumped her corpse in the bay.

Adeline stared at the video file icon for several minutes, her finger hovering over the screen. Did she really want to watch her daughter's murder from the point of view of the killer? Would it do anything to bring her back, make things right, or somehow erase the last ten years of estrangement?

No, it wouldn't.

But it would let her know what direction she should take next, and she would go through every single recording if necessary.

Adeline couldn't remember the exact trooper layout from that day, so she held her breath and selected one at random, Twenty-Four-Zero-One. The screen briefly went black before a mass of colored pixels burst out before resolving into a crystal clear three-dimensional video of the enforcer's P.O.V. Adeline felt a quick touch of nausea as the camera quickly moved left and right, showing a number of black-suited Talon enforcers march in step toward the rioters, which she could hear but not see. She stole a paranoid glance at her office door and turned down the audio. She didn't need to hear what happened.

In the lower left hand corner of the screen was the date and time, with the shifting global position directly beneath, both in Mahkanese. She tapped the right hand side of the screen twice and the video began quickly scrubbing forward. She watched as the enforcers marched up against the barricades, the seething mass of rioters throwing rocks, bricks, and Molotov Cocktails while also burning Mahk-Ra's in effigy. Soon the rioters broke through and began attacking the enforcer, or perhaps it was the other way around. It wasn't clear either way, nor did Adeline ultimately care. She knew what she needed to see, and nothing else.

Which was why it was so troubling when she suddenly came upon a black screen. Adeline paused the video and rewound, making sure it wasn't simply a glitch. She played it back, at standard rate, and watched as the video blinked off. She then fast-forwarded for several minutes before the video came back again. She glanced down at the time code and saw it had advanced nearly a half-hour. On screen the enforcer was in the midst of a violent struggle with the rioters, striking them with electrified batons, the humans' heads spraying blood in small geysers. This went on for quite some time—there had been a total of twenty-eight humans killed that day—so Adeline advanced the video further until she came to another section of black. Thinking, perhaps hoping, it was indeed really a glitch, she selected another IR at random, only to find the same sections blacked out. She selected another, and another, each time finding the same sections redacted from the videos. She had noted down the time code and global position of the two video breaks, recalling the first as the approximate time and location of her daughter's death, and assumed the second indicated when her body had been dumped into the bay. After the tenth or eleventh video Adeline leaned back in her chair, steepled her hands, and stared silently at the screen, understanding the implications.

"Franklin," she said as she walked out of her office an hour later.

"Yes, ma'am?" her assistant said, dutifully standing out of his chair.

"Franklin," she repeated as she adjusted her sleeves. "I'm going to be stepping out for a little while. Can you arrange for my car to pick up outside the Magistrate?"

"Certainly," he replied, though his face betrayed his befuddlement. "Would you like me to redirect your calls as well?"

"No, let them leave messages. Last I checked we weren't at war, at least not on this planet. I'm sure anything anyone might want me to deal with isn't so urgent that it can't wait until I return."

"Very good, ma'am. I'll make sure your car will be waiting for you."

Despite the innumerable armaments and security that surrounded what had once been called the Space Needle, the area still retained much of its park-like atmosphere, maybe even more so. Well-manicured grass surrounded the Needle, with benches, flowerbeds lining the brick walkways spreading out wheel spindles in every direction. It was a leftover from the Mahk-Ra's first attempt at a "hearts and minds" campaign shortly after the conquest. Adeline had always found the area reminded her of Washington, D.C. from before it was a crater.

Her car pulled up as she stepped off the Magistrate steps. Her chauffer left the engine running and went to open the passenger door for her. She gave him their destination as she climbed in. As he got back behind the wheel, she settled into her seat. The Director laced her hands together on her lap and watched the Magistrate pull away, her mind elsewhere.

Several hours later, Adeline found herself staring at a family portrait; a young father and mother, two children, a boy and a girl. The photo had been taken in a lush green park, or had been digitally altered to appear as such. Adeline had closed down the last public park nearly fifteen years ago, though she couldn't for the life of her remember the name. The family itself was all smiles, the father's right arm wrapped around the boy, the left over the mother's shoulder. The little girl, no more than a year old, sat in the mother's lap. Her daughter had been about that age right before the invasion, but back then their portrait had been painted and hung before the public.

She heard the front door unlock from down the hall, followed by the double-beep of the alarm system disengaging and then reengaging as the door shut. The corner of Adeline's mouth quirked into a smile, suddenly remembering the old days.

"Special Agent Harper," she called as he walked down the hall toward the living room. She waited until he was standing in the room before she slipped the photo back onto the shelf.

Harper's hand hung over his sidearm, an instinctual and, to Adeline's mind, understandable reaction. He glanced quickly to his left and right to confirm they were alone before let his grip on the gun handle loosen. "Director," he said, wiping his mouth with the back of his hand. "I apologize for the mess, I didn't expect you'd be—"

Adeline waved this away. "It's all right, agent, this isn't an inspection. Though," she ran a finger over the shelf, collecting a thread of dust, "the house could stand a cleaning."

"What can I do for you, then?" Harper said as he pulled off his coat and tossed it onto a ratty Chesterfield. "I'm afraid we haven't gotten any more leads since Jo and I saw you this morning."

"I need you to tell me where I can find the local Red Spear cell," she said, as much of a command as it was a request.

Harper briefly pinched his lips together. "I'm afraid I wouldn't know anything about that, ma'am."

Adeline gave him a crooked, knowing grin, and said deliberately, "Come now, agent. Remember what I said this morning about my access? How do you think I was able to find not only your home address but the key code to unlock your door?"

Harper looked back over her shoulder at his front door. "My family will be home soon. My wife... she's picking the kids up from school."

"Boy and a girl, yes? I understand your son has made some... interesting remarks in regards to our Mahk-Ra masters." Adeline let the silence hang between them for a moment, relishing the anger that flowed beneath Harper's face, before cheerfully adding, "I wouldn't worry, though. Thirteen, by Mahk-Ra standards, is still considered pliable, so I doubt the Talon will take any notice. Inflammatory rhetoric only becomes a problem when someone reaches fourteen." She smiled. "When is your son's birthday, by the way?"

Harper stuck his tongue in his cheek and let out a quiet, angry laugh as he shook his head. "Red Spear cells don't exactly put their addresses on the internet. And, as I'm sure you're aware, they keep their cells tight, so they're pretty damn hard to pin down."

"Yes, but something tells me you know more than you let on."

"I'm an agent of the Federated Bureau—"

"You're also human."

"And you're not?"

"Some think otherwise." She stepped closer to him. "I know you have formed a close friendship with agent JoHannas, which is admittedly rare between our two species, but even so, I still see a... resistance behind your eyes which tells me you have a lot to lose... Agent Harper," Adeline said with an amused tone, "are you a member of the Red Spear?"

"I ain't suicidal."

Adeline tilted her head to the side. "But..."

"I hear things."

"Do you, now?

Harper turned away and began pacing the room, a hand over his mouth. He was turning back round to her when he paused by the family portrait. "You two had a falling out, didn't you?" he asked suddenly.

"We did," she confessed without moving her gaze from him. Her heart hammered. "It was years ago."

"What was it about?"

"She found out who I was," she admitted. She felt the layer of dust still clinging to her skin, and began rubbing her forefinger against her thumb. "What I had done. She couldn't forgive me."

Harper didn't stop himself from letting out a curt laugh. "Can't say I blame her."

"Yes, well, it's a pity not all of us are angels."

"If you're asking me to apologize..."

"Isn't that what you're asking of me, agent?"

"I'd be a fool to ask anything of the woman who sold the world." Harper let out another curt laugh and glanced to the ceiling with a bemused expression. "South Lucile Street and Fourth Avenue South. There's a factory, what used be a factory, at least. You might want to drive by there in an hour or so."

"Need some time to send out the homing pigeons?"

"South Lucile Street and Fourth Avenue South," Harper repeated. "I recommend you travel light."

"Hm," Adeline sounded. "Thank you, agent. That will be all. And don't you worry. This conversation never happened."

She began to leave when Harper called after her, "Candle, Redwood, May."

Adeline stopped and looked back at the agent, his hands stuffed in his pockets.

"Maybe if you say it to them they won't shoot you," he added.

Adeline nodded. "Thank you, agent."

Her car had returned outside, her chauffer standing by the passenger door. Adeline could see the latent concern on his face, but he simply touched his cap and moved to open the door. "Ma'am. Are we heading back to the Magistrate?"

"South Lucile Street and Fourth Avenue South."

Her chauffer hesitated and gave her a nervous smile. "I'm sorry, ma'am, did you say South Lucile and Fourth?"

Adeline raised her chin. "Is there a problem?"

"Ah, no ma'am, no. None at all. It's just—It's just the area, you know. It isn't exactly the safest for someone of your... standing."

"I was quite clear with my instructions. If I had wanted your opinion I would have granted you permission to give it." Impatient, Adeline opened the door herself and began to climb in when she saw Harper's wife walking up the block with their two children, the daughter's hand holding on to her mother's. Her small, little hand.

Adeline slammed the door close before the other woman could recognize her.

Adeline rode the entire way in silence, her mind drifting forward, measuring every step she needed to take, while considering every danger ahead of her, every landmine she would have to avoid. It reminded her of the days before the war, when every waking moment had been secretly dedicated to the Mahk-Ra, before the world had even known of their existence. Adeline felt a wave of bitter nostalgia, as if a pleasant childhood memory of one's parents had been suddenly soiled by an adult realization of infidelity.

The car moved off the highway, down a poorly maintained ramp into what had once been referred to as Greater Duwamish. The tires rattled over twisted and broken train rails causing Adeline to clutch the armrest. With so much of North America's—and for that matter, the world's—industry shifting toward aiding the Mahk-Ra interstellar war effort, there was little need for the sort of production that had once filled the area, leaving it to ruin. To Adeline's eyes, it almost seemed as if everything had been drained of its color before washed in brown and grey. Or perhaps that was simply her mind.

"I'll be getting off here," she announced as the car pulled up to the corner of Fourth and South Lucille. A forlorn, crumbling factory sat across the street, its windows boarded up, a padlocked chain covering the door.

"Ah, ma'am... Are you sure?" the chauffer asked through the rearview mirror. "This is a really dangerous neighborhood."

"I believe I was quite clear. This should only take an hour, make sure I'm not waiting." She opened the door and stepped out.

She stood in the middle of the street, her hands clasped behind her back as she stared at the derelict building, feeling a dozen hidden eyes staring back. The car hung there for several moments before slowly driving away, the chauffer's hesitation palpable. Adeline paid it no mind. She was a patient woman. She would wait here as long as she needed.

As it turned out, she only needed to wait a half-hour.

They appeared all around her, moving out from behind broken brick walls, shattered doorways, and dilapidated cars. At first glance, none of them looked like freedom fighters, they were grandparents, mothers and fathers, young men and women; dressed in the sort of everyday clothing one would see in a major metropolitan area. It was only the hate in their faces and the guns in their hands, that told where their alliance truly lay. She kept her gaze forward as they closed in and stared at her in silence. A small bead of sweat trickled down the back of Adeline's neck, more from the sun that broken through the clouds than any sense of fear.

Several moments passed before the chain linked door in front of her creaked open. An older man, dressed in stained camouflage fatigues, an arm resting on the rifle strung across his chest, ducked under the chain and slowly walked toward her. His booted heels crackled against the shattered pavement. Adeline recognized his scarred visage instantly from her recent Red Spear Intel reports. Duncan Briggs, the former London-based terrorist responsible for more attacks on Mahk-Ra interests in Europe than any other human. The Mahk-Ra had tried to have him assassinated more times than she could remember. There had been some shake-up in the local cell after the incident with the Overseer ship. Briggs had been brought in to clean house.

"I see you got Harper's homing pigeon."

Briggs frowned. "Harper?"

Adeline smiled coyly despite herself. "Quite the reception," she said with the air of visiting dignitary. "I always appreciate an armed response."

"Pretty ballsy you comin' out here all on your own," Briggs said, his Scottish accent tinged with a decade of London.

She smiled. "I pride myself on my initiative. Though for someone of your notoriety I am surprised that you took the time to answer the door."

"When your houseguest is Joanne Adeline, you roll out the red carpet." A handheld scanner was passed over her body by one of his crew, checking for surveillance devices.

"Why're we talking when we should be shootin'?" an older man said from Duncan's left, his gun already aimed at Adeline's sternum.

"We're talking because you know who I am," Adeline said to Duncan in response.

"It's because of who you are that my friends' trigger fingers are itchin'," he said, broadly waving his hand at his compatriots. "Most of 'em might not be old enough to know firsthand what you did, but they know the stories quite well."

"I can imagine." Adeline shifted her feet slightly, relieving a bit of tension in her calves. "Besides, they should be hard pressed to not know my face. I am the Director of the North American region. I'm certain they've seen me on the net or television."

Duncan gave her a lackadaisical grin and shrugged.

"But the real reason why you haven't done what I am certain you all wish you could do is because you know why I'm here."

"Do we now?" Duncan said, frowning theatrically as he began to pace around her.

Adeline took a deep breath, feeling surprisingly nervous. "My daughter was part of your cell."

"She was," Duncan said at last.

Adeline looked to her shoulder as Duncan rounded his way in front of her. "She told you she was my daughter?"

"First words out of her mouth." He leaned in close, their noses almost touching. He was trying to scare her, but Adeline wouldn't give him the pleasure flinching. "It was like she was sitting in a confessional and I was her priest."

"Good. Then let's continue the familial tradition and go inside for privacy." She gestured to the sky with her eyes. "There is always someone watching."

Duncan glanced up to the clouds, knowing there would be drones passing over soon. "There is. But, why do you think we should trust you, of all people?"

Adeline took a deep breath and said, "Candle, Redwood, May."

Duncan stared at her placidly before he pressed his tongue to the inside of his cheek and nodded. He gestured to the abandoned factory. "Bring her in."

Two rebels stepped up on either side of Adeline, grabbed her arms, and pulled her toward the door. Adeline didn't bother to resist, she knew there was no point, they would kill her or they wouldn't. It was ultimately up to her which outcome would occur.

The inside of the factory was as derelict as its exterior, with an angled pillar of light cutting in from a large gaping hole in the ceiling, dust and soot glimmering. The concrete floor was lined with gravel and a thick powder, while the mechanical remains of some lost industry dotted the space like Terracotta soldiers. A part of her was almost impressed with the Red Spear, their fortitude and outright stubbornness at remaining a potent counter-force this long.

Duncan sat down atop a small, dust-covered table, leaving one foot firmly pressed to the ground. The two men holding Adeline let her slip free and stepped back, their guns ready, while the remaining freedom fighters surrounded them in a semi-circle. Adeline brushed the grit off her sleeves.

"So you're here to talk." Duncan opened his arms expectantly. "Talk."

"I want you to help me take down the Talon."

She had expected laughter, which made the silence that came all the more discomforting.

"Oh, that's just bloody rich, coming from you," Duncan said with an angry grin. "You shoulda gone into comedy you should. Probably woulda made a better livin' than you do now."

Adeline didn't bother to retort.

"Tell me why?" Duncan asked sounding almost amused by the absurdity of it all. "After all this time. After all you did, why

311

would you bring the war back to their front door."

Adeline arched an eyebrow. "Does it really matter?"

"Of course it fucking matters!" he shouted, slamming a palm down onto the table. "The woman who sold out her planet, her whole fucking species to the mocks. The woman who has more blood on her hands than any other monster in human fucking history, walks in telling me she's suddenly gone turncoat? Knowing why is the only fucking thing that matters right now!"

Adeline inclined her head, looked him in the eye, and calmly said, "Because they killed my little girl."

Duncan placed his hands on his hips and let out a sigh that might have been a laugh. "Is that all it really takes?"

"They beat her to death," Adeline said, her lower lip quavering. "Brutally, leaving her little more than a bloody sack of pulp. And when they matched her genetics and discovered who she was, they took her body and tossed her into the bay like she was trash. Then they did all they could to cover their tracks, going so far as to pretend my daughter didn't exist. They killed my daughter and then they lied to me. They lied to my face."

Duncan's eyes narrowed, deciding whether he believed her or not, but Adeline knew the balance was beginning to tip in her favor. "That's touchin'. Real touchin'. But you're still the one who handed them the world on a silver platter. For all we know, you're just staying true to form and selling us all up the river again. Why should we believe anything you say?"

"Because I have something to offer." Adeline carefully reached into her pocket, mindful of the guns that were quickly aimed in her direction. Her fingers wrapped around a small plastic and metal stick, warm from her body heat. It made everything suddenly become all the more real. There would be no turning back.

"Whatever it is, you best bring it out slowly." There was a smattering of guns engaging, safeties being switched off.

Duncan held out his hand. "Like I said, you make my friends real itchy."

Adeline kept her eyes locked on his as she leaned forward and placed the hard drive in his palm.

Duncan rolled the drive onto his fingers and caught it between his forefinger and thumb. He held it up like a teacher holding a student's note up in class. "What is this?" he asked. The smirk on his lips indicated he already knew the answer but wanted Adeline to say it aloud.

"A back up of my system at the Magistrate. I took the liberty of copying it before I came here. Proof that I am legitimate. It has everything you could ever want to know about the Mahk-Ra in this territory. Arms locations, passwords, key codes, troop deployments, both Earthbound and extraterrestrial. Even the identities of undercover agents in your organization... Any question you need answered," she nodded at the drive, "is in there."

Duncan delicately turned the drive over. "For all we know this could be all lies, or at the very least, half-truths to gain our trust. Worse, it could be a bomb or a tracking device that turns on when inserted into a computer. All we need to do is put it into one of our computers and... Boom. There goes the Seattle cell."

"There's always risk in revolution," Adeline said with a smug, lopsided grin. "I should have thought you would have known that by now, seeing as you're the professional."

His fingers curled around the drive. "In this industry, the only way to become a professional is by stayin' alive. And one way I do that is by not trusting Joanne fucking Adeline."

"The Mahk-Ra did and look where it got them," she said, turning back toward the door. "Go through it, double check it. Triple check it. Once you're satisfied, use the number I've given you on the drive to contact me." The two men that had dragged her in stepped up and blocked her way. She waved her hand dismissively at them. "Call off your watchdogs, Briggs, my ride should be waiting outside."

"Let her go," Duncan said with reluctance.

The guards and surrounding rebels parted like the Red Sea. Adeline marched through, ignoring the tingling sensation she felt in the back of her head. She just needed to put one foot in front of the other as if she were walking through her kitchen to make herself tea. They couldn't let them sense the trepidation, and oddly, the fear that had begun to boil in her stomach.

One of the rebels pushed open the chained doorway. Daylight spilled through the narrow opening, looking, briefly, like a cut in the fabric of reality. Adeline ignored the scowling, twisted look of disgust on the soldier's face, ducked beneath her outstretched arm, and the chain beyond. Adeline blinked as her eyes adjusted and saw her car waiting across the street. Her chauffer was in the driver's seat, leaning up against the steering wheel. His expression of abject dread and panic reminded Adeline of a circus clown from her youth. The driver jumped out of the car and made his way around to the passenger side in quick, tight, jogging steps.

"Ma'am, please hurry," he said in a hushed breath. He watched the factory door, anticipating gunfire. "Are you all right?"

"Get back in the car," Adeline snapped.

"Do you want to head back to the Needle, ma'am?" he asked after he had peeled out and launched the car down the street.

"Home," Adeline said, massaging her right temple. Her hands were shaking. From the adrenaline, she told herself, knowing it was a lie.

Harper and Duncan had both called her the woman who had sold the world. She had heard the term before, had even relished hearing it. It elevated her, placed her, rightfully, above every other human in the galaxy. But then why did it suddenly feel like a curse? Why did it feel like salt poured on a wound?

She knew the answer, but she refused to admit it.

What was it her daughter had said before she stormed out that final time? Adeline had tried to remember it, but all she could picture in her mind's eye was the door slamming, the swoop of her hair. Adeline tried to reform the young woman's face, tried to picture it the way it had been before, when they had loved each other, when they had been each other's world. But all Adeline could see was the puffy, distorted visage of her daughter's corpse. At first, Adeline tried to brush the image away, covering her eyes with her still shaking hand as if it would clear her mind. But she needed to remember it; needed to keep that horrible impression in front of her at all times. It was why she was betraying everything that she had been — everything she had built for the last twenty years.

Later, Adeline sat alone on her back porch, wrapped in a heavy flannel robe, a cooling cup of tea between her hands. The clouds had broken open, so she watched the sun set behind the trees. She had seen it once; miles above the Earth's surface, shortly before the war had begun. She remember thinking how small it looked, and wondered how insignificant it must seem to beings like the Mahk-Ra, who had seen blue stars, white stars; who conquered alien worlds as custom, who rode the vacuum like sailors had once done with the seas. Was it any wonder that she had said yes?

But then they had killed her daughter.

She glanced down at her tea, the small flecks of leaves collecting at the bottom. Tea was a luxury that her position allowed her. A luxury she used to share, but now drank alone.

The call was coming soon; she could feel it in her bones, rattling like the decades-old timer in her grandmother's kitchen. In the darkening twilight her phone, placed by her elbow on the deck table, seemed to have become monolithic; it was a talisman, a harbinger...

She jumped when it buzzed against the metal tabletop. She

carefully set down her cup and let the phone buzz three more times before she tapped the screen and brought it up to her ear.

"Is the line secure?" Duncan asked flatly.

Adeline leaned back in her chair and wrapped her free arm around her midsection. "You think I would have answered if it wasn't?"

A low choking sound came from the other end and Adeline realized it was Duncan chuckling. "Are you sure you didn't want to go into comedy?"

"I take it you're pleased with what I provided," she said, suddenly needing a cigarette.

"It was everything you promised and more. I had to kill a few good people since it turned out that they were, well, your people."

She couldn't help but smirk. "I always aim to please."

"I guess we should start talking next steps, shouldn't we?" he asked, his tone shifting from jovial to grave.

Adeline glanced up at the heavens. The stars were beginning to punch through the bruised sky. "If you wish."

"You have something special planned, don't you? But, I guess it wouldn't be a good idea to discuss it over the phone."

"No, it wouldn't be. But we don't have to, do we? You looked over everything; you already know what I want to do. I made it quite clear."

Duncan again made that strangled chuckle. "Just wanted to make sure we were on the same page. I must say... I was impressed, but not surprised. You've got balls, lady. With you on their side, I suppose I can finally see why they won."

"Two days from now," she said in reply. "That should give you enough time to obtain what I require. I will pick the location. Bring a couple of your men if you want. I will be alone."

"I look forward to it, Director Adeline."

Adeline hung up, dropped the phone on the table, and realized she was shivering. She debated going inside, but chose to sit outside a little longer, taking several long breaths of cold night air, savoring it while she could.

The next two days moved slowly. Even the resurgent cloud cover seemed to roll at a glacial speed. Adeline was careful, working her way through her schedule as she normally would, keeping her face placid and unreadable. During her conference with the Eastern governors, she made sure to listen to their concerns before tramping down their requests with her natural cold-hearted efficiency. Franklin still eyed her with concern, but kept his thoughts to himself.

And her chauffer, though shaken from the previous day's sojourn, was smart enough to keep his mouth shut. The understanding between them had been implicit, if he were to speak of what he had seen he would most certainly face the firing squad, for who would believe Joanne Adeline a traitor? Even her daily meeting with the Grand Commander was uneventful. He kept his face forward, his questions clipped and simple, his pace brisk as ever.

That was, until the second day.

S'Fek met her outside the Magistrate Building, which, in all the years she had worked with him, had never occurred before. Adeline kept her face steeled over as she exited her car. She had expected this, but not so soon. She would not comment on the change in procedure, would not even acknowledge that he was standing outside without his sunglasses. She brought her mind back to the conversation she had had with the then President of the United States just after the Mahk-Ra had appeared in the skies, and how she had feigned ignorance and shock. The President had been killed the next day in the first wave of attacks.

"Grand Commander," she said with a nod.

"Did you sort out the discrepancy?" he asked, immediately to business. Adeline expected him to turn on his heel and begin marching through the hallways of the Magistrate. When he

317

didn't, she stopped at the second step on the staircase, arms at her sides, her head craned back to look up at his black eyes.

"Yes, it's been taken care of," she replied, knowing full well what he was asking without needing elaboration. It wasn't as if the topic had been far from her mind. "I should have the report ready for you in a day or so."

"What was the source of the discrepancy?"

"Simple mistakes in reporting, nothing too significant. Call it human error." S'Fek nodded and began to move toward the entrance when Adeline suddenly added, much to her own surprise, "I also noticed that there were several gaps in the Incident Recordings."

The Grand Commander stopped short and slowly turned back at her. "Were there?" he asked in a dry growl.

"Nothing serious, I assume," she said, forcing her eyelids not to flutter with the lie. "Probably just a malfunction in the recording system. I'm having TechOps take a look. I'm certain it will be corrected."

They studied each other in silence for several seconds. Somewhere, very deep inside her mind, Adeline wondered whether S'Fek knew what she planned, if he had a drone follow her two days ago; if Franklin or her chauffer had talked; or, even more implausibly, if the Red Spear had sold her out. And while the ghost of panic boiled in her chest, she kept her expression, as always, composed and slightly impatient.

"Yes. See that it is," S'Fek said, at length.

Their meeting ended there. He walked off without another word. Adeline's hands unclenched and she noticed the four red crescent imprints in her palms.

When Adeline sat down at her desk she brought up the Talon IRs and accessed the base code, wondering why it hadn't occurred for her to do so originally. The system took a moment to access the code, the billion lines of text that made up much the IRs inner workings were something the boys in TechOps understood like the devout understood a book of worship, but Adeline only needed one simple word. She typed in a search request into the program and —

Adeline leaned back heavily in her chair, not sure why she had expected anything different.

And yet... And yet she couldn't help the chill that iced through her veins nor could she ignore the strange sense that there was a gun pressed to the back of her head. It had always been there, she supposed, ever since she first had become the Mahk-Ra's chief human ally. Everything and everyone had a period of efficiency; hers was bound to have ended sooner or later. Her daughter's death had simply expedited the matter.

"Well," she said aloud so she could hear the words, feel them vibrate through the air. "I suppose that's all there is."

Her meeting with Duncan occurred that evening in an abandoned school in Redmond. The building had no significance, no vital function; to both parties it was simply brick and mortar remains. Duncan and Adeline both entered the building alone, though Adeline had little doubt that Duncan had set up a contingent of sentries and snipers around the building.

They situated themselves in a bombed out classroom, shattered glass lined the floor between the rows of wooden desks speckled with splashes of maroon. Adeline ran her hand over the shape of a large bloodstain, the dust piling up against her fingers. Not all of the war had been fought in the sky and in the cities, she reminded herself; not all the victims had been soldiers.

"How did they find you?" Duncan asked as he entered the room. "Back then, before the war? How did they make you turn traitor?"

Adeline shrugged. "They did their research. They knew my husband was weak, that with all the power of his office, I alone truly controlled it. But they didn't make me do anything.

Everything I did I offered willingly, not for their sake, but for mine."

"You took a peak at their cards and decided to fold before your hand was dealt."

"I already knew my hand, Briggs, which is why I bet on theirs." From the corner of her eye, Adeline noticed the large black case in Duncan's hand. She nodded to it. "Did you bring me a present?"

Duncan carefully placed the case on what was once the teacher's desk and unlatched the locks with a grin. "Christmas came early."

There was a small hiss of air as Duncan deftly pulled the case open. Adeline saw what, to the untrained eye, looked like a small golden pin. It was little larger than the size of an old fashioned American quarter, the design simple and elegant.

"Lovely brooch you have there, Briggs."

Duncan gave her a croaking laugh. "Isn't it lovely?" He picked it up between his fingers and turned it over, the metal gleaming subtly in the moonlight. "Wonderful little thing. Makes our homemade IED's look like kid's play. It's exactly what you requested, mocktard tech, something they won't ever be looking for. You'll be able to wear it straight through the Needle's various security sweeps, even walk it right into Talon headquarters while people compliment you on how nice it looks."

"The Mahk-Ra are too proud to consider their own weapons used against them. It's why they lost Dro'midus."

Duncan gave her a puzzled look, but Adeline indicated its irrelevancy with a wave.

He handed it to her. Holding it in her palm, it was heavier than she had expected. She studied it closely, noticing the small wireless receptor on the back. "It's remotely activated," she said with little surprise. "I take it you don't trust me to do it myself."

Duncan's smile was her answer. "I assume you know the

size of the blast radius."

"I do."

"As per your plan, you need to contact us immediately after you plant it in Talon Central Command. We'll be able to track your movements, of course, there's a GPS installed in the bombs circuitry, but..." He rolled his hand in a circle as if that was all the explanation that was necessary. "We'll give you a good two minutes to get clear of the building before we detonate it. If you're not clear of it in time you'll hear a low pitch whine right before it pops."

"Only two minutes?"

"Only two."

A crooked grin tugged at the corner of Adeline's mouth. She knew he wouldn't even give her one. She doubted he would even wait for her to step fully through the doorway before detonating the bomb. But that was fine, that was expected and planned for. She wasn't going to go to Talon Central Command. She pinned the bomb to her lapel and found it was indeed, in its way, beautiful. It looked like something her mother would have worn. She smoothed out her suit jacket and admired it.

"You ever feel guilty?" Duncan asked after a moment. "For what you did to this world, to us?"

Adeline sighed audibly. "If you're going to lecture me, might as well use the chalkboard."

Duncan nodded slowly, his expression distant and cold. "Just wanted to make sure." He held out his hand. "Good luck, Director Adeline."

Adeline took his hand without hesitation, his rough, calloused palm like sandpaper against hers. "And to you, Briggs."

Adeline slept soundly that night and awoke shortly before the sunrise. She had kept the bomb on her bedside table, leaning it against the base of the lamp. She spent the morning slowly drinking tea while she watched videos of her daughter's

childhood birthdays, smiling wistfully at the precocious girl
that scampered around playing hide and seek with her friends;
whose rolling, bubbly laugh was infectious and uplifting;
whose pale blue eyes looked at the world and only saw magic.

She chose an outfit of a simple black suit with a white shirt.
She pinned the bomb on her lapel and studied herself in the
mirror. No, she didn't feel guilty. Had never, would never.
She had done what she had done and there was little point in
regrets and second-guesses. She rolled back her shoulders and
raised her chin.

The time had come.

Her car was waiting outside, just as it always had. Her
chauffer stood with the passenger seat open, his gaze on the
ground. She climbed in without a word and they drove toward
the Needle in silence. Halfway there she brought Franklin up
on her car phone, his youthful face filling the screen on the back
of the driver's seat.

"Good morning, ma'am. Is everything all right?"

"Yes. Franklin, I seem to have forgotten some of my files at
home. I'll need them later today for my meeting with the Water
Rationing Commission. Could you grab a car and go there to
pick them up? I know I only just left but I wouldn't want to be
late for my meeting with the Grand Commander. You know
how he can be."

"Yes, ma'am, I understand," he said with a nod. "I'll make
sure to have everything in hand by the time you're finished
with the Grand Commander."

"Thank you, Franklin. You've been a splendid assistant."

Franklin's brows furrowed briefly, stunned by the
uncommon compliment. "I—ah… Thank you, ma'am. I'll see
you soon."

"What's your name?" Adeline said to her driver after
Franklin hung up. "I'm afraid I never learned it."

"Gregory, ma'am," the chauffer replied through the

rearview mirror. "Gregory Chapel."

"Gregory Chapel." Adeline nodded her approval as she watched the city of Seattle roll past her window. "Gregory, do you have any children?"

"Ah… No, ma'am. A little young for that, though don't tell that to my mother."

"Did you know I had a daughter?"

"No, ma'am, I didn't."

"I had never wanted her. She was an accident, or rather, she was a surprise. You'll hear people say you can never truly prepare for having a child, and that is true. Especially when you don't think you can have one… You try and do all you can for them, make the world safer, better. And you end up loving them, with all of yourself. But then they become people, with thoughts of their own and you don't know them anymore and they—" Adeline's voice briefly caught in her throat. She rapped her knuckled against the door's armrest. "Everything I've done was for her, do you understand that? Everything I did was for her. And she—"

Adeline caught Gregory's eyes in the rearview mirror; his distant look of confusion and panic, and saw that there was little point in continuing. There would be no proselytizing, no grand statements, no confessions, or justifications. There would only be the task at hand. Through the front window she saw the Needle appear in the distance, and wave of calm suddenly washed over her. She glanced down at the bomb, knowing Duncan and his men were currently hunched over a computer terminal, tracking her movements, their fingers hovering over the trigger. She smiled wanly and kept her face forward as the car moved through the first gate and then through the second. Security personnel paced around vehicle, sweeping their bomb and weapon scanners over every inch of its metal frame. Adeline watched them through the tinted glass and tapped her nails impatiently against the armrest, knowing, or perhaps just hoping, that the scanners would fail to pick up the bomb pinned to her jacket.

When they finally waved her on, Adeline realized she had been holding her breath. Her heart was hammering.

The car turned onto the round-about surrounding the Needle. As it made its way around the curve, Adeline saw S'Fek-ra waiting for her on the steps of the Magistrate, alongside a dozen Talon enforcers, their guns at ready.

She smiled to herself. Finding herself strangely happy that this wouldn't be a surprise for the Mahk-Ra, that at the very least, they knew what she had become, what she had always been.

And perhaps, hopefully, her daughter's killer was among them.

Gregory parked the car in front of the Magistrate and glanced at the small army of Talon enforcers surrounding them and then looked back at Adeline, his face leeched of color. "Ma'am?"

Adeline stepped out of the car without an explanation or apology. There would be no chance of him getting away in time. A part of her felt guilty, but most of her didn't care. No matter how many innocents had to die, now, as before, as it had always been, was for that little girl with the pale blue eyes, for her daughter. Adeline had failed her once, and she wouldn't do so again.

The morning air was crisp; a slight wind rustled her hair. All around her the Talon's guns were activated. High above, the sun broke through the clouds.

S'Fek tilted his head forward. "Director Adeline..."

"Evelyn," Adeline said.

"What?" said S'Fek, a rare look of puzzlement on his face.

"My daughter," she said.

At the edge of her hearing, she could hear the bomb emit a low-pitched whine. Then, just before the roar of sound and flash of light enveloped them all, she raised her chin and added loudly so that every member of the Talon, that every Mahk-Ra in the universe could hear.

"Her name was Evelyn."

HUNTER X

RICHARD J. BREWER
AND GARY PHILLIPS

PT. 3
BLOOD AND HONOR

Johannas-ra had barely got Masstas-ra into the back of the Limo before his partner, Paul Harper, got in behind them and told the driver to get moving. Masstas seemed shaken but overall unharmed. Harper on the other hand had blood running down his face, a piece of shrapnel having clipped the side of his head.

Moses on a pony," said Harper, his head back against the car seat.

JoHannas opened a compartment on his side of the car and pulled out a small first aid kit and passed it over to his partner.

"You're hurt," he said.

"I'll live," said Harper. He opened the kit and pulled out a mirror, some alcohol pads and bandages. He began to dab at the cut on his head. "Looks worse than it is. Head wounds bleed like crazy."

"Where are we headed?" said the driver.

"What do you think?" said Harper. "Red Spear?"

JoHannas thought about that. "I wouldn't think they'd had

time to recover from the last purge. Many of them are dead or in custody, and the word on the street is that the few that are loose are in deep hiding. Plus, this was brutal. It looks to me like there will be several human casualties along with Mahk-Ra and Re. The Red Spear usually try to keep collateral damage to a minimum."

"Can you guys give me a direction while you figure out whodunnit?" said the driver, a human in a suit.

"Department of Freight and Transport," blurted Harper.

"I agree," said JoHannas as he quickly checked his computer pad. "It is the most secure facility in the vicinity. Only 2.6 miles away." His large fingers punched the pad's touchscreen. Then he said to the driver. "I have uploaded the most direct route to your GPS."

"Got it," said the driver and the car began to pick up speed.

Harper turned back to JoHannas. "Let's review possibilities. Possibly Red Spear, but it somehow feels too improvised, too ruthless, even for them. And it would make bigger headlines if they'd tried to destroy the actual ship. That would be more their style."

"I agree. Maybe a local gang. The Double Dragons, The Twisters maybe? Though I can't think of a reason they'd want to bomb the ceremony… unless… I know several gang members worked on that cruiser and old rivalries between gangs run deep."

"There is someone else," said Masstas-ra, speaking for the first time.

"Someone else?" said JoHannas.

"He's been designated Hunter X. He has been targeting high level Mahk-Ra here on Earth for some time."

"He's Mahk-Ra?" Harper asked.

"Human," Masstas-ra answered. "He has a history with… he was a member of our, well I suppose the Earth equivalent would be your Special Forces."

327

"A human who fought side-by-side with an elite Mahk-Ra unit in the off world conflict?"

The war hero's face was ashen.

"Why were we not informed of this threat?" asked JoHannas.

"I'm like you," said Masstas. "I do what I'm told by my superiors."

"They knew this might happen?"

"It was one of three possibilities," he said.

"Then why wasn't there extra security?" asked Johannas.

"Yeah," said Harper. "Why isn't the Talon swinging in here like the fucking horsemen of the apocalypse?"

Masstas-ra didn't reply. Instead it was JoHannas who spoke up.

"Because this was the least important of those possibilities," he said. "But it was the most likely one to draw an attack." He looked at Masstas with understanding. "Because of you. This Hunter X wants you, and the High Command sent you here to draw him away from the other targets."

"We're the staked goat," said Harper in realization.

This didn't sound right to JoHannas. No matter how important the other targets might have been, High Command would never risk the life of the greatest living hero of the Mahk-ra. His death would be devastating. There was something else. Something he was missing.

It was while JoHannas was trying to make sense of the whole business that the grenade hit the skimmer in front of the limo and everything went to hell.

A huge ball of fire erupted from the hood of the lead skimmer as the projectile exploded, dropping the vehicle to the ground and sending fire and shrapnel flying everywhere. The armored glass and paneling kept those inside the limo safe from those elements, but everyone was tossed about the inside of the car like dolls by the actual collision with the downed skimmer in front of them. At the same time, the trailing skimmer clipped the cabin of the limo, bursting the back window, as it tried in vain to rise over the Lincoln and avoid another crash. With its stabilizers damaged in the impact, the secondary skimmer flipped over and skidded into a parked car. Its machinery imploded and flames immediately erupted from the wreckage. Two dazed shock troopers crawled out.

The back of the limo was a chaotic mass of twisted metal, broken glass and bloodied bodies. JoHannas was the first to regain his senses. Harper was unconscious, his head wound turning the freshly applied bandage a dark red. Masstas-ra was awake and doing his best to reorient himself to the surroundings. The driver was dead. There was a pervasive smell of gasoline in the air. Unlike the skimmers, the Limo still ran on fossil fuel... highly combustible fossil fuel.

"We have to get out of this car," said JoHannas. He began to push at the door to his left. It had been damaged by the crash and resisted his efforts. He turned to Masstas. "Help me get this open."

"He'll be out there waiting for us," said Masstas, not moving.

"Then we'll face him on open ground," said JoHannas. "Better that then sitting here in this death trap, we need to get out. Now help me."

Reluctantly Maasta-ra climbed over to JoHannas and added his weight to the agent's efforts. With a creaking of metal on metal the door slowly opened until it was wide enough for them get through. JoHannas turned back and grabbed Harper by the arm to pull him free of the wreckage.

"Leave him," said Maasta. "We have to get to a secure place where we can wait for help."

"I will not abandon my partner," said JoHannas. "Would you abandon one of your own on the battlefield?"

"He's an Earther," said the Mahk-Ra hero. "What are they to us?"

"This 'Earther' is my partner," said JoHannas. "I will not

leave him."

With an air of exasperation Maasta reached over and grabbed Harper's other arm and helped pull him from the car. The rain had started again and as they exited the car, it slapped into Harper's face and he began to come around. With a groan his eyes fluttered open and focused on something happening outside the opposite window.

"Help's here," he said.

JoHannas followed Harper's look in time to see a police cruiser barreling toward them at top speed. But as he watched he saw the driver dive and roll from the car, leaving the cruiser to roar toward them like a missile.

"Move!" he said, speedily pulling Harper the rest of the way out of the car and dragging him away from the wrecked limo and the approaching police vehicle.

The cruiser rammed the limo, the force of the impact lifting the old prewar vehicle up onto two wheels, almost tipping it over onto its side before settling back to rest on the hood of the police car. Smoke and steam rose from the cruiser's engine. One of the shock troopers on the ground tried to raise his rifle but was immediately shot through the head by the supposed deputy. The other one bled out on the ground.

JoHannas barely had time to register what had just happened as he was too busy trying to get himself, Masstas-ra and the still dazed Harper as far away from the pileup of cars as possible, when a black object a little bigger than a fist came skittering across the hood of the now totaled limo. In the half-second it took for JoHannas to think "grenade" there was a blinding bang/flash of sound and light, followed immediately by darkness.

The world came back to JoHannas in increments. First was light, his sunglasses had been knocked off his face and despite the cloud cover and the rain there was enough sunlight to be painful to his unprotected eyes. Next was his injuries, cuts and aches seemingly all over is body. And finally sound. He could hear, despite the roaring in his ears, the sound of someone yelling. Moving his head he squinted his eyes, trying to block out as much of the sunlight as he could. He could make out two figures, one on the ground hands outstretched before him, the other standing over him, a gun in his hand. JoHannas reached for his own weapon but found it missing from its holster. He rolled painfully over onto his stomach and began to inch toward the two figures, belly-crawling. There was a jagged, raw wound in his thigh and he couldn't put weight on his leg.

"I'm not him," said the figure on the ground. JoHannas could tell by the voice it was Masstas-ra.

"I see that. Where is he?" said the standing figure, taller than average for a human JoHannas noted. A plain, grim face atop a sharply defined body, he could tell this human was not one to waste time.

"Dead," said Masstas.

"Bullshit!" Briefly he glanced toward JoHannas then the lead skimmer where the personnel in it were alive but trapped in the compacted metal.

"No, I swear by Mother Ra."

Hunter X leaned in and pressed his gun to the fallen Mahk-Ra's forehead. "When?" He said. "How?"

"Five cycles. I don't know particulars."

"And you're a double?" He said, pushing the alien's head back with the barrel of the gun to get a better look at his face. "Surgically altered."

"What you Earthers would call a doppelganger," said JoHannas, putting the pieces together in his head. It made sense. He found his spare sunglasses in the side pocket of his coat and put them on. He shifted his head to look at what he now knew to be a faux Masstas-ra. "Because the great hero of the home-world, the legendary Masstas-ra must continue to live, continue to inspire..."

331

"Forever," said the imposter. "Forever the warrior supreme. Forever the leader."

"Forever the lie," said Hunter X with disgust. "Even in death… the false hero."

Hunter X lowered his weapon. His shoulders sagged, the rain dripping down his face as he turned away from his downed target. In the distance, sirens could be heard. The Hunter stood, listening to the approaching back-up, his face one of tired resignation. For a moment, eyes flat like a bored copperhead, he turned back and regarded the terrified Masstas-ra and raised his gun. Then with a casual flick of his wrist, he holstered the weapon.

"You keep playing hero, pretender. Let the mocks and their human boot lickers have their illusion. I have real warriors to kill." He started away and called over his shoulder, "Take care of your partner, JoHannas-ra."

The alien agent watched as Hunter X jogged into a complex of apartment buildings across the road. Harper, who was awake now, was struggling to sit up. Rising shakily to his feet JoHannas limped over to his partner and sat down beside him.

"We're not dead," said Harper.

"Correct," said JoHannas.

"The Hunter?"

"Gone."

"Masstas-ra?"

JoHannas thought for a moment. "The great hero lives on. Apparently he will never die."

The rain beat down on the two agents.

Harper shivered. "That sounds deep. I'm going to let you explain that to me later," he said. "Right now I just hurt too much. It's my birthday you know."

"Yes," said JoHannas. "I am aware."

They watched as the first of the emergency vehicles came racing around the corner and down the street toward them.

"I was kinda hoping there would be cake. Candles."

"I *am* willing to sing."

"Please," said Harper. "My head hurts enough as it is."

"A legend died today," said JoHannas. "But he, like other legendary heroes of old, will rise from that death and continue on... and on and on."

"Ooookay." said Harper. "Just how badly were you banged up in that car today? Look, don't be offended, but if the Talon don't execute us in the next few hours, and we actually get to go to a hospital? I'm gonna ask for a private room."

"Understandable," said JoHannas. "Understandable."

And the rain fell from the sky washing away the day.

- END -

OCCUPIED EARTH

CONTRIBUTORS

Cliff Allen has spent the majority of his life living and working in California's great Central Valley. He has had an interest in science and technology for as long as he can remember, and enjoys nothing better than sitting down with a good science text and learning something new. Cliff is a lifelong fan of the space program, and that has led to an avid interest in science fiction as a literary form. He is proud to have his short story "Strange Alliance" included in *Occupied Earth*.

Craig Faustus Buck is an LA-based writer for both print and screen. Among his dozens of television credits, including *Magnum, P.I.* and *Simon & Simon*, he was one of the writers on the seminal miniseries *V: The Final Battle*. His short story "Dead End," was a 2014 Anthony Award nominee. His novella, *Psycho Logic* was published by Stark Raving Press that same year. His first novel, *Go Down Hard*, was published by Brash Books this year and was First Runner Up for Killer Nashville's Claymore Award. Among his nonfiction books, two were #1 NYT bestsellers. He wrote the Oscar-nominated short film *Overnight Sensation*. His indie feature, *Smuggling for Gandhi*, is slated for production in the fall. He is President of Mystery Writers of America SoCal chapter, a member of the board of Sisters in Crime LA, and an active member of the Writers Guild of America and International Thriller Writers. He is also an unheralded pitmaster.

Matthew Clemens is a long-time co-conspirator with Max Allan Collins, the pair have collaborated on over twenty novels – including CSI and Criminal Minds TV tie-in books, more than fifteen short stories, several comic books, four graphic novels, a computer game, and a dozen mystery jigsaw puzzles. Their latest Thomas & Mercer thriller *Supreme Justice*, was published last year.

Hailing from Brooklyn, **Adam Lance Garcia** was raised on comic books, movie serials, and lightsabers. Best known for his *Green Lama: Legacy* series and his original graphic novel, *Sons of Fire*, Adam writes for a number of publishers, including Moonstone Books and Pro Se Productions, as well as working as a full-time television producer and a part-time screenwriter. Learn more at adamlancegarcia.com.

Howard Hendrix is the award-winning author of six novels (four from Ace Books, two from Del Rey), four short story collections, three book length works of nonfiction, many short stories, poems, reviews and essays published in a wide variety of venues. He also writes guest editorials for *Analog* Magazine, and has taught at the college level far longer than most of his students have been alive.

Rachel Howzell Hall is the author of the critically-acclaimed mystery series featuring LAPD Homicide Detective Elouise Norton, who debuted in *Land of Shadows* (Forge). The second novel *Skies of Ash*, was published in May 2015, and the third in the series, *Trail of Echoes*, will be published in May 2016. Rachel, a Los Angeles native, is currently a writer for City of Hope, a national leader in cancer research and treatment.

David Hall is the Design Director for the digital arm of the Oprah Winfrey Network (OWN). This is his first story collaboration with his wife writer Rachel Howzell Hall. David was born and raised in Los Angeles. A lover of science-fiction, he awaits their next project.

Rob Hart is the author of *The Last Safe Place: A Zombie Novella*. His short stories have appeared in *Shotgun Honey, Crime Factory, Thuglit, Needle, Joyland, Kwik Krimes,* and *Helix Literary Magazine*. His debut novel, *New Yorked*, is available from Polis Books. The sequel, *City of Rose*, will be released in 2016. Previously, he has been a political reporter, the communications director for a politician, and a commissioner for the City of New York. Visit his website at www.robwhart.com.

Richard M. Johnson is a screenwriter, copywriter, playwright, and poet. His short stories can be found in several anthologies, including *Meeting Across the River, The Story Salon's Big Book of Stories,* and *6S*, volume 3. He is also a performer and photographer and uses both avocations as excuses to occasionally get out of the house and into the sun. And it's always a treat to try and google his name, because there are somewhere near eight-million "Richard Johnson's" on the internet.

Jessica Kaye is a partner at Kaye & Mills (www.kayemills. com), a law firm specializing in publishing and entertainment. She is an audiobook producer of hundreds of audiobooks, more than a few of which have been nominated for Grammy Awards. She is the founder and owner of Big Happy Family, LLC (www. bighappyfamilyaudio.com), a digital distributor of audiobooks and ebooks. Jessica created and co-edited the anthology *Meeting Across the River* (Bloomsbury, 2005).

Adam Korenman has been dabbling in writing for most of his life, but only recently began spilling the crazy thoughts down on paper. He is the author of *When the Stars Fade*, the first book in *The Gray Wars* heptology, coming soon from California Cold Blood—a Rare Bird imprint. He is an editor for CC2KOnline, the nexus of pop culture fandom, and runs a weekly column for the Video Game section. Adam is a Captain with the Army National Guard, serving with a company of tankers in California. He currently lives in Los Angeles with his wife, and is always happy to take the other half of a sandwich off your hands.

Lisa Morton is a screenwriter, author of non-fiction books, Bram Stoker Award-winning prose writer, and Halloween expert whose work was described by the American Library Association's *Readers' Advisory Guide to Horror* as "consistently dark, unsettling, and frightening." In 2014 she released the novels *Netherworld* and *Zombie Apocalypse!: Washington Deceased*, and 2015 will see publication of *Ghosts: A Haunted History* and a short story collection from Cemetery Dance. Lisa currently serves as President of the Horror Writers Association (www.horror.org), and lives in North Hollywood, California. She can be found online at www.lisamorton.com.

Marsheila (Marcy) Rockwell and **Jeffrey J. Mariotte** have written more than 60 novels between them, some of the most recent of which are The Shard Axe series and a trilogy based on Neil Gaiman's *Lady Justice* comic books (Rockwell, dark and urban fantasy) and *Empty Rooms* and *Season of the Wolf* (Mariotte, urban and supernatural thrillers). They've also written dozens of short stories, separately and together. Some of their solo stories are collected in *Nine Frights* (Mariotte) and *Bridges of Longing* (Rockwell). Their published or soon-to-be-published collaborations are "A Soul in the Hand," "John Barleycorn Must Die," "V-Wars: The Real HousewiVes of Scottsdale," and "The Lottons Show." Other miscellaneous projects include

Rhysling Award-nominated poetry (Rockwell) and Bram Stoker Award-nominated comic books (Mariotte). You can find more complete bibliographies and news about upcoming projects, both collaborative and solo, at marsheilarockwell.com and jeffmariotte.com.

Nathan Walpow's Joe Portugal mystery series includes four novels and a threatening-to-be-resurrected serial. His novella "Push," from Fight Card Books, is set in the world of professional wrestling, and is an expansion of "Push Comes to Shove," selected for the Best American Mystery Stories series. Nathan's novella "Logan's Young Guns," available as a paperback and an e-book, details how Annie Kevorkian and Johnny P. Jones met, years before the Mahk-Ra showed up; his short story "A Good Day's Work," originally in *Orange County Noir*, has been optioned for a movie. Nathan is a past president of the Southern California chapter of Mystery Writers of America and a five-time *Jeopardy!* champion. Visit his website at www.walpow.com.

ABOUT THE EDITORS

Richard J. Brewer, a native Californian, has always been a lover of stories and storytelling. He has worked as a writer, actor, bookseller, story editor, book reviewer, movie and television Development Executive, and audiobook narrator. He was co-editor of the critically acclaimed Bruce Springsteen inspired short story anthology *Meeting Across the River*. His most recent short story, *Last to Die*, was included in another anthology inspired by The Boss, *Trouble in the Heartland*, and was noted as one of the Distinguished Mystery Stories of the year in *The Best American Mystery Stories 2015*.

Gary Phillips is also editor of *Day of the Destroyers*, a linked retro anthology about a coup plotted against FDR. A reviewer said of his *Astonishing Heroes* collection, "It's a book for anyone who remains nostalgic for the golden age of Toei films, blaxploitation movies, and lusty grindhouse cinema." He has short stories in *Asian Pulp* and *Jewish Noir*, and his graphic novel about a money launderer, *The Rinse*, has been optioned for television. Please visit his website at www.gdphillips.com.